THE CHRONICLES OF FAERIE

# THE BOOK
# OF DREAMS

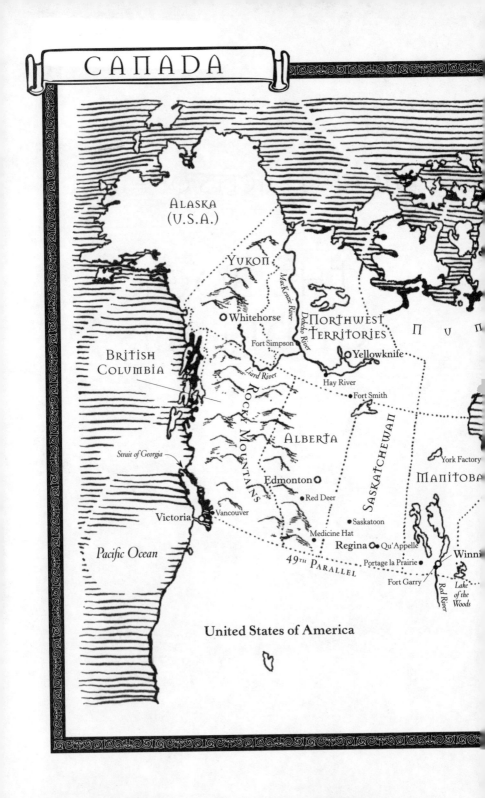

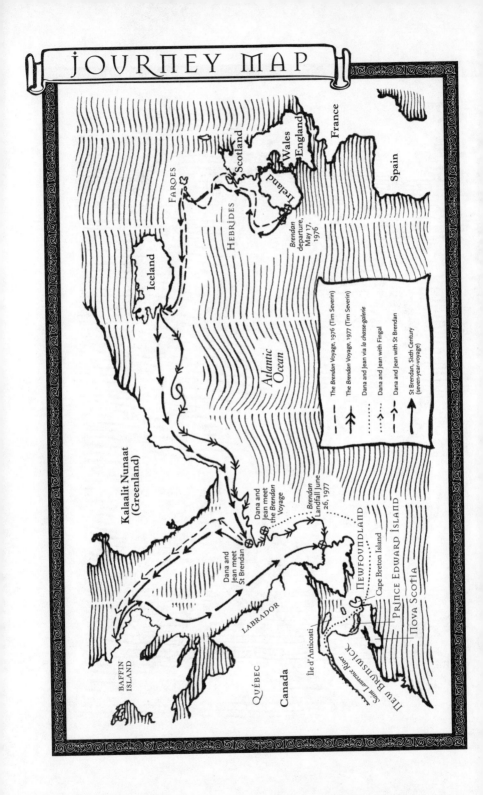

KALAALIT
NUNAAT

Inuit

Inuit

DENENDEH

Inuit

Hareskin
Dogrib

Tutchone

Slavey

Yellowknife
Chipewyan

Inuit

NUNAVUT

Inuit

Inuit

Tlingit

Tsimshian

West
Cree

Inuit

Inuit

NITASSINAN

Beaver

Plains
Cree

NUNAVIK

Beothuk
(extinct)

Haida

Iynu
(East Cree)

Innu
(Montagnais
& Naskapi)

Kwakiutl

Siksika
(Blackfoot)

Gros
Ventre

Mi'kmaq

Coast Salish

Nez Percé

Chinook

Absaroke
(Crow)

Métis

Anishinabe

G
R
E
A
T

P
L
A
I
N
S

Assiniboine

Algonkian

Iroquois

Wabanaki

Shoshone

Lakota
(Sioux)

Yana

Wyandot

Mohawk

Dakota
(Sioux)

Paiute

Pawnee

Shawnee

Yokuts

Cheyenne

Cherokee

Hopi

Dine
(Navajo)

Zuni

Apache

Apache

Choctaw

East Coast Algonkians

Toltec

Seminole

Aztec

Maya

TURTLE ISLAND

Also by O.R. Melling
*The Druid's Tune*
*The Singing Stone*
*My Blue Country*

In *The Chronicles of Faerie*
*The Hunter's Moon*
*The Summer King*
*The Light-Bearer's Daughter*
*The Book of Dreams*

Adult Fiction
*Falling Out of Time*

# THE CHRONICLES OF FAERIE

# THE BOOK
# OF DREAMS

## O.R. MELLING

Amulet Books • New York

The Library of Congress has cataloged the hardcover edition as follows:

Melling, O.R.
The book of dreams / by O.R. Melling.
p. cm. — (The chronicles of Faerie ; 4)
Summary: Now thirteen and depressed, Dana has been living with her father and his new wife in Canada for a year, and when she finds that her gateway to the land of Faerie has been mysteriously shattered, she must travel the length and breadth of Canada to find the secret that will reopen the Faerie world.
ISBN 978-0-8109-8346-5
[1. Fairies—Fiction. 2. Indians of North America—Canada—Fiction. 3. Voyages and travels—Fiction. 4. Magic—Fiction. 5. Canada—Fiction.] I. Title.

PZ7.M51625Bo 2009
[Fic]—dc22
2008024689

Paperback ISBN 978-0-8109-8418-9

Text copyright © 2009 O.R. Melling
Map illustration copyright © 2009 Bret Bertholf

Pages 697–698 constitute an extension of this copyright page.

Printed and bound in U.S.A.
10 9 8 7 6 5 4 3 2 1

Amulet Books are available at special discounts when purchased in quantity for premiums and promotions as well as fundraising or educational use. Special editions can also be created to specification. For details, contact specialmarkets@abramsbooks.com or the address below.

ABRAMS
THE ART OF BOOKS SINCE 1949
115 West 18th Street
New York, NY 10011
www.abramsbooks.com

*For Rosemary, soul sister*

# Acknowledgments

*Go raibh míle maith agaibh* to all in Ireland: Findabhair of the laughing fairies; the supporting cast of my family, especially Georgie Whelan, Pat Burnes, and Patrick and Georgina Black; Michael Scott; Martha and John O'Grady; Sherron St. Clair; Jenny O'Reilly; Kate and Marcus McCabe of the Ark, Co. Monaghan; Frank Golden and Eve Golden-Woods; the wonderful staff of the Tyrone Guthrie Centre; Victor/Victoria's Way in Roundwood, Co. Wicklow; Ven. Panchen Otrul Rinpoche and Ven. Tenzin Choeden (Margery Cross) of Jampa Ling, Co. Cavan; the Arts Council of Ireland and Cultúr Eireann for travel grants; and Wicklow County Council for a bursary award.

*Merci beaucoup* to those in Canada: Dr Nena Hardie, dearest friend in Toronto; the Creemore Durnfords, bagpipes and all; Yvonne and Deirdre Whelan for being themselves; Jean-Francois Pinsonneault *et sa fille*, Mélissa; Bette George for teachings and a bed "in the bush"; Lynn Bennett of TLA Inc; Michael Mesure for his wonderful work with FLAP (Fatal Light Awareness Program); the Native Canadian Centre in Toronto; and *Prairie Ceilidh*, the band who whooped me through the last lap.

A big thanks to those in the USA: John Duff and Brian Levy, dear friends and hosts in New York, and all at Abrams, especially my editor, Susan van Metre.

Last but not least, my heartfelt thanks to *Na Daoine Maithe* and the many *Man-i-tou* who kindly gave their inspiration and assistance.

# PROLOGUE

It was the early hours before dawn. A cool mist hung over the waters of the great lake, which lay still and luminous in the moonlight. The sandy beach was deserted except for the wolf. He was a big animal, black-haired, with a white star across his chest. His eyes glowed like amber. After exploring the bluffs overlooking the lake, he padded softly along the boardwalk. Now he stopped. Sniffed the air. On the edges of the wind came a stench that repelled him. *What was it?* It emanated from the city beyond.

There was a moment's hesitation. The wolf had only recently come down from the North and he was not yet at home in this territory. For the short time he had lived there, he had kept to the nature trails and the marshes bordering the river that ran into the lake. But he was no ordinary wolf. He wasn't afraid of urban streets and tonight he felt called to the heart of the city.

It was easy to travel in the dark. Traffic was sporadic and few pedestrians were abroad. Anyone who spotted him assumed he was a stray dog, too big to approach. Nearing the city center, he skulked through the shadows of office blocks, hotels, and apartment buildings. The streets were almost empty except for night-shift workers and the homeless who made their beds in doorways and bus shelters. He nosed the air with distaste. What couldn't be seen could be sensed: the sewers under the sidewalks, the smell of overcrowding, the fear and entrapment, bad dreams, failed hopes.

With relief, he reached the green circle of Queen's Park. Avoiding the pools of light shed by lamps on the walkways, he inhaled the night perfume of trees and flowers. Though the park was empty, it spoke to him of the day's events. Here, the evidence of two dogs who had scuffled together in play. There, a popcorn kernel dropped from a hand-pushed wagon and missed by squirrels. Farther ahead, the track of an electronic wheelchair crossing bicycle treads. The odor of humans was everywhere: an old man who fed pigeons as their white droppings splattered over his bench; students from the university weighed down with books; Sufi dancers inscribing the grass with prints as light as sparrows'.

A song floated on the currents of night air, wafting toward him. He raised his head to listen. It came from the government buildings beyond. He moved to investigate.

The Legislative Building of the Province of Ontario was an impressive fortress of rose-colored sandstone. The walls were arched and carved with friezes. Lion heads and gargoyles grimaced above the wide steps. The wolf peered upward at the vaulted roof. Owls were gathering to hold their own parliament. He could hear the concern in their low hootings. He was not the only one disturbed that night.

The song he was tracing grew louder now, as if calling to him. It didn't come from the dim galleries inside. Around the corner of the building, he found the singer.

It was a statue of a tall angelic man with shoulder-length hair and a loose robe skirting bare feet. He appeared to be walking across a low stone wall. He held a book in his hands. His head was bowed over it.

"What are you reading?" the wolf wondered out loud.

"A book of dreams."

The voice seemed to come from far away.

"Whose dreams?"

"Ah, that is the question."

Riddles. It was a night of mystery.

"Strange times," he said, "when statues talk."

"And wolves listen."

The wolf barked a laugh, but he was uneasy.

"Why were you singing?"

"To ward off evil. Something wicked this way comes."

"I knew it. I can smell it."

"Will you fight?"

"It's not my business."

"There is no neutral ground in this war. The thing hates all life wherever it is found."

The wolf shuddered. In his heart, he knew that the statue spoke the truth. The scent itself was almost overpowering. Sour and metallic. A noxious leak in the air. Like something rotten, yet it wasn't organic, so how could it rot? He wanted to gag. There was no point in debating the matter. He knew to which side he belonged.

Racing away, nose to the ground, the wolf followed the trail easily. The buildings around him grew taller, pressed closer, making him anxious. He had reached the financial heart of the city. All around him were the head offices of banks, insurance companies, and law firms. He stayed in the shadows, always on guard. When the sound echoed overhead, he flattened himself against the pavement.

It was a feathery, whispering, sighing sound, like an onrush of wind, filling the air. The susurration of wings surging like the sea.

Relieved, the wolf looked skyward. Of course. The season had begun. The Great Fall Migration. Through the darkness they flew, immense flocks of birds. For millennia they had followed this route, foraging for food by day, traveling by night. Each spring they set out for their breeding grounds in the north and each autumn they returned to warmer climes. It was a journey bred into their being.

The wolf was so caught up in the beauty of the birds'

flight that the new sound came like a blow to his ears. The thud of a small body as it fell to earth. The sound came again. And again. And again. Like hard rain. Like bullet casings. The wolf searched the shadows with keen eyes. Now he saw them, scattered at the base of the office towers, on the steps, and in the doorways. Tiny bodies, stunned or lifeless.

For millennia they had followed this route but suddenly, in so short a time, everything had changed. Before they could cross the great lake of Ontario, they faced a perilous test that so many would fail. The buildings and towers that stood directly in their path shed a niagara of glass and blinding light. In the dark, the combination of glass and light was deadly.

The wolf's lips peeled back in a snarl. The death of the birds had already upset him, but there was something else. Something worse. The guard hairs on his body bristled from top to tail. The thing he could smell was nearby. It leaned casually against a wall, watching the birds die. It was enjoying the sight, feeding on the misery with a cold ravening hunger.

The wolf growled low in his throat. The thing had no form that he recognized. It was a thick slimy mass, scaled and tentacled, glowing a sickly toxic green. Along with the telltale odor that was sour and metallic, its body seemed to vibrate with sound. The waspish drone buzzed loudly in the wolf's head, making his teeth chatter.

Without thinking twice, he launched himself at the monster.

Too late, the wolf realized that he was no match for his enemy. Before he could even get near to the creature, the viscid tentacles snaked through the air and caught him in a death grip. Slowly, mercilessly, the grip tightened, choking the life out of him.

Still, he fought back. This was his inheritance. A fierceness that was proud and lonely. A tearing, a howling, a hunger and thirst. *Blessed are they who hunger and thirst.* A wild strength that would die fighting, kicking, screaming, that wouldn't stop till the last breath had been wrung from his body.

The wolf's eyes closed as the darkness gathered.

Then human voices rang through the air.

Three people turned the corner, bundled up in sweaters and scarves against the chill of pre-dawn. Two were women—a pretty college student and a gray-haired matron with strong, good-natured features. They were accompanied by a man in his early thirties, lean-jawed and determined. All carried brown paper bags and butterfly nets. In hushed tones they joked about dragging themselves out of bed for early patrols. Holy quests in the dark. None of them were morning people. All of them were bird people.

Quietly, sadly, they stooped to retrieve the small bodies. Gently, reverently, they handled the slain.

"This one's alive!" the student cried. Her voice quavered with relief. Then a half sob. "Just barely."

The tiny body of a hummingbird rested in her palm, not much bigger than a dragonfly and as delicate and fragile. It moved feebly. She hurried to the others to offer her find. Under her breath she repeated her mantra. *I will not cry.*

With the quiet efficiency of a nurse, the older woman removed her gloves to inspect the bird.

"Broken beak. Wing damage, see how it droops? The eyes are swollen. Collision injuries. Michael—"

The team leader had already blown air into a paper bag and lined it with tissue. Softly, softly he placed the bird inside.

"I hate bagging them," the student murmured.

"Much better than a box," Michael told her. "If they panic, the paper has give and is less likely to hurt them. We'll look for the living now, bag them, and get them to the Center. Then we'll return for the dead."

"There are a lot more dead," the student said bitterly.

She glared at the buildings, lit up like Christmas trees, creating the fatal light that trapped its victims. She knew the statistics. Hundreds of millions died every year due to collisions with human structures. Why keep the lights on? It was neither cheap nor efficient. Some firms liked the prestige—*look at me on the skyline!*—others were simply too lazy to make the arrangements to turn them off. Old habits die hard.

So do small birds.

She returned to her work, face streaked with tears. The two older volunteers exchanged a look. Unless the girl hardened she wouldn't be able to continue. It happened to many. Like the birds on the sidewalk, they broke inside.

Hidden from sight, in an alcove where he had dragged himself, the wolf watched the three work. They had revived his spirits. He was already recovering from the deadly attack. The monster itself was long gone, having fled a power much greater than itself.

Banished by love.

# ONE

Gwen Woods hurried through Queen's Park wishing she had time to stop and enjoy it. On a sunny afternoon in the last week of August, the park was green and leafy and full of life. Squirrels foraged in the grass, stocking their dreys for the winter. Pigeons flocked to the old man on the bench who threw bread crumbs. A woman in an electric wheelchair stopped to watch Sufi dancers at their sacred ballet. The popcorn man bumped his handcart over the curb.

Gwen was in her early twenties, plump and pretty with golden-brown hair cut in a short bob. She was coming from a job interview and dressed in a beige suit with a pink blouse. Though she could hardly walk in her high heels, she kept trying to run in short bursts of speed. A quick glance at her watch told her she was late as usual.

Leaving the park, she dashed across the road and on to Massey College. The wrought-iron gates at the entrance were open. Inside was a quadrangle of grass and trees. A clock tower rose above a fountain pool stocked with goldfish in among green reeds and lilies. Surrounding the quad was the orange brick residence that housed professors and postgraduate students. Each room looked down on the square through long narrow windows. Those working at their desks were illumined by lamps and computer screens.

Gwen gave her name to the porter, and the room she wanted him to ring, then sat on a bench near the fountain to wait. Soothed by the plash of water and the stillness of the place, she felt a pang for her own student days. They seemed so carefree in comparison to the grueling search for a job, made all the worse by the fact that she was far from home. Her qualifications were recognized by the Ontario College of Teachers, but it was unlikely she would find a job this late in the year. Her only real chance was a temporary position; but in the meantime she was applying for office work in banks and insurance companies. If all else failed, she was looking at a stint in a bar or restaurant. There were bills to pay and the rent on her little apartment.

Even as Gwen grimaced to herself, she accepted the sacrifice she had been willing to make, the upheaval of her personal life and the likely damage to her career prospects. Would there be worse to come? She already knew the answer.

The worried look on Gwen's face was the first thing

Laurel noticed when she stepped into the quadrangle. It wasn't reassuring. The meeting itself was something she was already unhappy about. Laurel had just settled into her rooms at Massey and was about to begin her studies for a master's degree. Following in the footsteps of her paternal grandfather, she planned to be a professor of Irish Folklore. This meeting had, of course, to do with folklore. Not the kind found in books, but rather the kind that was alive and kicking.

The first telephone call had been awkward for both of them.

"Laurel Blackburn? Hi. I'm Gwen Woods. Sorry to bother you, but this is important. Very important. I've been told . . . I mean . . . mutual friends . . . in the other place—"

"Who told you?"

"What?"

"Who told you about me?"

"Oh. Uh. Granny. Grania Harte. She's an old lady. Irish."

Laurel could hear the hesitancy and knew that Gwen was having difficulty bringing up the subject. Along with the fact that they were total strangers, it was never easy to talk about Faerie. The spells woven around that magic land helped to obscure and protect it. And the Irish always said it was unlucky to talk about "the Good People."

"Granny's a fairy doctress," Gwen said, in a rush of

words. "A white witch you could call her. She lived in Faerie for seven years, where she gained her knowledge of the secret arts. She says she met you a few years ago?"

Laurel answered guardedly. "Yes, I remember. On a train crossing Ireland."

"She wants us to take a mission together."

Laurel's response was quick and unequivocal. "I asked to be left alone."

"I know. I understand. I think. But . . . please, could we meet? Just once? It's so hard doing this over the phone. I need . . . I mean . . ."

Laurel heard the desperation and relented a little. "It's the nature of the beast, eh? They don't like being talked about." Against her own wishes, she could feel herself softening. "All right. I'll meet you, but that's all I'm agreeing to. Can you come here?"

They sat together on the bench. Both were around the same age, but there the similarities ended. Laurel was diffident and reserved, a tall young woman of lean and athletic build. She wore slim-fitting jeans, a dark sweater, and high-heeled boots. Her fair hair was pulled back in a French plait to reveal finely honed features and hazel eyes. Though she was striking, there was an air of vulnerability about her and her manner was defensive.

Gwen guessed at the reasons for the other girl's wariness. She knew the story as it was told in Faerie: how Laurel's twin sister had died in this world to become High Queen of the other. It underscored a truth Gwen knew from her own experience, something that Granny often repeated in warning. *There has always been commerce between the Earthworld and Faerie, but while the rewards are enchanting the dangers are real.*

"I'm sorry about your sister," Gwen said quietly to Laurel. "For your loss, I mean. I know she's happy where she is."

Laurel shrugged. She wasn't the sort of person who discussed her private life with strangers, but she appreciated the sentiment.

"Have you met Honor?"

"Not yet," Gwen explained. "I heard about her from my friends. To be honest, I don't visit Faerie that often. I haven't returned since she became queen. I guess you visit often?"

"No. I don't. My sister comes to me in dreams and sometimes in person, but I don't go there."

Though they were sitting beside each other, Gwen sensed the great divide between them. She needed to build a bridge.

"I understand," she said quickly. "Or at least I think I do. We were born into this world. This is where we're meant to live. Faerie is so incredibly beautiful, so magical, it can make being here too pale. That's not right. This is where we belong."

"Yes," Laurel agreed, with sudden vehemence. "Faerie can be like a drug. Alluring. Dangerous. Best avoided."

The bitterness echoed in her voice. She had said more than she intended.

"Is that why you asked that no one contact you?" Gwen spoke carefully. "Are you afraid of being drawn back in?"

It was a tricky moment, but it had to be grasped. Gwen needed Laurel's help.

As the last of the summer breezes blew through the quadrangle, the ivy on the walls fidgeted nervously.

They were two young women newly launched upon the world, yet they were more. Much more. Both had traveled far, not only across the Atlantic to the green isle of Ireland, but also across the ocean of infinity to the land of Faerie. Both had undertaken quests, faced danger and death. Both were heroines of song and story.

When Laurel didn't answer, Gwen cleared her throat. It was time.

"Something terrible is coming. A great attack against Faerie. Against all our hopes and dreams."

A tremor ran through Laurel, but she didn't look surprised. She had already been warned.

"My sister spoke of a 'dark hour' some time ago." Laurel's tone was wry. "But of course the warnings were couched in the usual cryptic premonitions. How do they expect to get a clear picture of the future from the flight of birds or the movement of clouds? It's absurd. Did you get the message from a dream?"

"No. E-mail." Gwen grinned. "Granny has taken to computers. She talks about the World Wide Web like it's a new form of magic. But she does the old stuff too. She saw the attack in a scrying glass even before the High King contacted her. She can also predict things from the movement of clouds—nephelmancy it's called—which is close to austromancy, divining the wind." She pointed to the spray of water in the fountain. "Pegomancy interprets the pattern of water as it falls in a fountain."

Laurel looked amused. "You should be in Folklore Studies. How do you know these things?"

Gwen started to laugh. "Granny taught me. Maybe if I can't get a job as a teacher I should try being a witch. Ornithomancy is my favorite. Can you guess?"

"Something to do with birds?"

"Yep. Reading the flight of birds."

The air was lighter between them.

"I know your story," Laurel admitted. "My sister's harper sang it one night when I still dined in the halls of Faerie. How you led the Company of Seven against the Great Worm to rescue Fairyland. It's a heroic tale."

"We just did what we had to."

Gwen was embarrassed by the praise. She would never be able to see herself as a heroine. In books and movies, the lead females were always tall and beautiful as well as fearless. Not only did she not look the part, she remembered being scared out of her wits most of the time. That was the difference, of course, between reality and fiction.

"Faerie is really important to me," she said quietly. "Something worth fighting for. Plus my cousin Findabhair was in danger at the time. Truth is, I was in over my head before I knew what was happening. And I couldn't have done it without the others, Katie, Matt, Dara . . ."

Her modesty was disarming. Laurel's tone was warmer. "Why don't you call up the Company of Seven? You've worked with them before and a team would be good if something big is going down."

Gwen shook her head ruefully. "The Company is scattered. My cousin and her husband, Finvarra, are on tour. They're musicians. The others were happy to volunteer, but Granny says no. The mission isn't really ours. We are just being called to support the key player."

Laurel frowned as she remembered. "Honor said the same thing. It has to do with the girl, Dana Faolan? *The light that can bridge the darkness.* She's here in Toronto?"

"Yes. We're supposed to protect her. Granny was adamant about it. Her exact words were 'You must stand between the child and the quern-stones of the Enemy even if you be crushed yourselves.'"

Despite the sunshine, they both shivered. A gloom fell over them.

"The fact we've been asked to do this shows how serious the threat is. I mean, the girl has abilities beyond either of us. If you've heard my story, then I guess you know hers too? She's half-fairy. Light flows in her veins. I've been told she's still growing into her powers, but she took on her quest for Faerie at a much younger age than we did."

"Honor's worried about her," Laurel said. "Apparently Dana is not the same girl we know from the story. Maybe she has fallen under malign influences already?"

Gwen was shocked by the suggestion. But it made her think. Even before she had decided to be a teacher, Gwen was involved with youth groups and summer camps. She had a special affinity for the young, particularly ones with problems.

"Dana was only twelve in her Faerie tale," Gwen pointed out. "That's over a year ago. The change in her personality could be due to something less sinister." Gwen grinned. "She's a teenager now."

Laurel rolled her eyes, but she was grinning too. They were both at ease with each other and definitely in tune. Perhaps that was what made Gwen careless.

"So, I understand you're in the same boat as me?" she said. "In a long-distance relationship with an Irishman? My boyfriend, Dara—"

The air between them went suddenly frosty.

Laurel's features cooled and her eyes hardened.

Glancing at the clock tower, she stood up. "I have to go. I've got an appointment with my thesis supervisor and I need to prepare for it. I'm sorry, but I don't want to be involved with the mission. You'll have to do this without me."

"But . . ." Gwen was so surprised she could hardly think. "You . . . you're needed! Only humanity can rescue Fairyland. It's always been that way."

"I'm sorry," Laurel repeated, and her tone rang with finality. "I'm telling you what I told my sister. I'm no longer a Companion of Faerie. I won't fight their battles. Maybe it's time Faerie grew up and took some responsibility for its own survival. Time they learned to rescue themselves."

And she hurried away.

Gwen sat stunned. What had happened? She was sure she had been getting through to Laurel. She had felt the first inklings of real friendship between them. Yet somehow she had said the wrong thing and ruined everything! Disheartened to the point of tears, she stared blindly into the fountain.

The splashing water sparkled in the sunshine. Though pegomancy was not something Gwen was very good at, she began to see patterns in the weave of water and light. Granny had explained to her the truth of fortune-telling. *Everything is interconnected. Reality is like a hologram. Every piece contains the truth of the whole. All that happens—past, present, and future—can be read in what lies around us, if we only know the code. If we can read the language.* What was she looking at? Something horrible. A monstrous shape with snakelike tentacles. There was another form near it. A human male. Now the tentacles snaked out, piercing the man's body like grappling hooks.

Gwen let out a cry and looked away. She couldn't bear to see more. But she knew what it meant. With or without Laurel, her mission had begun.

# Two

Brunswick Avenue was an old tree-lined street of big brick houses with bay windows, gables, and stained-glass transoms. Most had landscaped gardens and rockeries overlooked by verandahs dangling with wickerwork planters and glass wind chimes. Midway up the street stood an abandoned convent, nailed and boarded. The nuns were long gone and the school they had founded had moved elsewhere. Where the street ended was a small park with flowerbeds and rosebushes, and looming over the park was the rambling brownstone in which Dana Faolan had lived for the past year.

The house was a maze of winding stairs, dim corridors, and rooms with high ceilings. It was divided into generous flats that were leased out to professors and artists. Dana's family had the third floor with a spacious living room, wide kitchen for dining, and studies for both her father and stepmother. The master bedroom was at the front of the house. Dana's small room was at the back. Once a large balcony, it was enclosed with windows on three sides.

The glass bedroom was Dana's haven. Like an eagle's

eyrie, it overlooked the treetops and the park below. The one solid wall was covered with pictures of Ireland and posters of animals, especially wolves. The floor was covered with a golden-brown rug that looked like a fall of autumn leaves. There was a cluttered bookcase, an iron bed piled with cushions, and a desk with her computer.

When Dana wasn't in her room, she could be found in the backyard. It was a gloomy place, shunned by the other tenants and overgrown with weeds and briars. Old washing lines hung limp and gray. There was a greenhouse with broken panes inhabited by a clan of stray cats. At the foot of an old apple tree was the rickety bench where Dana liked to read.

On that warm and sunny Labor Day, she found it hard to concentrate. Tomorrow she would begin high school, her first day in grade nine. The idea was terrifying. A new school. New faces. As if junior high hadn't been bad enough. She flicked through the pages of the book in her lap. It was one her aunts had given her, by their favorite author. He wrote about urban magic and fairies in North America.

*I wish.*

Dana's thought was bitter. There was no magic here. She leaned back against the apple tree and stared up into the branches. Her dark hair was lank on her shoulders, her face pale. Blue shadows rimmed her eyes. Under the bulky pants and sweater, she was thin and gangly. A great longing came over her and she let out a deep sigh. She couldn't have imagined being so lonesome and homesick. The past year had dragged on like an unending nightmare. Not a day passed by that she didn't miss Ireland.

She had found it impossible to settle in her new country. For one thing, she had no friends. And though she pretended she didn't care, Dana was aware of what she was missing that day. Most kids her age had gone in droves to celebrate their last day of the summer vacation at the Canadian National Exhibition. She knew from the previous year that there were carnival rides, an international food building, musical performances, and every kind of show and display. Her father had offered to take her again this year, but at thirteen you went with your peers, not your parents.

Her eyes misted with unshed tears. She fought them back.

"I'm such a loser," she muttered angrily.

The cat dozing on the bench beside her reached out to claw her arm.

"Ow!" she yelped. "Hey, you!"

A big tabby, sleek and strong, he was the king of the cats who lived in the greenhouse. His golden eyes appraised her coolly.

She grinned back at him.

"You're right. Stop feeling sorry for myself."

As she tickled his ears and scratched his chin, he purred like a motor.

"It's just hard sometimes," she murmured.

There were other problems that she wouldn't admit to. A tomboy and adventurer when she was small, Dana hadn't welcomed the changes that came with getting older. She wasn't interested in clothes or makeup or boys. And from the way things had gone so far, it was obvious to her that the older you got, the more you lost. Like Peter Pan, she didn't want to grow up.

Dana heard her father calling her to come in for lunch. She ignored him at first, then the rumblings in her stomach sent her into the house.

The hallway was filled with the aromatic scents of cumin, coriander, ginger, and cloves. All had been crushed together with a mortar and pestle before going into a pan of melted butter. Lunch would be spiced dahl and rice.

When Dana reached the kitchen door, she heard her father and stepmother preparing the meal together. Though they hadn't raised their voices, it was obvious they were arguing. At the mention of her name, Dana stopped to listen.

"I am only saying it is a shame she will not wear brighter clothes. I was sad that she chose only black. And such drab things as well!"

Her stepmother, Aradhana, was referring to their shopping expedition that weekend. New clothes for the new school year.

"We should be glad she isn't into fashion," Gabriel countered, though he sounded uneasy. "It's a good thing she isn't fanatical about her looks. There's too much of that with young girls nowadays. That's how anorexia starts."

"This is true, but also not true. It is important that young people take some pride in their appearance. It is part of their self-esteem. Dana dresses to hide herself. That cannot be good."

Dana was unsettled by her stepmother's words. They were too close for comfort. She cleared her throat loudly and entered the kitchen.

The two adults went immediately silent, looking guilty. Dana avoided their eyes and sat down at the table. This threesome had first come together in Ireland where Aradhana owned an Indian restaurant with her brother, Suresh. She was a beautiful young woman, as graceful as a gazelle, with black hair that reached her waist and soft dark eyes. Sometimes she wore saris, but mostly she wore jeans. When Gabriel fell in love with her, Dana had encouraged the marriage. She knew her parents would never be reunited, and she liked Aradhana.

"All set for the big day tomorrow?" Gabriel asked with false heartiness.

Dana ignored him.

He tried again. "We'll go out for dinner to celebrate the occasion. That's a promise."

"And we all know what your promises mean," she said coldly.

Gabriel opened his mouth to retort, caught a look from his wife, and closed it again. He began to fiddle with the silver ring in his ear, then rubbed his shaved head, the two things he did whenever he was upset. In his early thirties, he was a professional musician and also taught at the university.

"Will you dish out the rice, please, Dana?" her stepmother asked.

The fluffy basmati was cooked with coconut milk. Dana's mouth watered but she wasn't to be distracted. As she emptied the rice into a large bowl and passed it around the table, she continued her attack.

"If we were in Ireland, I'd already be in secondary school," she pointed out, "with all my friends."

Gabriel sighed but kept silent.

"And you promised me if I didn't like it here, we could go home. Well, I hate it! What kind of promise-keeping is that?"

Gabriel frowned. He had to answer. "Sometimes parents break their promises. It's impossible to keep them all. You'll discover that yourself one day."

Now the argument began in earnest, continuing through their lunch, till Gabriel finally lost his temper.

"That's it!" he exploded, "I'm fed up with this. You're like a dog at a bone. Go to your room!"

"As if I have anywhere else to go!"

Dana stormed out of the kitchen, slamming the door behind her.

Aradhana stood up to clear the table and patted her husband on the shoulder. While she did her best at times to play the mediator, she couldn't intervene every time the two fought. Sooner or later father and daughter would have to make their peace.

Gabriel shook his head with chagrin. He had lost it once again. He knew his daughter was unhappy, but there was nothing he could do. He had a good job and so did Radhi, and they both loved being in Canada. In fact, except for Dana, everything in Gabriel's life was going great. Though his friends and colleagues assured him that it was natural—their teenagers hated them too—he wasn't convinced. Did it really have to be this way? He was dismayed by the loss of her affection. Once upon a time they had been so close. A little family of two. When his first wife ran away and left him to raise their toddler alone, he had taken on the task with love and enthusiasm. Dana was his princess. He was her hero. Alas, the fairy tale was not ending happily.

In her room, Dana flung herself across the bed not knowing if she wanted to scream or cry. Miserable, she stared at her posters. The images of Ireland reminded her of everything she had lost: the little terraced house where she and Gabe had lived together, the gang of boys she played soccer on the street with, the sea-swept strand of Bray, the Wicklow Mountains.

And, as always when her unhappiness grew too hard to bear, she made her escape.

It was easy to do, as natural as breathing. Dana closed her eyes and let her thoughts drift. In the darkness behind her eyelids, the motes of light gathered. Slowly they began to dance together, weaving a vision.

*A high hill of dappled grass. A shining green slope. The pale mist of morning mingles with the light spilling from the clouds. On the crown of the hill, a megalith takes shape. Two great standing stones with a capstone overhead: a dolmen, a great stone archway. Green grass, gray stone, pale mist and light. The ancient magic of Faerie. A portal to beyond.*

No longer an image in her mind, it was there before her.

Dana ran up the hill toward the dolmen. Golden light issued forth to caress her face like the sun. Faint sounds of revelry echoed from within. Her heart lifted. This was what sustained her in her life of exile. Two homelands were hers, Ireland and Faerie. If she could not have one, at least she had the other. Half-human, half-fairy, this was her birthright, to walk between the worlds.

Dana had no sooner stepped through the portal than she found herself facing a great wall covered in ivy. She grinned to herself. There was often a trick or a test to undergo. The world of Faerie was like Chinese boxes— an elaborate puzzle of riddles and secrets, a maze of dimensions wrapped inside each other. She inspected the wall. It seemed to go on forever, both upward and sideways. She attempted to climb but her foot found no purchase and she immediately slipped back. She stood there, stumped. Then she heard the giggles. They came from behind the ivy. She giggled herself as she pulled at the leafage.

After a few tugs, the creepers obligingly gave way like green curtains on a stage. There in the stonework was an exquisite frieze that told a tale in multicolored mosaic.

*Fado, fado. Once upon a time . . .*

*Edane, the fairy Queen of Wicklow went a-maying with her ladies. Eastward they journeyed, toward the rising sun. The land was an endless garden. Beautiful were its trees and flowers, its lakes and streams; sweet, the music of the birds on the branch and those in the clear air.*

*When they reached the sugared peak of Little Giltspur, in sight of the blue sea, the Queen's ladies chose a sheltered place to hold their picnic. They fashioned a bower with the mayflowers they had gathered as they went. On a cloth of white linen, they laid out seedcakes dripping with honey and crystal glasses of cool elder wine. Then they called to their mistress to join them.*

*Edane only laughed and waved them away as she ran down the hillside, for she was chasing two butterflies, a Holly Blue and a Clouded Yellow. Soon she had left her ladies behind, as southward she flew in pursuit of her quarry. Her red-gold hair shone like fire. She wore a gown of pale silk that swept the ground.*

*After a time she came to an old forest that crested a high ridge. There she heard the music. It drifted through the air toward her, high silvery notes. Head tilted on her shoulder, eyes closed, she listened. The tune was like nothing she had ever heard before, powerful and beguiling. Following the sound, she moved lithely through the trees, drawn downhill irresistibly closer.*

*When Edane came to a clearing, she hid behind a bramble bush. Purple berries draped her ears and throat like jewels. Peering through the greenery, she gazed at the young man who commanded the glade.*

*His hair was dark, falling in curls that framed his lean features. He bowed his slender body as he strained to make music, his red lips pressing against the silver flute.*

*The Queen was enchanted by what she heard and what she saw. The Queen was enchanted by the music and the man.*

Dana smiled at the pictures, knowing the story of how her fairy mother fell in love with her human father. Alas the tale didn't end happily ever after, not only because they were mortal and immortal but because Dana's mother was already married to the King of the Mountain.

"Stop messing." Dana addressed her mother in one of the panels of the mural. "Come on, let me in."

The image burst out laughing, the wall disappeared, and there stood Edane, fiery hair wreathed in holly and ivy, eyes like blue stars.

"Welcome home, daughter," said the fairy queen in a melodious voice. "Welcome to the Fair Flowering Place where there is no grief or sorrow nor sickness or death."

"Just what I need," said Dana as they embraced.

They were more like friends than mother and daughter. Forever young and forever beautiful, Edane appeared no older than a girl of eighteen. Dana, tall at thirteen and soon to be fourteen, was quickly catching up. A fleeting concern crossed her mind. What would happen when she grew older than Edane? Dana pushed the thought away. She had come to escape her worries, not to add to them. After all, she didn't have to age either, at least not at the same rate as full mortals. Her fairy blood was strong. She could control how she looked, especially in Faerie.

Remembering that, Dana looked down at her clothing. With a single thought she transformed the baggy pants and sweater into a blue gown with a silver mantle. As she touched her head lightly, her hair was swept up with a crespine of pearls. In Faerie, she was beautiful.

Edane clapped her hands with delight.

"Come, dance with me!"

The shining kingdom was their playground. *Tír Tairngire.* Land of Promise. *Magh Abhlach.* The Plain of the Apple Trees. It was a country that revived the spirits of all who journeyed there, delighting the mind and nourishing the soul. The greensward of meadow was speckled with red poppies and bluebells. Streams overflowed with milk and honey. Sweet music chimed from the gold-leafed trees, and the "nobles of the wood," the birds of bright plumage, sang from the branches in the ever-new tongue.

*What is the number of the hosts which the light of the clear sky reveals?*

*What are the multitudes which dwell there on the other side of the solid earth?*

*And the bright sun, whither does it go?*

On a summer lawn, they danced a roundelay with many creatures. Wood mice and foxes, hares and hawks, ladybirds and damselflies, all footed lightly, singing and hooting and humming together. When the dancing stopped, they dined in a house of white stone with a roof of peacock feathers and a floor of spangled glass. A feast of fruits and sweet wine was served in dishes of gold and silver.

After the meal, they lounged on embroidered cushions as music wafted on the air like perfume.

Edane cupped her palms together and smiled to herself as golden light spilled out. She caught her daughter's hands.

"Do you make light?"

Dana was surprised. Truth to tell, she couldn't remember the last time she had tried.

"There's no need to here," she said defensively.

Her mother laughed and shook her head gently.

"What of the other place? You belong to two worlds. Are you not yourself in both?"

Edane flung a stream of light into the air.

"You come from a noble line, Dana. You are the daughter of a *spéirbhean*, a sky-woman. You belong to that tribe who herd the stars across the heavens, whose veins flow with light. We are descended from the White Lady of the Waters. That is your legacy."

The more Edane spoke, the more suspicious Dana grew. It was not like her mother to ask questions or give lectures.

"Who told you to say this?" she asked indignantly. "Has someone been spying on me?"

"We see everyone on every side and no one sees us," Edane said blithely. Then her eyes flashed with mischief and she threw up her hands. "I cannot do this! I cannot be like a human mother. I cannot tell you what to do. Remind you of your duties. Be good. Behave. It is against my nature!"

Edane burst into such wild peals of laughter that Dana couldn't help but join in. Here was another reason she loved Faerie. No one expected her to be responsible or mature. Indeed the opposite was encouraged.

Dana stayed for many days and nights. Days spent sailing in a glass-bottomed boat on warm green seas where mermaids dwelled. Nights spent sleeping in a hammock high in the treetops under stars that sang. Eventually, however, though she tried hard to ignore it, she felt the pull of the Earthworld drawing her back. No matter how much she enjoyed herself in Faerie, her human side inevitably wanted to go home. She resented the pull and yet was powerless against it. Otherwise she might never have chosen to return.

It was twilight. A hush had fallen over the sage-green fields. Dana strolled arm in arm with her mother. On the road ahead, the portal took shape. In flashes of mist and fire the great gateway rose up to span the worlds.

Edane reminded her daughter that no time had passed on the other side.

"I willed it so," she said lightly. "The order of things is ours to play with. We can open time like a fruit and spill out its seeds. For there is ordinary time and there is the

Great Time of eternity. Humanity dwells in fallen time. We live in the Dreaming."

With regret and resignation, Dana hugged her mother good-bye.

"I'll be back soon."

As soon as Dana stepped through the dolmen, she was back in her bedroom on that sunny Labor Day afternoon. A pang of dread struck her.

Tomorrow she would begin her first day in high school.

# THREE

Not long after Dana left Faerie, a young woman appeared beside Edane in a flash of light. Her skin was golden, her eyes sky-blue, and her pale hair was crowned with a wreath of red holly. Though she wore the shining raiment of Faerie, she seemed a little more solid than Edane herself.

"Your Majesty," said Edane, greeting her with a slight bow of the head.

Though Dana's mother was a queen in her own right and formal *courteisie* was usually reserved for the Court, this was Honor, the High Queen of all Faerie.

"Hi," said Honor. "At ease or whatever."

The two giggled. Honor was not long the High Queen and rarely said or did things properly. This made her very popular with her subjects.

"So, your daughter was here again? And she still won't visit me?"

Edane shrugged. "We spend our days in revelry, then she takes her leave. Her humanity pulls her back to the Earthworld. If I mention going to the Court she always suggests some other diversion. I tried to speak of the matters you mentioned, but it was no use. I do not fathom her at times and when this happens I think to myself, 'This must be her mortal side.'"

"Thirteen is a difficult age," Honor observed.

Edane looked perplexed a moment, then her features cleared.

"Ah, you would know this, being once mortal yourself."

Honor sighed. "I'm beginning to forget, but I do remember that. Puberty. What a nightmare."

"She is happy when she is here," Edane pointed out.

A slight frown crossed Honor's face. "That's what we need to talk about, dear heart. I fear Dana is using Faerie to escape reality."

"And what better place to do it!" Edane agreed. "How fortunate she is that she may claim her inheritance."

Honor hesitated. She would have to tread carefully. She knew that what she had to say went against the grain, the fairy perspective.

"I'm worried, Edane, that coming here so often is not good for her. It makes it hard for Dana to live in the world where she was born."

"She is of my blood and my world too," the other responded. "She is doubly in exile now that she lives *i n-ailithre*, in another country. She longs to return home. Both to Ireland and Faerie."

"Life is a journey through a foreign land," Honor said softly. Like a shining mantle, the wisdom that came with her sovereignty settled over her. "All are exiled from their true Home and ever travel towards it."

In the sky, the fairy constellations had begun their evening dance, pirouetting across the heavens in a grand ballet.

The High Queen linked arms with Edane as they crossed a wide sea, treading the path of moonlight that bridged the water. Honor's voice was low and musical.

"Because you are *spéirbhean*, full silver-blooded, you cannot know how these visits weaken your daughter. The High King and I are very concerned. She comes here to avoid her troubles. She is running away. And even as each act of bravery builds our store of courage, so too does each act of cowardice diminish us. It is important that Dana be strong in both worlds."

Edane was trying to listen, but the sky distracted her. A spiral galaxy had wheeled into view like a chariot, trailing lines of stars behind it. Holding onto the reins were two of her sisters, sky-women also. As soon as they spied Edane, the sisters waved wildly.

Honor could see that Edane was only half listening. The frustrating part of dealing with the Fey Folk! Notoriously flighty, they couldn't hold the moment, especially if it was a serious one. Only the High King could maintain any gravity for long. Edane was worse than most, not being of the earth but a Light-Bearer who fell from the sky. Totally airy-fairy.

Yet Honor had to get her message through somehow. Someone had to influence Dana, to make her see sense. Honor herself had once been a good friend to the girl, but Dana avoided her now. The one time the High Queen attempted to speak with her, Dana had turned sullen, as only a teenager can. She was obviously angry about something. The trials of growing up? The move to Canada? Somehow, somewhere, Dana had taken a wrong turn, gone down the wrong road, and it was not good, not good at all. Her time was coming and she wasn't ready.

"All the portents are strong," Honor said to Edane. "Soon a great blow will be struck against Faerie. Worse than any in the past. We are unable to see how or from where it will come, but we do know this. Dana is the key to our salvation. Her destiny calls."

The more Honor tried to impress the gravity of the situation upon Dana's mother, the more she could see the effort was hopeless.

Edane was gazing upward. Her sisters were steering their starry chariot in her direction. Now elegant arms reached down to catch her.

"I must away!" cried Edane.

Corybantic laughter filled the air. The sky-women reached for Honor too, but she smiled and shook her head. However tempting, she didn't need a mad dash through the cosmos right now. Ruefully she watched as Edane disappeared into the folds of night, along with any hope of reaching Dana through her mother. The High Queen was running out of options.

Stepping off the moonlit path, Honor headed west across the waters of the fairy sea. She walked through the night and the next day and the next, toward the land where the sun never set. Uncertainty weighed on her mind. She could sense the threat that hung over the Realm, lurking in the shadows, unnamed and terrible. But was she doing the right thing?

As the light grew brighter, the sea grew warmer. Soft winds breathed a sweet scent like roses. On the edge of the horizon hung the great golden orb of Faerie's sun. Honor could see the fiery plains where drakes and salamanders basked like red jewels. Solar winds ruffled her hair. Golden peaks spilled hot lava. She did not have to journey to that burning country, but the place she sought was near.

The small island floated like a lily on the waves. It was no more than a green hillock with a single tall tree. The tree appeared to be in bloom with a profusion of white flowers, but as Honor drew near she caught sight of the truth. The branches bore neither fruit nor flower, but a great flock of birds. Heads tucked under their wings, all were fast asleep, hushed and white like a fall of new snow.

*The soul-birds of Faerie.*

Honor knew that what she was contemplating was a huge risk. To waken the soul-birds was to waken Old Magic, an ancient and mysterious force that existed before the worlds came into being, before the great divide of good and evil. There was no telling what might happen if she woke that power. It was unpredictable. It could not be controlled. The only thing she knew for certain was that it guaranteed change.

And things *had* to change. So much was wrong and sure to get worse. All the prophecies and predictions were clear. Faerie's doom was upon them. Dana should be the one to counter their fate, but she was too weak for the mission. Honor could see that even if her beloved husband, the High King, could not.

"The rescue of Fairyland is a mortal task," he would assure his wife. "Since the two worlds came together, it has always been that way. Only humanity can fight our battles and they have never let us down."

"There's a first time for everything," she had argued.

And that was another exasperating thing about the fairies; their absolute faith in tradition. Had no one considered the possibility that humans could fail? Then what would happen? The Earthworld would lose the source of its hopes and dreams, and Faerie would lose its very existence.

Compounding Honor's doubts and fears was the rejection of her plea for help by her own twin sister. While

Honor accepted that Laurel had the right to say no, the wound had cut deep, further convincing her that the tide was against them.

The High Queen of Faerie stood at the bottom of the tree and gazed upward. Having failed to influence events through Laurel or Dana, she was ready to act on her own. There was a faint rustling in the branches above her, as the birds sensed her presence. But though the feathery bodies quivered, they remained asleep.

Despite her determination, Honor felt a tremor in her soul. Did she dare such a thing? To tamper with Old Magic?

"Desperate times call for desperate measures," she muttered.

And before she could change her mind, she raised her arms and cried out in full voice.

"*Sleepers awake!*"

Her cry had the same effect as the report of a shotgun. In an explosion of sound, the birds rose up in a frenzy. In a great white swell they banked overhead, an arabesque of sibilant flight. The sky throbbed. For one pure second of eternity, they hovered in the air, brooding over her with *ah! bright wings.* Then in a whir of wings and wind, they were gone.

Honor stared at the empty tree, the barren branches, the sky without birds. The deed was done. Only time would tell if she had helped or harmed.

# FOUR

Dana regarded her new school with a cold eye. It was
huge, twice the size of her last school. Everything
about it filled her with dread: the prison-gray stone, the
hostile glint of the tall windows, the interminable number
of steps that fronted the building. The big doors stood
open like a gaping maw to swallow the steady stream of
youth. Judging by the noisy greetings and laughter, most
were willing victims.

Slowly, reluctantly, Dana joined the crowd. Her steps
were leaden. The knapsack on her back seemed weighted
with rocks. She wore a loose-fitting jacket and black baggy
pants that trailed over her running shoes. Her hair fell
lankly over her face. A small silver ring shone in her left
nostril.

"Out of the question," was Gabriel's decree on body
piercing of any kind.

"You wear an earring," she had pointed out hotly.

The dispute was unexpectedly settled by Aradhana.
"There is a Western prejudice, husband, against piercing
the nose. In India it is a fashion for girls and women to

wear an ornament in this manner. I think you should allow her."

Though she would deny it if challenged, Dana's appearance was a silent protest against her life. The dark and bulky clothes cocooned her from the world around her. On the other side, in Faerie, she emerged like a butterfly, resplendent with fairy glamour. But the moment she returned to the Earthworld, she hid away again.

Head down, shoulders slumped, Dana shuffled through the long corridors. Lockers clanged. Friends hailed each other noisily. Squeals of excitement pierced the air. Forcing herself to stay calm, resisting the urge to flee, Dana located the classroom assigned to her on orientation day.

There were already a number of students there, most of them seated and talking quietly. Some were strangers, enrolled from other neighborhoods. With a sinking heart, Dana recognized the small group of girls who gathered near the door. Fashionably dressed, loud and pretty, they were a notorious clique from her old school. One of them raised an eyebrow as she passed by. The remarks were meant to be overhead.

"What's with all the black?"

"Is she a Goth?"

"Hardly. That would make her interesting."

Dana cringed, but told herself she didn't care. These were not people she envied or admired. Janis, the leader, was popular but not very bright. She had barely managed to pass grade eight. The other two were her lackeys, incapable of independent thought or action. While they had ruled the small kingdom of junior high, they were now little fish in a much bigger pond. Dana saw through their show of bravado. They were just as nervous and anxious as she.

Moving to the back of the room, she chose a desk in the last row. In her old school she had been known as a quiet girl, a loner without the protection of a circle or best friend. She had grown used to standing by herself at recess, leaning against the fence, usually lost in daydreams. She didn't want to mix with others and had rebuffed the few who tried to make friends with her. Unless specifically asked, she didn't participate in class, nor did she join in school activities, sports, or clubs. She resisted all efforts by her father and teachers to encourage her out of her shell. She did not want to be part of this world; she did not want to make friends.

"Some children are solitary," the principal had finally conceded to Gabriel. "You can either accept that or consider a psychologist."

Gabriel had decided to accept it, for now.

It helped that Dana did well at school. She liked to study, and her projects were always well researched and presented. With tutors and hard work she had caught up on Canadian subjects to earn high marks. The French language was still a weak point. Her father wanted her to learn it to be fully Canadian, but she had yet to reach the level of those who had begun the stream in earlier grades. Since she was already bilingual, being fluent in Irish, she was confident she could.

It was only when she had settled into her seat that Dana noticed the other student in the back, a few rows over. Now she understood why Janis and her coterie were making such a fuss. Here was surely the one whom they hoped to attract. Even Dana, who had no interest in boys, was not unaffected.

His raven-black hair fell loosely around his face. The narrow cheekbones and firm jaw hinted of strong character. His clothes jarred in the urban classroom but seemed to suit him: an outdoors look of rugged denim, dark-green shirt, and brown leather boots. He appeared older than the class average, but perhaps it was just his self-assured air. He did not look around, but sat relaxed at his desk, reading a book. Dana tried to catch a glimpse of the title. She was surprised at herself. There had been cute boys in her class before, and she had never paid them any attention. But this one was different. There was something about him . . .

Dana caught her breath. He had looked up suddenly to catch her gaze. His eyes were startling, a cool wintergreen. He seemed surprised to see her, as if he recognized her from somewhere, and he searched her features curiously.

The blood rushed to Dana's face. She turned away. It was not just from shyness. She was unsettled by that look, so keen and intense. When she found the courage to glance back again, he had returned to his reading. She was relieved, but also a little disappointed.

Once the school bell rang and the day officially began, Dana settled into her usual state of "betwixt and between." With half a mind, she listened to what she had to learn and made notes when necessary. With the other half, she looked out the window, lost in thoughts of Faerie.

Beyond the asphalt grounds of the schoolyard, a line of old oak bordered the road. Where their leaves were beginning to turn, faint stitches of bronze trimmed the green. Gray squirrels scrabbled in the branches, busy with their work. Dana smiled as she watched them. But what was that above the treetops? A white blur in the sky. At first she thought it was a bank of clouds herded by the wind, then she realized it was a great flock of birds. A mild shock ran through her. What were they? There were so many of them, all different shapes and sizes, but every one was snow-white. She felt her heart lift like a bird that wanted to fly too, and she followed their movement with longing.

A harsh voice broke Dana's reverie, followed by an outburst of laughter from the class. Words filtered through Dana's confusion.

*Woolgathering . . . daydreaming . . . featherbrain.*

To her horror, she found herself in the glare of

exposure. The whole class was staring at her with open amusement while the teacher scowled from the front.

It wasn't just the unwanted attention, the unkind words, or even the embarrassment. Something else alarmed Dana. She knew instantly in a way she couldn't explain that she was under attack. Struggling through her bewilderment, she faced her tormenter.

Mr. Crowley. When he had first entered the room, the universal reaction had been shock and dismay. He was not the jolly, pink-faced man who had made them all laugh at orientation. In a few short weeks some awful change had come over him. For one thing, there had been a drastic weight loss. Was cancer eating away at his insides? His skin seemed to hang on his big-boned frame, like the hide of a dead animal. And his hair was much thinner, falling in oily gray strands to his shoulders. There was a greenish tinge around his lips that pressed thinly together in a perpetual sneer. When he spoke, spittle gathered in the corners of his mouth and his tongue darted like a lizard's. And even his voice had changed; from a friendly baritone to a creepy whisper. But worst of all was the dead look in his eyes.

Dana shuddered as she met the cold gaze. There was something awful here, something far worse than his appearance. She could sense the ill will bearing down on her; an implacable hatred. It made no sense. What had she done? A buzzing noise rang in her ears, growing louder and stronger till her head began to ache.

She felt as if she were falling . . . falling backward . . .

*It is dangerous to approach evil. The best thing you can do is run away.*

Dana had no idea who or what was speaking to her, but the soft voice fluttered through her thoughts like wings. It was all the encouragement she needed. Mustering whatever resolve she could, she made her escape, journeying in her mind toward Faerie.

Despite her panic, Dana got there easily. In a matter of moments, she was running up the hill to reach the great portal. Music and laughter echoed from within. The warmth of the Summer Country bathed her face. But before she could step inside, it happened.

There was a blinding flash of light and a monstrous roar.

And her world blew apart.

As if in slow motion, she saw the great stones leap into the air. Then they crashed to the ground, shattering like glass. The pieces flew everywhere, strewn like bones in the grasses. Nothing was left standing.

Though reeling with shock, Dana grew aware of a second horror. The air was singed with a sour metallic smell. A sickly green mist whispered over the stone ruins. The buzzing sound rang out again, like a giant wasp about to sting her. She sensed a malevolent presence that didn't belong there. And in one heart-stopping second of clarity, she knew it was after her.

Too late, she tried to back away, to return to the Earthworld. The green mist was beginning to thicken, to take shape. Tendrils snaked toward her and curled around her throat. She began to choke. Drowning in terror, she clawed at the thing wildly, but the more she struggled the tighter it gripped. She couldn't scream. It was cutting off her windpipe. The buzzing sound was inside her head. She was losing consciousness.

Then words rang out like bells in the distance.

"*Tabernac*, so she look out the window. What's the big deal?"

It was like a splash of frosty water from a mountain stream.

With a sickening lurch, Dana fell into her body and was back in the classroom. She clutched her desk as she gasped for breath. Quickly she looked around. What was going on?

Mr. Crowley's face was contorted with fury, but his attention was no longer directed at her. It was trained on the young man a few rows over.

"Ah. Jean Ducharme. Or should I say, *Monsieur* Ducharme? Our transfer delinquent from Quebec. Swearing in class already. Have you been introduced to your peers who are hardly that since they are so much younger than yourself?"

The words oozed like an oil slick over clean waters,

but their target was not in the least perturbed. Jean Ducharme returned his teacher's glare with a mild look of disdain.

"I have fifteen years, *un peu* older than the others, *oui*. But my English is not good, so I am agreed to be here. In one year, I will meet my class. *Mais peut-être*, you cannot see this. You cannot see intelligence."

For a moment Crowley looked as if he might explode. Shuddering visibly, he regained control. His face cooled to a mask. His tone was icy.

"I wouldn't advise you to keep up that tone. I've seen your record. I could have you expelled in an instant."

A light smile played around Jean's lips, but he didn't bother to reply. Instead, he simply shrugged.

With a scowl, the teacher turned his back on the class and began to write on the board.

Wide-eyed, the rest of the class didn't hide their delight as they exchanged furtive glances. The year had barely begun and it was already showing great promise. They had all been immediately intimidated by the change in their teacher, but here was a new player challenging him. The girls cast approving glances at the hero in their midst. Dark-haired and handsome, older than the other boys, with a French accent and a shady past, what more could they ask for?

Only Dana was unhappy. Her thoughts raced wildly. She hadn't begun to absorb the horror of the attack against her and the destruction of her portal, when she found herself facing another dilemma. Like electricity in the air before a thunderstorm, she could sense it around her: the presence of magic. It was in the classroom. Had something followed her from the portal? Was it her attacker? She looked first at Crowley and then at Jean. Her mind was on fire. When the two glowered at each other, a look of recognition had passed between them. Or had she imagined it? No, they were connected, she was sure of it.

As the first shock wore off, Dana went on the defensive. There might be another assault. For the remainder of the class, she kept a careful eye on both her teacher and Jean. The two did not clash again, but settled into an uneasy truce, ignoring each other. Crowley also appeared indifferent to Dana, sometimes looking right through her as if she weren't there. She was beginning to think she was mistaken about him, when the bell went off. As she grabbed her books to leave, she caught him staring at her. A cat watching a mouse. The threat burned in his eyes before he could hide it. *I'll get you.* Trembling, she hurried from the room. She no longer doubted that he was her enemy. But why? How?

And what about Jean? She was not the only one interested in him. As the morning progressed, he was showered with glances like handfuls of confetti. Notes were passed among the girls. In the halls, spurts of French could be heard wherever he walked, as his admirers hoped to woo him with his own language.

In the cafeteria at lunch hour, clusters of girls hovered near his table. Some stood around awkwardly where he might see them, while others approached him directly to converse in French. The latter included young women from the higher grades. Word had spread like wildfire about the handsome new student who stood up to teachers.

Jean, for his part, was courteous to everyone who came near him. Those who spoke French, however badly, were rewarded with a half-smile and a fluent response that left them dazzled. He was so French. He was so hot. But despite all the fuss, he remained aloof, like a visitor who knew he would be leaving soon. As the circles of girls eventually drifted away, he went back to reading his book.

Dana had no desire to join the crowd around Jean, but she wanted to thank him for defending her in class. She was hoping to get closer, to investigate her suspicions. There was definitely something different about him. Could he be linked to the attack at the portal? But he seemed so . . . nice. A wolf in sheep's clothing?

As usual, Dana ate her lunch alone in a secluded corner. Like Jean, she had brought a book to read; but she couldn't concentrate. She was too upset. What had happened at the portal? What was after her? Along with her terror raged a deep sense of betrayal. Where was Faerie when her portal was destroyed? Where was Edane?

Why hadn't anyone mentioned danger? And why did no one come to help her? The more she thought about it, the more her heart beat wildly. The room seemed to close in on her. The din of too many voices. The screech of chairs scraping the floor. Like an icy hand around her throat, the truth seized hold of her.

*My portal is destroyed. My bridge to Faerie is gone. I'm alone and defenseless against an unknown enemy.*

A cold shiver ran through her. She felt sick with fear. Instinctively she glanced across the room. Once again Jean met her gaze. Was that a question in his wintergreen eyes?

Before she knew what she was doing, Dana was on her feet and walking toward him. Barely able to breathe, she willed herself across the unending stretch of floor. His quizzical smile seemed to encourage her.

She had almost reached him, when her way was blocked.

Janis had not seen Dana coming, as she was busy fixing her hair, and before she could finish the French phrase she had practiced, Jean interrupted.

"*Excus'-moi*, but we wish to speak," he said, indicating that someone was behind her.

Surprised and annoyed, Janis turned to find Dana. In one scathing glance she took in the rumpled clothing, the lank hair, the face without makeup. Curling her lip, she flounced away.

• • •

Dana was already regretting she had come this far, but Jean's voice was kind. "*S'il te plaît*, sit down."

She remained standing, and managed to stammer out her words. "I . . . I . . . wanted to say . . . *merci beaucoup* . . . thank you . . . for speaking up this morning. It was . . ."

"*Ce n'est rien*," he said, with a slight shrug. "Monsieur Crowley is not so nice, eh?"

As the calm eyes appraised her, Dana found herself mirroring Janis's scorn. If only she had made some effort with her dress and hair! If only he could see her in a fairy gown with jewels! For the first time since she could remember, she cared how she appeared in the Earthworld. He himself had a certain flair, though his clothes were casual. She noticed his watch had a wristband of beaded design. It showed a black bird, perhaps a raven. There was also a Native look to his boots.

She couldn't begin to know what he was thinking, but she was certain he found her unattractive, maybe even repulsive. She began to edge away.

"*Dis-moi*," he said. "What is this, your accent?"

"I'm Irish."

His smile was so swift and embracing that Dana felt her face go red.

"*Irlandaise! Magnifique!* The French and the Irish, we are always good friends. *C'est un beau pays, l'Irlande.*"

"Yes, it's a beautiful country," she said.

He caught something in her tone.

"You are not happy here?"

"Yes. No. It's . . . complicated." She didn't want to explain. She had yet to decide if she trusted him, this mysterious and charming stranger. "What about you? This isn't your home either?"

"I am Québécois. Born in Rivière-du-Loup, but we move around a lot. My parents, they are *artistes*. They get good jobs in *le théâtre* here. I choose this school to learn English better." A wry look crossed his face. "Maybe not a good idea."

"I'm so glad you did!" she exclaimed.

Dana thought she would die. Her face burned. He was so easy to talk to, she had been lulled by their conversation. Her stuttering had stopped, and in a natural progression, she had sat down at his table. Now she couldn't believe she had blurted out her feelings like that! Worse still, she grew suddenly aware of all the eyes that were watching.

Dana jumped up, almost upsetting her chair. She had to get away.

Jean looked surprised by her panic, and frowned. Before she could leave, he caught her arm. His voice was low.

"I want to say to you, about Crowley. Beware this man. For you, he is *dangereux*."

Before she could ask what he meant, he nodded toward

the entrance of the cafeteria. There in the corridor, staring through the glass doors, was their teacher. He looked from Jean to Dana and back again, eyes dark and furious.

"*Prends garde*," Jean said softly as he released her arm.

Confused and disturbed, Dana hurried away.

# FIVE

O n the same day and at the same moment in which
Dana was attacked, Laurel Blackburn pitched
forward with a cry. She was sitting in her academic
supervisor's office, discussing the subject of her thesis,
when the blow struck. It was as if a balled fist had punched
her gut. She doubled over. As the pain coursed through
her, a series of images entered her mind.

*A little girl with blond curls, about three years of age, reaches
out to touch a hot stove. She lets out a cry as it burns her hand.*

*The same little girl, two or three years older, falls off a
swing. Hitting the ground, she gashes her forehead.*

*Now she is nine, cornered in the schoolyard by a bully
who pushes her against the wall.*

Laurel recognized the child immediately, even as she
remembered the images. They were memories of times
when her twin, Honor, was in trouble. Being the stronger

and more daring of the two, Laurel had rescued her sister on each occasion.

The last vision was a new one.

*Through a dark wood overhung with shadows, Honor runs wildly. Her hair is tangled, her gown torn. Tears stream down her face as she cries out: "Our doom has fallen! The Summer Land is lost!"*

"Are you all right?" Laurel's professor asked her, concerned.

Laurel straightened up. The pain had left her, but the horror lingered on.

"Yes . . . yes, I'm fine. I'm sorry, but I must go."

And she ran out of his office.

Gwen, too, felt the blow that day. Late for a job interview, she was hurrying through a downtown shopping mall when it struck. Her knees buckled under her. She leaned against a store window.

"Oh God," she gasped.

The mannequins stared back at her blindly.

With the pain had come an image that hurt her all the more. It was only a brief flash, but the details were seared on her mind.

*A high hill cloaked with hawthorn. A gray sky above a*

*grassy slope. A chill wind blows over the desolate scene. Two figures sprawl facedown in the grasses, both utterly still. One is an old woman, the other a young man.*

As soon as she recovered, Gwen ran for the subway, abandoning her interview. She had to get home. Call Ireland. The place in her vision was well known to her; Dunfinn, the fairy fort on Inch Island in Donegal. Worse still, she knew the two people she had seen lying dead on the ground. The old woman was Granny Harte, fairy doctress and friend. The other was Dara, the young man Gwen loved.

The telephone was ringing as she opened her apartment door. She ran to answer it.

"Gwen, something terrible has happened!" Laurel's voice shook.

"I know. Can I come over?"

*"Please!"*

Laurel's rooms were spacious by student standards. A partition separated the bedroom from the wide living area that had a built-in desk against the window and shelves lining the walls. These were stacked with books and papers. There was a small sofa and armchair with a wooden coffee table. A burnt-orange rug warmed the tiled floor. Classical music played softly on the radio.

Gwen sat on the couch, sipping a mug of herbal tea. She could feel herself calming down.

"St. John's Wort?"

Laurel nodded, pouring herself a cup.

"A fairy plant. It dispels dark forces."

"Tell me what happened," said Gwen.

Laurel paced the floor. No longer reserved and self-composed, she was evidently distraught. Her face was pale, her eyes frantic. The long blond hair straggled on her shoulders as she ran her hands through it anxiously.

"Honor and I always had this twin thing. We would know if the other was hurt or in trouble. The day she died, I collapsed. I knew she was gone."

Laurel choked on her words. Gwen murmured sympathetically and waited for her to continue.

"This was the same but even stronger, as if she were consciously trying to contact me, to get a message through. I'm worried sick. There's been no sign of her since that vision. I have an awful feeling that she can't reach me. I tried to fall asleep to dream my way into Faerie, but I'm too upset."

"I felt something too." Gwen described her own experience. "I called Ireland right after you rang. All I got was Granny's answering machine. She and Dara were to meet the High King today at Dunfinn on Inch Island." She fought back the tears. "That's where I saw them . . . lifeless."

Overwhelmed with emotion, the two young women stared at each other.

It was Laurel who rallied first.

"You don't know that for certain," she insisted. "You're assuming the worst and you don't have the facts. For all we know these could be premonitions or warnings. We might be able to prevent them. We've got to think rationally."

Gwen heard the "we" and it steadied her up.

"You're right. I'm being a dope. We've got to get the story. Find out what's happening."

"There's something else . . ." Laurel hesitated, then made a reluctant confession. "I rang Ireland too."

With sudden insight, Gwen guessed what she was talking about. Laurel's tale was familiar to her: how the other had quested in the west of Ireland to find the Summer King. During the course of her mission, Laurel had discovered that the fairy king was to blame for her twin's death; but she was already in love with his human side born separately in the Earthworld.

"You called Ian?"

Laurel turned away. Her voice was strained. "We broke up a year ago. I stayed away from Faerie since he spends half his time there as the Summer King. I decided it was best to leave it all behind me and get on with my life. When I couldn't contact Honor . . . well, I thought he might know something. I rang his flat and his work but there was no answer, so I called his father, the Reverend Gray." A quaver crept into Laurel's voice. "Ian's missing. He didn't show up for work today and he didn't call in.

That's not like him. He's a vet, with his own practice. His parents are really worried. So am I."

She returned to her pacing.

"I thought it was over, but I've obviously been fooling myself. As soon as I heard he was missing, it was like an arrow in my heart. I thought I would die."

"So whatever has happened involves him too," Gwen said, thinking. "But I thought this mission had to do with Canada, not Ireland."

"Ireland isn't the common denominator here," Laurel pointed out. "It's Faerie."

That was when the penny dropped for Gwen; the bigger picture that loomed over the nightmarish vision of Dara and Granny.

"How could I be so stupid? It was just . . . Dara . . . I . . . Yes, this is it. The great attack against Faerie that Granny foresaw. The darkest hour."

Laurel nodded. "We know what we must do: rescue Fairyland."

Again Gwen was heartened by the "we" but needed to know for sure.

"You've changed your mind, then? You're in this with me?"

Laurel grimaced wryly. "That's the way it goes, eh? Just like you said. You're in over your head before you know it. Honor and Ian are the two people I love most in the world. I can't bear the thought of losing them."

They regarded each other solemnly, two heroines who had quested once before for Faerie.

"We need a plan," said Laurel.

Gwen agreed. "I'll keep trying to find out about Dara and Granny. Hopefully Honor will contact you again, or maybe Ian. We've got to find out what's going on. Meanwhile, our original task was to look after Dana. I have some protective charms and herbs. I was going to put them around her, secretly of course."

"Excellent idea," said Laurel. "I have a few spells of my own that I learned on Achill Island. 'Red thread tied round branch of rowan.' Stuff like that. We should do ourselves as well."

"Of course. We could be targets too," Gwen said without flinching. "I've got the addresses of Dana's home and school. I've even applied for a job at her high school, as a teacher's assistant. That would have been perfect, but no luck. We should get going on this as soon as possible. Today, at twilight or midnight. Threshold hours are the most potent. I suggest midnight. Less chance of being seen. Is that okay with you?"

Despite the gravity of the situation, Laurel smiled at Gwen's air of command. It was such a contrast to her friendly features and plump femininity. Here indeed was the captain of the Company of Seven. A warrior in pink.

"The sooner we do it, the better," Laurel agreed. "Something is on the move, working its way through the city. Have you read the papers? A crime wave is hitting the streets."

"I should've acted before now," Gwen said with a pang of guilt. "The move and the job hunt have really slowed me down."

The same guilt struck Laurel. "It's my fault too. If I had joined you when you asked . . ."

Gwen dismissed the point with a wave of her hand. "I could've made more of an effort to win you over. You want to know something? I wasn't really that happy that you were being called in. I liked being the only adult on this side of the water. It left me in charge."

Caught off guard by her words, Laurel let out a quick laugh. "Well, you're the only American."

"Good thing," rejoined Gwen, and they both laughed together.

"You should laugh more," Gwen said.

"With you around I have a feeling I will." Laurel's features softened. "After things ended with Ian, I couldn't go back, not to Ireland or Faerie, even though I wanted to. It was my fault, you see. We were always arguing and I just found it too difficult to reconcile our differences. He wanted to keep trying. He believed in us. But I said no." She shrugged sadly. "I think I'm just one of those people who ends up alone."

Gwen reached out to touch her arm.

"You're not alone. We're in this together."

• • •

Later that night, shortly before twelve, Gwen and Laurel met at the corner of Brunswick and Bloor. Both wore dark clothing to blend with the night. Each had a bulging knapsack. Gwen had brought branches of ash and whitethorn as well as bunches of primroses gathered on May Eve. Laurel had sea salt, twigs of rowan and broom tied with red thread, dried daisy chains, and old knives and scissors. Gwen had been taught her charms by Granny, the Wise Woman of Inch. Laurel had learned hers from the sea fairies of Achill Island.

"Any news?" Gwen asked.

Laurel shook her head. "Still no word or sign from either of them."

Gwen's shoulders slumped. "Same for me. I tried to reach the other members of the Company of Seven: Katie on her farm and Matt at home. All I got was voice mail or busy signals. I've sent e-mails too, but no replies. My cousin Findabhair is still on the road with her husband. I left an urgent message with their manager."

Laurel could hear the huge effort Gwen was making to stay optimistic. They were both clinging to the hope that, despite all appearances, their loved ones were safe.

"Come on," Laurel said, "we've got work to do."

They hurried up Brunswick Avenue to Dana's address. When they reached the big brownstone, they stared in dismay. It was a huge area to cover. Despite the late hour, lights shone in many of the rooms. The charms had to be placed in spots that were both secret and safe; where they wouldn't be seen or removed or blown away by the wind. And would it be possible to strew the doors and windowsills without being noticed? At least the house was surrounded by trees and bushes. Plenty of places to hide if anyone came out.

"I'll take the backyard," Laurel said in a low voice. "You do the front."

Gwen was grateful that she didn't have to climb over the fence.

The two hurried away but it wasn't long before they joined up again.

"Finished?" they asked each other, exchanging looks of surprise.

It was only when they were a safe distance away that they broke their silence.

"I put some stuff on the sills," Gwen said, mystified, "but then I stopped. I got the strangest feeling— "

"Me too! That it wasn't necessary?"

"Yes! Because— "

"The house is already protected," Laurel concluded.

They had stopped under a street lamp. Bathed in a soft yellow light, both were breathless and excited.

Gwen looked back up the street. "A beautiful presence," she said softly. She could hug herself she felt so good.

"And jolly as well." Laurel wanted to laugh, but she also felt shy. "Full of fun and laughter, but also sacred and powerful. The way I imagined Santa Claus when I was little."

"We're not alone," Gwen whispered.

"Other forces are gathering around the girl," Laurel agreed. "This is good. This is very good."

For the first time since the blow was struck, the two were hopeful.

"Right, then. Let's get a taxi to her school," said Gwen. "We've got plenty of charms left for the job."

"School and home," said Laurel, nodding. "That should do it. Where else would you find a thirteen-year-old?"

Reaching Bloor Street, they kept watch for a cab. Despite the late hour, the avenue was busy. Restaurants, pubs, and coffee shops were bustling with late-summer trade. There was a mild chill in the air, but the night was still amenable to strollers.

"How about lattes and Nanaimo bars in the little café?" Gwen suggested.

"Work first, then treats."

"You are so like my cousin," sighed Gwen.

When they arrived at Dana's high school, their hearts sank. Not only was the building locked and shuttered, it was ablaze with security lights and video cameras. Gingerly they approached the first window. Laurel flung a handful of salt through the metal grate, while Gwen pressed a primrose petal onto the sill.

Neither was prepared for what happened next.

Flower and salt burst into flames, even as a blast of hot air flung the two of them backward.

They hit the ground hard. Both had the wind knocked out of them. Gwen cracked her elbow. Laurel smacked her head. Stunned, they lay there a moment. Then, groaning with pain, they helped each other up.

"We're too late," said Laurel.

"It's been claimed by the other side," agreed Gwen. "We're not safe here."

Glancing around them fearfully, they hurried away.

Back at Laurel's, any thought of treats was long forgotten.

"I was afraid of this," Gwen said, sickened. "We're failing already."

"We're dancing as fast as we can," Laurel countered, but she also looked grave. "With her school compromised, Dana's in serious danger. We've got to join up with her."

Gwen frowned. "Granny's instructions were clear. It's her mission, not ours. We are just to be like guardian angels. Watch over her from afar."

"That doesn't make sense," Laurel argued. "We can protect her better if we are with her. Things are getting serious. And she's only a kid."

"She's more than a kid. She has power of her own." But Gwen sounded uncertain.

"The situation has changed since you last spoke with Granny," Laurel pointed out. "The plan must change too."

"All right, we'll contact her," said Gwen, though she didn't look happy. Talking about Faerie was never easy; could they do it with a complete stranger and a teenager at that? She thought out loud, as much to reassure herself as Laurel. "I'm good with young people. And she'll recognize you since you look like the High Queen. It shouldn't be too difficult getting her to trust us."

"Okay," said Laurel. "First thing tomorrow, we tackle her."

Had that meeting taken place, all of them might have suffered less, but it was not to be. Things were about to get worse.

# Six

It was Aradhana who noticed how ill Dana looked when she came home from her first day at school. Dana's face was so pale, she was almost translucent, and her eyes had a feverish look. She was sent to bed immediately.

"Are you feeling any better?" Radhi asked gently when she came into the room with a cup of chamomile tea.

Dana smiled wanly but was unable to muster a livelier response.

"Your temperature is very high," her stepmother said worriedly, placing a cool hand on her forehead. The scent of jasmine was comforting.

In the days that followed, Dana grew worse, as if some poison were working its way through her system. Unable to eat, she complained of mysterious aches and pains. Her sleep was fitful and broken as a recurring nightmare plagued her. She would find herself back at the portal and under attack. Cords of sickly green mist snaked around her to choke off her air. In the distance, a shining figure reached toward her in vain. Dana could hear the terror in her mother's cries. It was Dana's attempts to call back that would wake her up. Then she had to face the dreadful truth once more: she was all alone and cut off from Faerie.

"It's most likely a virus," the doctor told Gabriel. "No use treating it with antibiotics. We'll give it a few days and if there's no improvement, I'll order some tests. Between you and me, it could be psychosomatic. Some kids are traumatized by starting high school. They adjust with time."

Gabriel sighed. He had thought as much himself, though his wife didn't look convinced.

When the doctor was gone and Gabe had left the room to make dinner, Aradhana sat down beside the bed. Her voice was quiet as she clasped Dana's hand.

"Is everything all right between you and your mother?"

Dana stared into the dark, thoughtful eyes. Her stepmother's question showed how special Radhi was. Both Gabriel and Aradhana had discovered the truth about Dana's mother before they left Ireland. Gabriel soon forgot what he had learned about his first wife, remembering only that she had promised to stay in touch with Dana. It was the nature of Faerie. The spell of forgetting was woven like a wall around it. Adults in particular could not hold the reality of fairy existence for long. If they did remember, they inevitably dismissed the experience as a dream or a figment of their imagination. There was a time when Dana wished she could have shared that side of her life with her father, but his forgetting made things easier. She could move between the worlds without permission or explanation.

Up to that moment, she had assumed that Aradhana, too, had forgotten the true story.

"I respect your privacy," her stepmother said now. She chose her words carefully. "Your life with your mother is not any of my business. But I want you to know, my Irish Barbie, that if you need to speak of such matters, you may do so with me. In India we live with many gods and spirits. They are not strangers to us."

Tears pricked Dana's eyes. She felt as if she were at the bottom of a dark well, looking up at her stepmother who peered over the edge. She wanted to call out to Radhi, but found she couldn't. All she could do was shake her head.

By the end of the week, Dana began to feel better, as if the shadow that had fallen on her had finally dispersed. When her father announced they were going to her grandmother's in Creemore for the last family gathering of the summer, she couldn't have been happier.

The village of Creemore was just an hour and a half drive north of Toronto. It was given its name in the 1840s by Judge James R. Gowan. He called it after a townland in his native county of Wexford in southern Ireland. The founding father of the village, Edward Webster, also came from that townland, but his family had emigrated to

Canada long before the judge. While there is no recorded history of the moment, Edward and Judge Gowan may well have christened the village together over a malt whiskey in Kelly's Tavern on the main street.

The modern Creemore was a picturesque village of tree-lined avenues, old churches, and stately homes of red or yellow brick. Nestled in the valley of the Mad and Noisy Rivers and surrounded by rich farmland, it was a quiet, sleepy place during the week. Every weekend, however, it would fill with tourists as well as the city dwellers who kept summer cottages in the Purple Hills. The main thoroughfare of Mill Street was a browser's delight with quaint storefronts, hanging flower baskets, and hand-crafted street signs. Antique shops, art galleries, and tea rooms bloomed like roses. The village also boasted North America's smallest jail, little more than a shed.

Dana's grandmother, Maisy Gowan, was "bred and buttered" in the village, as she liked to say. Though married, she was called by her maiden name since she belonged to one of the oldest and most respected families in the town. A small, sturdy woman of endless energy, she wore her salt-and-pepper hair in closely cropped curls. On Sundays she dressed in a skirt and blouse with pearls or brooches and sometimes a hat, while the rest of the week saw her in tracksuits and running shoes. In her late sixties, she lived a busy life, working in her garden and keeping up the family home. She also served on various committees including the Creemore Tree Association, the Creemore Horticultural Society, the Purple Hills Arts and Heritage Society, and the Royal Canadian Legion.

The Gowan home was just off the main street. Built by Maisy's grandfather in 1901, it was a fine big house of red and cream brick with stone quoins on the corners and gabled windows. Geraniums blossomed on the sills. A wooden veranda encircled the house, furnished with a swing seat, a rocking chair, and wickerwork tables. A wide front lawn ambled down to the road, shaded by maple and cherry trees. In the past, the rooms were heated with wood stoves whose pipes went up to warm the second floor before connecting to the chimneys. According to Gran Gowan, the house was never as cozy once "newfangled" central heating was installed. But old-fashioned comfort was still to be found in polished pine floors, iron beds with goose-down quilts, and open fireplaces. In the backyard was a drive shed where the horse and carriage were once kept. Now it housed Gran's pride and joy, a dark-green Triumph Herald that once belonged to her husband.

Dana loved her grandmother, who doted on her and also her two aunts, Yvonne and Deirdre.

Though they were older, Dana's aunts looked and acted like teenagers. At thirty-two, a painter and sculptor, Yvonne was a brash blonde who dressed in dramatic colors, usually scorched orange or red. She liked tight skirts and slinky dresses, stockings with seams, stiletto high heels, and ruby red lipstick. Younger at twenty-nine, Deirdre, also called Dee, was a filmmaker who specialized in radical documentaries and political animation. Having shaved her head for years, she now sported a blue brush-cut. Slashed jeans and leather jackets were Deirdre's preference, worn with hobnailed boots, but sometimes she added strings of pearls to "soften" the look. Given their own idiosyncratic tastes, the aunts would not interfere with Dana's appearance despite their older brother's pleas.

"There's no such thing as a good influence," Yvonne told him. "As Oscar Wilde said, 'All influence is immoral.'"

"Is she saying 'grunge' do you think?" Dee wondered. "It's a valid statement."

"What," snorted Gabriel, "'I will not wash?'"

"'I will not be a slave to conventional forms of beauty,'" his sister corrected him. "Didn't you see my doc on youth and fashion? Does no one in my family look at my work? I'm a prophet in my own home, unrecognized and undervalued."

"I know all your work," Yvonne pointed out, "and Gabe was out of the country for that one."

In the end, of course, Gabriel knew it was hopeless. His sisters would never side with him against Dana. He was a parent: "one of them." She was a daughter: "one of us."

• • •

The barbecue and corn roast was held in Gran Gowan's back garden with its broad lawn bordered by a fence and tall privet hedges. The smell of charcoal mingled with that of hamburgers and hot dogs sizzling on the grill. A pot of boiling water bobbed with yellow cobs of corn. On a cloth-covered table were baskets of crusty bread and soft rolls along with bowls of potato salad, coleslaw, mixed greens with tomatoes, sliced beetroots and pickles, and various pots of mustard and relish. Ice clinked in wet jugs of homemade lemonade sprinkled with white sugar. As Gran Gowan did not approve of alcohol and barred it from the premises, the aunts had been forced to stash a cooler of beer in Dee's bedroom. Getting it up the stairs without their mother noticing involved stealth and timing, but they were practiced hands. Gran also didn't approve of the vegetarianism of her son and granddaughter who had brought lentil patties to accompany the corn and salads.

"I have no objections to Aradhana not eating meat," Maisy stated in her no-nonsense way. "It's her religion and I would never stand between someone and their God. You two, on the other hand, are just being contrary."

As the afternoon meandered on and they all had eaten their fill, the croquet set was arranged on the lawn.

"We'll divide into teams," Yvonne declared. "Radhi and Gabe, Maisy and Dana, Dee and me."

"Place your bets, ladies and gentlemen. We're going

to take you to the cleaners," said Dee, swinging her mallet like a golf pro.

"There'll be no gambling here," Gran Gowan said.

"Don't mind those two," Gabe said to his wife. "They're all bluff and bluster. It's the dark horses we'll have to watch out for, Dana and Mom."

Dana listened to the banter as she lined up for her shot. She felt safe with her family, and was happy to forget about the nightmare of the previous week. *Clack* went her bat as it hit the hollow ball that rolled over the grass. When it sailed through the wire hoop, everyone cheered.

By late afternoon the barbecue had cooled and the table was cleared. Aradhana went to her room to rest, while Gabe and his mother sat on the chesterfield in the parlor to watch the news. The two aunts stayed outdoors, sneaking gin into their lemonade from a flask. They sent Dana into the kitchen to fetch more ice. That was when she overheard her father and grandmother talking in the next room.

". . . dreadful," Gran Gowan was saying, "even paler than usual. And she still has no friends! I've said it before, Gabriel, and I'll say it again, Toronto is no place for the girl. You've taken her from a small town in Ireland and dropped her into a big foreign city. A year has passed and she has not settled in. Every time I see her, she looks unhappier than the last. She should be here with me in Creemore. I know you love her, but you're too busy with your new job to look after her properly and you have a wife now as well. Dana was used to having you all to herself."

"Dana loves Radhi!" Gabriel protested.

"Don't interrupt your mother. That's not the point. I'm not going to stand by any longer and watch that bright, lively child grow more miserable by the day. She's withering away. It's not natural. She would flourish here. Creemore is a close friendly community. She'd go to the high school in Stayner—a good size, but not too big—and there are plenty of young people to be her friends, like that sweet Holly Durnford down the road."

"Dana's eccentric, like her aunts," Gabriel argued defensively. "They had no friends either, and they grew up here in Creemore."

Gran Gowan was stumped by that truth for a moment, but she recovered quickly.

"Well, they had each other. Dana has no siblings. Which is another point. You're married now and not getting any younger. It's time you started thinking of a family. There is already too much of a gap between—"

"Aradhana and I will have kids when we're ready!" Gabriel's voice thundered. This was forbidden territory.

"Hmph," said his mother, retreating quickly.

Dana could hear her father spluttering. Here was undoubtedly one of the reasons why he had lived in Ireland for so long. Gran Gowan had no qualms about interfering in her children's lives.

Dana backed away from the door. Why was everyone always talking about her? As if she were nothing but a problem! She was overcome by the shame, the unfairness, the sheer awfulness of her life. It only compounded the nightmare of the week gone by. Her eyes flooded with tears. She barged through the screen door and out into the garden.

"Where's the ice, O slow but faithful one?" Dee called out.

Her aunts were lounging on deck chairs on the far side of the lawn, where Gran Gowan was unlikely to detect the scent of liquor.

Dana didn't answer, but raced blindly around the side of the house and onto the street. She had no idea where she was going; she just wanted to get away. Too miserable to see anything, she didn't notice the car parked across the road— a black sedan with tinted windows. Nor did she notice that it moved off to follow her as she ran down the street.

Now, like a panther stalking its prey, it pulled up beside her. The passenger window slid noiselessly down.

Shocked by the sight of the driver, Dana stopped.

"Hello, my dear," came the whispery voice. "Fancy meeting you here. Small world, isn't it? I missed you at school all week. Are you feeling better now?"

Mr. Crowley looked even thinner than she remembered him. His frame was skeletal and his face, gaunt and gray. The only part of him that seemed alive was the eyes that burned into hers, though they, too, had something hollow about them.

"Would you like to come for a ride with me? Yes. Open the door. Yes. Get in."

Alarm bells rang in Dana's head, yet she found herself inexorably drawn to the car. Her hand reached out to open the door. She knew it was wrong—*what am I doing?*—but she couldn't resist. Crowley's voice was mesmeric. His eyes transfixed her.

"Yes. Get in," he insisted. "Come with me now."

Dana was almost in the car when she heard a shout. Slowly, with huge effort, she turned to see her aunts. They were running toward her.

"*Get in!*" Crowley urged.

His will seemed relentless; but the shouts of her aunts jarred against it. The two forces pushed and pulled at her. As the aunts drew nearer, Dana saw the panic on their faces. Dee was ahead, boots pounding the pavement, with Yvonne close behind despite her high heels.

Crowley cursed and leaned over to grab Dana.

Just as Deirdre arrived in time to grab at her also.

The car door slammed and the sedan screeched away.

Dee clasped her niece.

"What's the license number?" Yvonne shouted, catching up to them.

Deirdre squinted at the speeding vehicle as it disappeared down the road.

"I don't have my lenses in," she said, nervous and jittery.

Yvonne was the same.

"For chrissakes, how can you go around half-blind like that!"

"New perspectives. Fuzzy edges."

"Great. A myopic filmmaker."

"We're babbling," Dee warned. "Shock."

"You're right," her sister agreed. "We should call the police."

They both pulled out their cell phones as if they were pistols.

"Did you get a good look at him?" they asked Dana. "What did he say?"

Dana was bewildered. She was glad that Deirdre was holding on to her. Her head hurt and she felt loose and disconnected, as if she were unraveling. She had a vague sense that something terrible had just happened, but she couldn't remember what. At the same time she was confused by the memory of a harmless conversation.

"I . . . it was . . . someone asking for directions."

"Oh yeah?" Dee demanded. "Then how come he took off like a bat out of hell?"

"And what were you doing getting into the car?" Yvonne asked, more gently. "You know better than that, kiddo."

Dana shook her head as she looked from one to the

other. Tears trickled down her face. She had no idea what was going on. Could her life get any worse?

The aunts were calming down. Their terror at seeing their niece being abducted began to ebb away as they found themselves questioning what they had seen. The more they thought about it, the vaguer were their impressions. The only thing they were really sure of was Dana's distress.

"Tea room," Yvonne announced, throwing her sister a look. "Hot chocolate and chocolate buns with heaps of chocolate sauce and chocolate doughnuts."

"When in doubt, administer chocolate," Deirdre agreed.

The Mad Hatter Tea House was a favorite of the aunts. Everything about it was "darling." The wood-framed building was painted eggshell blue with yellow trim. A line of pink flamingos marched past the front window. Inside, the big room was chock-a-block from floor to ceiling with shelves of teapots. Big ones, small ones, plain and patterned, delicate china or glazed ceramics, they came in every shape and color; a black-and-white cow, a hen on her nest, ladies in long skirts, a honey hive with bees, a piano, a chair. Each was a work of art and no two were alike.

The three settled into an alcove by the lace-curtained window. Though the menu offered sandwiches and other savories, they went immediately to the desserts. By the time they had tucked into the chocolate-mousse cheesecake and chocolate-chip cookies, they had forgotten why they were there.

"Gran will kill us," Dana said, her mouth full. "She made a rhubarb tart."

"Hah! We'll eat that too," said Dee.

Yvonne dialed her cell phone.

"Maisy, we've gone for a walk," she said, winking at the others. "Put the pie in the oven. We'll be back soon."

The aunts had huge appetites and ate like horses without any visible effect on their weight. "Good breeding," their mother maintained. "Hyperactive madwomen" was their own prognosis.

"So why did we get so upset when that guy asked you for directions?" Yvonne wondered.

Dana shrugged.

"Toronto paranoia," Dee concluded. "Do you ever get the reverse kind? When you think you're following someone?"

"Oh yeah," said Yvonne, dropping brown sugar cubes into her coffee. "Everywhere you go, you keep seeing the same person and you think 'My God, am I trailing them?'"

Sitting between the two, Dana felt her spirits lift. She was always in good humor when her aunts were around. They expected nothing of her and accepted her as she was, regardless of her mood. She wished she could tell them about the attack at school, but it wasn't possible.

They knew nothing of fairy life, and she couldn't begin to explain what happened when she didn't know herself.

"I still miss Ireland," she confided instead. "It's like an empty feeling in my stomach that won't go away."

"Try the cheesecake," Dee said. "It's almost as good as—"

Her sister frowned her into silence.

"You're just like your dad," Yvonne said with sympathy. "We weren't surprised Gabe stayed so long in Ireland. Aside from escaping Mom, of course, he was always crazy about everything Irish—music, books, history, language, Irish this and Irish that."

"Irish Guinness," Dee added.

"The trouble is," Yvonne continued, "you haven't seen enough of Canada. All you've seen is Toronto and Creemore."

"Toronto's good," Dee interjected. "Creemore's good."

"Yeah but," said Yvonne. "There's so much more. Like Hugh MacLennan said, 'This land is far more important than we are. To know it is to be young and ancient all at once.'"

"How do you remember these things?" her sister said admiringly.

"There's been no time to travel," Dana pointed out. "We've had so much to do from the time we got here. Find a place to live, Gabe and Radhi's marriage, their new jobs, my new school."

"I rest my case," said Yvonne. "No time to smell the roses, to appreciate where you are and what you've got."

"I appreciate you two," Dana declared.

Her aunts beamed back at her.

"And we're crazy about *you*," Yvonne said. "We're really glad you're over here and we just hope someday you will be too."

The three returned to Gran Gowan's in time for the rhubarb pie and a family game of Scrabble. As the night grew darker, Dana was eventually sent to bed. Climbing under the soft quilt, she was nagged by a stray thought. There was something she had forgotten. Something that happened during the day. What was it? But no matter how hard she tried, she couldn't remember. Giving up at last, she fell into a troubled sleep.

Later that night, when the others had gone to bed and the lights were out, Crowley returned.

# SEVEN

*D*ana was standing on the sidewalk in front of her
grandmother's house. She had no idea how she had got
there or what she was doing.

A black sedan drew up to the curb. The door swung open.
A whispery voice issued from the dark interior of the car.

"This time you will get in. Yes. You cannot resist."

Crowley wasn't lying. Though it was the last thing she
wanted to do, Dana did as she was told. As soon as she sat
in the passenger seat, the door shut and locked of its own
accord. Now the seat belt slithered over her shoulder to bind
her fast.

"You're mine!" he hissed triumphantly.

"Where—?" Dana's voice was small and strangled. She
found it difficult to think or speak. "Where are we?" she
tried again.

Creemore was gone. Outside her window was a bleak and
blackened landscape. As far as the eye could see, everything
was dead or dying, sered by fire. The earth was gashed and
torn, and thrown aside in clots of dank mud. Swamp willows
crawled from the roscid hollows. A polluted snye trickled like

*ink past a wood of withered larch and spruce. The sky was ashen.*

*"This is a dream," Dana told herself. "There's no reason to be afraid."*

*"To the contrary," he said with a cold laugh that made her shiver. "You have every reason to be afraid."*

While Dana's dream held her spellbound in Crowley's car, her real self was sleepwalking through her grandmother's house. With no knowledge of the fact, she had slipped out of bed and padded downstairs in her bare feet and pajamas. When she reached the kitchen, she searched through the bundle of keys that hung on a hook near the stove. Then she left the house.

Still trapped in her nightmare, Dana stepped across the damp grass to where the old Triumph Herald was parked. Not yet stored away for winter, the antique car stood in the driveway. She unlocked the door, slipped behind the wheel, and put the key in the ignition. Reversing the car onto the road, she drove into the silent streets, past the stately homes of Gran Gowan's neighbors, beyond the Creemore Public School and Recreational Center, out beyond the town's border and into the countryside.

The wolf had journeyed far that night, leaving Toronto miles behind him. In short, steady bursts, he reached his peak speed of forty miles an hour. Tired of the pockets of nature he had found in the city, he was heading northward to the promise of mountains. *Caledon. Albion.* Once across the Nottawasaga River, he wandered in the Hockley Valley, through fields of baled hay, wild daisies, and goldenrod. Avoiding villages, hamlets, and farmsteads, he traveled uphill along the rim of the Niagara Escarpment. From there he could see the glimmer of Georgian Bay farther north. Would he go that far? He felt something tugging at him, though he didn't know what.

The star on his chest blazed white against the black hair that blended with the night. The great head tapered to a glossy nose and wide mouth. His nostrils quivered as he caught the scent of other wolves in the area. Preferring to run alone, he didn't answer their howls, but he was pleased to know they still roamed the region. Too many of his kin had been driven out by man and coyote. There were other animals abroad in the night and he detected them easily: red fox, porcupine, raccoon, deer, weasels and muskrats, hare and grouse. The sour scent of a black bear surprised and delighted him. How good it was to meet wildness again!

*In wildness is the preservation of the world.*

Joyously, effortlessly, he loped on with smooth strides.

Only when he had crossed the Boyne River into the Mulmur Hills did the wolf sense the other preternatural creature abroad in the night. His hackles rose. The guard hairs on his body stood on end. He growled low in his throat. The foul odor was unmistakable. His enemy was near; the monster that had tried to kill him in the city. Evidently it, too, was traveling that night. Was it hunting him? He hunkered down in the tall grasses at the side of the road, alert in the darkness.

The longer the wolf waited in the grass, the more confused he grew. He did not feel like prey, yet all his instincts urged him to flee.

He didn't.

For deep inside he had heard it. The blood call. The cry from kin. From where it came, or how, he couldn't be certain but this he knew: one of his own was about to die. Had he stopped to ponder, the wolf might have guessed that it was this very call that had caused him to wander that night. But he wasn't thinking. He was acting on instinct. Over hill and valley he raced, through the Mulmur forests, toward the Devil's Glen. On a height near a waterfall above the Mad River, he stood in the moonlight. Below, along the edge of the gorge, lurched the only traffic on that lonely strip of road.

The old car was speeding, pushed to its limit as it headed northwest. The night was cool and clear, lit up by the moon. The land rolled gently, fields of hay bordered by stands of forest. Careering around the steep curve of the mill town of Glen Huron, the Triumph sped onto an isolated stretch of road. The ground grew marshy as it trailed the Mad River. Now the car bumped onto a gravel track. A warning sign said "Summer Road Only." August storms had already caused damage, leaving deep ruts and depressions. As the car struggled over them, going ever uphill, the wheels bumped and slid. Dense tracts of ash and maple crowded the verges. Lit up by the headlights, the red candles of the sumac glowed like blood.

Skirting the edge of the Bruce Trail, the Triumph traveled along the gorge that had been carved by the river as it flowed off the escarpment. The line of hills in the distance marked the boundary of the provincial park called the Devil's Glen.

Dana's foot pressed the accelerator to the floor. The engine screamed in protest. The car shuddered like an animal in pain. Its windows rattled like teeth. A new sign on the road—"Unopened Concession"—indicated worsening conditions ahead. The tires spat gravel as the car lurched in and out of the corduroy ridges.

*"Nearly there," Crowley whispered to Dana in his car, in her dream.*

"Nearly there," Dana's lips whispered as her hands gripped the steering wheel.

She was coming to a bend in the road. Beyond it fell a sheer drop of cliff. She did not turn the wheel.

Outside, the trees seemed to lean toward the car. Branches of pine tapped at the windows as if to waken her. But Dana's mind had been taken too far away. She didn't hear the trees. She didn't see the forest.

Though the wolf usually steered clear of humans, he felt drawn to the Triumph Herald. His sense of alarm was acute. He could see the car nearing a bend, but the wheels weren't turning. It would plunge over the cliff. A suicide? His amber eyes glowed. Now he jerked back with surprise as he caught sight of the driver. Rigid at the wheel sat a young girl, staring blindly ahead of her.

There was no time to wonder or question. The wolf threw back his head and howled. Then—in a magnificent arc of poised muscle and bone—he leaped from the height and onto the road.

*In Crowley's car, in her nightmare, Dana jolted upright. The call of the wolf echoed through the gloom of the burnt landscape. A wild cry of freedom that was life itself.*

*"NO!" screeched Crowley at the wheel of his car. He reached out to grab Dana.*

*Too late, she was gone.*

In the Triumph Herald, Dana woke with a start. Though stunned, she immediately saw her peril. The car was speeding toward the edge of a cliff. On the road in front of her, lit up by the headlights, stood a great black wolf with a white star on its chest.

She didn't stop to think. She pulled at the steering wheel with all her might. Had the car been modern, lighter and faster, it would certainly have turned over and she could have been killed. Instead, the old Triumph, slowed by its weight, obligingly crashed into the nearest tree by the road. It didn't buckle; the solid chassis held, but Dana was catapulted forward with a painful wrench even as the windshield shattered. Her head struck the dashboard and she was showered with broken glass. Blood trickled down her face. She could taste it in her mouth. Overcome with shock and terror, she looked wildly around her.

What was she doing in her grandmother's car? On a dark road at night? In bare feet and pajamas?

Slowly she moved her arms and legs, instinctively checking for injuries. No bones broken. There were cuts and bruises, but she didn't feel any pain. She was reeling with incomprehension. The car was crushed against a tree, but it too had survived. The key still turned the ignition. If she could just stop shaking, she would be able to drive. She needed to get help. She needed to get home.

A dark shape appeared at the window.

Dana was about to scream when she heard a familiar voice.

"*Ouvre la porte! Vite!* Open the door!"

Her mind spun. What was this? How could that be

Jean, the boy from her class? He was peering through the window. Pulling at the door. It was locked. What was he doing here? He kept looking around. His fear was contagious. She sensed the danger too. Whatever had brought her to that place was near.

A wave of hysteria overwhelmed her. *Jean was her enemy!* He had to be. The thought was followed by a stab of doubt. An image of her teacher flashed through her mind. A black car. A burnt landscape. Were they working together? How else would Jean be there?

"*Câlisse*, girl! Open the door!" Jean shouted. "*Qu'est-ce que tu fais?* It's coming!"

A buzzing sound rang in her head. The air thickened with a sour, metallic stench. She recognized the signs.

"It's here!" she screamed back.

Like a missile plummeting downward, it arrived with a deafening screech. A horrible thud hit the roof of the car, as if a body had landed on it. The fetid odor was overwhelming; she almost fainted with the stench. The buzzing increased till her teeth began to chatter.

Dana scrambled to turn on the ignition and shoved the gears into reverse. With a great crunching noise, she backed the car full throttle away from the tree. Jean was thrown sideways. She could only hope that the thing had been thrown off too. Turning the wheel back the way she had come, she put her foot to the gas.

Despite the squeal of protest, the car took off like a

bullet. Dana was shaking uncontrollably. Tears poured down her face. A quick glance in the mirror brought new horror.

Two figures struggled on the road behind her. One was the great black wolf that had blocked her path. It reared up on its hind legs as it fought with ferocity, tearing and biting, snapping and snarling. The other was a ragged and tentacled thing that glowed with the fluorescence of decaying matter.

Dana sped away, overcome by the truth. The monster on the road was the same as the one that had attacked her at the portal! It had followed her to the Earthworld and was still trying to kill her! She wanted to scream, she was so terrified. Instead, she fought for control. She was safe for now. She had managed to escape. Yet something felt wrong. What about Jean? Should she have left him there? Was she right to think he was allied with her enemy? But how did he get there? And what about the wolf? Should she have abandoned it? Didn't it save her? She was utterly lost, sick and distraught. Nothing made sense.

Despite the prickles of her conscience, Dana kept driving. Her instinct for self-preservation urged her on. All she could think of, all she wanted, was to get back to Creemore.

She was grateful that the Triumph was like her dad's old car, a standard with the steering wheel on the right-hand side. Despite her state of shock, she was able to drive it. She had grown up watching Gabriel drive and once in a while, out in the countryside, he would let her behind the wheel. The car had taken a bashing. Cold air blew through the shattered windshield, chilling her to the bone. Only one headlight was functioning to show her the way. The shadows of the trees loomed over the dark road. The road itself was torn and broken. She had to slow down to traverse the ruts. Luckily there was no traffic at that hour of the morning. She wasn't about to trust anyone. Her enemy was out there. With a vague sense of the direction she had to take, she eventually reached a familiar signpost. Passing Glen Huron, she was on the last stretch home.

Driving into Creemore, Dana nearly wept with relief. She was frozen from the cold night air and the shock of what had happened. Hardly able to think, she was acting automatically.

There on the front lawn of her grandmother's house stood a ragged little group lit up by the red flashing light of a police car. Dana's aunts huddled together, blankets wrapped around their skimpy nightwear. Without makeup, their faces looked pale and bleary. Gabriel stood beside them, dazed, holding Aradhana's hand. At the center of the gathering was Gran Gowan looking, for the first time since Dana had known her, very old and frail.

A policewoman was ushering them back into the house

when the Triumph drove up. Everyone turned to take in the crushed car, broken windshield, and Dana behind the wheel, caked with blood.

Despite her state, Dana caught the look on her aunts' faces. Not even the antics of their own youth matched this. She drew up the car in front of the police cruiser and stepped out shakily. Gabriel was already running toward her. She opened her mouth to speak, but no words came out. As her father's arms reached out to embrace her, she collapsed.

The rest of the night was a blur. Kind hands bathed her and changed her pajamas. Radhi's soothing touch. The scent of jasmine. Then a soft quilt settled over her and hot water bottles were placed at her feet. People came in and out of her room, speaking in low voices. One was a doctor. *No questions now. Shock. Mild concussion. Cuts and bruises. Nothing serious. Keep her warm. Watch her.*

Hovering between sleep and waking, she could hear them in the hall.

". . . the whole neighborhood," Gran Gowan said, querulously. "We are thoroughly disgraced!"

"Oh, come on, Mom." That was Deirdre. "It's nothing new. We used to terrorize the town. They haven't exactly forgotten. Old Nalty still glares at me every time I pass him."

"And that's not what you're worried about, Maisy,

you can't fool us," Yvonne added gently. "She'll be okay. You'll see."

Then came the most painful sound Dana had heard that night. The defeated weeping of a little old lady.

Gradually the voices trailed away as everyone went to bed.

Dana's door opened again. A chair was placed beside her. Gabriel's voice trembled in the darkness.

"I know I've let you down, Dana. I haven't been a good father. But you've got to know that I'm trying to do what's best for you, for all of us. I love you, princess, no matter what has happened. That's all that's important, that you know I love you. Can you tell me what's going on? Will you let me try to help you?"

She kept her eyes shut. She didn't respond to his plea. How could she? He needed an explanation and she didn't have one. Even if she tried to tell him, he wouldn't be able to hear. He had forgotten the fairy side of her life and she didn't think he would want to remember. The other world had taken his first wife away, now it was trying to kill his daughter. Her throat ached with the things she couldn't say. She longed for someone who understood, who could help her through this nightmare. Why had Faerie forsaken her?

Never in her life had Dana felt so alone.

# EIGHT

"I can see why you like this spot," Laurel said when she spotted the statue.

Gwen had suggested they meet at the Mackenzie monument on the west side of the Ontario Legislative Building. The sculpture by Walter Allward was different from the other statues of rulers and politicians that adorned Queen's Park. Perhaps this was the reason it was hidden away in the leafy shadows behind the building.

"He reminds me of a fairy king," Gwen said with a little smile.

Laurel gazed wistfully at the figure cast in bronze. He was striding across a low stone wall with a book in his hand. His features were noble and majestic. There was something about him that reminded her of Ian. As the Summer King, cloaked in a blue mantle with a brooch shaped like flame, her former boyfriend had the same air of command. When in Faerie, he wore his raven-black hair to his shoulders, bound with a circlet of sapphires. In the Earthworld he preferred jeans and a leather jacket, with his hair cut short and a jewel piercing his eyebrow.

While dealing with his two sides had been exciting, it didn't help that the human part could be temperamental. Add Laurel's own volatile nature to the mix and their relationship had seldom been peaceful.

"We got along best when we danced together," Laurel murmured, more to herself than to Gwen. "We used to waltz all night on the summer lawns of his palace in Hy Brasil."

She let out a sigh, then forced herself to return to the present.

Gwen had collapsed on a bench nearby. Having run all the way from the subway to avoid being late, she was still catching her breath.

"Another interview?" Laurel asked, noting the suit and high heels.

"Eat first, then talk," she pleaded. "I'm starving!"

Sitting together, they opened their lunches. Laurel raised her eyebrow at the sight of Gwen's sandwich: a large crusty roll stuffed with slices of pepper salami and mozzarella. She herself had rye bread with shavings of cucumber on a spread of cream cheese.

Gwen noticed the difference too, and grinned. "Some people are slim, some are rounder. I like my food."

Laurel felt a twinge of envy. Gwen obviously liked herself as well.

"Thanks for bringing me here," she said to Gwen. "It's magical. I never noticed this spot, though it's so close to Massey. I don't know the city very well. I grew up in Niagara Falls."

The last of the summer sun shone through the trees and lit up the pink rosebushes around them. Though the road beyond was busy, the sounds of traffic were muted by the dense foliage.

"There are little bits of magic all over Toronto," Gwen said in between mouthfuls. "I started to find them soon after I got here. It's a question of perception, isn't it? Not just where you look, but *how*. There's an old bank near Front Street. I spotted it the day I applied for a job at *The Star* newspaper. There in the cornerstone of the building, half-hidden behind tall weeds and overlooking a parking lot, was a beautiful centaur, carved in white marble! He looked as if he were supporting the bank on his shoulders. I could hardly believe what I was looking at, he was so beautiful. I stood there admiring him for ages. Then just as I turned to leave, I swear, he winked at me!"

They both laughed.

"I'm not surprised you see these things," Laurel said. "You have a very different attitude toward Faerie than me. It's like being brought up in the same family, but not having the same experience. Faerie has only been good for you; I can't say the same." Her features looked pained. "First it took my sister away, then came the disaster that was Ian and me. You know, most times I wish that world never existed."

Gwen looked sympathetic and didn't speak at first. Then she asked curiously, "So how come you're studying folklore?"

Laurel was caught off guard. Her smile was wry. "*Touché.* That's the one thing I can thank Faerie for. I really didn't know what I wanted to do with my life. I always loved sports, but I never settled into one or trained long enough to be a professional. If it wasn't for Faerie, I think I would have drifted through university without knowing what to study or where I was going. I really am fascinated by the subject. As you know from my story, my granddad also became a professor of folklore after his involvement with Faerie."

Gwen finished her sandwich and unwrapped a chocolate bar. "You want to know something?" Her voice was quiet. "I haven't suffered as much as you, I know that, but it hasn't been easy. Being in love with a mortal king is no picnic either. Dara is the hereditary King of Inch Island. While that doesn't mean much in modern Ireland, it does mean a lot to the islanders and even more so to Faerie, not to mention Dara himself. Though he doesn't live on Inch all the time, he won't go too far away. We've talked about marriage, but then comes the hitch. No matter how much he loves me, he won't emigrate. As for me"—she let out a huge sigh—"I'm American. I love my country. I mean, I found it hard enough crossing the border to come here. How could I cross the ocean?"

The hint of despair in Gwen's voice touched Laurel. With sudden insight, she saw that Gwen's constant good spirits were a hard-won battle. There was no solution to the dilemma of a long-distance relationship. Their love was not a fairy tale. They could not live happily ever after in two separate places.

"Well, never mind all that," Gwen said, brushing the crumbs off her lap. "Let's get down to business. Any luck with Dana?"

Laurel shook her head. "She didn't go in or out of her house all morning."

Gwen's face creased with worry. "And there was no sign of her at school today. Something has happened to her!"

"I don't think so," Laurel countered. "Her parents have been going to work as usual, and they look happy enough. They wouldn't be acting normal if something was wrong. We must be missing her somehow."

"We're being blocked," Gwen swore. "That's it!"

Laurel frowned. "Do you feel a spell around you? I don't."

"Me neither," Gwen admitted. "But I swear I'll go crazy if we don't make some headway soon. I feel like a rat on a wheel. We're running in circles and getting nowhere."

"How's the job hunt going?" Laurel asked with sympathy.

"It's not," she groaned. "My feet are killing me, bloody high heels, and I hate interviews. Sucking up to people just to get hired, it's degrading."

It was so unlike her to be negative, Laurel knew things were bad.

"And I'm worried sick," Gwen continued. "Not one phone call or e-mail from Ireland. It's not like Dara. It's not like any of them. The only good news is that there aren't any reports of strange deaths in the Irish media. I've been monitoring them on the Web."

The image that constantly tormented her flashed through her mind yet again: her boyfriend, Dara, lying facedown on the ground, limbs motionless. She was close to tears.

Laurel, too, was living with the nightmare of no word from her loved ones. As each day passed with no sign of Honor or Ian, she felt the threat around her loom closer. And it was all the more sinister for being insubstantial. How were they to fight shadows?

"What can we do that we haven't done already?" she said, exasperated.

"I've been thinking about that." Gwen pulled out a brown envelope from her shoulder bag. "I'm going to Ireland."

Not for the first time Laurel marveled at the iron will behind Gwen's mild manner. But she was even more surprised when Gwen handed her the envelope. Inside were hundreds of large bills.

"There's a small fortune here!"

Gwen nodded. "It came by courier the day Granny contacted me about our mission. It's from my friend Matt, the businessman in the Company of Seven. He's a millionaire. Years ago, he was the sales rep of this company that was going bust and he got all the workers together to buy shares so they could keep their jobs. Then the Celtic Tiger hit, the economic boom in Ireland, and now they're rich."

"I love stories like that," Laurel said with a grin. "But you can't give me this. Your friend meant you to have it."

"I've split what Matt sent. That's your half. It's his way of helping the mission. If we need to buy anything or rent a car or whatever." Gwen looked suddenly uncertain. "I doubt he meant me to take a free trip, though."

"It's the right decision," Laurel assured her. "We're in the dark. We don't know anything and communications are down. I'd go too if I thought it would help."

Gwen looked grateful for support. "Only one needs to go," she said, "and I'm unemployed with nothing to lose. You must keep trying to reach Dana."

"That's the plan, then," Laurel agreed. "Good luck. Call me as soon as you get there."

Gwen was packing when Dara rang. She dropped the receiver at the first sound of his voice.

"I'm here! I'm here!" she cried, scrambling to retrieve it.

Her heart almost burst with relief and joy. *He wasn't dead!* She could see him so clearly in her mind: the nut-brown hair framing strong features, the mischievous look in his eyes, the slightly crooked grin. The first time they had met was on an island road when he knocked her down on his bicycle. She was only sixteen, under a fairy spell, and unable to move. Thinking he had hurt her, he hoisted her over his shoulders and carried her to Granny Harte's cottage. On holidays in Ireland, Gwen had become entangled with Faerie when her cousin Findabhair was abducted by the High King, Finvarra. When Dara heard the story, he was quick to join her. Gwen had liked him from the start, though she was too shy and insecure to show it; but it soon became obvious that he liked her too. She would never forget the sunny day they wrestled in the cold waters of Lough Swilly, and the heart he drew in the sand around his name and hers.

He loved to tease her and make her laugh. "You have a brilliant laugh," he would say. When she told him that she had never had a boyfriend, his reaction was instant. "I can't believe no one has fancied you!" And of course when she asked him if he thought she was fat, his response was better still. "You're not skin and bones if that's what you mean. You're lovely. I couldn't help but notice when your clothes were wet."

Though they lived in separate countries, their love had survived across time and distance. They spoke daily on the phone, sent e-mails and letters, and took holidays together whenever they could. Each ignored the cloud hanging over them, the fact that neither wanted to emigrate. They were young. They still had hope.

"Are you well, love?" Dara asked her now.

"Yes, I'm fine! Are you?"

He didn't answer the question, nor did he give her the chance to ask again.

"How is the girl? Is Dana all right?"

His words were abrupt. She heard the urgency and answered at once.

"I think so. I mean most likely, yes, or we'd know otherwise. We haven't been able to reach her in person but we've been to her home and—"

"Thank God."

His relief was audible.

"Dara, what is it?"

Ever direct, he gave her the full brunt of the news.

"It's worse than we could have imagined, even with the warnings. The gateways have been destroyed. All of them. The bond between Faerie and the Earthworld has been severed."

Gwen caught the cry in her throat. She forced herself to stay calm. She was the Captain of the Company of Seven. She could keep a cool head.

"What are the consequences?" she asked immediately. "How long can the worlds exist without each other?"

From her own mission for Faerie, she knew that the destinies of both worlds were inextricably linked. She had faced Crom Cruac, the Great Worm, the guardian of the balance between the worlds.

*I lie curled on the branch of the Tree of Life that bears both Faerie and your world like two golden apples. Two orbs, two moons that eclipse each other, one fantasy, one reality, balanced side by side. Humanity cannot exist without its dreams, but for any dream to exist there must be a sacrifice.*

Dara's reply confirmed her fears.

"You know yourself, we are responsible for Faerie's existence. Without us, the Summer Land is doomed."

"Then so are we," she said gravely. "Faerie is the Land of Dreams. Humanity needs to believe in something greater than itself. We need our dreams to keep us going."

"The strike is against both worlds," Dara agreed. "But how it has been brought about is still a mystery. Granny has gleaned only the smallest part of the truth. We are still suffering the consequences of the death of the First King."

"What?!"

Of course Gwen knew the story, it was part of her own tale. How Finvarra, the first High King of Faerie, had lost his immortality when he fought Crom Cruac as one of the Company of Seven.

"But that matter was resolved," she argued, "when the

Midsummer Fire was lit by the Summer King and Faerie was healed."

"Apparently not," was all Dara could say. "More lay in the shadows than we could know. Foul plans were set in motion before the Fire was lit. Who or what enemy laid them is uncertain, but we now face the dire results."

Gwen fought against the panic that threatened to overwhelm her. The Rescue of Fairyland was mankind's eternal duty, but this was obviously much bigger and more sinister than anything previously faced.

"What can we do?" she whispered.

"The girl is the key," Dara said, "even as Granny foresaw. The Light-Bearer's Daughter must restore the gateways and soon. The worlds have begun to drift apart. By the power of the next convergence—*Samhain*—they will align once more. But unless a bridge is there to bind them, they'll drift again. And if they do, it will be forever."

Gwen knew that the worlds collided at certain times in the year. These occasions were celebrated in Faerie as feast-days even as they were once held sacred by the Celtic peoples: *Imbolc*, the spring festival at the beginning of February; *Lá Bealtaine*, May Day; *Oíche Lár an Tsamhraidh*, Midsummer's Eve in June; *Lá Lughnasa* or Lammas Day in August; and *Samhain*, the autumnal feast and the beginning of the Celtic new year, which began on *Oíche Shamhna*, Halloween.

"It's almost two months till Halloween," she said with

some relief. "At least that gives us time. What must Dana do and how can we help her?"

The silence on the other end of the line was worse than a scream. Gwen's stomach clenched. *Here it comes.* Because she knew him so well, she had sensed it the moment she had heard his voice. Dara was hiding something.

"We don't know," he said at last. "We had hoped to learn more about Dana's destiny from the Faerie Council, but that's when . . ."

Gwen's vision flashed through her mind. Dara and Granny sprawled on the ground.

She barely got the words out. "What happened?"

He didn't try to cushion the blow. He was the King of Inch. Like many such kings in modern Ireland, on Tory, Aran, and other islands, he had no official authority; but the title was held proudly through the generations. In the realm of Faerie, it meant much more. The hereditary kings were the only Irish rulers acknowledged in that land. Dara had already proven his kingship in defense of the Summer Country. He was a hero there.

He spoke quietly, without emotion.

"On the day the gateways were destroyed, every member of our Company was attacked. Matt and Katie are both in the hospital. Some kind of coma. Matt collapsed over his desk at work. They thought at first it was a heart attack. Katie was found lying unconscious in a field, her cattle around her. As for Granny and I . . ."

For a moment his voice wavered. Gwen's stomach clenched. She knew he couldn't bear to hurt her. What terrible thing was he afraid to tell her?

"What?" she pressed, reminding herself that he was alive and talking to her.

"We were struck blind, Gwen. We are both blind."

"Oh, my love," she sobbed.

Now that the worst had been said, he moved to support her, speaking calmly and steadily to ease the shock.

"We were entering the portal at Dunfinn when it exploded. The High King and High Queen were on the other side, waiting to greet us. The great stones flew into the air and we were blasted backward. I lost consciousness. When I woke on the hillside everything was dark. I thought it was night. We had gone to the fort just after lunch. I crawled around till I found Granny. She was wounded but awake. That's when we realized the truth."

Gwen tried to hide the fact she was crying, but he stopped when he heard the muffled weeping. She was angry with herself. She knew she was making it all the harder for him.

"Go on," she said at last, taking a deep breath.

"We've been in the hospital since then. We were released today. Judging by the state of Katie and Matt, we didn't fare too badly. We're disabled but not defeated. We'll manage, I can promise you that. Granny has ordered a computer that responds to word commands.

She'll be in touch with you as soon as it's up and running. I've moved in with her for now. We can help each other. You know the two of us. The indomitable Irishry. We just need time to adapt. The worst of it is we can't come to join you. We'd be more of a hindrance than a help right now."

Gwen was still trying to absorb the enormity of what had happened.

"I felt the blow," she said, dazed. "I saw you struck down. And Laurel, the High Queen's sister, felt it too. But how come we weren't hurt?"

"Granny says the protective spirits of North America can counter any spell. But you're not clear of danger. Whoever or whatever dark force this is, it is bound to come after you and, particularly, Dana."

A chill ran up Gwen's spine as she remembered Dana's school. She told Dara what had happened there.

"You must look out for the girl!" he urged. "She's our only hope. This is her destiny. How she must fulfill it we don't know yet, but Granny will keep trying to find out. You can count on that. And as soon as we know something, we'll let you know. Until then, you must guard her. You must keep her safe."

"We can do it," she assured him. "Laurel and I are on it."

Gwen managed to sound more confident than she felt. She was determined to match his resolve with her own. He had enough to deal with. She could hear the weariness in his voice. He was obviously still recovering.

But even as their conversation drew to a close and the initial shock wore off, she began to feel the first waves of real pain.

"Dara," she murmured.

"You must be strong, my love. There is always hope. And I am happy to know that you are not alone in this."

After she hung up, Gwen stared dazedly at the telephone for a while. It took all her willpower not to ring him back and tell her she was flying out that night. And when she had won that battle, she canceled her flight. There was no doubt in her decision. She would stay and do her duty. He wouldn't be happy if she did otherwise and neither would she. Whether big or small, they had their parts to play. Their love would have to wait.

Gwen was about to ring Laurel to tell her the news when the phone rang again.

"Gwen?"

"*Findabhair!* Thank God you've called! Are you okay?"

It was more than a year since Gwen had last seen her Irish cousin and that had been a flying visit. Findabhair was so immersed in her musical career along with her husband, Finvarra, that she had little time for anything else.

"Aside from being knackered, I'm grand," came the

familiar voice. "Too many days on the road. Too much *craic agus ceol*. I got your message. Sorry, but I haven't had a free minute till now. What's up?"

"We've got a serious problem," Gwen began. "Faerie—"

"Trouble in Paradise?" Findabhair's tone was wry. "Are we surprised?"

Quickly Gwen outlined the situation. Even as she spoke, she thought she detected a slight coolness on the other end of the line, or was she imagining it? Long-distance calls were rarely satisfactory. California was even farther away than Ireland.

"How soon can you and Finvarra get here?"

"Whoa, that's not on," Findabhair said quickly. "Sorry, but we're in the middle of a major tour here. It took over a year to put this together. A lot of planning and money. We can't leave our backers high and dry. There are concerts booked solid along the West Coast and then across Canada. We'll be in Toronto mid-November. We'll meet up with you then."

Gwen could hardly believe what she was hearing. Perhaps she hadn't explained properly? Hadn't conveyed just how bad things were?

"That will be too late!" she cried. "We've got to open the portals on Halloween. It's our only chance! Don't you—"

"You're not listening to me, cuz. You'll have to count

us out. I'm sorry about Dara and Granny and the others.
I really am. But we're not in a position to help them right
now. We can't sacrifice our lives for Faerie again. It's
someone else's turn."

Gwen could hardly think. "But you were once High
Queen and Finvarra was the First King! How can you
abandon the Summer Land like this? You know how
important it is!"

"And you know I haven't been there since Finvarra
lost his kingship." Findabhair's voice went cold. "He
can't go back, and I'd never go there without him. We did
our bit for Faerie and we paid the price. We owe nothing
to the Realm."

As the truth finally hit home, Gwen was left speechless.
Neither Findabhair nor Finvarra would come to Faerie's
aid. The bitterness in her cousin's tone shocked her. How
long had it been there? A quick survey of the past showed
Gwen what she had failed to notice. It was actually several
years since she had last met Finvarra. Only Findabhair had
made the effort to stay in touch. Even then, the meetings
were always brief, and they rarely if ever talked about the
other world. There it was before her, as plain as day to see,
her cousin's disaffection from Faerie. How could Gwen
have been so blind?

She knew the answer to that question. Laurel had more
than hinted at it from to time. When it came to Faerie,
Gwen wore rose-colored glasses. She couldn't see anything

wrong with that magical land. Nor could she bear to think that others might not love it as deeply as she did.

"Oh Finn," she said. "I've been so stupid. I didn't realize how unhappy you were about—"

"Don't," said her cousin. There was an echo of sadness in Findabhair's voice, but then her usual dry humor came through. "It's not your fault. You were always a dope."

"That's me," Gwen agreed with a little sigh. "I miss you, cuz."

"I miss you too. But I'll see you in November. I promise. We'll have a long chat then. And Gwen?"

"Yeah?"

"It'll work out. You'll see. As long as he has you, Dara will be fine. I really believe that. And you'll get the job done. Look, you quested all over Ireland without me, remember? You were the real hero of the Hunter's Moon."

"Thanks," Gwen said, and she meant it. "Good luck with your tour."

When her cousin rang off, Gwen knew she should call Laurel with the latest news. But she didn't. Instead, she turned out the lights and lit candles around the room. Sitting on the sofa, she gazed out the window. Her apartment was on the thirteenth floor, high above the city, with a bird's-eye view of rooftops, streets, and patches of greenery. In the lambent quiet, she watched the night fall.

Gwen was mourning the loss of the Company of Seven. Her friends and comrades-in-arms would not be with her in Faerie's hour of need. Even as the Earthworld was severed from the Land of Dreams, so too was she cut off from those who sustained her.

"I should call Laurel," she told herself. "We've got work to do."

Still she didn't move. Cloaked in loneliness, she stared out at the dark.

# Πίηε

For the week following Dana's nightmare with Crowley, Gran Gowan got her wish, and kept her granddaughter in Creemore. The Triumph Herald was repaired at a body shop for vintage cars, and the family doctor gave Dana a clean bill of health. The police decided to let the matter go, dismissing it as teenage antics in an otherwise respectable and law-abiding family. Remembering Dee and Yvonne, the sergeant simply rolled his eyes. He was glad to hear the girl normally resided in Toronto.

As soon as the others had gone back to the city, Maisy Gowan turned her full attention to her wayward charge. The first thing to go was the nose ring. Then the black clothes. Several shops in Creemore stocked young people's fashions. Dana was allowed to choose her new wardrobe as long as the colors were bright. A visit to the beauty salon was, for Dana, the oddest experience, especially since the clientele were her grandmother's age. However, she liked the hairstyle she got, trimmed and tapered, and she listened politely to the advice on makeup and skin care. In fact, Dana was prepared to do anything to gain her grandmother's forgiveness and regain her trust. It was a bonus that she liked what she saw in the mirror.

Dana also enjoyed spending time with Gran Gowan, strolling through the town, sipping hot chocolate in the Tea Room, and chatting on the veranda as the evenings grew short. All of it helped to push the horror of that terrible experience away. And though Dana offered no explanation for what happened that night, she had shown enough remorse to satisfy her grandmother. By the time Dana returned to Toronto, the two were fully reconciled.

Back at home, there was a tearful reunion between father and daughter. Gabriel was delighted with the change in Dana, not only the brighter appearance but her more open manner.

In her own bed that night, Dana stared at the ceiling. She couldn't sleep. Tomorrow she had to return to school. The time with her grandmother had been a respite, the calm before the storm. Though much of what occurred on the Mulmur Road was a hideous daze, she knew one thing for certain: both her teacher and Jean were somehow involved. The very thought shook her to the core. How could she face them? More importantly, how could she protect herself? She was overwhelmed by the mystery, helpless and powerless.

Sick with dread, Dana turned fitfully to face the

window. She always opened her curtains at night. Outside, the street lamp shed light on the treetops. Leafy shadows danced into her room. She blinked for a moment. What was out there, in the branches? A pale blurred shape. Her eyelids felt too heavy to lift. Falling into sleep at last, a thought fluttered through her mind.

*You must change your life.*

The next morning, Dana steeled herself as she walked into the classroom. Her first surprise was that Crowley was gone. In his place was a plump and pretty young woman with a pleasant manner. She handed Dana a note for her parents. The school regretted the unforeseen departure of Mr. Crowley, but hoped everyone would be satisfied with his replacement.

The second surprise was that Jean was also missing. His seat was empty. Dana was baffled. What could this mean? With a pang of disappointment, she accepted that it confirmed her suspicions that the two were connected; yet she couldn't shake the uneasiness that plagued her. Something wasn't right. Every time she remembered Jean sprawled on the road, she felt a wave of shame.

It was in the cafeteria at lunch hour that she heard the news. Two senior girls ahead of her in the queue were talking.

"Did you hear that French boy got mugged? Found in High Park in a really bad way. Early in the morning."

"What was he doing out so late?"

"Clubbing, probably. He could pass for nineteen."

"Couldn't he just. I mean, isn't he hot?"

"He was pretty badly beaten. I read in the paper he was still unconscious. They think a gang got him."

"You don't think he's—?"

"Nah. Well, I hope not!"

A wave of nausea swept over Dana. She leaned against the counter. It was all her fault! How could she have left him? Her act of cowardice filled her with self-loathing.

*You must change your life.*

As the whisper shivered through her, Dana knew it was true. Lost in her unhappiness the past year, she had forgotten how to be strong, how to stand up for herself. Once upon a time she had quested alone in the mountains of Ireland, facing the world boldly. But somehow she had let herself grow weak and powerless. That had to change. Jean had been harmed because of her. It was up to her to do something about it.

She interrupted the older girl who seemed to know the story.

"Where is he? Do you know? What hospital is he in?"

The girl's look was cool. How dare a first-year butt in like that? But Dana's glare was enough to convince her to cooperate.

"He's in Intensive Care at St. Michael's."

• • •

Rushing out of the cafeteria, Dana bumped into her new teacher.

"Whoa, what's the hurry?" said Ms. Woods. Her smile seemed a little nervous. "I'm glad I've caught up with you. I was looking for you."

"Yes?"

Dana shuffled impatiently. She didn't have time for this. She had to get to the hospital. But how could she leave the school without anyone noticing?

"I was hoping to have a talk with you," her teacher was saying. "Since I'm new here, I'm interviewing everyone in the class, one by one. Nothing formal. Just a little chat so we can get to know each other."

Dana's impatience turned immediately to suspicion. Despite the smile, the blond curls, and the pink dress, she sensed that Ms. Woods was not as soft as she appeared. Was there a hidden agenda behind her request? Dana wasn't about to trust another teacher, not after her experience with Mr. Crowley. Was Ms. Woods his replacement in more ways than one? She had to think fast, to get out of this.

"You want to interview me alone without my parents' consent? Sorry, it's not on."

Though her voice quavered as she challenged her teacher, Dana was determined to stand her ground. She couldn't risk being trapped alone with a stranger.

Ms. Woods was taken aback by the outright refusal and, seeing her chance, Dana fled down the hall.

· · ·

Her teacher's attention put an end to Dana's plan to skip classes that day. Everywhere Dana turned, Ms. Woods seemed to be there, hovering in the background, watching her covertly. On guard at all times, Dana spent the day avoiding her.

As soon as school ended, Dana hurried home and went straight to her stepmother.

"I need to visit a friend in the hospital."

Aradhana's expression was pained. "Your father has grounded you, Dana. You know that. I cannot go against his wishes. It is not an unjust punishment given what happened in Creemore. You will have to ask him yourself when he comes home."

"I can't wait that long!" Dana cried. "And he might say no. It's too important! Please, Radhi. I'm begging you!"

Dana's intensity jolted her stepmother. Dana had never raised her voice to her before. Aradhana grasped the girl's shoulders.

"Will you tell me, now, what is going on with you?"

Dana's eyes filled with tears. She shook her head.

"I . . . I can't."

Aradhana's voice was firm. "If you cannot trust me, I cannot trust you. That is the matter in a nutshell." There was a pause as Dana's stepmother grew thoughtful. Her voice softened. "Has all this to do with the other world?

Is that why you won't speak of it? You know I understand such things. Tell me and I will listen."

Dana almost gave in. She yearned to confide in someone. She felt so alone. Yet still, she wasn't ready to open up. She was afraid to. Her stepmother vowed to understand, but how could she? Dana herself hardly knew what was happening. Her shame over Jean also kept her quiet. What would Radhi say when she heard about *that*?

"I can't tell you, Radhi. I want to, but I can't." Dana's voice rose as she pleaded. "You've got to believe me. I need to see this friend. I need to help him if I can and even if I can't, I need to try."

Aradhana's features showed her struggle. She was evidently torn. Gently she put her arm around Dana's shoulders. The scent of jasmine wafted in the air.

"Someday, Dana, I hope you will learn that to ask for help is a strength, not a weakness. I will let you go without further questions, but first you must let me do something for you."

Aradhana brought Dana to her study, a little solarium at the side of the house. Vases of fresh flowers stood on the windowsills. Indian rugs and tasseled cushions covered the floor. A small altar was set up in a corner, draped with red and gold silk scarves. Statues of Hindu gods and goddesses were surrounded by incense burners, candles, and brass bowls of offerings. Amidst the statues were photographs of Aradhana's parents and relations, her brother Suresh and his restaurant staff, she and Gabriel on their wedding day, and Dana in her school uniform back in Ireland. Of all the figures and images, one stood out above the rest. Bedecked with pearls and a golden crown was the plump merry god with the head of an elephant, the Lord Ganesha.

Aradhana placed her hands together and bowed before the altar.

"I was six years old when my mother died," she began in a low voice.

Slowly, gracefully, she lit the candles and a stick of incense.

"On that day I lay across my bed, weeping with grief. My child's heart was broken and inconsolable. I would let no one near me, not my *aya*—my beloved nurse—nor my father or Suresh. I screamed like a wild cat if anyone touched me and in the end, they left me alone."

Gently she bathed the statues with drops of perfume.

"That is when he came to me. First I caught the fragrance of jasmine, then I heard the golden rattles. The ones he loves to play with. My head was buried in my arms, but I could not resist looking up. There he was, resplendent in white silk and adorned with pearls. He lifted me in his arms and kissed my face and when I looked into his beautiful dark eyes I saw that he was weeping too. Weeping for a motherless child. I wiped away his tears and he wiped away mine. And when I had stopped crying, he danced with me, the way my mother used to dance with me. He didn't have to say the words, I understood his promise. He would always be with me, my dear guardian Ganesha."

Dana felt her heart lifting. Radhi *did* understand.

"One day I hope you'll come to Faerie with me," she said to her stepmother.

Aradhana shook her head, but her tone was mild. "It has been many years since I walked among the gods. It is much harder for adults, Dana. The *sadhus* and the *gurus* go that road but the rest of us are bound to this world, to the business of living. And that is how it should be. It is here we belong for the time that we live."

Now Aradhana placed her hands together in prayer. Touching her forehead, lips, and heart, she bowed to her guardian.

"O Joyous One, beloved God most dear to my heart, Remover of Obstacles, hear my prayer. I love this girl as I would my own daughter. I appeal to you now to come to her aid. Bring to her your strength and guidance. Remove the obstacles that block her path. Beloved, will you come to her?"

Aradhana's eyes closed and her lips continued to move in silent prayer. After a time, her face lit up like a sunburst. When she turned to Dana, her voice rang with happiness.

"He will help you."

Dana hugged her stepmother. "I'm so glad you married Gabe."

"So am I," said Aradhana, all smiles. "Now I must get dressed for work. Your father will not be home till teatime. You may go to the hospital, I will write Gabe a note, but I expect you to return as soon as possible."

"I'll do my best," Dana promised.

The Toronto underground transit system was a modern marvel that Dana had taken to from the day she arrived in Canada. There was no subway in Ireland, and though Dana had gone on the Tube in London and the Métro in Paris, she would definitely give "the Rocket," as it was affectionately called, first prize.

The silver train glided like a sea snake through the dark tunnels beneath the city. Metallic shrieks echoed loudly as it scraped the tracks. As the train turned swiftly around the bends, the carriages rocked from side to side. Normally Dana would pass the time observing the other passengers or noting the colors and signage of each station. Today she sat hunched in her seat, sick with worry.

*Museum.* The station was lemon-yellow and bright like the sun.

She could see him in her mind, Jean Ducharme, wintergreen eyes studying her curiously. That disarming smile. The way his face lit up when she said she was Irish.

*Irlandaise! Magnifique! The French and the Irish, we are always good friends.* He had stood up for her that first day in class. Then later, he had warned her against their teacher. *For you, he is dangereux.* How could she have thought that he was aligned with her enemy? Whatever the reason he was on the road that night, she should have opened the door. She should have let him in the car.

*Queen's Park.* Royal blue for the Queen of Canada.

They said that he had been attacked by a gang, that his injuries were severe. It wasn't a gang, she knew, but a malevolent monster. The monster who had come to kill her. When she fled, leaving Jean behind, it had gone for him instead.

The train drove into the next station on a blast of wind. Chimes rang out as the doors swished open, then shut.

*St Patrick.* Pale green with a dark green trim. Green for a saint from the Emerald Isle.

He was still unconscious. What if he never woke up? What if he died? Oh, how could she live with herself!

"Poor little girl with lots of worries, eh?"

The voice came from in front of Dana. The words were obviously directed at her, and they seemed to fall on top of her head. No wonder, she realized, as she looked up. The speaker was quite short. Dana frowned. She had been warned not to talk to strangers, especially on the subway. Too many weirdoes, as her aunts would say. But this little man did not look sinister.

His skin was the brown of oak leaves in autumn. His clothes were a quirky design of black and white with a black floppy hat, white T-shirt, and checkered shorts with suspenders. His feet were shod in white leather sandals showing hairy toes. Along with dark sunglasses, he was wearing a clunky, old-fashioned Walkman that spilled out jazzy music. Instead of turning the Walkman down, he raised his voice.

"A problem shared is a problem halved."

His accent was broad, very nasal and Canadian, almost singsong in tone, quite pleasant on the ears. His look was pleasant too, and so kind and friendly that Dana couldn't help smiling back. The train was crowded with office workers on their way home. Safe enough, she decided, if he tried anything strange.

"I . . . a friend . . . is in the hospital," she told him. "St. Michael's."

The little man bobbed his head vigorously, displacing his earphones. "St. Michael's a good one. Patron saint of fairies, eh?"

Dana was startled. She studied him closely. He peered back at her over the edge of his sunglasses. The eyes were big, an earth-brown color darker than his skin. There was something innocent and childlike in his gaze, but there was no recognition. And she felt none herself. Still, she liked him and that encouraged her to talk.

"Do you know the old folktale about Saint Mike?" she

said. "How he defended the fairies after the Great War in the heavens? The fairies were in disgrace for refusing to take sides."

"There's no neutral ground in some wars," the little man murmured.

"What?" said Dana.

He shrugged and clammed up.

"Anyway," she continued, "apparently Saint Michael argued that while the fairies weren't good enough for heaven, at the same time they weren't bad enough for hell. He suggested they should live on Earth. Some say that's how Faerie and our world got connected in the first place."

"He'd make a good lawyer," the little man commented.

Dana laughed. She leaned toward him confidentially. "I don't really believe that story. You know what I think? I think Michael is their patron saint because he's their dream, their ideal. What could be better or more beautiful than a fairy? *An archangel.*"

The little man cackled with glee. "Oh, that's a good one. I like that. Well worth some advice." He glanced out the window. "The Lady's station. Isn't this your stop?"

*Queen Street.* Light blue, the favorite color of the Queen of Heaven.

Dana had lost track of the time and her journey. She jumped up and made a dash for the door. Behind her came a shout.

"Put your hands over his head! That should do the trick!"

*What? How?* She spun around. Too late. The door slid closed. He was lost in the crowd.

Dana stood dumbfounded as she watched the train rumble down the track. Then she shook herself out of her daze. Impossible. They didn't exist, not here, not in Canada. But as she hurried toward the exit, her heart felt lighter. First Radhi and now the little man. They had taught her a lesson. People could be magic too.

# Ten

Queen Street was bustling with office workers and shoppers. Dana hurried past a construction site that reverberated with the noise of drilling, men shouting, and trucks unloading. On the road, traffic moved slowly. A streetcar rumbled by, packed with rush-hour passengers. In the press of the crowd a ragged figure looked out at Dana, but she didn't see him. She was threading her way up the street toward the hospital. Behind her glinted the department store windows of the Hudson's Bay Company. Ahead rose the red brick walls of St. Michael's.

She didn't need directions. From a billboard high on the wall, a benign visage gazed gigantically down: a cloud-white angel against a blue sky. He wore his wings like a feathered mantle; his head was bowed and his arm raised. *Help Us Watch Over You. Give to Toronto's Urban Angel.* Cheered by the image, Dana headed for the entrance of the Victoria Street wing of the Intensive Care Unit.

The moment she set foot on the ramp that led to the glass doors, Dana knew she was in trouble. It was the smell that alerted her: a metallic odor that soured the air.

Then came the buzzing noise in her ears that made her feel immediately nauseous and faint. Terrified, she looked around. The side street was empty. Then something stepped from the shadows.

She hardly recognized him. Crowley was more emaciated than the last time she had seen him, and his face was disfigured with hideous scars. The look in his eyes was shocking. From the depths glared a raging hatred. Worse was to come. Out of his body snaked writhing tentacles, green and viscid, like toxic matter. Now she knew for certain that Crowley and the monster were one and the same.

She made a bolt for the doors. A tentacle whipped toward her and coiled around her waist. Its grip was like a vise. She screamed in pain. More tentacles shot out to bind her body. One curled around her throat and began to choke her. The buzzing sound was all around her, as if she were being attacked by a swarm of bees. His whispery voice echoed with the cold glee he took in killing her.

*You are such easy prey. Poor little girl. All alone and afraid. It is so easy to defeat you. You lack the will to defend yourself. You would be dead already but for the wolf.*

Somewhere in the midst of terror and panic, Dana rallied. Those scars on his face! The wolf had done that! The thought gave her strength. She began to struggle. His grip tightened, and the awful voice continued to mock her.

*Your hero is not here to save you. I have dealt with him.*

She was overcome with shame. Her worst fears were confirmed. Jean was attacked when she left him on the road. He had tried to help her and she had abandoned him.

*Why was I sent to kill you, I wonder? You are no threat to anyone. A weak and foolish child with no defenses, no allies, no power.*

She was too long without air. Her skin had turned blue. As her head fell back in a swoon, the high walls of the hospital loomed above her. The fortress she had failed to reach. The image of the urban angel stared down. Was that reproach she saw in his eyes?

*Help us watch over you.*

And deep in the back of her mind, she heard her stepmother's words. *To ask for help is a strength, not a weakness.* Even her enemy knew the truth. She had no allies, and her isolation made her weak.

She couldn't speak, she was almost unconscious, but in her mind she formed the words.

*Saint Michael, patron saint of my mother's people, grant me sanctuary.*

As if in a dream, she saw the image move. The arm that was out of sight in the billboard came into view, wielding a weapon. The sword of light descended through the air, slashing at the monstrous limbs that bound her. Crowley recoiled, screeching with agony. Dana was set free. Without a second thought, she raced up the ramp. More shrieks erupted behind her, but she didn't stop to look. Catapulted forward, she charged through the doors.

As soon as she was inside, Dana knew she was safe. Though she was trembling with shock, she began to calm down. Deep in her heart she had heard the still voice. *He shall cover thee with his feathers and under his wings shalt thou trust.* This was not a place where Crowley could follow.

Stopping to catch her breath, she looked around the lobby. To her right was the reception desk. Ahead were the elevators. On her left was an alcove built into the wall, illumined by lamps. It housed a marble statue of Saint Michael, the original of the image on the poster outside. Overcome with gratitude, Dana approached the white effigy of the great archangel.

At the foot of the statue were flowers and cards from patients and their families. *Thank you, St. Michael, for your intercession.* She repeated the words softly.

His head was bowed, his features serene. Calmly he regarded the vanquished demon at his feet. One arm was raised in triumph, the other held a sword against the serpent's neck. From his shoulders unfurled a swan's span of feathered strength. His composure bespoke a different world, a different way of being, not human but immortal.

A plaque on the wall told Dana about the statue, but nothing about the celestial being himself.

*For almost a century, the statue of St Michael the*

*Archangel has graced St Michael's Hospital as a symbol of hope for employees, patients and their families.*

*The artist and date of creation are unknown, but the name of "Pietrasanta" chiseled on the back of the statue indicates that the stone is from the same quarry in Italy where Michelangelo procured marble for his famous Pieta.*

*How the statue of St Michael made its way to Canada is unclear. What we do know is that during the latter part of the 19th century, the Sisters of St Joseph found the statue, dirty and blackened, in a second-hand store on Queen Street and bought it for $49—a sum they had accumulated from the sale of old newspapers.*

*Plaque unveiling*
*St Michael's Feast Day Celebrations*
*September 30, 1996*

Dana stared at the demon under the archangel's foot, the writhing body, the ophidian eyes. Saint Michael had the power to conquer his enemy, but how could she defeat hers?

Dana asked herself hard questions. She recalled Crowley's taunts. Were they true? Was she powerless? For the second time that day, she remembered how much stronger she had been only a year ago, so daring and full of spirit. And what of her birthright? Was she not of the immortals herself? The silver blood of Faerie ran through her veins. Light lived inside her. All her gifts and strengths had been buried deep, like treasure in a bog. And she herself had lost her way, sinking into that bog. Could she rise again?

With quiet resolve, Dana walked to the elevator. She had a job to do. She had come to right a wrong. Though she had no idea if or how she could do it, she was here to save Jean.

Admission to the Neurosurgery and Trauma Intensive Care Unit was strictly controlled. There was a waiting area with chairs and magazines, and a locked door with an intercom system. The door was already opening even as Dana grasped the handle. She smiled to herself. She knew who was helping her. His angelic presence permeated the brick and glass, indeed the very air itself. This was his hospital, his domain. As he guided her through the corridors, she saw that she was somehow cloaked from prying eyes. Doctors and nurses passed her without a glance.

When she reached Jean's room, two attendants stood outside the door, one in a green uniform, the other in dark blue. They spoke in low tones.

"Definitely a gang beating. The extensive injuries are typical. Head trauma. Deep shock."

The second attendant was visibly upset. "Mindless violence! I hate it when the city goes this way. Wait and see, there'll be more. It always comes in a wave. As if something evil sets up shop and starts to feed."

The first shuddered. "I hope you're wrong!"

As soon as they left, Dana went inside. She almost cried out at the sight of him. Hooked to monitors and intravenous drips, Jean was covered in bandages and plaster casts. The only distinguishable feature was the dark tousle of hair.

Fighting back waves of guilt and sorrow, she approached his bed.

*Put your hands over his head. That should do the trick.*

Dana looked down at her hands. They were trembling. Once upon a time she could cup them together and a pool of light would well up in her palms. It was her inheritance, a gift from her mother. But a long time had passed since Dana had last called up her light. As a silent protest, she had refused to bring it to the place she considered her prison. Eventually she lost the memory of how to produce it, though she never admitted this to her mother or even to herself.

Dana knew she needed the light to help Jean. She had nothing else to offer him. But what if she couldn't? She was almost afraid to try. She looked at him with pity. Even unconscious, his body twitched with pain. She had no choice.

Taking a deep breath, Dana placed her hands together and willed the light to come.

Nothing.

Her heart sank like a stone. She tried again. And again. By the fourth time, she was crying, utterly devastated. She had lost her gift. She had squandered her inheritance.

Dana buried her face in her hands. And that was when she saw it, through the film of her tears: a faint dusting of gold at the tips of her fingers. The tiny specks were almost imperceptible. Hardly the pool of gold she once possessed. It was better than nothing, but would it be enough?

She held her hands above Jean's head. The light fell like soft rain upon him. Slowly, softly, it formed a halo. She closed her eyes. For a moment, she saw the green hill and the broken portal. She turned away. This was not her destination. Instead she thought of Jean, wherever he might be, and she reached out with her mind to find him.

*"Tabernac!* What you are doing here?"

He stood before her, tall and lean, the raven-black hair loose around his face, the wintergreen eyes bright with astonishment.

Dana shivered at the sound of his voice. It was like a cool mountain stream. She was so happy to see him she almost laughed, but the laugh died in her throat as she looked around. The place was horribly familiar. The burned and blackened landscape she had seen from Crowley's car. It was even worse close up.

They were standing in a mire of dank peat and cess-pools. Olid vapors rose around them like wafts of bad breath. Nearby was a brake of barren trees, pleached and prickly like a field of barbed wire. In the distance lay a bleak prospect of crags that seemed to claw at the dull sky. The air was acrid with the sour, metallic smell that Dana had come to associate with Crowley.

"I remember this from my nightmare!"

"Le Brûlé," said Jean, nodding.

"You know it?!"

He shrugged. "It look like a place I get lost in one time, in eastern Québec. They are all over the country. Spruce bog. In English, 'the Brule.' Not so good. You step in the wrong way"—he made a drowning motion—"you go down."

"Quicksand?" She looked around warily. "I know it from the night Crowley tried to kill me. He took me here in his car, but at the same time I was somewhere else. On the Mulmur Road." She stopped, overcome with shame. Then she burst out with, "I'm so sorry, Jean! For leaving you there! I was scared and confused. I didn't know who to trust, but still it was wrong. I acted like a coward."

"*Ce n'est rien.*" He shrugged again. "It was a strange night, eh? Who could know what happen?"

She was surprised by his indifference. Did he think it was all a dream, back then and now? But though he seemed to have no interest in what went on, she needed to know.

"Did Crowley attack you? I saw a wolf fighting the monster. How—?"

"Yes, he attack me," Jean interrupted quickly. "The thing it was our teacher, yes, but something else. It pick me up and throw me and then I am here. In this place."

"What about the wolf?" Dana asked. "Where did it come from? How did—?"

Again he cut her off. It was obvious he didn't want to talk about it. He changed the subject quickly.

"*Dis-moi*, are you really here or do I dream you?"

"I'm here," she said. "I've come to help you."

"I think maybe not." His look was quizzical, but there was no sarcasm in his voice, only grave doubt. "For days I try. The bog is *dangereux*, but worse are the *feux follets*."

"The what?"

"*Feux follets*. Crazy fire. They come from the ground."

"You mean will-o'-the-wisps?"

Jean frowned. "I don't know this word, but it sound too nice."

He turned to show her his back. Dana gasped. There were scorch marks on his shirt and the back of his jeans. Worse still, where the fabric had been burned away, his skin was raw and red with burns.

"We've got to get you out of here," she swore.

Again Jean looked doubtful, but Dana was thinking fast. "Can we fight fire with fire?"

She cupped her hands together. Regardless of Jean's talk of Canadian spruce bogs, this was obviously a dreamscape created by Crowley. Since it was made by magic, she hoped her power might be stronger here. Now as the light welled up and spilled over her palms, she breathed with relief.

"If I could just do that back in the real world," she murmured.

Jean's eyes widened when he saw the light. Frank and curious, he studied her features.

Unable to hold his gaze, Dana looked away. But she was pleased and proud that she had something to offer.

"Okay," he said quietly. "Maybe we got a chance. I been here awhile and know some things. See the mountains? Every time I try to go that way, the *feux follets* they attack me. *Alors,* this tell me, I want to go there. Maybe with your fire we do it!"

The ridge was on the other side of the bog, beyond the copse of dead and withered trees. There was no discernible path leading to it. Jean set off with Dana close behind. They skirted the woods, following a sluggish stream where the ground cover was sparse.

"Don't look to the water," Jean warned over his shoulder.

Dana immediately glanced at the stream, though she hadn't given it a thought before he spoke. She had been concentrating on keeping up with him. But there in the sickly flow of the snye, she caught her reflection. Bloated and grotesque, it wavered in the turbid waters, half-strangled by oily, tubular plants. Spellbound by the image, she watched herself thrash wildly even as she tasted the greasy stem that was invading her mouth.

"*Câlisse!*" cried Jean.

He had turned just in time. She was leaning over the water, about to fall in.

"I say not to look!" he yelled, pulling her back.

"Everyone looks when you say 'Don't look'!"

Dana sounded annoyed, but she was angry with herself. She had to be more careful. How could she rescue him if she got trapped herself?!

They were approaching the far side of the bog. The stream had widened to a dark turgid river that was impossible to cross. The only way forward was through the woods. Ragged branches of swamp willow and black spruce clutched at each other. The dank ground was gashed and pitted and gnarled with old roots.

Dana was taken by surprise when Jean reached out to grasp her hand. His felt dry and warm. Though she was overcome with shyness, she was also glad. He knew the way they should go, and it was easier to follow him. Together they pushed through the brittle brush and briars. The bog made sucking sounds under their feet. Wading through a pool that bubbled like oil, they were splashed with foul-smelling mud. At last the copse began to thin out and the jagged outline of the ridge rose up ahead. The ridge was only a short distance away, but the moment they broke free of the trees, any hope of a quick escape died.

Up from the ground rose a globe of greenish light. Small as an apple and seemingly harmless, it paused in midair, as if looking around. Now another rose up, as big as a grapefruit, then another, larger still, the size of a football. As more and more joined the swarm, their appearance grew increasingly sinister.

"In Québec," Jean said in an undertone, "we say the *feux follets* are sinners so bad they are not welcome in hell."

Dana stared at the fireballs that now hissed and spat. The sickly green color was all too familiar, as was the waspish drone that reverberated through the air. Though they were known in Quebec, these things were undoubtedly Crowley's own distorted versions.

"How often have you faced them?" she asked with horror.

"I stop counting," he said with a shrug.

His quiet courage steadied her. This was why she had come. Despite his strength and bravery, this was where Jean failed.

The swarm was growing increasingly agitated. Before Dana had time to cup her hands, the crazy fires bore down.

"I think now we run, *non?*"

"Yes!" cried Dana.

Heads down, shoulders hunched, they raced for the ridge. It meant charging the *feux follets* full-on. It was like dodging gigantic bullets or burning hailstones. While Jean swerved with the skill of one who had done this many times, Dana held her hands high and called on the light.

As if they sensed she was a threat, the fires sped toward Dana. The green flashes blinded her. The buzzing noise was deafening. One struck her left hand. She cried out as it burned her. And lost her concentration. Another struck her right hand. More searing pain.

Jean was beside her, running silently. As he ducked to miss a globe, another struck his back. She saw the scorch mark on his shirt. The red weal on his skin.

She had to do something. Into her mind flew an image of him lying in the hospital. With sudden certainty she knew that he would die there if she didn't stop the attack.

"This is for you!" she cried.

A golden banner of light streamed from her hands.

And she flung it over him like a shining cloak.

The *feux follets* went mad. But as soon as they drew near, they drowned like flies in molten gold.

"And this is for me," she thought as the guilt and shame was burned away. A baptism by fire.

"*Bravo!*" Jean yelled.

"Keep running!" Dana panted, not letting up her stride.

Yes, it was working. The crazy fires were in disarray. As more and more were destroyed by the light, they finally retreated.

And as Dana and Jean reached the foot of the ridge, the landscape faded away around them.

Dana was back in the hospital, beside Jean's bed. His eyes fluttered open. Gently she moved her hands away from his forehead, but not before he had caught sight of the remnant of gold.

"*Qu'est-ce qui se passe?*" he whispered. "What are you?"

She was overwhelmed with relief and joy. She had done it! He was free from the nightmare in which Crowley had imprisoned him.

But this was not the time for explanations. He needed to rest, to recover.

"I'm something different," she said softly. "Get better and I'll see you soon, *mon ami.*"

As his eyes closed in a deep and healing sleep, she left the room.

# Eleven

Dana's dream began badly. She was floating in a black void, as if underwater. Her first instinct was to draw on her light. The clash of metal rang out as she cupped her hands. They were encased in gauntlets of iron, the bane of Faerie! A wave of despair washed over her. She struggled against it. The dark would not claim her without a fight. As soon as she began to struggle, she felt herself move upward. Using the iron gloves as weapons, she pummeled the void, rising like a bubble toward the surface.

In a burst of black spray, she emerged from the darkness and found herself treading water in a mountain lake. Above her, the sky was ablaze with sunset. All around were the great shadows of the mountains. She swam to shore.

The dark tarn lay in a high hidden pasture. The grass glistened with evening dew. The earth was cool and damp beneath her bare feet. The iron gloves had disappeared. She was dressed in a white gown that reached her feet. She didn't wonder why she was dry after her swim, nor did she question what was going on. She knew she was dreaming.

Now she walked through fields lined with bushes of

yellow whin that glowed palely in the dimness. She came to a wooden archway that stood alone and unsupported. It was guarded by statues of Indian goddesses. An inscription was carved on the lintel overhead.

*It's a funny old world.*

Dana knew where she was. Gabriel had brought her here when they still lived in Ireland. A sculpture park outside of Roundwood in the Wicklow Mountains, it belonged to an eccentric philosopher. The park featured statues made in Mahabalipuram in southern India. One figure in particular dominated the collection.

"Ganesha!" Dana murmured.

Her stepmother's prayers were answered. He had come!

She hurried into the park and there, as she remembered it, was the great statue of Ganesha in shining black granite. He looked round and jolly, with plump limbs and toes, big belly and trunk, a generous spread of leafy ears, and long eburnine tusks. Sitting cross-legged on a dais, he held a book in his lap. When Dana glanced at the pages they were blank at first, a tabula rasa. Then letters began to form, darting like tiny fish in a pool. They spelled out words: *The Book of Dreams*. Dana noted the message, though she had no idea what it meant. She gazed expectantly at the statue, but nothing happened.

Not far from where she stood, a green garden hose lay coiled in the grass like a snake. In India, priests would bathe the temple statues with water and various oils and perfumes. In the sculpture park, guests were invited to shower Ganesha. Dana retrieved the hose and stood on tiptoe to spray the statue. In the last rays of the evening sun, the water sparkled with light, cascading over the gleaming black figure.

The first sound Dana heard was a chuckle. It rose from deep inside the belly of the god. Then came the tinkle of anklets as his left foot twitched. The chest heaved slightly and the limbs stretched out. Color seeped like life into the cold stone. The white pearls of Hyderabad and the blue gems of Bangalore shone on the silver-gray elephantine skin. Now the eyes shot open, bright with wisdom and mischief and laughter.

Dana jumped back. Dream or no, he was overwhelming!

THE LORD GANESHA.

*Flap flap* went the great ears like giant fronds in the wind. *Haarrooo* blew the trunk's trumpet call.

He didn't give her the chance to bow. Leaping from the dais, he caught her hands and danced her around the park with sweeping strides. Now the other statues came to life. Ganesha playing the tabla. Ganesha playing the sitar. Ganesha playing the flute. A wild sweet music rang through the air, singing of hot winds and red soil, bright silks and glass bangles, banyan trees and scented temples. *Indiahhhh.*

"You came!" Dana cried with delight. "Just like Radhi said you would!"

"My daughter calls, I answer."

His voice was rich and dark like chocolate. Hooting and laughing, he scooped her into his arms and swung her high as if she were a baby. Then gently he placed her back on the ground.

"I have many forms, many abilities, but I come to you this night as the Remover of Obstacles. For a short while only, I will lift the veil. For a short while only, I can remove what keeps you from your land and people. But you must act quickly. Your enemy is near and dreams are fragile. This one will soon be torn asunder."

Dana understood the warning. At the periphery of her vision, she could see a greenish mist creeping toward the park. As it moved, it consumed the grass and the bushes and all the colors of her dream. Her heart beat wildly.

"Where should I go? What should I do?"

Ganesha took her hand and walked her back to the lake through which she had arrived. On the shore was a little coracle with oars.

"Go quickly, daughter. What you seek awaits you on the other side."

"Thank you, thank you so much!"

She lifted his hand and kissed it reverently.

The Lord Ganesha smiled.

"Fare thee well, child. Give affectionate greetings to my beloved Radhi. Tell her to laugh more, as it makes me happy. I have come to you at her request, but I will do so no more. Your gods are all around you, child of Faerie, you need but open your heart to them."

Dana climbed into the boat and took up the oars. Ganesha pushed her off with his trunk.

The lake was as smooth as glass. The oars sliced through the water as if it were quicksilver, propelling the skiff over the surface with ease. As the sun set, the sky turned a midnight-blue, sprayed with stars. The night was still. The only sounds were the dip of the oars in the water and the lap of the low waves against the hull. The gentle rocking of the coracle was like a cradle. How long she rowed Dana couldn't be certain, but at last she saw a rim of land ahead. She strained to move faster.

As landfall drew near, Dana cried out with happiness. There on the shore stood a shining figure with red-gold hair.

Dana jumped from the boat and flung herself into her mother's arms.

"Child of my heart, blood of my blood," Edane murmured.

"Where have you been?" Dana asked, urgently. "What's going on? What has happened?"

Edane led her daughter into the dunes beyond the shore. A small campfire burned amidst the marram grass. The flames flickered in the darkness.

"We are on the border of Faerie," Edane told her quietly. "The Lord Ganesha fashioned a dream to make a bridge that could bring you here. There was no other way, for there are no bridges left. We must be quick, dear heart. The stuff of dreams is delicate."

Dana crouched by the fire. A little meal had been laid out on stones in the sand. Dishes of gold held fruits and wild berries, and tiny seedcakes dipped in honey. A jeweled goblet brimmed with wine.

"Eat and drink while I speak," Edane said. "Your fairy soul is in need of sustenance."

Even as she consumed the food and the wine, Dana tasted the truth of her mother's words. How much she had hungered and thirsted for this, the fruits of the other world! In the long days of separation from the land of her spirit, she had been slowly starving to death. But though she was soon refreshed and nourished, a cold dread was rising inside her. She had never seen her mother so subdued and solemn.

Edane was roasting hazelnuts in a bronze pan over the fire. A sweet woody smell filled the air. Dana remembered doing the same for Honor, the High Queen of Faerie, when she was trapped in Dún Scáith, the Fort of the Shades. Her dread increased. This was not a good sign.

"Hark to me, daughter," Edane said. "Our doom is upon us. The portals between Faerie and the Earthworld lie riven. Not only the gateways throughout Ireland, but all the doors of perception that open to the fairy world. All commerce between humanity and Faerie has come to an end."

Dana was stunned. This was beyond her worst imaginings.

"I thought it was just me," she whispered. "How did it happen? Who—?"

Edane shook her head. Her voice trembled with distress. "It is an ancient tale interwoven with new threads of which you are one. There is no time to tell it here, and how it came to be is not as important as what must be done."

With trembling hands, she fed Dana the roasted hazelnuts, one by one.

"The High King sends you this message. *The hour of your destiny has come. You are the light that will bridge the darkness. Only you can restore the gateways.*"

Dana's eyes widened with shock. A short while ago such a huge task, such a burden, would have broken her; but she had retrieved her light and rescued Jean, danced with a god and eaten otherworldly food. Though she was reeling at the thought of what lay ahead, some part of her had already accepted the quest.

"You must find the Book of Dreams," Edane said. "It holds a secret—"

She was about to place another nut in Dana's mouth when she dropped it. With a cry, she searched frantically in the sand at her feet. It was nowhere to be seen.

"It's okay, Mum," Dana said, but Edane looked stricken.

"The High Queen was to bring these to you. I pleaded that I might come in her stead, for I feared that I might never see you again. Oh, what have I done?"

Dana felt a wave of the same panic. She was about to undertake the greatest mission of her life and the wrong person was guiding her! She forced herself to be calm. Her mother was already distraught. No use both of them losing their heads.

"Okay, so I'm to find a book," she said. "How? Where do I look? Should I return to Ireland? Or is it somewhere in Faerie?"

Edane frowned as she tried to remember. "The Book of Dreams is in Canada. It is as the High King foresaw long ago. Your destiny lies there."

Dana was appalled. "*Canada?* That doesn't make any sense. There's no magic there. And I can't quest in that country. I don't know it at all!" A map of Canada flashed through her mind. "And it's *huge!*"

She might as well have been asked to search the ocean.

"The High Queen believes without a doubt that you are able for this," Edane insisted. "The Book of Dreams belongs to you. It is your inheritance."

"I don't understand. What does that mean?"

The question only heightened her mother's confusion and distress. Again, Dana saw the grave error that had been made. Honor knew the answer to that question. Edane did not.

Now Edane stiffened suddenly and looked out across the water. A greenish mist was creeping over the lake toward them.

"Too little time! I have not said enough!" Her blue fairy eyes welled with tears. She was already fading away. "Your enemy will do anything to stop you. Courage, my daughter. You are the Light that I bore. Remember always, I love you."

Dana reached out for her mother. "I love you too!"

The sickly green mist had reached the shore and was crawling like worms toward Dana.

"Wake up!" Edane screamed.

Dana woke in her bed, arms grasping the air.

"Mama," she whispered.

Her face was wet with tears. She got out of bed and walked to the window. It was the darkest hour, just before the dawn. The road below was deserted. The street lamps shed light through the trees. The birds had yet to begin their morning song. In the distance came the silvery sound of wind chimes.

There was no question about the reality of her dream. It was a cry for help from Faerie. Not only had her portal been destroyed but all portals everywhere. Her soul trembled at the thought. The bond between the two worlds had been severed. Each side stood alone in the dark. The message in the dream was also clear. *The hour of your destiny has come.* A pang of fear shot through her. She had been given a terrifying mission: to save two worlds! How could they expect so much of her? What if she failed?

Dana steadied herself. Fail or not, she had to try. For better or worse, the job was hers.

A sweet fragrance lingered in the air around her. She heard the faint sound of music. She was not alone. Great powers had already moved to help her. The words of Lord Ganesha echoed in her mind. *Your gods are all around you, child of Faerie, you need but open your heart to them.*

Standing at the window, she watched the night transform. Slowly the darkness gave way to the inky blue of pre-dawn; then the half-light that heralded the arrival of day. In the changing of the hours, her resolve hardened. She would go out into Canada and quest for the book. *Your enemy will do anything to stop you.* Her mother's warning explained Crowley and the attacks against her. She would have to protect herself. It was time to end her isolation and ask for help. But caution was important. How could she tell friend from foe? For now, there was only one she was prepared to trust.

Below in the street, across the road from her house, he stood. She had been watching him as he skulked through the park, half-hidden in the shadows. The amber eyes glowed as he stared up at her window: the great black wolf with the white star on his chest.

# †WELVE

Jean did not return to school till the end of September. During the time he was away, Dana prepared for her mission. At home in her room, she practiced calling up the light. Her first efforts were miserable, as if she was drawing power from a broken circuit. Refusing to despair, she persevered until slowly but surely the connection was made. Her light grew stronger, brighter. When at last it welled up like a pool of gold in her hands, she bathed her face in it, laughing and drinking and eating the pure light. Like fairy food, it nourished her spirit. And even as the light grew stronger, so too did Dana. She began to delve deep to discover her powers, though she wasn't always sure what she might find. She had never asked her mother about her birthright. Edane preferred to play games and dance and party, and her daughter was of like mind. Oh, how Dana regretted rejecting the High Queen's offer to tutor her! Given that Honor herself had had to learn fairy arts, she would have been a perfect teacher.

No use crying over spilled milk, Dana told herself.

Alone and without guidance, she explored and practiced. Certain fairy gifts were familiar to her as she had used them occasionally in Faerie: *glamore*, flight, enchantment, and shape-shifting. But they were far more difficult to wield in the Earthworld. On top of that, her skills were halved due to the fact she was part human. Still, she had enough to work with, and as her powers increased, so too did her hope that she might succeed in her mission.

All the time she was training, Dana kept on guard. Since the attack at the hospital there had been no sign of Crowley. While she wanted to think he had been defeated, her dream warned her otherwise. The sickly green mist had undoubtedly come from him. He seemed to be able to find her wherever she was. That realization would have terrified her if she wasn't also aware of other presences around her. There were times when she felt oddly safe and secure, as if someone was watching over her like a guardian angel. Was it Lord Ganesha?

At school, she had become adept at avoiding her new teacher. Though Ms. Woods appeared to be kind and good-natured, Dana had already made up her mind. There was only one person she intended to trust on her mission, and she was waiting for him.

The day Jean returned he walked slowly into class, avoiding the curious stares of the others. Though he bore no evident scars from his ordeal, there were shadows under his eyes, and he looked pale and thinner. He didn't glance once in Dana's direction, nor did he respond whenever she tried to catch his attention. She finally had to accept that he was ignoring her.

Dana was crushed. Had he forgotten their time in the Brule together? Perhaps he only remembered the night on the road, when she had left him to die? There was also another possibility: he might well have no memory of either event. Her heart sank at the thought. That would be the worst case of all, for then she would mean nothing to him. She would just be another girl in his class. Dana couldn't accept that. She wanted, *needed* him to join her. There was no question of what she had to do. She needed to convince him somehow. Her heart sank further. What could she say to him?

After a long morning spent mustering her courage, Dana confronted Jean in the hall between classes.

"*Ça va?*" she said, unsure how to begin.

Jean frowned and shrugged, then tried to move away.

She blocked his path. "Wait. Please," she pleaded. "I know it was my fault you were hurt. I'm really sorry, believe me. It's no excuse, but I honestly didn't know what was going on. I thought you were my enemy or at least on his side."

Jean's frown deepened. She saw the wariness in his eyes. There was anger there too, but also confusion. Did he or did he not remember? The moment had come. It was now or never. She moved closer to him. Then, turning in such a way that he could see her hands, though she shielded them from others, she called up the light.

Nothing happened. She was too nervous. She had never shown her gift to another human being before.

Jean made an impatient noise and was about to leave when at last the light shone. His eyes widened. But he didn't look as shocked as she had expected. He grasped her hands and stared at them.

"What are you?" he demanded quietly.

"You asked me that before," she answered, in the same low tone. "I'm more than I seem. I'm something . . . different."

"*Le Brûlé!*" he swore suddenly. "*Les feux follets!* It was no dream! *Maudit, c'est incroyable!*" The green eyes flashed. All the anger and confusion vanished. Excitement lit up his face. "*Dis-moi.* What is happening? What *aventure* is this?"

Dana was abashed by his intensity. She could feel the full strength of his personality concentrated on her, and it threw her into a muddle.

"The w-w-olf," she stammered. "The . . . the one that follows you? He tried to save me that night. I want to thank him and maybe . . . could I meet him?"

It was as if a mask was clamped down on Jean's face. His eyes went cold. He backed away from her.

Dana understood. She, too, was protective of her

otherworld friends. She, too, guarded her secrets. But, as she herself had learned only recently, sometimes you had to open up. Sometimes you had to share your secrets. He was the one person she was ready to trust, and she needed him to feel the same way about her. Casting aside her usual shyness, she rushed out her words.

"I've shown you my light. It's a gift from my mother. She's a fairy queen. A sky-woman. But I think it's my human side you'll accept more. My last name is Faolan. *Faol* is the old Irish word for 'wolf.' My father's people are the Clan of the Wolf. We belong to the wolf. She's our guardian."

It worked! He was caught, she could see it. A strange delight shone in his eyes. He grinned with a sudden flash of white teeth.

"*Alors*, the wolf in you wish to meet my wolf?"

She nodded vigorously.

"And you don't fear?"

"No!" Dana declared from her heart. "I love the wolf!"

"*C'est vrai?*"

Jean's grin widened. Mischief sparked in his eyes. He was so hugely amused, she was nonplussed. Was there some joke she was missing?

Jean leaned toward her. His grin seemed to stretch from ear to ear. Disoriented, unsure what she was seeing, Dana found herself staring into a maw of white canines. *Grandma, what big teeth you have.*

A laugh growled low in his throat. "Like you, I too am more. I too am *différent*."

A yellow-gold color seeped into his eyes, drowning the green irises. Now the amber glare of the wolf stared out at her.

Instinctively Dana backed away.

"You!" she gasped. An unreasoning fear gripped her. This was more than she had bargained for. This was not the wolf she knew. "You're a werewolf!"

His grin was wicked. "So, not all wolves you love, eh?"

Dana recovered quickly, ashamed of herself. "I'm sorry . . . really . . . I . . . I never met a werewolf. Not in Ireland or Faerie."

Jean shrugged good-naturedly. The wintergreen color returned to his eyes.

"I am not werewolf," he said. "I am *loup-garou*. You know what is this?"

She shook her head.

"It's a French-Canadian thing. I tell you later. *Maintenant*, we go with chemistry. You know how to do this?"

For a moment Dana was totally confused. Her face flushed red. Did he mean—?

"Oh," she said with sudden understanding. "Our science homework? Yes. It's an experiment with hydrogen. I've done the first part."

"*Bon*. I sit with you."

· · ·

Dana entered the science lab in a happy daze. New and peculiar feelings were bubbling away inside her. She felt as if she had taken a turn in the road and was now wandering through exotic territory. It was exciting and disturbing and promising and terrifying all at the same time. For better or worse, she was no longer alone on her mission. A new kind of magic had entered her life and with it, a boy. She wasn't sure which was more fascinating.

There was a lot of laughing as they struggled with a Bunsen burner that refused to light.

"We do the *feux follet*, we can do this," Jean assured her.

At lunch in the cafeteria, he joined her in the line.

"You eat with me, *non?*"

He was obviously not shy with girls. His manner was both casual and confident.

Battling her own shyness, Dana followed him to a secluded corner. She was painfully aware of the looks cast in their direction. At one table, the older girls she had questioned about Jean raised their eyebrows at each other. At another table, Janis and her circle sat stupefied.

Indifferent to their audience, Jean drew up his chair close to Dana's. If he was aware of her discomfort, he didn't show it. Unwrapping a baguette of ham and cheese, he tore into it hungrily. His manner toward her was both casual and intimate.

To cover her embarrassment, Dana spoke quickly,

keeping her voice low so no one else could hear. "How did you become a werewolf? Were you bitten by one?"

He waved his hand dismissively. "*Mais non,* I tell you I am not this thing. I am *loup-garou.*"

Mesmerized, she watched as he took another voracious bite of his sandwich and almost swallowed it whole.

"It happen to *mon grand-père* . . . my grandfather . . . and he tell me of the others, my great-grandfather and his great-grandfather. The first one, he come from Poitou in France but it only happen here, *je pense.* He don't go to Mass for seven year, so he become a wolf at night. He can be normal again if he confess the sin to a *curé.* A priest *catholique.* Then he go back to the Church and he is *loup-garou* no more."

Dana thought for a moment. "The men in your family didn't go to a priest?" Then she grinned. "They liked being a wolf."

"*Mais oui.*"

Jean's teeth flashed white. He threw back his head to laugh.

Dana couldn't help but join him. Their laughter was so loud and wild, they drew more looks. She no longer cared. She was caught up in the wonder of a Canadian fairy tale.

Enjoying her response, Jean was happy to continue his story.

"Unless the man confess, it stay in the blood of the

*famille*. But not all the peoples. My father is not *loup-garou*. But my dear *grand-père* he see that I am. He wait for me outside the house the night I have seven year. When I turn, there is much fear. *Terreur*. Here I am a *petit* boy in my bed, then I am on the floor with four legs and so much hair and big teeth. I am all—how you say?—shivering. Then I hear the call to me. This howl in the night. This *cri de coeur*. A cry from the heart, yes, that is *liberté* . . . freedom . . . the freedom of the wild. It is like a fire in my head, in my blood. I jump out the window to start my new life."

"Was it less scary being with your grandfather?"

"*Mais oui*, but also with the wolf comes courage."

"Of course," Dana murmured, remembering.

"That first night we run together, I never forget. *Mes parents*, they live in Trois-Rivières at that time but *grand-père* he live in Labrador City. He invite us to visit at his house for my birthday. He know I am to turn that night and he want me to run free in the wild place with him. *Câlisse, c'était merveilleux!* I have not the word to describe. It is the winter. The land is all white with snow and the ice. The trees, they are tall and black like arrow that shoot into the sky. We run across many lake that are frozen and across many hill with snow and many river that are like a road of ice . . . *c'était très beau*."

Eyes shining, face aglow, he was lost in his memories. Dana could see that he was far away, running with the wolves through the cold white interior of Labrador and Quebec. Oh, how she yearned to be there with him!

"Is it up to you when you turn?" she asked. "Do you have any choice about becoming a wolf or not?"

"*Toujours.* Always I choose. Except when the time is full moon. Then the moon, she call to the wolf and the wolf he come out whether the human like it or not."

Again, the wide grin.

"And during the day?"

Dana saw immediately that she had said the wrong thing. Jean's face darkened suddenly. His features seemed to close in on themselves.

"It is not good to turn wolf by day. Then you stay wolf forever. You can never be human again. But I don't want to talk about this."

She didn't press him. From her own experience, Dana knew all too well that magic was a two-edged sword. Enchantment could be beautiful and exciting, but it was also perilous. Fairy tales did not always end happily. She could sense an old wound, some deep loss he had suffered. Instinctively, she rested her hand on his.

"Back in Ireland, when I was lost in the mountains, a wolf came to be my friend. To guide me. She was my *anamchara.* That means 'soul-friend' in Irish. She . . . she died. I loved her so much. I . . . I've never told anyone about her . . . till now."

She could see that her words affected him deeply. His

features worked with emotion and he seemed unable to speak at first. Then he took her hand and kissed it lightly.

"The first time I see you, you feel like *famille*. The life of the wolf can be lonely, *non?* But he always know his people. Your wolf friend, she is gone. I will be in her place. I will be your soul-friend. How you say this *beau* word in your language? *Anamchara?* In my language, it is *âme soeur. Alors*, now tell me. Why do this monster want to kill you?"

For a moment Dana was overwhelmed, not only by his charm, but by the generosity of his offer. This was what she had so dearly hoped for: that she could set out on her quest with a companion by her side.

"I don't know who or what he is, only that he's an enemy of Faerie," she began. "He took over Mr. Crowley somehow. I guess to get closer to me." Even as the thought struck her, Dana went pale. Felt sick. How many more innocent people would suffer or die as this thing tried to kill her? She fought back the fear and the nausea. There was only one thing she could do to stop it: succeed in her mission. "He's trying to keep me from finding something. It's a bit like the quest for the Holy Grail, except it's not a treasure, but a book I'm looking for. The Book of Dreams."

As Dana told her story, she grew afraid that Jean might not want to join her. After all, it was not his battle, the mission had nothing to do with him. He already knew from his experience with Crowley that the dangers were real, could even be fatal. Why would he want to risk his life for someone he hardly knew? She faltered at the end of her tale and waited anxiously. How would he respond?

The wintergreen eyes glittered with excitement. There was not a moment's doubt, not a second of fear.

"Already I meet the monster before the night I try to save you. He attack me in the city. He is my enemy too. In my heart I know this—he hate all the thing that live, all that is good. *Alors,* I do this quest with you! We go together."

Dana caught her breath. She could hardly speak she was so happy. How much her life had changed in so short a time! As if she had stepped out of the shadows and into the light.

"So where do we look?" said Jean.

With a thump, she was back to reality.

"It's somewhere in Canada," she said lamely. "That's all I know. Talk about a needle in a haystack!"

"Needle?" He looked confused. "Haystack?"

"Sorry, it's an expression," and she began to explain.

His face cleared. "Ah *oui,* it's the same in French. *Chercher une aiguille dans un botte de foin.*"

A shiver ran up Dana's spine. She loved to hear him speak his own language.

"I have an idea," he said suddenly. "You can run with the wolf?"

She frowned nervously. "I . . . I've done it before. But it's been a long time."

He gave her a stern look. "It is necessary you run with me. I can be no help if you don't."

Her throat tightened. She had no idea if she could do what he asked. All her recent attempts to shape-shift had gone very badly. It was one of the most difficult of fairy arts. But she could see that he was growing impatient.

"Yes, of course I can," she stated, with more confidence than she felt.

"*Bon!*" he said. "When we do this? We go the whole night, *n'est-ce pas?*"

"How about on the weekend?" she suggested, thinking fast.

She needed time to prepare, not only for the magic, but to cover her tracks. If she was going away overnight, she would have to do it in secret.

"*Bon,*" he said again. "Saturday. We meet *chez toi.* Your house. I know where you live. I go there as wolf."

"I saw you that night!" she said. "What—?"

He shrugged, but didn't bother to explain. He would make no apologies for the lupine side of his character.

They were still discussing their plans when their teacher approached them.

"You're hard to get ahold of, " Ms. Woods said to

Dana, smiling tentatively. "But it's really important that I speak with you. I understand if you're afraid or suspicious. Believe me, I know what's going on. Well, I know something. I want to help you."

Jean looked surprised and leaned forward with interest, but Dana's eyes narrowed.

"I don't need your help."

Ms. Woods glanced around her anxiously. Her presence in the cafeteria was already drawing attention. Teachers usually kept to the staff room. Some of the nosier students edged closer in an attempt to overhear. Who was in trouble? What had they done?

"If you would just come with me," she urged Dana, in a low voice "where we could talk in private. If you'd like to bring your friend, I don't mind."

"Leave me alone," Dana said. "If you come near me again, I'll report you."

Ms. Woods was taken aback. Yet it seemed for a minute, as she regarded the two of them, that she also looked pleased.

"Very well," she said. Her sigh seemed to echo sadness. Then, reluctantly, she withdrew.

"You don't like?" said Jean, as he watched their teacher leave the cafeteria.

"I don't trust."

"She seem *très gentille*. She don't feel bad like Crowley. But who can know for sure, eh?"

"Exactly," said Dana. "I'm not taking any chances. The less people involved, the safer it is. We don't need strangers."

"*D'accord.* So, we got a date for Saturday?"

Dana blushed furiously.

# Thirteen

It was late when Jean finally appeared outside Dana's house. She was watching for him at her bedroom window, ready to go in jeans and parka. She had grown worried that he might not come, but there he was, in the shadows beyond the street lamp: the great black wolf.

Dana glanced toward her bed, at the lump under the duvet. What should have been a simple enchantment had taken all week. In theory, she knew how to fashion a changeling: bind leaves, twigs, branches, and clumps of earth with a string of words, a spell, to make a human shape. Getting the materials from the backyard and up to her room was the easiest part; but the magic itself eluded her at first and the early attempts left a rotting mess on the bed. Days of frustration and sometimes tears finally brought the desired result. There lay the counterfeit Dana with dark curls of hair, fair skin, similar height and weight, wearing her pajamas.

Gabriel and Aradhana had retired earlier that evening,

but there was always a chance they might look in on her. Aside from the musty smell that lingered in the room, all seemed normal.

Dana leaned over the sleeping form for a final check.

The eyes shot open.

"Go 'way," it said grumpily.

Dana jumped back. The eyes closed again.

*Perfect*, she thought. *And creepy.*

She tiptoed into the hall and down the stairs. By the time she had shut the front door and crossed the road to the park, Jean had returned to his own shape to greet her.

Hands plunged into the pockets of his jacket, he leaned toward her eagerly with a big smile on his face. Though the rest of him was human, the eyes glowed like polished amber.

She was happy to see him, but at the same time suffered an attack of bashfulness. She had grown used to meeting him at school, sharing lunch, and talking between classes. His manner was so natural and easygoing, she was able to relax in his company. But this was different. They were no longer surrounded by the security of the school routine and the presence of other students. This was just the two of them, alone in the night. And she could hardly believe what she was doing. Behind her, a light shone through the blinds of her father's bedroom. What would he do if he looked out the window and saw her meeting with a boy!

Jean caught her arm and drew her into the park.

"*Je m'excuse*, I am late," he explained in a quick whisper. "I wait for *mes parents* to sleep. They know I go out sometime, but then they worry. Especially since the night I get hurt. *Alors*, I go *en secret*."

"Me too," said Dana. "So where are we going? Is it still a surprise?"

All week he had refused to reveal their destination.

"I bring you to the place of my friend," he said. "He is one who is special. A medicine man. We go to him for help."

"Medicine man?" She looked confused.

"You don't know this word? There are other—*jongleur*, *sorcier*—I don't know in English. How you say a person who go between the world?"

"You mean like me? A fairy?"

"*Non*, he is human. He is born in this world but he travel to the other one. He do this for power and to know many thing, but also to help the peoples when they are sick."

"Of course!" said Dana, annoyed with herself for being so slow. "In Ireland we call them a fairy doctor or doctress. I didn't know there were people like that over here."

His exasperation was quick. "You think these things are only *irlandais*? This country has *beaucoup de magie*! Open your eyes, eh!"

Dana heard the echo of the Lord Ganesha's admonishment. *You need but open your heart.* And suddenly she caught sight of a truth she had refused to see. Eyes opening, heart opening, a door opened in her mind.

"I was so sure there was nothing here," she said, shocked by her own blindness. "And that's all I saw. Nothing."

"*Alors, regarde chérie,*" he said with a wicked grin. "Canadian magic."

Even as he grinned he was already turning. Dana drew back involuntarily with a frisson of terror. Her instincts told her to flee. It was a natural reaction. As the old Irish adage warned: *Bí ar d'fhaichill ar an strainséir.* Beware the stranger!

His features disappeared first as the face elongated to an elegant snout. Now his back arched and he dropped to the ground, landing on all fours. *A stranger to humanity.* Hands and feet changed to great paws. Nails grew to claws. Black hair sprouted from every pore, piercing his skin and then his clothes, covering both like a coat. He expanded in size. *A stranger even to her fairy self.* There before her stood a great northern wolf, with enough bulk to hunt the moose and the caribou. As the broad head reared back, she saw the point of the white star that emblazoned his chest. When he opened his mouth, a great red tongue lolled out. The fangs looked lethal. And yet, somehow, that wicked grin was Jean's.

Turning to leave, he trotted a short distance away and stopped to look back at her. The amber eyes were as cool as the moon. He snapped a quick bark. *Your turn*, it clearly said. *Turn.*

Her moment of truth had come. Metamorphosis, for fairies, was as natural as dancing, and the wolf itself was Dana's totem, yet no matter how often she had tried that week, she had not been able to alter her form. The changeling spell had been difficult enough, and that was only a simple enchantment; shape-shifting proved impossible.

Dana hesitated, afraid to tell him. She could sense the wolf's impatience, his lupine hunger to run wild, run free. With a final bark, he took off without her, dashing into the night.

A cry escaped her. If she didn't move quickly, she would miss her chance. He would leave her behind. The thought of facing him later with lame excuses was unbearable. She clenched her body in a furious effort to transform.

The first thing she felt was the howl of the wolf inside her. It rose up like a pressure against her ribs, an excruciating pain, as if the creature were trying to claw its way out. She opened her mouth to scream. An impossible stretch of jaw. Now the howl tore through every cell in her body. It was a cry of longing. A cry of grief for her *anamchara* who had died in the mountains. A call-note of sorrow from her fairy self caged too long in her humanity, yearning to be free.

As the life force of the wolf struck her, Dana fell to the ground. She landed on her dewclaws, and the immediate discomfort pushed her upright on all fours. There was no time to lose. She sniffed the air to catch Jean's scent and bounded after him, a hunter on the trail of her prey. The last changes were quick and graceful and occurred as she ran—fur and fang, sleek sinew and muscle.

Racing at a breathless pace, Dana had to wonder: how had she kept the wolf trapped for so long?

To run with the wolf was to run in the shadows, the dark ray of life, survival and instinct. A fierceness that was proud and lonely, a tearing, a howling, a hunger and thirst. *Blessed are they who hunger and thirst.* A strength that would die fighting, kicking, screaming, that wouldn't stop till the last breath had been wrung from its body. The will to take one's place in the world. To say I am here. To say *I am*.

Traveling westward, she caught up with Jean. He let out a glad bark to acknowledge her arrival and together they loped in smooth strides. The cool night air flowed past like a river. The two kept a steady pace, occasionally breaking into short bursts of speed. Dana knew they could run this way for hours, but she was already losing track of human time.

Racing through Toronto's streets, the wolves moved

swiftly and silently over the sidewalks, across the roads, through green patches of park. They stayed in the shadows and sheltered spaces, but it wasn't really necessary. No one paid them any heed, neither the drivers whose cars sped through the dark night nor the pedestrians who had their own reasons for being out so late. Those who did notice them assumed they were a pair of stray dogs. Dana realized the truth: the vast majority see only what they want to see and what they believe to be real. Most people ignore the extraordinary and anything that might challenge their view of life; anything that might frighten them.

An Irish fairy in the shape of a wolf, running beside a *loup-garou*, Dana was part of that silver thread of magic, that other world stitched into the fabric of reality. She could sense it all round her, humming like static on electric wires, fluttering like ribbons through the silent streets. The stuff of dreams. *There are more things in heaven and earth, Horatio, than are dreamt of in your philosophy.*

As they passed through a Chinese neighborhood, Dana was startled to see huge creatures crouched ominously on the rooftops. At first she thought they were demons or gargoyles, then she realized they were dragons. Ruby red, dark blue, yellow and green, they perched atop shopping malls, restaurants, and businesses. Many were fast asleep with no sign of life except for the puffs of smoke that rose lazily from long snouts. Others dozed like giant iridescent lizards with one eye open, tails batting leisurely against scaly hides. Some, but not all, had wings tucked at their sides. One of them winked at her and Dana suddenly knew. These dragons were the guardian angels of the community. They had emigrated with their people to bring them prosperity and luck.

The two wolves continued westward as if tracking the sunset. On reaching the rolling green of High Park, they skirted the cold waters of Grenadier Pond, stopping at the edge of the South Kingsway. As it was Saturday night, there was still plenty of traffic. The pair waited patiently to cross the road. Once across, they slipped into the marshes that fringed the Humber River. As they skulked along the riverbanks, past white oak and cottonwood, they surprised a blue heron asleep in the reeds. The river flowed southward into Lake Ontario, but they journeyed north to Étienne Brûlé Park.

The black wolf that was Jean came to a halt. Shivering violently, he rose up on his hind legs. Slowly at first, then more quickly as the change gathered momentum, his snout, fur, and claws receded even as his humanity emerged.

Following his lead, Dana unraveled too. Breathless with the speed and thrill of the journey, she couldn't speak at first. Oh, how alive and happy she felt!

Jean grinned a welcome. The same intensity burned

in his eyes, still glowing amber. He waved his arm at the dense greenery of trees and bushes around them.

"This is one place I go when I am *loup-garou*. There are other. Warden Wood, the Don Valley, High Park . . . All are good for the wolf. They are also place to hide *le canot* that run *la chasse-galerie*."

"The what?" said Dana.

She could see he was barely suppressing his excitement and she guessed this was the secret he had been keeping all week.

Jean started to search the underbrush. Pulling at something large on the ground, he dragged it out of the greenery.

"A boat?" she exclaimed.

It was a long graceful canoe, not a modern fiberglass construction, but a Native craft of birch bark artfully stitched over ribs of wood. The blood-red color glowed in the dimness. The sides were painted with many images and patterns. Dana could discern the shapes of raven and wolf, but there were other figures that made her uneasy. Grotesque faces grimaced at her with unmistakable malice. She backed away. There was something here that reminded her of Crowley. Something menacing.

Jean clambered into the canoe and retrieved the oars in the bottom of the boat.

"*Allons-nous!*" he said to her over his shoulder.

"What?" she spluttered. Was this some kind of joke?

But she didn't feel like laughing. She wanted to get away from that canoe as soon as possible.

"Let's go!" he said again. "*Vitement.* Time fly. So we do."

Dana hung back. Her old doubts about Jean crept into her mind. She knew for certain that the boat was bad. All her instincts screamed in alarm.

"No," she said, taking another step back.

She was planning her escape. Having reclaimed her ability to shape-shift, she would try to change herself into a bird. No wolf could catch her if she flew away. Still, she hesitated. She wanted so much to trust him.

"Jean, what's going on? There's something wrong here. I know it."

He had been concentrating on what he was doing, laying out the oars fore and aft. Taking up position in the stern, he obviously meant her to go in the bow. Now as he turned his attention to her, he regarded her gravely. There was a touch of sadness in his look.

"You think I will hurt you, *chérie?*"

"No," she said, struggling to be clear. "It's the boat. I don't trust *it.*"

He gave a little shake of his head, and his voice was apologetic.

"You are *sensible, n'est-ce pas?* Sensitive, I mean? And I am *stupide.* I don't tell you everything so you don't fear. *Je suis desolé.* This is not right. You are not *enfant. Alors,* I explain."

He rubbed his hand gingerly along the side of the canoe as if it were a horse.

"This is a spirit boat. With it, I run *la chasse-galerie*. It fly through the air, like a canoe go over water. This is the good thing. Now I tell you the bad that you feel. The boat, he belong to a *diablotin*. A demon. A devil. This we fight—*comment dit-on?*—wrestle. Yes, that is the word. It is necessary we wrestle it. There is a battle of will between the one who own the boat, the demon, and the one who row. This is what make *la chasse-galerie*. This is what make the boat fly."

The alarm bells lowered in volume. Dana could hear the truth in his voice.

"You've done this before?"

"*Mais oui.* All the time when I want to go where is too far for the wolf. Like tonight. This is the surprise I have for you. We go to the north of Québec where live my friend."

Despite the last of her misgivings, Dana was thrilled. A journey to northern Canada! And with him!

Jean's tone grew persuasive as he argued his case.

"But think, *chérie*, this is not so strange a thing, eh? All the peoples do this all the times, eh? We fight the demon inside us, *non?*"

Dana wished she could say she didn't know what he meant, but of course she did. With sudden unease, she reflected on the year gone by. Had she fought her demons or had she succumbed to them?

Jean stood up in the boat and reached out to coax her in.

"You come with me, yes? I make this good for you."

With a deep breath she took his hand and stepped into the canoe.

"Dark forces can be dodgy," she muttered.

"Without the dark," he shrugged, "it don't go. But you and me, we are strong together. One last thing it is necessary to remember. Don't call to God no matter what happen. If you do, the demon he let go of the boat and we fall from the sky. *Comprends-tu?*"

Dana understood perfectly. There was always a risk when you played with the dark.

Kneeling in the front, she took up her oar. It felt light and easy to handle. She had never been in a canoe before and wished she could sit behind Jean to copy his movements. Apparently, the more experienced person went in the back. But though Dana felt anxious and unsettled, she was also excited. The night's adventure had only begun.

A shiver ran through her when Jean called out the challenge that was also a spell.

"*Nous sommes ici!*" he cried. "We play the game of chance and fate! *Nous risquons de vendre nos âmes au diable!* We play for our soul! *Canot d'écorce, qui vole, qui vole! Canot d'écorce, qui va voler!*"

Regardless of her feelings about the spirit boat, Dana would have been disappointed if it didn't fly; but she didn't have to worry. Like a dead thing slowly coming to life, the canoe began to shudder. Cold currents of air rushed toward them. She sensed the invisible demon in the atmosphere around them. As it clutched the sides of the boat, she felt its ill will and its eagerness to seize those who risked their souls for a night ride. She knew she was in mortal danger.

The canoe shook violently. Her teeth rattled in her head.

"*Fais-nous voyager!*" Jean roared. "*Par-dessus les montagnes!*"

As the last words of the spell were uttered, the boat leaped upward. It was as if an unseen hand had plucked it from the ground and flung it into the sky.

For a moment they hovered over the park, hundreds of feet in the air, hanging above the treetops like a star.

"*Regarde,*" Jean called to Dana. "When we run *la chasse-galerie*, the boat he sail through time and space. He give us eyes."

Below her, the air rippled like water. She had a bird's-eye view of the modern-day park; the site for campfires, parking lot, and public washrooms. Then a wave seemed to wash over the scene. The trees were suddenly denser, much bigger and older. There was a clearing not far from the river. Smoke rose up from structures of hide and wood. It was still nighttime and few were awake, but two men sat companionably by a campfire. One was Native, the other white, but both wore the same clothing of deerskin and fur. The white man looked up. Even from a distance Dana could see he was young, still in his teens. It seemed that he saw her too, floating in midair. His glance was swift and piercing, like an arrow.

"Who's that?" she asked Jean.

Jean laughed with pride. "Étienne Brûlé. He come here long ago when the park is a village of the Wyandot peoples they call the Huron. Étienne is the first white man to visit the Great Lakes. He have only eighteen year when he come to Canada with the explorer Samuel de Champlain. Like you, Étienne was *sensible*. He see many thing."

Jean waved down at the young man, who waved back. "Now we go!" cried Jean.

A surge of power coursed through Dana as she paddled furiously. The canoe itself seemed to tell her what to do. She delved the air with her oar, first right, then left, as if paddling the craft over the surface of a lake.

Swiftly flew the spirit boat over the forest and across the black flow of the Humber River.

Below them the landscape unfurled like a map. To the south gleamed the waters of the great lake of Ontario. Toronto sparkled with a thousand lights, like a jewel on the north shore. The magnificence of the city took Dana by surprise; the ivory-white spire of the CN Tower, the leafy parks and avenues, the elegant skyscrapers jutting upward like crystal quartz. There were no cities like this in Ireland. Even Dublin, the capital, was merely a big town compared to this glittering metropolis.

Up, up they flew into the atmosphere. The city lights blinked below like the gold and silver specks of the stars overhead. The canoe rocked on the cool currents of air.

Worse than turbulence in a plane, Dana thought, her heart in her mouth.

She was glad of her parka. The wind was harsh. When they passed through clouds, they were left chilled and damp. Above the clouds was the dark of night where the moon hung like a sliver of nail, a pale lunula. Toronto fell away behind them. The countryside spread out in broad flat fields and low rolling hills ribboned with roads.

It was hard work, paddling the canoe. The air, like water, resisted their flight. And so too did the spirit boat itself. In fits and shudders it would buck like a bronco, trying to toss them out. Sometimes it veered crazily in another direction. Fighting it furiously, they struggled to keep it on course.

"It wants to go somewhere else!" Dana shouted to Jean.

"*Mais oui,*" he called back. "It want to go to hell!"

She heard the truth behind the joke and paddled all the harder. This was the perilous game, the terrible risk they were taking. Whoever mastered the boat mastered their fate. Dana took heart from the knowledge that Jean had done this before. And all by himself! Sensing him behind her, like support at her back, she was determined not to let him down. From time to time he called out instructions and words of encouragement. When he praised her newfound skill, she glowed inside. Gritting her teeth, she worked so hard she began to sweat despite the cold. In the end, she had to admit she was enjoying herself thoroughly. There was something to be said for taking up the challenge and pitting one's will against the dark. Wrestling with demons. You can't really know what you are made of until you are tested.

Guided by the Polar Star, they headed northeast, crossing the sky like a ship at sea. To the south glimmered the speckled band of the 49th parallel, the most populated region of southern Ontario. To the north lay a great soft cloth of darkness, the shadow of the vast terrain that was the Canadian Shield. To the east wound the St. Lawrence River on its way to the gulf and the ocean beyond.

Another bright city sparkled ahead of them, a tiara crowning the brow of a hill. Ottawa, the capital. Dana gazed down curiously at the silver-green spires of the Government of Canada and the white vein of the Rideau Canal that shone frostily in the starlight. Jean called out the names of the many bridges that clasped the slender arm of the Ottawa River: *Pont Champlain, Pont des Chaudières, Pont du Portage, Pont Alexandra.*

Ottawa, it seemed, was the marker buoy that pointed

the way home. Steering the spirit boat due north, Jean urged them on to greater speeds. They were shooting the rapids of wind, flying on night's dark wing into the heart of Quebec.

"*À gauche! À gauche!*" he cried to Dana. "Left side only!"

The land below became an ink-black shadow of rock and bog. The ground bristled with the pointed spears of black spruce, jack pine, and barren tamarack. Chains of lakes and winding rivers gleamed a faint silver. Except where sporadic points of light shone like lone ships on the sea at night, there was an overwhelming sense of the absence of man and the triumph of nature. *In wildness is the preservation of the world.* They were crossing the taiga, coniferous bogland on the fringe of the northern boreal forest that draped like a green scarf over the shoulders of North America. Beyond lay the tundra, a cold lonely land oblivious to the humanity that crouched on its borders.

How far into Quebec they journeyed Dana wasn't sure, but the occasional signs of communities grew fewer and farther between. After a particularly long spell of darkness, Jean pointed to a flickering light ahead.

"We are here! I bring us down. Don't paddle!"

She could hear him chanting in French as they began to descend. It was a steep drop to the ground. Her stomach lurched as they hurtled downward. She let out a yelp.

"*C'est* okay!" he called out.

She put her paddle aside and held on to the canoe. The descent was rapid, cold and rough. The ground seemed to rush toward them with frightening speed. It was all happening so quickly that she caught only flashes of what lay below: a dense forest, a small lake, and a narrow winding road.

Dana was just getting used to the free-falling motion when she spied it ahead of her.

A smear of greenish mist trailed in the air.

It was almost imperceptible, but she knew instantly what it was. Now the twisted features came into view, scarred and familiar. The eyes burned like red coals.

Crowley!

The phantasm charged straight at her.

"Oh, God!" she cried.

The words were out of her mouth before she could stop them.

"*NON!*" shouted Jean.

Too late.

Like a bird whose wings had been clipped in mid-flight, the canoe lost all buoyancy and plummeted downward.

Jean and Dana clung to the gunwales. The canoe was pitching from side to side in a last-ditch effort to toss them overboard. No doubt the demon of the canoe had recognized an ally. The two clung on for dear life, but their luck was running out. There was nothing below to break their fall. Only hard ground. They were riding a juggernaut on a dash to their deaths.

Jean grabbed his oar and began to paddle with fierce strokes.

"*Dans l'bois!*" he cried.

Dana spotted the trees in the distance and understood. If they could land in the branches of an evergreen, they had a chance. But the forest was far away.

And the ground was rushing nearer.

She saw in an instant they would never make it. They were bound to fall short. Jean roared as he paddled furiously, every inch of his body bent on the task. Now Dana roared too, hurling herself forward against the bow of the boat. Calling on the power of her fairy blood, she drove the canoe with the sheer force of her will.

It was enough.

Leaping forward in a last gasp of flight, the spirit boat crashed into the top of a tree.

In the tense stillness that followed, the only sound to be heard was the protest of branches beneath the weight of the canoe. The craft teetered precariously. The tree's weave held. Finally the boat settled, perched askew in the boughs like a great misshapen bird.

"*Maudit, câlisse, tabernac,*" swore Jean.

He moved quickly to see if Dana was all right. She had fallen back into the bottom of the boat. Bruised but otherwise fine, she sat up shakily.

Jean peered over the side of the canoe.

"*Pas de problème.* We climb down. *Le canot* go first."

She expected him to be furious. With one careless word, she had nearly killed them.

Jean's eyes glittered, but not with anger. He flashed a wide grin.

"That was some ride, eh?"

Dark hair tousled in the wind, white throat bare, he threw back his head to let out a wild laugh. It turned into a howl.

For a moment, Dana was stunned. Then she threw back her head and howled along with him.

# Fourteen

Climbing down the prickly spine of the evergreen was difficult. Pushing the spirit boat ahead of them through the tangle of branches was trickier still. The sturdy craft was undamaged by the fall but, like a canoe snagged in lakeside rushes, it resisted their efforts. Struggling downward, Dana kept an anxious lookout for Crowley. Had they managed to outrun him in their race with death? Or was he lurking nearby, waiting to attack?

At last they wrestled the boat to the ground and landed after it.

The northern night was cold and silent. High above the treetops, stars sprayed the sky. The scent of frosted pine tinted the air. They were surrounded by the white hush of snow.

Jean dragged the canoe into the undergrowth. Noting the spot, he tied a piece of string on a branch above it. At Dana's questioning look he grinned.

"One time I forget where I put him."

Her eyes widened. They would be stranded in the middle of nowhere!

"Do you know where we are?" she asked.

"*Mais oui, c'est mon pays.* This is my country." His voice rang with pride. "This is where the wolf run and where my friend live. Many mile to the east is Labrador City. That is where my *grand-père*—"

A tremor of pain crossed his features. He didn't continue.

Dana was curious, but she didn't trespass. Their friendship was too new. She caught the gratitude in his eyes when she didn't press him, and there was something else. He seemed to be studying her. As always, the intensity of his gaze made her look away.

"*C'est ça,*" he said suddenly, as if coming to a decision. "Before we go to my friend, I like for you to meet someone else."

The amber light seeped into his eyes. He threw back his head and let out a howl. When an echoing bay came from deep in the woods, Jean howled a second time. Again came the response, but it was closer now as the other wolf drew near.

As Jean continued to call, Dana kept watch, but she was still surprised when the great animal charged from the trees. Silver-gray in the starlight, the wolf was huge, with a powerful head and gaping jaws. It had the northern coat of long hair, as well as thick underfur and a large bushy tail.

Dana let out a cry as it leaped at Jean.

The wolf's great paws struck Jean's chest and knocked him down. Landing on top, the wolf growled low in its throat. But Jean was quick to recover. Grappling the beast in a headlock, he twisted sideways till they were both rolling on the ground. Now Jean leaped to his feet, arms stretched to wrestle. The wolf crouched low, ears pricked forward, ready to pounce. The two began to circle and feint, sometimes bounding forward, sometimes dashing back.

By this time, despite the throttling and biting, Dana knew they were playing. When the greeting game was over, Jean put his arms around the wolf's neck. Panting, the two stared at each other, man and beast. Dana could see the pain in Jean's features.

"We don't run tonight," Jean told the wolf. "I go with my friend to the Old Man. You come too, eh?"

The gray wolf studied Dana a moment, then loped into the woods.

Jean lurched to his feet. His eyes were wet. As he lowered his head, he let out a tortured sound.

Without thinking, Dana moved quickly to put her arms around him.

"What is it? Tell me!"

The night seemed to hold its breath there in the forest of snow and pine, with the moon and stars watching above. She had caught him by surprise, but he didn't try to break away. His body trembled as it leaned against hers.

He rested his head on her shoulder and spoke in a hoarse whisper.

"One time when I am small . . . when I have ten years . . . I stay with my *grand-père* in Labrador City. I . . . I climb a high tree to the top and then I fall down. My legs, they are broken. Maybe my back too. I bleed inside. The *hôpital* is far away. It's winter and the road are all ice and snow. My *grand-père*, he put me in a blanket on the sled. A man, he can't go so fast but a wolf, he is strong . . ."

Jean pulled away from Dana. He clutched his stomach as if he were in pain. His face was twisted with grief and guilt. She knew, in that instant, that he had never spoken these words to anyone else.

"It is day. It is not the night. My *grand-père*, he . . . he . . ."

Jean let out a cry like a wounded animal.

"He turned wolf." She finished for him, feeling the echo of his pain inside, for she carried the same wound. "He knew what it meant and he did it anyway. He turned wolf in the daylight so he could save you. And he can never turn back."

Again, without thinking, Dana reached out to hold him. Great sobs racked his body as he wept unrestrainedly, letting flow the tears he had blocked for so long.

Only when he grew still did she dare to speak.

"You have to accept the gift," she said softly in his ear. "His sacrifice. His love for you."

She felt the surprise shudder through him. Drawing back a little, he took her face in his hands and stared deep into her eyes.

"How do you know to say this?"

Tears flowed down Dana's face in response. "Remember I told you about my *anamchara*? My wolf guardian? She died . . . to save me."

They held each other for a long time, like two lost children who had finally found their home. Slowly the darkness lifted around them, as the first hint of dawn crept onto the horizon.

There was a moment, just before they broke apart, when Jean's face was so close to Dana's, she could feel the warmth of his breath. It occurred to her suddenly that he was about to kiss her. Overcome with panic, she stiffened and closed her eyes.

Nothing happened.

When she opened her eyes again, he had already stepped back, hands plunged into his pockets. For the first time since she had met him, he did not meet her gaze, but looked away as if embarrassed. When he spoke, his voice sounded tight.

"We go to my friend, *n'est-ce pas?*"

Dana was confused. She was certain he had been about to kiss her, but then he didn't. Was it her fault? Did she do something wrong? Or maybe it was just her imagination? Wishful thinking. She had so wanted him to. And now he was acting strangely. There was an awkwardness between them that wasn't there before. She was mystified. She knew nothing about boys and couldn't begin to guess what he was thinking. As she followed him through the forest, she told herself to stop being silly. This was no time for fantasies. They had work to do.

Their feet crunched over the snow as they walked.

"My friend, they are Iynu of the Cree peoples," Jean told her. "The Cree are the biggest nation in Canada, but here in the north of Québec they are small. They share the land with the Naskapi and the Montagnais."

"*Croí.*" Dana repeated the word in Irish, as it had the same sound. "That means 'heart' in my language."

Jean smiled. "*C'est beau.* 'Cree' is the name the French give them. The East Cree say they are Iynu."

"I've been in Canada a year," she commented, "and I've never met a Red Indian."

Jean winced. "This is not so good to say. In English they are 'Native peoples.'"

"Sorry. That's what the Irish call them. We don't learn about . . . Native peoples." She sighed. "I do know their history is sad, like ours."

Jean nodded. "But *l'histoire* is not over while the peoples live. The First Nations, they are strong again."

Dana could hear the passion in his voice. "Your canoe looks Indian, I mean Native. Did the medicine man build it?"

"He help me to make it and he teach me how to call the demon. With the spirit boat I can visit and see *grand-père* who live here too. After he turn forever, he don't stay in Labrador City. They will kill him there. Here is better. The Native peoples, they don't hate the wolf so much. They say he is their brother, like the dog."

When they broke from the forest, they faced a stretch of open ground. Most of it lay cloaked in snow, but there were patches of moss-covered rock and coarse grass. In the distance, a scatter of buildings stood haphazardly like tents, as if the inhabitants didn't intend to stay long. Behind the buildings gleamed a strip of lake. Nothing indicated they were on reserve lands. This far north, signposts were meaningless. If you didn't know where you were, you were hopelessly lost.

There was no highway or other access to the wider world beyond, but a dirt road led from the forest to the community.

They passed a big dilapidated shack that was boarded up.

"The Hudson Bay Trading Post from the old time," Jean told her. "It don't open now but the peoples still are hunter and *trappeur*."

"You don't think that's wrong?" Dana asked, surprised.

"The wolf is hunter too, eh? I don't like when the peoples hunt for fun and they make a big joke about killing the animals. It's not the same here. These peoples, they don't kill the animal for nothing. They do it for their life, for how they live."

Farther ahead was a small wooden church with a cross on the roof and a graveyard behind it. Beside the church was a low flat hall that served as school, library, and community center with offices for the band and government officials. Most of the houses were wood-framed bungalows with aluminum siding, television aerials, and satellite dishes. There were no gardens or driveways. The cars parked randomly were all four-wheel drives accompanied by snowmobiles. Life was organized around the reality of nine months of snow.

There was no one about at that hour of the morning. A few houses shone with yellow light and the flickering reflections of television sets. All around, the landscape glistened white with snow, outlined by dark forest and the hills beyond. Above, the sky was ablaze with stars.

Jean pointed to the lake that glinted icily on their left.

"There's no road so the airplane bring the store, the food, the priest, the teacher." He started to laugh.

"What?" said Dana, laughing with him.

She was glad to see him cheerful again. The awkwardness between them had disappeared.

"The airplane land on the lake in the summer and the winter. In the winter, he land on the ice. When he go again the little kids they run behind to catch—how you say?— the air that comes?"

He made a whooshing sound.

"The draft?"

"Yes, I think so. They hold open the coats and it's like they are wings. The air pick them up and they fly maybe a *mètre* from the ground." He was laughing again. "You see the plane go across the lake and all these little birds, they run and jump and fly behind it."

"Did you try it? I bet you did."

"Maybe," he admitted.

They were still laughing when they reached their destination. The house was a wood-framed structure like the others, but there was no wiring for television. The door posts and lintel were intricately carved with the shapes of animals. As Jean knocked, Dana studied the designs of wolf and raven.

The door was opened by a young man, not much older than Jean. He was lit up by the glow of a bare bulb behind him. Darkly handsome, he had glossy black hair that fell to his shoulders and lively eyes. His chest and feet were bare. It was obvious that he had just jumped out of bed and thrown on his jeans. He looked slightly annoyed, as well as concerned, but the minute he saw Jean he let out a yelp and grabbed him in a bear hug.

"*Loup! Enfin! Ça va?*"

The greeting was followed by a lot of horseplay as the two fell into the hallway. Loud whoops and laughter were interspersed with rapid-fire French and words of another language Dana guessed was Cree. She followed behind them and waited patiently till they broke apart.

The young man looked at Dana with frank curiosity as Jean introduced them.

"We speak English, okay? She come from *l'Irlande*. Dana, this is my friend, Roy Blackbird."

"*Salut*. Hi there," said Roy, offering his hand.

His grip was warm and friendly. They grinned at each other with instant liking.

"So you finally got a girl, eh?" he said to Jean. "A real cutie."

Jean ignored the statement. Dana blushed.

Despite the kidding, there was a peculiar gravity to the moment that descended over the three of them; a sense that they had met before. In other times and other places, these three had stood side by side in the fray. *As it was, so it would be, now and always.*

Roy ushered them through the dim house. Doors opened into rooms of bare walls and plain furniture. Dana saw immediately that no woman lived here. The place lacked decoration and the comforts of a feminine touch. Its purpose was evident: to provide shelter for men who spent most of their time outdoors.

"Should've known it was you," Roy said to Jean. "Guess who's been up all night drinking tea and smoking? Wouldn't go to bed, like he knew someone was coming."

He led them into the kitchen where a big woodstove

dominated the room. The floor was bare linoleum. A government calendar hung on the wall. The furnishings were simple and functional, plain cupboards and shelves, a Formica-topped table with wooden chairs, a refrigerator, and a battered washing machine.

In a chair beside the stove, an old man sat hunched over his cup of tea, smoking a pipe. He wore denim jeans and a heavy plaid shirt. His silver-gray hair was twisted in long braids. A red-and-black blanket was draped over his shoulders like a mantle. The edges of the blanket were woven with the same designs that were carved on the door.

It was the blanket that Dana noticed first, then she met his eyes.

The room fell away. Dana staggered slightly. It was as if she had suddenly come to the edge of a precipice. She felt weak and dizzy. Never had she encountered such a powerful force, not even in Faerie. But though his gaze showed something profoundly deep and ancient, at the same time there was great humor in it. Dana found herself wondering if life wasn't some huge joke being played on humanity.

He looked away from her and greeted Jean.

"*Bienvenue, Loup.* I been waitin' for you. I had a dream. We got work to do, eh?"

His voice was like his gaze, deep and grave yet full of laughter.

Before Jean could answer, the old man stood up and nodded solemnly to Dana. She was overwhelmed by a desire to bow or curtsey, to show him respect. She knew how he would be addressed in the formal courtesy of Faerie. *Lord. King. Majesty.* But how to approach him here, in this world?

She stooped to take the edge of his blanket and brought it to her lips.

"I am honored to meet you, Sire."

The dark eyes crinkled. His laughter rumbled like thunder.

"Don't be too humble. It lacks dignity. Call me *Nee-moo-soom*. Grandfather. The boys call me the Old Man."

He took hold of her hands. She felt the rough rasp of his skin, like the bark of a tree, felt also his immense strength. He turned her palms upward and stared at them intently. Though she made no effort to call it herself, the golden light shimmered. He let out a grunt, then gently dropped her hands and gestured her to sit.

"Welcome, Sky-Woman's Daughter. You got news of the Summer Land?"

Though Dana had recognized that he was special, she was still astounded. Tears pricked her eyes. This was the first time another human being had known exactly who and what she was, had recognized and greeted her as herself. The irony that it should happen in Canada—and not Ireland—was not lost on her. She sat down shakily in the chair beside him. Jean had already drawn up a stool, while Roy pottered around, filling the kettle with water, getting mugs from the cupboard, setting out milk and sugar. When the tea was made, everyone sat quietly sipping the hot brew.

Grandfather regarded Dana with calm dark eyes. He puffed on his pipe, waiting for her to speak. When she did, her voice shook with emotion.

"Yes, my mother is a *spéirbhean*. A sky-woman. And she lives in the Summer Country that has many names. I am of fairy blood, but I'm also human. The news isn't good. That's why I'm here. To ask for your help."

The Old Man nodded. "My people tell stories about the *ma-ma-kwa-se-suk* who come as if from nowhere, who live underground and in the rivers and the hills. They are also called *u-pes-chi-yi-ne-suk*. 'The little people.' Some say they are the ones who make the flint arrowheads you find in the ground."

"Elf-darts!" Dana exclaimed. "We say the same thing in Ireland!"

Grandfather tapped his pipe against the stove.

"When I was a young man, I went off with my uncle across the country. We wanted to see the land, test our skills with strangers, and hear the stories of other nations. In the east we sat at the fires of the people called Mi'kmaq. There I heard the tale of how summer came to Canada. How their hero-spirit Glooskap—like the one we call We'sa-ka-cha'k—went to the Summer Land to ask their queen for help. He wanted her to chase away Old Man Winter, who was killing the people with too much cold. Glooskap sang her a song and she liked it. He was handsome and she liked that too. So she came back with him. Everywhere she walked, sunshine spread out from her feet. She melted the frozen ground and the snow and the ice. And she melted the cold heart of Old Man Winter. They sat down together and had a talk. He promised he wouldn't stay all the time and he'd let the summer come every year."

Dana was amazed by the story. She recognized it as yet another tale of Faerie, a land whose history could never be fathomed.

"That explains something," she said, grinning suddenly.

"What?" asked Roy.

"We get awful summers in Ireland. That fairy queen must have given you ours!"

Everyone laughed.

"And I thought Faerie only belonged to Ireland," she added, shaking her head.

"We are all part of the Great Tale," Grandfather said. "We are all family."

Dana felt her soul shiver at his words. She knew it was time to tell her story. Hesitating at first, because she was ashamed of parts, yet knowing she couldn't leave anything out, she related everything. When she came to the part where she left Jean on the road with the monster that was

Crowley, her voice faltered. Roy looked surprised and angry, but Jean interrupted to tell how she had fought the *feux follets* to save him. His friend was satisfied with that, and the Old Man looked pleased.

"In the long ago past," Grandfather said, "we would make many preparations before going on a difficult journey. There was little time for you to prepare, Sky-Woman's Daughter, but you did well and you have grown in your travels."

Dana felt like crying. She had come for his help; his praise and approval was more than she could have hoped for.

Grandfather stood up slowly. It was obvious he had come to a decision.

"Since we have been fenced into reserves, ours is a different life now. But the council fires have not gone out and we still have our medicine. *Pu-wa-mi-win*—the spirit power that comes through dreams—is with us still. You've come to me for counsel. Some would say it's not our battle, it's for your people only. But we all got duties and obligations to each other. When bad times come, they strike where they will. Only last week, word came that strange footprints were seen near the Peawanuck Nation on the Hudson Bay. It's been a long time since rumors of the We-ti-ko traveled. Dark spirits are walking the land."

Dana was guilt-stricken. "This is all my fault . . ."

Grandfather waved her words away. "No use saying

it's your fault or anybody else's. Evil comes when things are out of balance. We all got to deal with it. *Comprends-tu?*" Grandfather said to Jean.

"*Je comprends,*" said Jean.

"*Moi aussi,*" said Roy.

They were all standing now. Dana knew without being told that a pact had been made. Whatever might come, these three were with her.

"We go to the Medicine Lodge," Grandfather said. "The girl will journey. You boys will stand guard."

"*Grand-père* is here too," Jean told him.

"Good," said the Old Man. "We need all the power we can get right now."

He glanced out the window at the darkness beyond.

"It's coming."

# Fifteen

Roy moved the jeep to the front of the house and let the engine run. Jean did not climb in immediately. The air was cold and his breath streamed like mist in front of him. In the east, a wintry light was seeping into the sky. He looked around with an anxious frown.

Roy caught his look. "A wolf smells his own kind over a mile away. You know that. He'll follow."

"*C'est vrai,*" Jean said with a sigh. "Still, I worry."

"*Je comprends.*" The other nodded.

Roy stayed behind the wheel as Dana and Jean climbed in the back. They left the front seat for Grandfather, who had told them to wait while he made his preparations. Though the heaters were on full blast, the jeep was freezing. When Dana shivered, Jean put his arm around her. Caught by surprise, she stiffened. He quickly removed it, to her regret. The earlier awkwardness returned. She tried to shake it off.

"Thanks for bringing me here," she said to him. "I couldn't get better help than Grandfather."

"He has power," Jean agreed.

"He got it young," said Roy, leaning over the front seat. "There are many stories about my grandfather. Remember what he said about traveling across the country? That was back in the 1930s. He was sixteen years old and his uncle was twenty-four. First they went east and then they went west. Between freeze-up and spring break-up, they walked and snowshoed over three thousand miles. Before they came home, they sat at the fires of many nations."

Roy and Jean sighed together. Dana knew they were wishing they had been there with him.

"Even before that," Roy continued, "the Elders saw he was *stabo*, a man who stands alone, who has no need of others. Some dreamed it. Others felt weak when they came near him. Those are the signs."

"That's what I felt!" Dana broke in. "When I met him, I felt dizzy!"

"It's his power," Roy explained. "He has it from the *mista'bow*, the spirit who guides him. Today, when he sings and drums in the Lodge, he'll ask his guide to help you."

Dana was overcome with awe. A brief silence filled the jeep, then Roy changed the subject.

"I sent in the application to FNTI," he told Jean.

"*Fantastique!* I'm glad you do!"

Jean punched his friend's arm with delight. He told Dana that Roy had long been talking about entering the

Aviation Program at the First Nations Technical Institute in Tyendinaga.

"They got a residence and everything," Roy said. "I don't like to leave the Old Man but like he says, it's only Ontario. I'll get back as much as I can."

"I visit him too," Jean promised.

"It'll be great," Roy said happily. "After two years, I can go for my commercial pilot's license. I'll fly like a bird for Air Creebec!"

There was more talk about the flight training program but everyone went quiet when Grandfather stepped from the house. He looked magnificent in his ceremonial garb. The coat and leggings of deerskin were embroidered with porcupine quills. His moccasins were sewn with blue and red beads. Most resplendent of all was the great black mantle of ravens' feathers that hung from his shoulders. Under one arm was tucked a drum and under the other, a rolled bundle.

When Roy and Jean hurried from the jeep to assist him, he waved them away.

"*Je suis ancien,*" he said, "*pas invalide.*"

The young men grinned.

Soon the jeep was speeding down the road and out of the community.

They drove north, around the lakeside, toward a range of hills cloaked with forest. Though the air had lightened to a milky fog, stars still gleamed in the sky.

Grandfather turned to Jean in the backseat. "Have you told Sky-Woman's Daughter how you and Roy came to be brothers?"

Jean started to laugh even as Roy let out a whoop and slapped the steering wheel.

"Will I tell her how you hunt me down?" Jean called to his friend.

Roy and Grandfather laughed out loud.

They were all so merry, Dana had to laugh too. She couldn't have been happier, driving across the frozen north of Quebec in that jeep with those men.

"When *grand-père* disappear," Jean told her, "*mes parents* move from Trois-Rivières to Labrador City. My father search for many years. It's sad but I can't tell him the truth about his father. *Grand-père* he tell me always it is necessary to keep the secret. It is necessary to keep safe the wolf. But for him and me, the move is good. I run with *grand-père* all the time and he's not so lonely. But sometime, because I am young, I want to go more far. To the north where there are no trees and sometime to the west. That is how I come here."

The jeep was approaching the dense forest that bristled with jack pine, black spruce, and birch. Though the trees looked like an impenetrable barrier, they were soon bumping onto a narrow trail and into the woods.

"I come here," Jean continued, oblivious to the jolting of the vehicle, "where live the best young hunter and *trappeur* in the land. *Son nom?* Roy Blackbird. He see me one night and the trouble begin."

"The black wolf with the white star on his chest!" Roy exclaimed. "He was *magnifique*. There he stood in the moonlight, a dream of power. I told the Old Man, 'I got to hunt him.'"

Grandfather shook his head. "I warned him. 'This is sacred. For such an animal to appear can mean your life or your death. We don't hunt our brother, the wolf, unless he takes our food.'" The Old Man shrugged. "Like most young, he didn't listen."

"The black wolf was in my head and my heart," Roy swore. "I couldn't rest till I got him. I tracked him from dusk till dawn. He brought me deep into Nitassinan, the lands of the Innu."

"A good chase," Jean agreed.

"We were equals," Roy said, grinning at Dana in the rearview mirror. "Cunning against cunning. Strength against strength. I would sing the song of the wolf. The song I made to help me catch him. The hunt went on for weeks until we headed into winter. Now I knew the time was coming, the hour of his death. For the wolf, like all animals, grows weaker in the winter. I began to regret the day I would kill him. It came to me that I would be sad in the world without him."

Grandfather nodded. "This is a truth the good hunter knows. Animals can live without humans, but we can't live without animals. We'd die of lonesomeness."

"Why didn't you stay away?" Dana asked Jean. "Why didn't you stop being a wolf till he gave up the chase?"

Jean shrugged. "I don't think that. How to say? Something go between the hunter and the one that is hunted. I feel it with him. In my blood. For me, it's not right to hide the wolf. It's the coward act."

The jeep came to a stop in the heart of the forest. No one moved as Jean finished his tale.

"That last night, he trap me in the mountains near to *un escarpement*. It's too high to jump. I am too *fatigué* to run. I see him hold up the gun. Death is near. I don't think to turn human. I am wolf. I wait to die."

Jean paused.

Dana held her breath.

"*Rien*," he said at last, echoing his amazement from that time. "No shot. No bullet."

Dana let out her breath.

"Couldn't do it," said Roy. "Even before I cornered him, I had a feeling I wouldn't. Good thing, eh?"

The two grinned at each other.

"I see the gun point to the ground," Jean concluded. "Then this hunter, this great enemy, he lift his hand to say farewell. Also, to salute me. Then I know he's my friend. My brother. I make the decision. In front of him, I turn. Except for *grand-père*, I don't do this before."

Roy let out a whoop to acknowledge that incredible

moment when he saw a wolf change into a man. "Lucky I seen some strange things with the Old Man or I would need clean pants, eh?"

When the laughter died down, Grandfather spoke quietly. "It's good to tell stories of courage and friendship. And it's good to laugh together. This gives us heart. Now we do what we came here to do."

Just beyond the jeep was a clearing in the trees and within the clearing stood the Medicine Lodge.

The framework of the Lodge was made of saplings, strong and supple enough to bend without breaking. The slender poles were slanted to the middle and lashed together with lariats of *shagganappi*, tough twisted rawhide. A circular hoop on top of the structure positioned the canopy of moose hide that covered the frame. A corner flap was left open as a door.

Beside the Lodge, a fire pit had been dug, with logs and kindling waiting to be lit.

Jean let out a low whistle. "The Shaking Tent."

"We made it two weeks ago," Roy said. "I asked the Old Man who it was for and he said, 'We'll know when they get here.'"

There was enough room inside for several people, but Grandfather told the young men to stay outside and light the fire.

"You guard the circle," he told them gravely. "Allow no one or no thing to enter."

Roy and Jean stood shoulder to shoulder, a determined look in their eyes. Dana knew they would die before anything came into that space. Once again, she sensed that she had always known these two and that they had always stood by her.

A sudden noise could be heard in the underbrush. Out bounded the gray wolf that was *grand-père*. In the early morning light his coat shone like polished silver. He ran up to Grandfather and bowed his head in greeting. The two gazed at each other for a while. *Grand-père* let out a series of barks and whines. The Old Man frowned.

"He has seen things in the woods. That is why he was delayed. He hid in the bushes and watched. Some of what he describes are known to me, *esprits du mal* of the northern lands. The Bag o' Bones they are called, skeleton creatures who fly on the wind and perch in the treetops. But there is something else he speaks of that is unknown. It is like Ka-pa-ya-koot—'he who is alone in the wilds'— but it is not the same. *Grand-père* says it comes first in the shape of a green cloud."

"Crowley!" said Dana. "My enemy!"

"He is near," Grandfather said. "Come."

The Old Man led Dana inside the tent and closed the flap behind her. The air smelled of damp earth and the musk of moose hide. Though the space was pitch-black, she was surprised to realize she wasn't afraid. She felt strangely at home.

A match was struck. The scent of sulfur grazed the air. Grandfather lit an oil lamp and shadows danced across the walls. He invited Dana to sit on the ground as he knelt to unravel his bundle. The hide unfurled in the shape of a deer leaping in flight. Feathers, pebbles, bones, and small carvings were arranged on top of it.

"What is the sacred number of your people?" the Old Man asked her.

"Three," she answered, without hesitation.

He lit a bunch of sage and sweetgrass and smudged the air three times around her. The smoke smelled sweet and soothing.

"Four is the sacred number of my people," he said, smudging the air around himself four times.

Now he set fire to a little pile of tobacco in a bowl and placed it at the center of the hide. Humming and singing, he moved with quiet purpose. His words seemed to curl with the smoke that filled the Lodge.

"This place was given to me to make the dance. I have never mocked it. I rely upon it."

Despite the calm of the Old Man's voice and movements, Dana felt anxious. Tension crackled in the air around her, as if a storm were brewing. She sensed that what they were about to do was dangerous. But there was no question in her mind of turning back. This was her quest, on behalf of her people, and with great good fortune she had found allies in her cause.

Grandfather called on the spirits of the East, South, West, and North as he shook his rattle in the four directions. Rattling above his head, he called on the spirit of Father Sky. Tapping the rattle on the ground, he called on the spirit of Mother Earth.

Dana could feel the power that was gathering in the tent. Whispers and low murmurs shivered in the air. Invisible presences pressed against her. With every word the Old Man spoke, the feeling intensified.

"All creation flowed out of the mind of the Creator. Not only earth and fire, water and plants, animals and humans, but also the mysteries, those who inhabit the other worlds and those who can walk between the worlds, the spirit helpers, the demons, the dream-speakers, the wind-walkers."

Now he crouched in front of Dana. His eyes were like an eagle's, piercing her soul. His hand waved over the deerskin and the sacred objects upon it.

"This is the Medicine Wheel. This is the circle that is life."

"*Roth Mór an tSaoil*," Dana repeated softly, in Irish. "The Great Wheel of Life."

The Old Man looked pleased.

"You will journey well. Close your eyes, Sky-woman's Daughter, and I will drum. Let the beat of the drum be the beat of your heart and the beat of your wings. Let it carry you where you need to go."

For a moment Dana felt overwhelmed. Poised on the edge of the darkness, she was suddenly afraid. To bolster her resolve she concentrated on why she was here. Two questions rose in her mind. *Where is the Book of Dreams? How can I find it?* She didn't speak the words out loud. Her trust in the Old Man was complete. Closing her eyes, she surrendered herself to the spirit of the journey. She knew she would go wherever she needed to go.

The beating of the drum began.

It was strong and steady, like a heartbeat, rapid like a wing beat. Great soft leathery blows reverberated against her eardrums. Softly pounding. Softly pummeling. Softly pulsing. The sounds beat against her skin as if she herself were the drum, thrumming and throbbing. She began to feel drowsy. Her head fell to her chest. There were more drums drumming now. And other sounds too. Wood crackling in a fire. Dogs barking. Wolves howling. Voices singing. Now she heard the high-pitched screech of a bird. Was it a hawk?

An eerie siren wailed overhead as a blast of wind struck the Lodge. The tent shuddered wildly. The poles creaked and snapped as they twisted out of shape. The moose hide flapped as if coming apart.

Though her eyes were still closed, Dana felt an immensity of space open up around her.

Another waft of sage and sweetgrass engulfed her.

Louder and louder came the voices, driven relentlessly

by the beat of the drum. The clamor was explosive. The center couldn't hold.

*Oh-oh-oh-whi!*

Was that the Old Man calling?

*Yei! Yei! Yei! Yei!*

She felt weak with terror. Everything seemed to be bursting its seams. She, too, was being pulled apart. Her eyes fluttered, as if to open.

*"Do not fear the shaking of the tent."*

Grandfather's voice came from far away. Dana's heart leaped as she realized the truth.

Something wonderful was happening.

Her journey had begun.

# Sixteen

*Splash!*

Dana gasped as the icy water struck her face. Those nearest to her laughed and continued to paddle. She was no longer in the dark Lodge. Opening her eyes, she found herself in a canoe, like the spirit boat, but much bigger and crowded with men and supplies. Her companions were burly men, dark-haired and bearded, dressed in buckskin with fur caps on their heads. Some were Native. All had the weathered skin of those who lived outdoors.

*Coureurs de bois.*

The words flew through Dana's mind like birds, carrying with them the knowledge of what they signified.

*Runners of the woods.*

Explorers and adventurers, hunters and fur-traders, these were the intrepid men destined to become folk heroes in the passage of time. Traveling the mighty waterways of North America, from Hudson Bay to the Gulf of Mexico, from the Atlantic Ocean to the Rocky Mountains, they crossed plain and woodland, mountain and prairie. They learned the languages of the Native peoples and adopted their ways to survive. Often they married and lived amongst the tribes. Oh, the fierceness of them! Full of life and vigor, voices raised in song, strong backs to the work, paddling in unison, they guided their canoes over the rush of the river.

*Assis sur mon canot d'écorce*
*Assis à la fraîche du temps*
*Oui, je brave tous les rapides*
*Je ne crains pas les bouillons blancs!*

*Les canayens sont toujours là!*
*Eh! Eh! les canayens sont toujours là!*

(Seated in my bark canoe
Seated in the coolness of the day
Yes, I brave the rapids
I do not fear the white foam!

The Canadiens are here, hurrah!
The Canadiens are here!)

The canoe bounded over the foam, plunging and rising on the crests of white water. Only skilled oarsmen could guide this frenzied movement to avoid the rocks that jutted out like knives. With their oars, they held the bark craft steady, reading the waves and the shapes of the currents and keeping in the best stream to ride the rapids. They were one with each other, one with the canoe, a live thing swifting downriver. Twisting and turning! Shooting round bends! Leaping like a salmon!

On both sides of the river crouched the jungle of black forest. The majestic trees soared to the sky. The air was so fresh and clean, it was like champagne. The aromatic resins of pine and balm of Gilead oiled the breeze. The leafy shadows rang with the cries of birds and animals: the melancholy call of the loon, the screech of the hawk, the roar of a black bear. A moose crashed through the trees. On the riverbank, the brown furry bodies of muskrat and beaver scurried busily. Like the air, the waters too were clear and clean, brimming with whitefish, maskinonge, trout, and bass.

Dana was utterly thrilled. It was all so real and vivid, so unlike any experience she had ever had. She, too, delved the water with mighty strokes. She, too, sang lustily in the raucous tongue of the *voyageur canadien*.

*Je prends mon canot, je le lance*
*À travers des rapid's, des bouillons blancs*
*Et là, à grands sauts, il avance*
*Je ne crains mêm'pas l'océan.*

*Les canayens sont toujours là!*
*Eh! Eh! les canayens sont toujours là!*

(I take my canoe and I launch it,
Across the rapids and the white foam,
And then by great leaps it advances,
I am not afraid even of the ocean.

The Canadiens are here, hurrah!
The Canadiens are here!)

Caught up in the beauty of the scene and her work in the canoe, at first Dana didn't recognize the man who paddled beside her. With a thick black beard and long hair tied back in a ponytail, he looked very handsome in his buckskin clothes.

"Jean!" she cried out in surprise.

"*Qu'est-ce que c'est?*" he shouted back, over the noise of the river and the others singing.

Apparently he didn't know her, at least not as Dana. Perhaps this wasn't Jean, but one of his ancestors? After all, she reflected, Jean was Québécois, of an old family from France. The blood of the *coureurs de bois* surely flowed in his veins. But was she in the past or traversing a dream landscape? Either way, with him beside her, she felt easier in this brave new world.

*Vive la Canadienne!*
*Vole, mon coeur, vole!*
*Vive la Canadienne!*

*Et ses jolis yeux doux, doux, doux—*
*Et ses jolis yeux doux!*

(Hurrah for the Canadian girl!
Fly, my heart, fly!
Hurrah for the Canadian girl!

And her gentle, gentle, gentle, sweet eyes.
And her gentle, sweet eyes!)

They moved swiftly through the vast wilderness. Where the river swirled around jutting rock and cedar-crowned islands, the shores seemed to tremble. Where the river widened, the waters rushed into ink-black pools. A cold steam rose above the rapids. Dana paddled blissfully. The solitude was so profound, she was shocked when an arrow landed with a *thwock* in the side of the canoe.

"*Attention!*" Jean shouted.

Dana didn't duck fast enough. He pushed her down as a hatchet spun past. It sank into a tree on the far side of the river.

The others in the canoe were now shouting and cursing as they paddled faster. There was no question but that they were under attack. Dana looked around wildly. She heard the howl of a wolf. A gray streak ran through the trees on the shore.

Beside her Jean frowned, as if remembering something.

*"Grand-père,"* Dana whispered.

The other men were tense. Something strange was happening. Many blessed themselves with the Sign of the Cross.

*"Que'est-ce que c'est que ça?"* they asked each other.

"What is it?" Dana called to the wolf.

The wolf ran along the riverbank to meet up with someone. As the canoe caught up, Dana saw it was Grandfather. He looked younger, more vigorous. His hair was as black as the cloak of raven feathers that fell from his shoulders. He was gazing up at the sky. Now he raised his rattle and shook it like a fist. The jingling sounds rained over the forest. Behind it, like thunder, came the drums.

Following Grandfather's gaze, Dana saw the clouds roiling in the upper atmosphere. An angry storm was brewing.

The Old Man's voice boomed through her mind.

"Your enemy. I see his face. The hatred in his eyes is indescribable. This is personal. It is *you* he hates."

"What do you mean?" Dana cried.

Yet something inside her understood. She remembered that first day of school when Crowley singled her out. She knew in an instant that his malice wasn't new. That he already knew her. But how could that be?

Now the storm struck with full force. First the rain lashed down in sheets. Then the air chilled so that the rain turned to hailstones, hitting them like pellets sprayed from a gun. The river rose in spate. The canoe careened. The men needed every bit of skill and strength they had to keep the craft from capsizing.

Grandfather's voice was urgent as he called to Dana.

"You must name your enemy! It will lessen his power!"

"But I . . . I don't know him!" Dana yelled.

Even as she searched the dark sky for any sign of Crowley, she searched her mind for any hint or clue that could answer the question: who was her enemy?

There was more movement on shore. A young man stepped out of the trees, a bare-chested warrior with hide leggings and breechcloth. His hair was tied back in a braid, his skin oiled and painted. As she recognized Roy, Dana saw how like his grandfather he was. He fitted an arrow to his bow and aimed at the sky. With a war cry, he released it. The arrow flew into the clouds and burst into flame.

The storm retreated.

"Name your enemy," Grandfather insisted again. "You know him."

The river grew calm. The *voyageurs* quieted down but were still uneasy. Dana understood that Roy had bought her some time. Yet no matter how hard she tried, she couldn't grasp what she needed to know.

The drums were beating faster. Or was it her heart pounding?

She let out a cry.

No longer in the canoe with the *coureurs de bois*, she was airborne in the spirit boat. High above the ground, she was flying like an arrow into the heart of the storm. Below was the rushing torrent of river, above was the tempest.

Kneeling amidships, Dana was the only human aboard and the only one paddling. Behind her, astern, was the gray wolf that was *grand-père*; ahead, in the bow was the black. He turned around to look at her. His golden gaze was somber.

"Jean," she whispered, and her heart lifted.

He turned back to stare ahead into the storm.

Dana felt strengthened by the presence of the wolves as well as the two others who had joined them. The great black ravens perched on the gunwales on either side of her. She wasn't alone as she flew into the darkness to face her enemy.

The attack was sudden and horrific. On the winds of the storm came the most terrifying creatures, screeching and chattering like nightmarish gulls. They appeared to be human skeletons with some organs still intact—the tongues, windpipes, and lungs that allowed them to scream. Their voices were dreadful to hear. Swooping down like vultures, they rushed at the canoe. Dana felt faint. Each time they dove near, it took all her willpower not to jump overboard.

One of the ravens cawed at Dana, then lighted on her shoulder. A familiar voice sounded in her ear as Grandfather spoke.

"They are hungry ghosts. Bag o' Bones we call them. They live in the clouds. In the fall, when the wild geese leave and the winds and the snows come, you can hear them in the treetops as they chatter and cry. From the northwest they come, out of the lands of Hudson Bay. To the southeast they go, deep into Labrador. Your enemy has called them. Darkness will go to darkness."

The great raven spread his wings and flew into the sky. The other raven that was Roy followed after. With sharp beaks they pecked at the skeletons, with talons they clawed them, and with strong wings they beat them back. The screeches of the creatures were deafening. The ravens cawed. Black feathers fluttered, white bones rattled.

Dana fought back her horror as she realized what was happening. Once again, Grandfather and Roy were buying her time. She had work to do. She must name her enemy.

"I know the name he goes by," she thought wildly. "It's Crowley."

But she already suspected that the name had been stolen, along with the life of the man who owned it. So this was a new name on an old evil to cloak the truth.

Now the storm clouds parted like a black veil above her. Over the beat of the drums came the sound that Dana had come to dread, even as the metallic smell soured the air. The buzzing noise drilled through her brain. All ability to reason or reflect was lost. Panic choked her.

"Be of good courage," came Grandfather's voice. "When all is lost, grab hold of the truth."

And suddenly she understood. Here, be it dream or other world, nothing could hide. She was about to see her enemy as he really was.

The ragged shape took form in the air, a greenish, writhing mist. Inside the clammy mass wavered Crowley's tortured features. Then another human face flickered briefly. A slash of red streaked through the green. Shocked, Dana recognized her enemy from the time she had quested in the Irish mountains: the monster who killed her wolf-guardian!

"I know who you are!" she cried out, though every part of her reeled with the knowledge. "You're the shadow of the Destroyer!"

The green cloud exploded, sending out shock waves of air and water.

The spirit canoe was thrown into a tailspin. Capsized in midair, Dana was flung out.

She was falling

falling

into the country far below.

Free of the waspish noise, she could feel her mind expanding with the view.

A great river wound across the land like a cold white serpent scaled with ice. *Dehcho.* All around the river, the land slept beneath a blanket of snow, frozen muskeg laced with small lakes. The ground bristled with dark fir. As far as the eye could see was a vast terrain of ice, snow, frost, and cold.

*Mon pays ce n'est pas un pays, c'est l'hiver.*
(My country is not a country, it's winter.)

Her free fall was slow and oneiric. A dream of flying, not falling. Slowly she grew aware of a pattern in the flow of ice on the water. Was it deliberate? The ice seemed to speak in the way it moved. Now she sensed the same message in the creep of moss over frost-shattered stone. What could it mean? Who was speaking to her? Something moved in the east. She strained to see it. Like a line of spilled ink it came trailing through the snow. *La Foule.* The Throng. The mass migration of the caribou, a flowing river of the wild reindeer's run. They too seemed to say something in the way they ran, their grand movement a cipher inscribed on the earth.

Here was a script far older than any mankind had invented. The secret language of the land. This was the heart of the message in her journey. If only she could read it! What was it telling her?

Now she was falling into a dark rug of land pitted with

lakes. She recognized the forest where she and Jean had landed in the spirit boat. The treetops quivered with Bag o' Bones like ragged crows. When they came flying at her, screeching and chattering, she fell right through them. She could see the clearing where the Medicine Lodge stood. It looked so tiny, like an anthill in life's forest. She looked for Jean and Roy, but she was falling too fast. Everything was a blur.

With a thump, she landed inside her own body, back in the tent, beside the Medicine Wheel where Grandfather was drumming. Was the journey over? Her heart sank. She had named her enemy but she hadn't found what she was looking for.

The drum was still beating. She took encouragement from that.

"I won't leave the wheel till I find the answer!"

As she sent her cry out into the universe, she opened her eyes to gaze on the Medicine Wheel. The deerskin, which she now realized was caribou, bore markings she hadn't noticed before. She was surprised to see the chevrons and spirals. They were the same designs carved on the ancient stones of Ireland and the portals of Faerie.

Grandfather's drum was sounding a new beat. Low and chthonic it came from deep in the earth, from the heart's core. Stronger magic was being made.

Dana's head throbbed. She could hardly breathe.

Swirls of tobacco smoked the air. She was getting closer, she could feel it.

The markings on the Medicine Wheel began to quiver. They looked like stars spiraling in a galaxy. No, like birds in flight, high in the atmosphere. Or were they clouds racing across the sky? She kept her eyes on the designs as they played over the deerskin. She had seen these patterns only a short while ago, in the ice and the moss and the wild run of the caribou. She struggled to understand them, to decipher their code. If she could read the patterns, she would have the answer.

"*Roth Mór an tSaoil,*" she murmured. "This is the great wheel of life. *My* life."

Suddenly the pieces fitted together. They made the shape of a book.

"The Book of Dreams!" she cried, reaching out to grasp it.

But before she could touch it, the book fell open and the pages of white paper fluttered like wings. They flew upward in a flurry of white leaves, white feathers. White-winged birds were swirling around the tent, around Dana's head. They sang in a beautiful tongue, a language she didn't know, though it was strangely familiar. Painfully so. Her ears ached to hear the words. Her heart longed to understand them.

She caught the gist of what they were singing, something about a Promise and a Faraway Country.

Tears filled her eyes. The song was so grand, so beautiful, so true.

And now another marvel in that marvelous journey. She was so taken by surprise, she let out a cry. The caribou hide suddenly leaped to its feet, a great wild deer with antlers branching. It still bore the designs of the Medicine Wheel on its flanks. For one quivering moment, it stood there paralyzed, nostrils flared, eyes wild with terror. Then it bounded out of the Lodge and into the night.

Dana didn't stop to think. She jumped to her feet and chased after it.

Outside the tent, she paused at the sight of Jean and Roy. They stood guard by the fire, watching the trees around them. They didn't appear to see her, but *grand-père* hunkered down and growled low in his throat.

"*Qu'est-ce que c'est?*" Jean asked him.

But Dana was already away, racing into the trees, after the caribou.

At first she thought she was a wild deer herself, running on four legs with speed and agility. *Hind's feet in high places.* But she didn't feel like a deer. She felt savage and ferocious, propelled by a hunger that raged through her blood. She was beginning to realize what she was when she saw the others, running alongside her. Hair bristling gray and black, they streaked through the trees: two fierce wolves with fiery eyes. She was hunting in a pack with *grand-père* and Jean! Above the treetops, cawing loudly, were the birds known to hunt with wolves, two black ravens.

Dana's blood was afire. She could smell her prey, smell its fear and its death. In the heel of the hunt, it all made sense. The deer was the answer, the secret she sought. She had to pursue it, to track it down, to eat and drink it.

Both were caught, the Hunter and the Hunted, on the Great Wheel of Life.

The trees began to thin out. Dana was gaining on her quarry. She could hear it panting. There were flecks of foam on its flanks. Her heart almost burst with the strain of the chase. It was just ahead of her now. Something huge and nameless, but she could almost name it. Something on the tip of her tongue, at the edges of her vision, in the back of her mind. She was approaching the answer.

The deer ran into a clearing. The mists of morning rose from the ground like the breath of the earth. A fire had been lit. An early breakfast was being cooked. There were figures seated around the fire, faint shapes barely visible like trails of sunlight. They turned at the sound of her arrival.

She couldn't see them clearly. They were already being dispelled, all flickering and flashing and fluttering in the air, a spray of white feathers, white leaves, white pages.

"Please!" she cried. "Don't leave me! Tell me!"

*Boom! Boom! Boom!*

The drum was loud and rapid. Like someone

hammering on the door, banging to be let in. She knew it was Grandfather calling her back from the journey, calling her home.

"No, wait!" she cried. "I've almost got it! I'm almost there!"

Her wail quickly changed to a howl when the caribou suddenly crashed out of the trees. Antlers lowered, it charged at Dana. She didn't stop to fight. She turned and ran, back through the woods the way she had come.

The Great Wheel had turned. It was her time to be hunted, her turn to feel the terror of the stalker, Death.

Ears flattened against her head, eyes white with fear, she fled the thunder of the hooves behind her. At any moment the horns could impale her.

With a final gasp of desperation, she broke from the trees where the Medicine Lodge stood and flung herself through the door into the tent.

The drum was silent.

She opened her eyes.

Grandfather was rolling up his bundle. The air was thick with stale smoke.

"I was so close!" she sobbed. "I almost had the answer!"

There was no time for tears or regrets. No time for reflection. The tent was shaking violently. The ropes that bound it together were coming undone. The hide was flapping against the framework. The poles strained and snapped. Things were falling apart.

"What is it?" Dana said, though she had already guessed.

Grandfather finished wrapping his bundle. He stood up.

A storm was raging outside the Lodge. Gusts of wind battered the tent. The cry of the gale grew louder, moved closer.

The Old Man's eyes were dark.

"Your enemy is here."

# SEVENTEEN

Outside the tent, the three guardians were still on duty. The fire had gone out in the lashing rain. The ground was being churned into an icy sludge. Both Jean and Roy were drenched, while *grand-père*'s fur clung to his skin. Each time the wind gusted, all three were whipped with streaks of water, like cat-o'-nine-tails. Heedless of their misery, they stayed at their posts.

"Home!" Grandfather shouted as thunder rumbled in the distance.

They all ran for the jeep and piled inside. Though morning had broken, the storm darkened the air. Trees tossed and swayed in threatening motions around them. Trunks creaked, branches snapped. As soon as Roy attempted to move the vehicle, the wheels spun vainly, spewing up snow and ice and mud. The storm was pitched to a frenzy. Lightning raked the sky. Peals of thunder crashed above. *Grand-père* buried his head in his paws with a whine of pain. The wheels continued to spin.

"We push!" Jean swore, climbing back out of the vehicle.

Grandfather went to follow, but Roy caught his arm.

"Take the wheel, Old Man."

Roy got out behind Jean. Dana came after him.

"Stay inside!" the boys shouted.

"No!" she yelled back.

The three of them pushed with all their might as Grandfather put his foot to the gas. At last the jeep leaped out of the rut. A bolt of lightning suddenly hit the Medicine Lodge. First came the strike, like the report of a gun. Then the explosion as the tent burst into flames.

Everyone scrambled back into the jeep.

"I'm so sorry, Grandfather!" Dana said as the Lodge burned.

Roy was behind the wheel again. Grandfather took out his rattle.

"*Ce n'est rien.* It's only a thing of hide and wood. The power is here and here," he said, touching his head and his heart.

Now came the full brunt of the assault.

A blast of wind struck the jeep. It was as if a rhinoceros had charged them. The vehicle juddered like a wounded animal. The headlights burst.

"*Go!*" Grandfather cried to Roy.

Roy sped away as fast as possible, though he could hardly see in front of him. A gray fog had descended and the headlights were out. Trees kept looming up as if to attack. As he veered to avoid them, his passengers were flung from side to side.

"I can't see the trail!" he shouted.

The Old Man began to chant as he shook his rattle.

"We need light," he called over his shoulder.

Jean was already rummaging wildly in the back of the jeep. Under the tools and tarpaulin, the hunting and fishing gear, he found a flashlight.

The battery was dead.

*"Tabernac!"*

The jeep grazed a tree and bounced off sideways. Again they were hit by a deadly fist of wind. Already off balance, the vehicle tipped dangerously, about to turn over.

Grandfather's song rose higher. His rattle shook louder.

Using all his strength and then some, Roy pulled at the wheel to steady them. Onward he drove, cursing the darkness.

"We need light," Grandfather called again, looking directly at Dana.

Despite all the times she had called on her light, Dana couldn't imagine having enough power to counter this darkness. Yet she had to try. Putting her palms together, she produced only enough to brighten the inside of the jeep. She caught Roy's surprise in the rearview mirror, but there wasn't enough light.

"Can you help me?" she asked Grandfather.

His reply was stern. "Sky-Woman's Daughter, your friends are in danger. Those who stood guard and helped you on your journey. *O nobly born, remember who you are!*"

His words were the catalyst. Acting on instinct, Dana clapped her hands with sudden fury. Like a shooting star, the light flew out from her palms. Piercing the windshield in a fiery arc, it lit up the woods beyond and revealed their trail.

Roy let out a whoop as he steered the jeep onto the track. Jean clapped her back with approval and a quick "*magnifique!*" With the way shining before them, the jeep sped through the trees. As they broke from the forest, leaving the storm behind them, howls of delight mingled with the real howls of the wolf.

It was wonderful to return to Grandfather's house, where wet clothes were changed and hot tea brewed, where there was toast and sardines and cheddar cheese. Grandfather sat down by the stove and took out his pipe. *Grand-père* stretched out on the floor, flank to the heat. As his fur dried, the air thickened with the smell of steamed wolf. The others sat down in a half-circle. All looked satisfied with the night's work.

Grandfather spoke first. "Now, Sky-Woman's Daughter, the best hunters dream the way to heaven and on their return they make a map. Tell us your journey."

"You were there, all of you," she said, looking around at them. "*Grand-père* as well. Don't you remember?"

Roy and Jean looked amazed.

"Our spirits were with you," the Old Man agreed,

"but the journey was yours. You must have got a good one. Your enemy's real mad."

"I know who it is now!" she cried. "He tried to kill me in Ireland." She shook her head. "But I don't understand. He was defeated. The Mountain King drowned him in the Irish Sea."

Grandfather's voice was firm. "He is not dead. And he has great power. He called up a storm demon."

A thought in the back of Dana's mind rang like an alarm bell. Something her father had told her about the Irish Sea. The sickly green color of the monster suddenly made sense.

"It's radioactive," she said suddenly. "The Irish Sea! England dumps nuclear waste into it every day. That must be how the monster survived and why it changed."

"Then it come after you?" Jean said. "Across the ocean?"

Dana's face paled as she nodded. "To finish what it didn't do in Ireland."

Sitting beside her, Jean reached to take her hand. As he gripped it she gave him a grateful smile.

"So you know your enemy," Grandfather said. "This is good. Did you see the thing you seek?"

"Yes! The Book of Dreams. But it kept shape-shifting. It was part of the patterns and the white birds and the land. Oh it's all so mixed up . . ." She floundered.

"Was there a song?" the Old Man persisted.

"Yes!" she cried again. "How could I forget? The white

birds were singing it! It was so beautiful, but I couldn't understand the words." She struggled to remember. "The words were in the land as well. The patterns I kept seeing everywhere; the secret language in everything." She looked lost again. "This doesn't make any sense, does it?"

Grandfather's pipe was empty. Roy and Jean had taken turns to offer him tobacco from a pouch near the stove; now they signaled to Dana to do the same.

"You give tobacco to him," Jean told her quietly, "when he give you a teaching."

As the sweet scent of the smoke filled the room, the Old Man spoke in a measured tone.

"It has always been the way of the First Peoples to live in harmony with the land. The land, the plants, the animals, and the people all have spirit. It is important to encounter and acknowledge the life of the land. From such encounters come power, as the power of the spirits rises up from the land.

"You've lost two homelands, Sky-Woman's Daughter: the land of your birth and the land of your spirit. And you lost power because of that. Now you want power from this land 'cause what you're looking for is here and this is the place where you live. But you don't know the land and you don't know its spirits. When the land tries to speak to you, you can't hear. You're deaf to the words. You don't know the language.

"You're an outsider here, Sky-Woman's Daughter,

and you learned that truth in your journey. The land won't yield its secrets to a stranger."

Dana nodded mutely. It was a hard lesson, but she understood it all too well. Weren't these her own doubts? How could she quest in Canada the way she did in Ireland? She loved Ireland with all her heart and soul. Her new country was a foreign territory and she had made no effort to settle in it. Only because of Jean had she even begun to see its beauty.

"I want to change that," she declared, with sudden resolve. "I want to do what you and your uncle did. Like I did in Ireland, I want to travel the land so I can get to know it. Maybe, then, if I'm not a stranger anymore, it will tell me its secrets?"

She could see that Grandfather was pleased even before he spoke.

"This is a good plan. You will go on a vision quest, to acknowledge and encounter the land. Let the Four Directions be your map—North, South, East, and West. Go the road with heart, and the spirits will guide you."

There was a note of finality in his voice. The night had come to an end. The storm was long gone. From outside came the sounds of doors opening, voices calling through the air, engines starting up. The community was waking, coming to life.

*Grand-père* sat up, alert and quivering.

"Don't worry, my friend," Grandfather said to the

wolf, "we'll get you back to the forest. Is your spirit boat near?" he asked Jean.

"*Oui.*"

"Be careful when you fly. The one who hunts Dana will always be near. The demon of the canoe is his ally now." Then he turned to Dana. "You have more than one enemy," he warned her. "He has called up other bad spirits to join him. You saw the Bag o' Bones when you journeyed. There are others who will come. The We-ti-ko who cries in the cold heart of winter, whose own heart is ice. D'Sonoqua who kills in the west and eats her prey. There are many dark spirits known to the First Nations. Then there are those of Jean's people, *les diablotins, les feux follets, les lutins, les fantômes,* and more. When the white man came, he brought his devils too and he himself was *le Diable* to us. These will join with your enemy, for they are his brothers and sisters. In the spirit world, all are kin."

"So many against me!" Dana said, dismayed.

There was great kindness in Grandfather's eyes.

"Be of good courage, Sky-Woman's Daughter. You are not alone either. Others will come to your side. I dreamed this long ago. When darkness calls to darkness, light will go to light. For even as they are kin, so, too, *we* are family."

It was time for Dana and Jean to leave. Roy offered to drive them and *grand-père* into the woods where the canoe was hidden.

"I don't know how to thank you," Dana said. Her voice shook with emotion.

She was reluctant to leave. She felt safe and at peace in the presence of the Old Man.

He clasped her hands in his. "You got strong power, Sky-Woman's Daughter. Make sure you use it." Then he turned to embrace Jean. "A word to you, *Loup*. The place where a man lives shapes his character. Cities make men weak. Too many people, too much misery and bad spirit. The land of the forest with its lakes and rivers is the land of your heart. Keep its spirit with you."

Finally Grandfather laid his hand on *grand-père*'s head.

"It's good to have your kind under my roof. The raven and the wolf will hunt together again."

Outside, the day was clear and frosty. Their breaths streamed like smoke in the air. The community looked worn and exhausted after the storm. The ground was littered with broken branches, loose stones, and clods of earth. The few people who were out were wrapped up warmly. A man called out a greeting to Roy, who waved back.

In the jeep, they were all too tired to talk. Jean put his arm around Dana. She leaned against him. Roy grinned and winked at his friend.

"How's your girlfriend?" Jean asked him.

"Which one?"

Deep in the woods, Jean said good-bye to *grand-père.*

"*À bientôt,*" he murmured, holding the wolf's great head in his hands and staring deep into his eyes. "Don't forget me. I return soon."

The beast shook his mane of gray hair and licked his grandson's forehead. Then he loped away into the trees.

Jean watched him go. Then he turned heavily to Roy.

"*J'ai peur* . . . he forget one day. Who he is. What he is. Maybe I come back and find he's all wolf. Maybe he forget me."

Roy mirrored his sorrow. "Me and the Old Man, we watch out for him."

"You're a good friend."

"I'm your brother."

They embraced.

Before Roy left, he chucked Dana's chin and gave her a big smile.

"Look after *mon frère.* 'Bout time he got himself a girl."

Dana smiled back shyly. "Thanks for everything. I'm really glad we met."

"*Moi aussi.* We'll meet again, eh?"

After the jeep roared off with Roy beeping his last good-byes, Jean pulled the spirit boat out of the bushes.

"I'm knackered," Dana said, sighing with exhaustion.

The last thing she felt like doing was paddling home.

Jean clearly felt the same way, but he shrugged it off.

"We have no choice, *n'est-ce pas?* We rest here, we are late at home. I think *nos parents* can't take this?"

"Oh, God, no," Dana agreed.

"Don't say this word in the *canot*," he reminded her.

She clapped her hand over her mouth. "Should I gag myself?"

Dana stifled a giggle. She was giddy with fatigue and overexcitement, but at the same time she felt ready for anything. The high adventure she had had was singing in her blood.

Jean looked concerned for a minute. His intense gaze studied her face. A grin slowly formed on his lips. He seemed to make up his mind about something.

"We need some fire to fly this boat," he told her.

Before she could ask what he meant, he had pulled her against him and was giving her a long kiss.

There was a second when Dana struggled; but only because he had caught her by surprise. The moment quickly passed and she understood what he meant about the fire. The heat of his mouth and the joy of the kiss burned through her veins. And he kept the kiss going longer than she thought possible without taking a breath. When he let her go, she saw the same fire in his eyes that had scorched her heart.

They clambered into the canoe and grabbed the oars. The energy between them crackled in the air like sparks of electricity.

"*Allons! Allez!*" Jean cried.

Dana let out an echoing yell.

"*Coureurs de bois abú!*"

Soon they were airborne and flying.

Far above the clouds, the sky blazed with the red-gold splendor of dawn. As Dana felt the bite of the upper atmosphere, she turned her face to the sun.

Jean began to sing as he paddled, and she joined in. She would never forget the songs of the *voyageurs*.

A screech was carried on the wind toward them. The twisted visage of Crowley appeared briefly in the clouds. But he hadn't a chance, no luck at all. The canoe shone like burnt gold as it sailed through the morning, a flaming arrow. And the two singers in the boat sang with the unquenchable fire of new love.

*Vive la Canadienne!*
*Vole, mon coeur, vole!*
*Vive la Canadienne!*

# Eighteen

Flying faster than they had imagined possible, Jean and Dana reached Toronto by mid-morning. They landed in a secluded spot in the Humber Marshes. Though they had flown over many towns, no one had looked up or taken any notice of them.

"Is the canoe invisible?" Dana wondered.

"*Je n'sais pas.*" Jean shrugged. "I think they don't believe, they don't see, eh?"

Pale and tired, the two dragged the boat into the bushes and made their way to the nearest subway.

Both were too exhausted to talk as the train rumbled eastbound. Dana got off first, barely managing a good-bye. Jean had farther to travel and was already nodding back asleep. His head bumped against the window as the train pulled away.

Dana dreaded going home. She was certain that the changeling couldn't have lasted. How would she explain another disappearance?

On reaching the house and sneaking in the back door, she discovered there was no need to worry. Gabe and Radhi were apparently enjoying a lazy Sunday morning. Dana's room had been undisturbed. The bed was still made up as she had left it. Under the duvet, the changeling was a mess of dirt and wet leaves. Dana removed the soiled linen and stuffed it into her closet. She would clean up later. Crawling onto her mattress, she collapsed into sleep.

Several hours later Dana woke with a start, overwhelmed by the sense that she had forgotten something. Memories of her adventure flooded into her mind: the spirit boat, Jean and his friends, the journey with Grandfather, the vision quest that awaited her and . . . the kiss, oh the kiss! She jumped out of bed. How wonderful life was!

Washed and dressed, she reached the kitchen door in time to overhear yet another argument about her.

"She is a teenager," Aradhana was saying. "They sleep late because of their hormones and the upset of their body clock. It is not laziness."

"You always take her side!" Gabriel complained. "Are you going to be like this with *our* children too?"

"All children in this family will be treated the same."

"That's not what I meant and you know it!"

Gabriel's exasperation ended in a fit of spluttering punctuated by a hiccup. That made the two of them burst out laughing. Smooching noises followed, which Dana chose to ignore, but still she was pleased. Apparently her absence hadn't been detected since no one had tried to

wake her, thanks to Radhi. Once again Dana acknowledged how lucky she was that her father had married this
wonderful woman.

A pang of guilt struck her. Gabriel and Radhi were
only newlyweds. Had she helped them settle into their
life together? She knew the answer to that. The past year
hadn't been easy for any of them. For the first time since
she got there, Dana reflected that the move to Canada
might have been hard for the others as well. For Radhi,
it had meant leaving her beloved brother behind and the
restaurant they had run together. For Gabe, the changes
had been equally drastic. After ten years out of the
country, he was back in the vicinity of his strong-willed
mother. As well as that, there was the full-time job, so
different from his work in Ireland where he had been a gig
musician, part-time teacher, and even occasional busker
on the streets. There had been less money back then, but
also less responsibility and far less pressure. Being newly
married was, in fact, a bonus for Gabe, as his wife made
life easier for him.

*I sure don't,* Dana reflected.

She couldn't remember the last time she and her dad
had had fun together. Once upon a time, they were so
close they could read each other's mind, finish each other's
sentences. Truth is, she had blamed him for the fact that
she didn't like Canada the way he and Radhi did.

Well, things could change.

Dana burst into the kitchen and gave her father a quick hug.

"Morning, Da. I'm making pancakes. Would you like some?"

"Good *afternoon*," he responded, though there was no force to the reprimand. He was too surprised by the greeting, as well as the offer. "Hmm, yes, pancakes would be nice . . . for lunch."

"I'll make them Canadian-style, with bananas and maple syrup."

Now he looked worried. She always insisted on "Irish" pancakes, cooked thin and rolled up like crepes with lemon and sugar.

Aradhana smiled and poured herself some tea.

"So, how's work these days, Gabe?" Dana asked brightly.

"Well it's . . . There's . . . I mean . . ."

It took a few more questions, but she eventually got him talking about his students and the usual power politics in the department. Even as he talked she saw his features relax, saw how pleased he was that she was interested, that she cared. It was like the old days when he told her about his gigs. He even mimicked the voices of some of his colleagues till the three of them were laughing hysterically.

It was after lunch that Aradhana remembered to tell Dana about the phone call.

"A boy called Jean rang for you earlier. He asked that you call him when you are awake. His number is by the telephone."

"A *boy*?" Gabriel's good humor disappeared in an instant. "Who? How? When? Where?"

The look they both gave him formed a united front, a wall. He threw up his hands, knowing he had lost before he even began.

And they all laughed again.

When Dana rang Jean, the kiss they had shared hung in the air between them. After the initial hellos, an awkward silence fell over the line.

"You are fine today?" Jean managed at last.

"Yes," Dana replied.

Long pause.

"You?"

"*Oui. Bien. Très bien.* I sleep a long time."

"Me too."

"*Pas de problème* at home?"

"No. You?"

"*Non.*"

Another long pause.

Dana was racking her brain to think of something to say. They had just shared the most amazing adventure together, why couldn't she talk to him?!

Jean cleared his throat.

"So . . . I see you tomorrow at school?"

"Yes. Yes. See you then."

She was both relieved and disappointed to end the call. As soon as she hung up, she screeched for her stepmother.

*"Radhi! How do you talk to boys?"*

The next day at school, it was easier. Face-to-face, Dana felt more comfortable with him. He was so at ease with himself, it helped her to talk and to act naturally as well. Besides his open, friendly manner, Dana liked the way he looked. Now she understood why he dressed as he did. His clothes suited the North—the leather boots and tight jeans, the woolen shirts, the beaded armband. Her own appearance had become more dramatic, with bright tops to liven up her jeans and Indian jewelry Radhi had given her. She had started to wear her hair in different styles, sometimes loose on her shoulders, sometimes braided or piled on her head. But it wasn't only her new appearance that made her attractive. Having emerged from her cocoon, she was bursting with life. Her happiness brimmed over in smiles and laughter.

Apparently, Jean wasn't the only boy who noticed the difference. When the others started looking her way, Jean moved his desk next to hers.

Dana was delighted with the move, but it took all her willpower not to blush whenever he leaned too close. She kept thinking about the kiss they had shared. To distract herself, she would concentrate on what they needed to talk about: the task at hand, the next step in the quest.

"I've been thinking about what Grandfather said. Where we start doesn't seem to be so important, as long as we do the four directions. Maybe we should just pick one and go?"

"*D'accord.* But if we go far we need time," he pointed out. "*La chasse-galerie* is fast, but not like a rocket."

"This weekend would be perfect to start. With the Thanksgiving holiday we'd have an extra day. But how will we do it? I can't just take off. My dad would have a fit. And where will we go?"

Their heads were close together as they talked in low voices. The first class of the morning had yet to begin. They were so engrossed in their conversation they didn't hear the sniggers. One of the boys put his hand over his heart and was making exaggerated grimaces of true love. And neither noticed their teacher enter the room and walk casually in their direction. She hovered nearby, taking her time to open a window.

As soon as Dana grew aware of Ms. Woods, she signaled to Jean. They both stopped talking and opened their books. Dana was certain the teacher had been eavesdropping, but how much had she heard?

At the end of the day, Dana returned to her homeroom to pack up her books. That was when she found the note tucked discreetly in the corner of her desk. Handwritten on cream-colored paper with a border of gold spirals, it contained an urgent message.

*Time is running out. The worlds are drifting apart. You must restore the gateways on Halloween or they will be closed forever. You are not alone. The Companions of Faerie are with you. Please let us help you!*

The letter wasn't signed, but Dana was sure of its author. She sniffed at the paper. There was a faint smell of apples. She wished she could show it to Jean, but he had left for hockey practice. He was already being hailed the best on the team. Dana looked around. A few students lingered in the classroom, preparing to leave. Ms. Woods sat at her desk, her blond head bent over test papers, seemingly busy; but the suspense in her posture was obvious.

Dana read the note again. Could she believe it? She vaguely remembered hearing about friends of Faerie in North America, including the High Queen's twin sister. Ms. Woods didn't look anything like Honor. Could it be a trick? Another attempt by her enemy to get her alone? The mention of a deadline was disturbing. Halloween was only four weeks away. Edane hadn't said anything about it; but then, Dana realized with a wince, her mother wasn't the most reliable source.

Torn with doubt, Dana glanced again at Ms. Woods. If her teacher had knowledge of the mission, wouldn't it be best to find out? But what if this was a trap? And anyway, did Dana really want her help? The thought of someone else involved didn't appeal to her. She liked that it was just her and Jean.

As Dana approached her teacher's desk, Ms. Woods looked up hopefully; but the smile died as Dana hurried past. First she would talk to Jean. Together they would decide what to do about the note.

Going home on the subway, Dana kept a lookout, as always, for the little man. Would he show up again? Had she imagined he was special? Now that she had met Jean and his friends, now that she was deep in a Canadian fairy tale, she viewed the world around her with different eyes. There *was* magic here. Knowing that, she looked for it everywhere, in the tunnels of the subway, on the crowded city streets, in the green patches of park. As usual it played hide-and-seek, a veiled presence lingering at the edges of reality.

She left the subway at Spadina station. From there it was only a short walk home to Brunswick Avenue. The moment Dana stepped outside the station doors, she was struck by a blast of wind and music. She stood stock-still, a wolf catching the scent. Silvery notes winged through the air. It was an Irish tune. No, not quite. There was something different about it. She hurried toward the sound.

At the major intersection of Bloor and Spadina, the early rush-hour traffic had begun. Cars jammed the road. People crowded the sidewalks. On the other side of the street was a small square. White flagstones were laid around a grassy knoll planted with young trees. Scattered over the flagstones was a sculpture of huge black dominoes. The tiles were laid out as if for giants to play. Wooden benches bordered the square, and there was a space marked out for street performers.

The musicians were out of sight, behind the wall of people who had gathered to listen. Across the road, Dana strained to see as she waited impatiently for the lights to change. The music echoed over the noise of the traffic, teasing and taunting her: a tumult of merry reels and jigs. With a mild shock, she spotted a familiar figure in the crowd. Despite the blue jeans and leather jacket, she would have recognized her anywhere: Honor, the High Queen of Faerie! How did she get here?

Dana waved wildly to catch her attention. Would the lights *never* change?

She was certain Honor had seen her, but when at last the light turned green and Dana raced across the road, there was no sign of the High Queen. Was she imagining things? Dana's disappointment was soon forgotten as she caught sight of the musicians.

Shabbily dressed in torn jeans and old sweaters, the three men were remarkably ugly in a humorous way. All were of stocky build and very short, no more than five feet, with bulbous noses and bulging eyes. The fiddler had a mane of hair like a nest of red curls, with a bushy beard to match. The tin whistler's ponytail was a piebald black and gray. The drummer, who played a handheld bodhran, was as bald as an egg. All of them had tufts of hair growing from their ears and nostrils.

The music was fast and frenetic. They played as if their lives depended upon it. In a dazzling display of virtuosity, tune chased after tune without stopping for breath. The tin whistle trilled like birds at dawn. The drum rumbled like thunder. The fiddler's bow skipped over taut strings, a dancer leaping.

Standing in a half-moon around the musicians, the audience jiggled and jittered like puppets on a string.

"Ize the bye!" someone shouted, and everyone cheered at the Newfoundland expression.

"Newfies go home!" cried a lout from an apartment balcony up the street.

When some of the crowd shook their fists at him, he quickly retreated.

Oblivious to all, the red-haired fiddler was bent almost double as he strained and sweated over his instrument. He finished the medley of airs with a frenzied flourish. There was an uproar of applause. Coins cascaded into his open case.

Dana edged to the front of the crowd. The men were

less comical close up. There was a wild and disreputable air about them. She could smell the alcohol wafting from their direction. Then the fiddler caught her eye. The look he gave her drew her up short. As if he knew her somehow. And there was something sly about the wink that made her uncomfortable.

He suddenly broke off what he was playing and began a new tune. First came a shivery quiver across the fiddle strings. Then all three of them let out a high-pitched whoop. Now they burst into song together. Their voices were raucous. The words and the music rushed toward her in a wave.

> *Cold wind on the harbor*
> *And rain on the road*
> *Wet promise of winter*
> *Brings recourse to coal*
> *There's fire in the blood*
> *And a fog on Bras d'Or.*

*THE GIANT WILL RISE WITH THE MOON.*

With a breath-stopping pull, Dana no longer stood on the street in Toronto.

She was somewhere else. A damp, green place cupped by a range of hills. Behind her, a wintry sea crashed onto the shore. She could smell seaweed. The taste of salt was on her lips. With a surge of joy, she thought she had been transported back home to Ireland. Then she caught the sharp scent of pine in the air. The hills were sparsely dotted with fir. The landscape was more bleak and rugged than any she knew.

*The wind's in the North*
*There'll be new moon tonight*
*And we have no circle to dance in her sight*
*So light a torch, bring the bottle*
*And build the fire bright.*

## THE GIANT WILL RISE WITH THE MOON.

It was evening time. The light was dusky, but no stars were out. On her right, in the distance, was a scatter of houses. To her left, a rough road meandered into the hills. Her eyes followed the worn path that wove from the road to the highest peak in the hills. Her heart beat quickly. On top of the hill was an ancient stone circle. Jagged rocks stood out against the sky like a great crown. At their heart burned a bonfire. The stones flickered fitfully, illumined by the flames. Dana blinked. The stones became men; short, stocky men like the street musicians! They were singing and shouting and waving bottles in the air.

*'Twas the same ancient fever*

*In the Isles of the Blest*
*That our fathers brought with them*
*When they went West*
*It's the blood of the Druids*
*That never will rest.*

## THE GIANT WILL RISE WITH THE MOON.

With a dizzying lurch, Dana found herself back on the city sidewalk. The musicians had finished their song and were packing up to leave.

She ran over to the fiddler as he closed his case.

"Wait," she said. "Please. Are you here to help me?"

The three stopped to stare at her. All had gray eyes, like the sea in her vision and just as cold. Though they barely reached her chin, she suffered the sensation that they were immense. As tall as the stones she had seen on the hilltop. She was completely unnerved. How could she have thought them comical, even for a moment?

"I . . . I'm about to go on a journey," she stuttered.

They continued to regard her stonily.

"But I don't know where I'm going," she said desperately.

Still they kept silent. Their looks were veiled.

"The song you were singing . . . about the giant?"

"It be one of Stan Rogers." The fiddler spoke at last. His voice was flat, as if to deliberately discourage her.

"Where does he live?" she asked.

"He don't bide here no more," came the answer.

Looks were exchanged between the musicians, but she couldn't fathom their meaning.

Dana could have cried with frustration. It was obvious they weren't going to divulge their secrets. Regardless, she was grateful for the music and the clues it seemed to provide. She had already taken out some money to give them. Since their cases were shut, she handed it to the fiddler. The red-haired man grinned with sudden mischief.

"Ho byes. A generous hand, a generous heart. When I thinks about it, maybe we ought to tell her what she wants to know."

The drummer shook his head. "You knows it ain't like that. We can't do no more."

The tin-whistler agreed. "We've done our bit, that's for darn sure."

Dana caught her breath. "Do you have a message for me?" she pleaded. "Are you here to help? Are you Companions of Faerie?"

She was met with blank looks.

The drummer smirked. "A little birdie told us about ye. Asked a favor. And now we've done it."

More questions rushed into Dana's mind, but before she could open her mouth, the fiddler raised his hand.

"Look, lass, what's to be said was said in the song. You

seen the Place of Stones in the music. You'll know it when you sees it in the world."

Though the fiddler's tone was almost friendly, the other two were growing more agitated by the minute. Fidgeting impatiently, they looked at their watches and then glared at her. Though she wanted, needed, to know more, she found her courage failing. The three were rank with the smell of whiskey and there was a dangerous edge to their annoyance.

"*Go raibh míle maith agaibh,*" said Dana, thanking them in her own language as she backed away.

With a last glance at his watch, the tin-whistler eyed the Irish pub up the street and smacked his lips. Tipping his cap in farewell, he dashed away, running across the road against a red light. The drummer raced after him without another word to Dana. Only the fiddler lingered.

"Don't be afeard where ye go, lass," he said quietly. "The morning star shines in the east and there be my own country."

Then he, too, darted across the road, dodging the traffic, ignoring the blare of horns from irate drivers. Arms and legs akimbo, he held his fiddle above his head as if he were forging a river. When he reached the other side he turned back to her, beaming.

"Mind now," he shouted, "we are all family!"

Dana couldn't wait to ring Jean with the news. There

was no question now about which way they should go. To the east it was. And the song was the other clue. What was the place mentioned? She had heard them say "Bradore." It sounded French. Somewhere in Quebec? Jean was bound to know.

"Bras d'Or?" he repeated, when she called him. "*Oui, je connais.* It's not Québec, *non.* It's a big lake on Île Royale. Cape Breton Island. I never see this place but I think you will like it. They say it look like Scotland and also your country."

"Well, that's where we start," Dana said, delighted.

They were both over the moon that they had a destination.

"So how we do this?" said Jean.

"There's someone who might help."

Dana told him about the note from Ms. Woods.

"So, she do know about the mission," he said. "Remember she try to talk with you? What do you think?"

"I'm not sure I trust her, but between you and me we should be able to tell if she's an enemy or not. Maybe one could ask questions while the other watches her reactions."

"Good cop, bad cop?" Jean suggested.

"Something like that," Dana said with a laugh.

"*Bon,*" said Jean. "We do this tomorrow."

As it turned out, Ms. Woods had already moved to

help them. Dana discovered that fact when Gabriel got home from work.

"Your teacher rang today. Radhi got the call before she went out. Something about a field trip this weekend? Did you forget to tell us?"

Dana was too surprised to answer right away, but her father didn't notice.

"That rules out Thanksgiving in Creemore. Your gran will be disappointed but it gets me off the hook. Don't repeat that."

"So," said Dana, recovering, "can I go?"

"Sure. It sounds good and I can't believe there's no cost. She says she's looking after transportation and everything. Talk about last-minute arrangements. Do you have a list of things to bring?"

"No, but I know what I need. The usual stuff."

Dana's head was spinning. Between the musicians and Ms. Woods, things were happening very fast. It seemed forces were moving at last to help her. Or was it that she had finally let them? The words of Lord Ganesha echoed through her mind. *Your gods are all around you, child of Faerie, you need but open your heart.*

She rang Jean back only to find he was about to call her. His parents had just come home and Ms. Woods had rung them too.

"So, she's put the two of us together in this," Dana said uneasily.

She was not happy that Ms. Woods was taking charge and making plans on their behalf. But Jean was pleased.

"This is good, eh? We take the help she give us. But still we go and demand who is she and what is she. We do this tomorrow."

In the end, Dana agreed to the plan, as it obviously made sense.

But they didn't get the chance to put it into action.

For earlier that day, Gwen Woods had met Crowley.

# Nineteen

The day Gwen was offered a teaching job at Dana's school, she went straight to Laurel to tell her the good news. The porter at Massey College recognized her and waved her through the gates. As she hadn't called ahead, Gwen caught Laurel off guard. There was no time for the other to hide that she'd been crying. Her eyes were red and swollen from weeping.

"I need to be alone," Laurel mumbled, keeping the door half-closed.

"I don't think so," said Gwen, gently pushing her way through.

By the time they were both sitting down with cups of green tea, Laurel was ready to talk.

"I can't stop thinking the worst. If everyone in Ireland was attacked, then Ian would have been too. He could be lying somewhere in a coma or . . ."

Gwen listened with sympathy. The same thought had occurred to her also, but she had kept it to herself. "He could also be safely in Faerie," she pointed out. "You said he lives in both worlds. If he was there when the portals went down, he'd be stuck on the other side."

Laurel nodded and blew her nose. "That's what I believe on good days."

Gwen glanced around the room. This was obviously not a good day. Given that Laurel was a perfectionist, the state of disorder spoke volumes. Clothes littered the floor. Books and papers were strewn everywhere. Gwen had already noticed the photograph on the desk, which hadn't been there before. Encased in a silver frame was a young man with raven-black hair, striking features, and the startling blue eyes of Faerie. He looked thoughtful and romantic, but also moody; like an Irish poet.

"Ireland's a small place," Gwen said. "Do you want me to ask Dara about him? Maybe he and Granny could do some kind of search, with or without magic. I'm sorry, I should have thought about this before."

"You have enough to think about," Laurel said, "and so do they. The mission is the important thing."

"Ian's important too," Gwen argued. "Everyone is. She reached out to squeeze Laurel's hand. "We need to hold on to hope. It's the only way we'll get through this."

Laurel sighed and admitted quietly, "My hope is to see him again."

"That a girl. Are you ready for some good news?"

Laurel was delighted to hear about the job. She rallied

immediately, looking stronger and happier. The tide appeared to be turning in their favor at last.

"You'll be Dana's teacher!" she exclaimed. "This can't be a coincidence!"

*"There's no such thing as coincidence,"* they said together, then laughed.

Gwen was glad to see the change in Laurel. "It'll be a piece of cake to approach the girl now. She's far more likely to trust her teacher than some stranger off the street."

Dara was also overjoyed when Gwen rang him with the news. All of them needed a boost to their spirits. Despite every effort to date, Granny had been unable to counter the spell that held the Irish Companions in its grip. Katie and Matt were still unconscious; she and Dara were still blind. Nor had she divined a way to restore the gateways. Though her auguries continued to point to Dana, they showed little else.

"The situation's hopeless, but not dire," was Dara's comment, made with his typical dry humor. "We're working away. Granny's the brain and I'm the dogsbody. She has me out on the road at all hours, getting lashin's of this and lashin's of that. I can't drive, but I've got two feet and a cane. And don't I know the island like the back of my hand?"

Both Granny and Dara agreed that Gwen and Laurel should join up with Dana. The enemy's attacks called for direct action and with no communication from Faerie they had to make their own plans. Gwen's new position at the school seemed to support the idea.

But Gwen's hopes of making immediate contact with Dana died her first morning on the job. The girl was not only absent that day, it turned out she had been away since the first week of school. When Gwen made inquiries, she was given reports on an illness and a car accident, with doctors' notes attached.

"No wonder we couldn't reach her!" Laurel said, when Gwen rang to tell her. "She must have been attacked!"

"Maybe. But the medical reports didn't sound serious. Could it just be a coincidence? But we know the party line on that . . . She's expected back soon. We'll just have to wait till then."

The day Dana arrived back in the classroom, Gwen saw instantly that their fears were confirmed. She looked pale and fragile, like a porcelain doll, and her eyes had a haunted look. There was no doubt that she had suffered a trauma of some kind; and though she appeared both shocked and relieved to see a new teacher, she also seemed distracted, and kept looking around. Was she searching for someone?

From the front of the class, an astute teacher can tell a lot about her pupils. The faces turned toward her reveal a great deal about their feelings and attitudes, and the ease or hardship of their lives. Some students are naturally bright and cheerful, others sullen or rebellious. There are those who are utterly uninterested in being taught and those who demand to be challenged and stimulated. Then there are the ones whose features are closed like a door. For whatever reason, usually painful, they just want to be left alone.

It was to this last category that Dana belonged, Gwen saw immediately. The girl was evidently a loner. Despite her long absence, no one greeted her when she entered the room, nor did anyone ask how she was. Moving quickly to the back of the class, she slumped into her desk. At lunchtime, she sat by herself in the cafeteria, reading a book.

From the day Gwen took up her post, she introduced the practice of interviewing her students to get to know them. This provided an ideal opportunity to be alone with Dana. Gwen had decided she would casually introduce the subject of Faerie when they met. Given that the girl was obviously shy and withdrawn, Gwen knew she had to tread carefully. Still, she was not prepared for an outright refusal.

"You want to interview me alone without my parents' consent? Sorry, it's not on."

Before Gwen could react, Dana had sped down the hall. For the remainder of the day, despite all Gwen's efforts, the girl managed to avoid any further encounters.

• • •

"Something to do with her last teacher?" Laurel suggested when she and Gwen met that evening for supper.

Laurel was picking her way through a Caesar salad. Gwen had a plate of spaghetti with a creamy sauce and strips of smoked pancetta.

"Definitely," said Gwen between mouthfuls. "I did a little detective work in the staff room. His name was Crowley. Seems he went through some kind of major change since the summer. Lost weight, became withdrawn, acted weird. No one liked him anymore. In fact, I got the distinct impression they were afraid of him."

Laurel looked shaken. "This sounds all wrong. Was he possessed by something? Gwen, you've got to be careful."

"I am, don't worry. I'm up to the yin-yang in protective charms, plus I've put them around the school. The place is clear now, I guess with him gone. But do you see the good of this? Crowley has disappeared and Dana is still here. Whatever happened, she survived and he didn't. Looks to me like we're being helped."

"Could she have fought him off herself?"

Gwen was scooping up the sauce with her spoon. "I'd like to think that, but I can't. She's no warrior. There's no sense of power there at all. She seems weak and nervous. How can she possibly take a mission? No wonder your sister was worried."

"We've got to join her immediately. Granny and Dara say so too. We're running out of time."

Gwen frowned. "I agree, but I don't want to rush things and scare her off. She won't trust anyone after being attacked. Certainly not her new teacher if the old one was the bad guy!"

"Maybe I should talk to her?" Laurel suggested, but her voice was hesitant. "Since I look like Honor."

Gwen saw the grimace. Laurel didn't feel the same way Gwen did about children or teens. It didn't bode well. The girl needed to be handled sensitively.

"Give me a few more days," she suggested, to Laurel's obvious relief.

The waiter with the dessert cart was on the far side of the room. Gwen called him over despite the other's protests.

"This is my treat. Don't be a killjoy. We're celebrating my first real paycheck as a full-time teacher. And none of your low-fat nonsense," she added.

Laurel held up her hands in surrender.

Gwen waited till the dishes of gelato were served, garnished with chocolate-covered wafers. Then she brought up the new topic as tactfully as she could.

"Granny says she might be able to help with Ian . . . though she can't make any promises. But she needs something personal of his. Do you . . . ?"

"Yes." Laurel concentrated on her dessert as her face flushed with embarrassment. "I have one of his shirts. Oh God, this is so—"

"Well, it's a good thing you do," Gwen said in a no-nonsense manner, "or she wouldn't be able to work the spell. So eat up all those calories and we'll get back to your place and send it off by courier. The sooner Granny has it, the sooner she can find him."

Gwen's tone helped Laurel to regain her composure.

"Thank you," she said quietly.

"Oh stop it. What are friends for?"

The next day at school, Gwen was astonished by the difference in Dana. The girl looked transformed! The haunted look was completely gone, and though she still sat in the back of the class, there was something dignified, even queenly about her aloofness. There was also an air of triumph about her, as if she had succeeded at something. She looked immensely pleased with herself, like the cat that had got the cream. In the days that followed, Gwen saw a steady increase in strength and vitality. Dana's features seemed to glow. But at the same time, the girl became even more evasive and wily. No matter how often Gwen tried to cross paths with her or speak in private, Dana managed to slip away. She was adept at escaping, disappearing around corners, out of classrooms, down hallways.

"As elusive as a fairy," Gwen said ruefully to Laurel.

They were taking turns watching over Dana. Like guardian angels, they followed her from home to school and back again to make certain she was safe.

Though they didn't admit it, they were also spying.

Gwen now believed that Dana had a mission; that someone, somehow, had set her on the quest to restore the gateways. All the changes in the girl pointed to it. There was a definite air of determination and purpose.

Laurel wasn't convinced. "How could she know anything? The portals are down. There's no contact with Faerie. If there were, we'd have heard something by now."

Gwen recognized the logic of Laurel's argument, but she trusted her instincts. Dana was questing and growing from it. If only the girl would let them in!

Gwen's chance arrived the day Jean returned to school. She knew one of her students had been mugged, but she hadn't connected him to Dana. After all, Toronto was a big city with the usual crime rate, and this particular boy had notes on his file about absenteeism, rebelliousness, and defiance of authority. When he first entered the classroom, he didn't even look at Dana.

It was at lunchtime, when Gwen was passing the cafeteria, that she saw them together. Her attention had been caught by the sound of wild laughter. She was so surprised to see Dana with a friend that she stopped and stared. It was Jean, the boy who was attacked! Gwen's mind raced, putting two and two together. She studied Dana. The girl looked flushed and happy. With a pang, Gwen saw the relationship and knew what it meant. She could have been looking at herself and Dara the first time they met, brought together by a Faerie mission. The reminder brought an ache to her heart, but she was also glad. If her intuition was right, Dana was not only on the quest but she had a companion.

With some trepidation, Gwen decided it was time to act. She would have to talk fast. Teachers rarely entered the student cafeteria and she didn't want an audience. At the same time, she needed to convince these two that she was on their side and ready to help them.

Dana's instant rebuff was so forceful, it took Gwen's breath away. Hardly the weak and nervous girl of first impressions! Rejection notwithstanding, Gwen was delighted. She looked from Dana to Jean, liking what she saw. The young man showed strength of character. Someone to be trusted. Together they inspired confidence. There was hope for the mission.

The moment she was alone, Gwen rang Laurel with the latest news.

"No offense, Gwen, but we need something more tangible than your instincts. *Give me the facts, ma'am, just the facts.* She knows the portals are down since she, like us, would be cut off from Faerie. And she obviously knows an enemy is after her, if she has been attacked. But that doesn't mean she knows what to do or that she has the power to restore the gateways. We've got to meet her and find out what's happening."

"Our original task was to watch over her," Gwen

argued. "Not to interfere. We each had our own mission and this one is hers. If she doesn't want our help, we've no right to force her. We've got to trust she can do it. It's her destiny."

Laurel made an exasperated noise. "There's your rose-colored glasses again. Destiny doesn't guarantee that everything will turn out all right. This is too important to stick to tradition. You're endangering Faerie."

"That's unfair," Gwen protested.

She was hurt by the remark, but Laurel was relentless. "Fair or not, time is against us. I say grab Dana by the scruff of the neck and find out what she knows. If you don't, I will. This can't go on any longer. We've been sensitive enough for her sake. The mission is more important than any of us."

It wasn't their first disagreement about strategy, but it was the worst. Laurel's tone was belligerent. Gwen felt cornered.

"All right. I've got an idea. I'll write her a note. If that doesn't work, you can confront her yourself."

"Fine," said Laurel, and she hung up.

Gwen sighed as she stared at the phone. She missed the Company of Seven.

On entering the classroom the next morning, Gwen saw immediately that Jean had changed desks to sit beside Dana. The two were deep in conversation, oblivious to everyone else around them. It wasn't Gwen's nature to eavesdrop, but she couldn't help herself. Sidling along the aisle, she took more time than was necessary to open the window near them.

She heard very little before Dana spotted her, but it was enough. Confirmation at last! Gwen was elated. Dana was on the mission and so, too, was Jean. They had been discussing how to get away for the long weekend. Here was the opportunity Gwen had been hoping for, the chance to show her good faith and gain their confidence.

When Gwen called Laurel that day, they devised a plan together. Gwen would arrange "a school trip" for Dana and Jean. She had the money to finance their travels and she would accompany them. Between the note declaring Gwen a Companion of Faerie and the offer of assistance, they were bound to accept her.

"You'll miss Thanksgiving," Laurel said. "My parents were looking forward to meeting you." Her voice was sheepish. She was feeling guilty about the fight the night before, especially since Gwen had been proven right. Gwen being Gwen, of course, hadn't said, "I told you so."

"I'll visit another time. Tell them I really appreciate the invite. But it makes sense that I'm the one to go and not you. It's your Thanksgiving and you should be there. Maybe you'll come to New Jersey for ours next month?"

"You're sure about this?" Again, the guilt.

"Hey, I'm the one who's off on an adventure. Isn't that better than a turkey dinner?" Gwen gasped with mock horror. "Did I say that?"

"You've convinced me now," Laurel said, wryly. "Okay then, I'm going to head off today to beat the rush on the buses. I expect a full report when I get back."

"You've got it."

"And Gwen?"

"What?"

"Be careful, eh?"


The plan was a good one, but like all plans it wasn't foolproof. With only two days till the Canadian Thanksgiving weekend, Gwen had to act fast. First things first, she needed parental permission for the two students to travel. That was the easy part, a few phone calls. It was her efforts to make contact with the young people that failed disastrously. She had hoped to catch Jean before he went home, but hadn't counted on him leaving early for hockey practice. But the real catastrophe was Dana's reaction to the note.

The handmade paper was a gift from Dara. The golden spirals were a Faerie design. Gwen had taken her time to write the note, knowing it was important that the message appeal to Dana. As a last flourish, she had sprinkled the envelope with her favorite apple-scented perfume. The note was left on Dana's desk where she couldn't possibly miss it.

At her own desk, Gwen pretended to mark papers, watching Dana from the corner of her eye. She held her breath. Now her heart lifted with hope as the girl approached her. But without looking back, Dana hurried from the classroom.

Hopes dashed, Gwen sat stunned a moment. Then, grabbing her coat and purse, she ran after the girl.

Gwen was well used to trailing Dana from her turn on watch, but today everything conspired to confound her. First the school principal stopped to have "a little talk" in the hall and praise Gwen's work. She almost screamed with frustration. That delayed her getting to the subway. Dana's train was already leaving as Gwen hurried down the stairs, cursing her high heels. Racing back up the escalator and into the street, she hailed a cab. Early rush-hour traffic meant slow progress, and the one-way street system on Brunswick Avenue left her only halfway to Dana's house. Throwing money at the driver, she jumped out of the cab. A quick look around showed her instantly that she had arrived just in time.

On her left, a short way up the street, Dana was unconcernedly walking home. On Gwen's right, near an abandoned convent that dominated the street, something was taking shape in a gurge of green matter.

*Something wicked this way comes.*

Gwen wasn't sure what she was looking at, but she

could see it was all wrong. The smear of green mist took a human shape, tall and pale with hideously scarred features. But it wasn't human. Out of its body writhed long tentacles like tumid worms. Gwen caught the smell. A sour, metallic odor that clawed at her throat. Now a loud buzzing sound, like that of a giant wasp, drilled into her head.

The ghastly thing was not looking at her. It had turned toward Dana. The hatred that burned in its eyes was shocking. Gwen didn't stop to think. Before the monster could move, she ran to fight it.

The thing was now fully formed, both man and hideous creature at the same time. Barreling into him, Gwen caught him off guard. He fell back as she kicked and punched, but then a skeletal hand shot out like a claw and gripped her arm.

With horrible speed, he dragged her to the yard behind the convent.

*"You dare to challenge me?"*

Gwen shuddered at the sound of his voice. Something dead and remorseless echoed from the human throat.

*"First you, then the fairy girl. I will enjoy this little feast."*

Sticky tentacles coiled around Gwen's waist. A quick snap of her back was no doubt his intention. He had to get Dana before she reached her house.

"Not on my watch," Gwen hissed through clenched teeth.

She was neither weak nor powerless. The protective charms she carried were meant to combat a creature like this. Better than packing a pistol. She had slipped the first one from her pocket as she raced across the road. Clutched in her hand was a little sprig of green holly with a twist of red thread. Before the monster could tighten his grip, Gwen dropped the charm onto him and uttered the spell.

*Let the briar that spreads, let the thorn that grows, pierce and perish your flesh.*

Though she had barely managed to croak out the words, the effect was instant.

He released her with a screech and fell to the ground. Every part of him was pierced with fairy thorns. He writhed in agony.

Staggering back, Gwen grasped the next charm. She knew the battle had only begun. Though it was a long time since she had fought for her life, her adrenaline was rushing, her courage rising. Once a warrior in Faerie, always a warrior.

The second charm comprised dried leaves and flowers in a pouch of woven hemp. Gathered on May Eve, they were seven herbs that nothing natural or supernatural could injure: vervain, St. John's Wort, speedwell, eyebright, mallow, yarrow, and valerian. Quickly, she shook them into her palm. They had to be swallowed one by one. Would she have time? As soon as she gulped down the blade of yarrow, its power coursed through her veins. She was instantly stronger. Now for the speedwell. Yes! Her limbs quivered. She would move more swiftly. The eyebright would improve her sight and reflexes —

Her enemy had recovered. He charged at her. His rage was palpable. He was burning with it. The waspish noise exploded in her brain. The metallic smell was overpowering. Smoke rose from the pavement where he stepped. He spotted the pouch in her hand and lashed out furiously.

Tentacles flayed the air, each one a sharp and deadly weapon. The speedwell helped Gwen to dodge the full assault, but she couldn't avoid them all. One tentacle sliced across her face to gash her forehead. Blood ran into her eyes. The world went red. Another whistled through the air and tore at her hand.

She let out a cry.

The pouch of magical herbs was ripped from her fingers.

Now Gwen reached for her last weapon: a thin switch of hazel, peeled bare. It was tucked into her belt, like a dagger. Brandishing it like a sword, she sprang forward with a cry and laid into him with her own fierce fury.

Back and forth, they wove in a dance of death.

Gwen darted with the swiftness the speedwell gave

her, while the yarrow strengthened her arm as she smote and jabbed. Whenever she landed a blow with the wand, the creature shrieked with pain. Sacred and powerful, the hazel had secret properties that defied all demons. Though Gwen herself knew only a little of its mysteries, she was a trueheart and a braveheart and it responded to her touch.

But the monster was a mystery too, if a dark and loathsome one, and it had power of its own. The thing that had taken Crowley's body was much older and more terrible than Gwen could have imagined. Despite the grave injuries she inflicted upon him, slowly but surely he gained the upper hand.

She continued to fight valiantly. Long before she had begun to lose, she knew she had won. Dana was safe at home and out of harm's reach. Gwen had done her duty, she had served the cause well. Her king would be proud of her.

Gwen's time was coming. Despite the strength of the yarrow, her arm was growing tired. Despite the swiftness of the speedwell, her steps began to falter. The hazel could work its magic only as long as she could wield it. All this she knew as she continued to do battle against a much stronger enemy.

The monster's blows rained relentlessly down. The tentacles lashed out tirelessly like massive whips. Gwen could no longer fend them off. She staggered dizzily. When the blows landed, she screamed. The pain was unbearable.

Now her arms went limp at her side.

Now her tears fell, without shame, for a life lost too young.

Now the monster coiled around her once more.

She felt his rage and his ravening hunger. There would be no mercy. There was no hope. Yet even as she felt her body begin to crack, she found the last remnant of strength to utter a cry.

*Come, holy word, singing word, and the good word also! May the power of these three holy things set me free from evil!*

As her words shimmered in the air like silver, the monster recoiled. The cry seemed to reverberate outward, a clarion call to all that was bright and beautiful. But it lasted only a moment.

Now, with implacable malice, Crowley bore down on her. The stink was overwhelming. The foul smell of the murderer. She felt herself falling backward into darkness. Her heart fluttered wildly like a bird in its death throes. And as her eyes closed on the world, she whispered the name of the one she loved most, her greatest grief in parting.

*Dara.*

# Twenty

The next morning at school, Dana and Jean were surprised that Ms. Woods was absent. When the vice-principal hurried into the room, flustered and annoyed, they exchanged glances. No explanation was given as he began to teach them, but it was obvious that something was wrong.

"What's this?" said Jean, at lunch. "You think she run away from us?"

Dana was mystified. "It doesn't make sense. She sent the note and called our parents. I thought that meant she was on our side. But then she didn't mention the Book of Dreams. So she doesn't know about the quest, even though she knows about the gateways. That could put her in the enemy camp. And what about the Halloween deadline? My mother didn't say anything about that."

Jean looked equally confused. "She can be bad, she can be good. Maybe she try to trap us? Maybe she try to help? How do we know?"

"We don't," Dana said, thinking about it, "until she turns up again. But I think we should go this weekend anyway. We'd be following Grandfather's advice as well as the musicians'."

"*D'accord.* We take the chance she give us, and when she come back we see what happen."

Though Dana was glad to have a plan, she felt uneasy. What could their teacher's disappearance mean? What if Ms. Woods was in trouble? Should they do something about it? But what could they do? Whom could they tell?

"We go tomorrow," Jean was saying. "That give us *biens le temps,* many time to go to Cape Breton."

Dana agreed. "We should take sleeping bags," she suggested, "and maybe some food. Bring everything to school. Our parents will expect us to leave from here."

Immersed in the details of their trip, Dana soon forgot about her teacher. The thrill of adventure was rising. The fact that Jean was going with her made it all the more exciting.

The following day, when school was over, Dana and Jean collected their things from their lockers. Since they wouldn't be going for the spirit canoe until after dusk, they went out for supper.

In the restaurant, sitting across from Jean, Dana suffered a bout of sudden shyness. This was very like a date. Doing her best to stay calm, she agreed with his suggestion to share a pizza, with pepperoni and ham on his half and olives and green peppers on hers.

"In Ireland you can get sweet corn as a topping," she told him.

"*Câlisse,*" he said, with a shudder.

He ordered garlic bread for two.

"If one eat garlic, it is necessary all eat garlic," he said with a grin.

Dana choked on a crumb of pizza crust and went red in the face. To cover her embarrassment, she changed the subject.

"Do you feel bad lying to your parents about this?"

He considered her question. "*Non,*" he said at last. "For them, the truth is not good. I can't tell my life as *loup-garou* or what happen to *grand-père*. It is more pain for them. *Et toi?* You feel bad?"

Dana sighed. "Sometimes I wish I could share the magic with my dad, and also my stepmum. But the dangerous stuff rules that out. They would only worry or, worse, try to stop me. In the end, it's better that I keep it to myself."

A trace of sadness echoed in her voice. Jean said nothing, but his look was sympathetic. He didn't have to say that he understood, for he, too, knew the loneliness of living with secrets. Dana's hand was resting on the table. He reached out to clasp it, and they stayed that way till their food arrived.

The sun was setting behind the city towers when they

reached the Humber Marshes. Together they dragged the spirit boat out of the bushes.

"I bring this for you," Jean said, producing a knitted cap from his pocket. "*Tuque québécoise.* The best thing for the head!"

Grinning, he pulled it over her head and ears. It was identical to the one he wore himself, red with black stripes and a long tapering end.

"I brought a thermos of hot chocolate," she said.

"Like we go on a bus?"

They laughed.

As the canoe rose from the ground and shot over the currents of air, they soon left Toronto far behind. From the moment they were airborne, Dana kept watch for Crowley. Would the boat's demon call out to him? Despite her worry about an attack, the rowing itself was much easier. Though the dark force of *la chasse-galerie* struggled against them, they paddled with the skill and strength of a team. Their previous journey had bonded them like true *voyageurs*.

Dana knelt in the bow, gazing ahead. Once they reached Cape Breton, it was up to her to spot the place she had seen in the music. But first they had a long journey ahead of them. They were flying away from the setting sun into the eastern night. Ahead of them lay the great province of Quebec bordered by the St. Lawrence Seaway. They intended to follow the mighty waterway as if it were a road.

High in the atmosphere the wind was biting. Dana was glad of the tuque Jean gave her, as well as the parka she wore with scarf and mittens.

"Tell me stories about your country," she called back to Jean. "In Ireland we say that a song or a story shortens the road."

"I have *beaucoup*," he warned her. "*Mon grand-père* and before she die, *ma grand-mère*, they tell me many."

"I'm all ears!" she assured him.

He told her tales of John the Bear, Teur-Merisier, Talon-Rouge, and Ti-Jean the Giant-Killer, after whom he suspected he had been named. There were also tales of the devil—*le Diable, beau danseur*—who seemed to have a penchant for French-Canadian parties and dances. He would always appear as a dark, handsome stranger, richly dressed, with a fine beaver cloak and ebony cane. In the heart of winter he drove a magnificent sleigh pulled by a glossy black horse with silver bells and harness. The prettiest maid at the dance would inevitably be fatally attracted to him. But just as he was about to carry her off and steal her soul, some innocent would unmask him, usually a child. Proof of his true identity would be confirmed when his cloven hoof was revealed—the cause of his limp!—or the floor was seen to have been burnt in the places where he had danced. Then the Devil's game was up, and he would be chased away as everyone made the Sign of the Cross and the *curé* came running with Holy Water.

"Now you tell the story," he insisted, "or sing *une chanson irlandaise.*"

"This is like a road trip with my da."

She was about to take her turn with a song when she noticed something strange below. The land seemed to have patches of darkness and light, as if it were day in one place and night in another. The more she gazed down, the more confused she grew. She wasn't sure what she was looking at. There were moments when she saw things she couldn't possibly see from that far up, as if she were only feet away. Then she realized the truth. Like gazing into a crystal ball, she was viewing the land with magical sight. As well as the bright vistas of modern cities and townlands, she could see layers of time on top of one another, as if time itself were a heap of events, a great collection of moments.

"I'm seeing all kinds of things down there!" she exclaimed.

"*Mais oui.* Remember when you see Étienne Brûlé? This happen sometime with *la chasse-galerie.* The flying, she make *une ouverture sur le Grands Temps.* A big hole in time? No, I don't mean this."

Dana understood. "An opening in the Great Time. It's the same with Faerie! Time and space go all weird around it. More like a circle than a line or, better still, a spiral."

"*Oui, c'est ça! Exactement!*" He waved grandly at the panorama below. "*Regarde, chérie.* See my country."

As the spirit boat passed over Montreal, another

name came whispering through the cobbled streets and around the corners of tall buildings and sidewalk cafés. *Hochelaga.* At the foot of a hill not yet called Mont Royal stood a thriving Iroquois community. Palisaded like a town, with fifty longhouses, it overlooked tilled fields of corn and maize.

On sped the canoe past Trois-Rivières and Cap-de-la-Madeleine to la Ville de Québec. Again the layers peeled away like an onion. Beneath the majestic walls of the city and the great star-shaped fortress called le Citadel, Dana could see another settlement. *La Habitation* was a simple quadrangle of wooden buildings with a stockade and moat. It stood on a point where the St. Lawrence narrowed, a *kebek* as the Algonquian people called it.

A new sound reached the flying canoe. Musket fire and the roars of men.

On the Plains of Abraham, in the shadow of Quebec City, two armies gathered. Two old countries waging war for new land. Thousands of British troops were mustered on the grassy field below the western walls of the fortress. They had already bombarded and destroyed much of the city. If the French had only waited for reinforcements, they would have had a chance. But they were already moving out to engage in battle.

The spirit canoe quivered violently and stalled.

"We go!" Jean shouted. "*Vite! Rapidement!*"

But they didn't leave. It was as if the canoe were caught

in a hidden current. It began to circle around the scene.

Dana didn't want to look, but found herself mesmerized. It was nothing like the battles she had seen in movies or on television. Everything was chaotic, brutal and bloody. Limbs blown off with musket balls. Men screaming horribly. Her stomach heaved.

Frantically steering the boat away at last, Jean called Dana out of her daze. But even as they left, she remembered the outcome from her history book. The fight for Quebec was short and bloody, less than half an hour, but both leaders died. General Wolfe lay dead among his troops on the battlefield, while the Marquis de Montcalm perished from his wounds the following day.

Though they didn't get caught again as they continued eastward, Dana began to notice a pattern in their journey. Whenever the land told a story of death and destruction, the canoe would judder with delight. *He was a murderer from the beginning.* Feeding off the darkness below, the demon would gain in strength and ferocity. Then Dana and Jean had to struggle with all their might to keep control of the craft.

The demon was particularly strong whenever they encountered the devastation wrought by the settlers on the First Peoples of the land. Without pity or remorse, the Europeans burned villages and crops; enslaved men, women, and children; and slaughtered all who opposed them. Sometimes in the crowd of slaves or the bodies of the slain, Dana thought she recognized Grandfather and Roy. She would turn away with shame. She couldn't bear to watch.

Upstream of Quebec, they passed a small island. Dana felt a sharp ache in her heart. The wooded isle was sculpted with coves and capes. On a rocky promontory overlooking the river stood a Celtic High Cross carved in stone: a tombstone to mark the site of mass graves.

"My people are buried here!" she cried with sudden knowledge.

The sorrowful sound of keening was carried on the wind, a wake of fiddles and the clatter of bones. *Oileán an nGael*. The Island of the Irish. She heard the whispers of the thousands who had perished in this place. Some had crossed the Atlantic in "coffin ships" to escape the Great Famine. Others had come seeking new lives and freedoms. Here they died of disease and malnutrition, meeting death in their dreams.

"I know this *complainte*," Jean told her. "This is Grosse Île. Like Pointe Sainte-Charles too. With them lie the French also, who try to help. Like I tell you, *chérie*," he called to her sadly, "the French and the Irish are always good friend."

They continued to follow the St. Lawrence as if it were a highway. The great river had yet to freeze and was busy with sea traffic. Amidst the modern vessels, Dana caught sight of ancient canoes and ghost ships.

How long they traveled along that shining seaway, Dana had no idea. Hours seemed to pass like minutes and sometimes a minute seemed to contain eternity. Again and again, the land told its tales with all the color and verve of a storyteller. Then a silence fell over the country, like a book closed at bedtime, and they paddled on through the darkness beneath the sky of stars.

They heard the gulf before they saw it, a mournful sound in the distance, the plangent murmur of the sea. When they reached the estuary of the Gulf of St. Lawrence, it looked as wide as an ocean.

Jean steered the canoe south. To their left, in the distance, was the dark silhouette of Île d'Anticosti standing guard at the gateway of the great river's mouth. To their right, ahead of them, was Prince Edward Island.

They had journeyed through a long night into the rising sun. The waters of the gulf gleamed in fiery splendor. The sky blazed gold. Soon they came in sight of Cape Breton Island.

Dana scanned the rocky landscape and the sea-washed shores. Nothing looked familiar.

"Let's go inland," she suggested, trying not to sound anxious.

What if they had come all this way for nothing? What if they couldn't find the Place of Stones? She suffered a pang of doubt. What if it didn't exist, except in a song that she could hardly remember!

They had begun to descend. Jean was looking for a place to land.

"We don't fly near the lake," he warned. "There is fog on Bras d'Or."

His words triggered her memory. The line of the song echoed through her mind.

*There's fire in the blood and a fog on Bras d'Or.*

"That's it!" she cried. "The fog! Fly through it!"

There was a moment after they had sailed into the mist when they both regretted the decision. It was a moment of intense cold and damp and milky blindness. Both were all too aware that a huge, deep lake lay somewhere beneath them. If they were going to land on a body of water, they would prefer to see it! Both held their breaths as they continued to paddle, and only released them again when they flew out of the haze.

And there, in the clear light of day, was the place Dana sought.

Where the lake opened its arms to embrace the Atlantic was a little cove with a scattering of houses. The village was sheltered by a ridge of low hills. The highest peak had a crown: a jagged circle of stones.

"The Place of Stones!" Dana called out, delighted.

They landed the canoe on the pebbly shore of the cove. The air was salty with sea spray. Other boats lay upturned on the stones, small wooden craft painted in bright colors.

"It's like the west of Ireland," said Dana.

"There is nowhere to hide *le canot*," Jean observed, looking around.

The hills nearby were all grass and gray rock. There were few trees in sight.

"It should be safe here," she assured him, thinking of home. "This is fishermen's country."

Still, he didn't look happy at the thought of leaving the canoe out in the open.

"How about a picnic?" she suggested, to distract him. "Time for breakfast."

They spread out a sleeping bag over the stones and opened their knapsacks. He had rolls of ham and beef, while she had cheese and egg-salad sandwiches.

"You don't eat meat?" he asked her curiously. "Never?"

"I won't eat anything that had a face."

"This I can't do," he said, shrugging. Then he wolfed down his food.

As they ate their meal, they discussed whether they should rest or explore. After traveling all night, both were pale and bleary-eyed.

"The Place of Stones is on the highest hill," Dana said, surveying the range.

"Maybe we go to the village first, eh?" Jean stifled a yawn. "We see who live there."

"Sounds good to me."

Dana stuffed a few chocolate bars into her pocket, then rolled up the rest of her things in her sleeping bag and stowed them under the canoe. Though she was tired, she felt she could keep going for a while yet.

Jean was regarding her strangely.

"What?" she said.

"I like that we do this together, you and me."

His words made her smile. She felt exactly the same way. Only a year ago, she had quested alone in the mountains of Ireland. How much more wonderful it was to have a companion!

Hand in hand, they walked toward the village. They were ready for anything.

# Twenty-one

It was barely a village, only a handful of small houses perched on the rocks like a scatter of gulls. There were no paths or gardens. The cottages were made of stones that were wedged together without mortar or cement. The roofs were thatched, some as tightly as cloth, others less tidily, with weeds and wildflowers sprouting from the eaves. Lace curtains hung in the windows and pots of red geraniums sat on the sills. The place had an Irish or Scottish air. There was no sight or sound of the inhabitants, but they were apparently at home. Smoke curled from the chimneys, sweetening the air with the scent of burning wood.

Dana and Jean stopped at the first house. The heavy silence was unnerving. When they knocked on the door, no one answered. A big ginger cat on the windowsill eyed them coolly. The door was of the kind Dana had seen in rural Ireland. Built in two pieces, the top could open separately, like a window, to let in fresh air. The old people would lean on the bottom half and call out to their neighbors who passed on the road.

"Maybe we enter?" Jean suggested. "This look like

the kind of place my *grand-mère* say '*la porte est sur la clanche.*'"

"The door is on the latch?" guessed Dana. "That's what the Irish say too!"

She hesitated. If the villagers were friendly, wouldn't someone have come to meet them by now?

The half-door opened. An old woman peered out at them. She was dark-haired and dark-skinned, with gaunt features and bright lively eyes. Her nose was hooked like a beak; her clothes were black, and she wore a feathery shawl over bony shoulders. Head cocked sideways, she peered at them before speaking.

"I am the Cailleach Dubh," she announced in a shrill, chattering voice. "You are welcome to Ailsa Craig. Enter."

The cottage was a single-room dwelling with white-washed walls and a loft overhead that was reached by a ladder. A cavernous hearth dominated one end of the room. A black cauldron hung on a hook over the fire. Half the space was domestic with an old settee, table and chairs, and a wooden dresser filled with dishes and crockery. The other half, near to the door, was a makeshift shop and pub. A high counter ranged in front of shelves lined with canned goods, dried herbs, rolls of twine, and various tools. Bunches of onions and garlic hung from the ceiling. There were stools at the counter and chairs nearby. The floor was checkered with black and red flagstones worn down by the tread of countless feet.

Dana and Jean sat near the fire while the old woman made tea in a black kettle. She moved with an ungainly grace, kicking her long skirt in front of her. When she poured the tea, it trickled out like treacle, a dark brown mixture with leaves floating on top; but with dollops of cream and sugar, it tasted surprisingly good.

"Did ye ever hear the tale of tea?" she asked them, eyes sparkling with mischief. "When 'twas first brought from China, the people of Europe hadn't a notion what to do with it. They boiled up the leaves, threw away the liquid, and ate it like cabbage."

She made a face and pretended to spit. They laughed with her and felt a little more comfortable.

Dana took the chocolate bars out of her pocket and placed them on the table.

"There's an Irish saying that you shouldn't arrive at a house with one arm as long as the other. Can I offer these to go with the tea?"

The old woman slipped one into her pocket and placed the other on a plate, cutting it into small pieces.

"You've good manners," she said, pleased. "In turn, I will help you. Why have you come here?"

"We're looking for something," Dana said. "The Book of Dreams."

The old lady nodded. "Well, you had best ask the giant about that. Blessed with serendipity, Fingal is. Not too smart in the head department, but he's good at finding things."

Dana grew excited. "The song that brought us here was about a giant! Can we meet him?"

The old woman didn't answer. Glancing out the window, she was suddenly distracted. Now she spoke quickly to them.

"Hear me now and do as I say. You be the first of my visitors this day, but not the last. Mind, there be enemies in every tale. If you are found here, all will be lost. Do you understand me?"

Even as she spoke, she hurried them over to the ladder and up into the loft.

Upstairs she pointed to a single bed with a straw mattress and patchwork quilt.

"This is the best place to hide," she urged them.

Dana frowned and didn't move.

The Cailleach snorted impatiently. "If you enter our world, you must bide by our rules. There is nowhere else you can go."

With a shrug to Dana, Jean crawled under the bed. She followed after him, though she didn't look happy about it. Nothing made sense.

The old woman trailed the quilt over the side of the bed till the two were covered. Then she went back downstairs to tidy her house.

Dana and Jean were snug enough in their hiding place. The floor of the loft was made of slender branches woven together like a mat. It was rough but pliant, and comfortable to lie on. Best of all, they could see through the weave into the room below.

"I think we are in a *conte merveilleux*," Jean whispered to Dana.

"A wonder tale?" Dana thought about that a moment. "It does remind me of something." An unpleasant idea struck her. "What if she's a witch and wants to eat us?"

Jean squinted down at the cauldron over the fire.

"The pot fit only one, Gretel," he said with a snicker.

She gave him a dig with her elbow.

"I'm serious," she hissed. "Remember what she called herself? The Cailleach Dubh? At first I understood her name to be the 'Dark Wise Woman.'"

"It sound nice."

"Yes, but *cailleach* can also mean 'hag' or 'witch.'"

"Now you say! Okay, we don't sleep. It is necessary we regard her."

The first hour was easy. Despite their fatigue, they were too anxious to close their eyes. They kept a sharp watch on the old woman as she swept the floor and stocked the shelves. When she was finished her housework, she busied herself preparing food.

Dana grimaced as cod heads were lined up on the table, their empty eye sockets glaring. The old woman stuffed each head with a wet doughy mixture and put them in the cauldron. Dana felt better as more items went into the pot. There couldn't be room for much else in there.

As time passed without incident or excitement, the two found it harder and harder to keep awake. Their eyelids grew heavier by the second; their limbs, sluggish. It became more and more difficult to fight off the sleep that their bodies craved. Whenever one fell into a doze, the other gave a quick nudge; but eventually and inevitably both nodded off together and there was no one to wake them.

They slept without dreaming, perhaps because they were in a dream already. Minutes turned to hours. Outside, the sun rose in the sky and burned away the mist that hung over Lake Bras d'Or. The surface of the water gleamed like glass.

A loud knock on the door woke them!

Before either could figure out how long they had slept, the shock of the new visitor drove all thought from their minds.

Into the house he strode, a fierce black-robed rider in high leather boots and with a goad in his hand. Through the half-door came the sounds of his horse snorting restlessly and pawing the ground. Dana nearly choked when the man passed underneath her. His shoulders were empty. He was *headless*. In fact, he carried his head under his arm like a hat! It had the color and texture of moldy cheese and glowed with the phosphorescence of decaying matter. Gruesome wet lips grinned from ear to ear, as the dark wicked eyes surveyed the room.

Dana covered her mouth to keep from crying out.

The Cailleach looked unruffled.

"Good day to you, Dullahan, will you have a drink?"

A hoarse voice issued from the bloated lips of the head.

"Gi'e us a beer."

A glass of black porter was put on the counter.

Upstairs, the two watched with fascinated horror. How would he drink it?

As the glass was held to the head's mouth, it guzzled thirstily.

"*Maudit, câlisse, tabernac,*" Jean muttered.

Dana bit her lip. She wasn't sure if she wanted to scream or laugh.

*Slam* went the glass on the counter. *Pop* went the head onto the horseman's shoulders. He stretched his neck to work out a cramp, then threw a gold coin to the old woman, who caught it adroitly. Then, with a salute of farewell, the Dullahan marched out the door.

The Cailleach had no sooner bitten the coin and put it away in her pocket than another knock was heard. Several creatures came in, each more beautiful than the last: two men and a woman who held a child by the hand. All had scales instead of skin, an iridescent aquamarine, and their hair was like long green strands of seaweed. Their fingers and toes were webbed. Around their shoulders hung capes of sealskin.

Were they mermaids or merrows or selkies? Dana wondered.

She had hoped to discover the answer from their talk, but they didn't stay long. In a smattering of French and Scots Gaelic, they bought a few bags of salt and left.

The third party of visitors created an uproar. Their arrival was heralded by a whirlwind of noise that battered the thatch of the roof and the walls of the cottage. Jumbled all together were many sounds: the flapping of wings of a flock of large birds, the rolling wheels of many carriages, loud laughter and singing, bells ringing, dogs barking. Then came a banging on the door, like the hammers of hell. Voices were raised and raucous, a drunken crowd shouting to be let in.

"'S FOSGAIL AN DORUS 'S LEIG A 'STIGH SINN!"

Not in the least bothered, the old woman remained at the counter. She stood on one leg, head cocked as she listened.

The noise receded from the door and moved around the cottage toward the back wall. Circling the house, it came again to the front and then the door opened with a blast of wind.

In trooped the oddest sight yet. They weren't quite giants, but they were bigger than men. They had to stoop as they entered. They were broad, with great bellies hanging over their belts. Their hair and beards sprouted like birds' nests. Half their number were black-skinned with raven locks. The other half were ruddy red with manes of ginger. All wore denim dungarees and buckskin jackets. Some had caps or tuques pulled over their ears. Their feet were shod with homemade larrigans, laced stovepipe leggings with moccasined soles. They were a handsome lot in a rough, wild way, but there was a definite air of danger about them.

Their leader wore a headdress over his face and shoulders. It was made of the great hollowed head and hide of a bull, with the horns intact. Commanding the center of the room, he chanted loudly.

*Tháinig mis' anseo air tús*
*A dh'úrachadh dhuibh na Calluinn*
*Chá ruiginn a leas siud innseadh*
*Bha í ann bhó linn mo sheanar.*
*Théid mí deiseil air an fhardaich*
*'S tearnaidh mí aig an dorus*
*Craicionn Calluinn 'na mo phócaid*
*'S maith an ceo a thig bho'n fhear ud:*
*Chan eil duine chuireas r'a shróin é*
*Nach bí é rí bheo dheth falláin.*

(I came here first of all
To speak to you of the Calluinn
It's for the best that this continues to be told
Even as it was from the time of my grandfather
I'll go sunwise around the house

And I'll arrive at the door
The Calluinn skin as my pouch
And good will be the smoke coming from it:
There's no one who will hold it to his nose
That won't have health all his life.)

When he finished speaking, the man lifted the bull hide from his head to reveal a face half-red, half-black. Marching over to the old woman, he offered her the skin. In an oddly formal manner, she inhaled its odor. Then he brought it to the others so they could sniff it one by one.

In the rafters, Jean and Dana caught a whiff of the raw brutish smell.

"*SLÁINTE!*" the man roared at the finish. "HEALTH AND LONG LIFE TO YE!"

"*SLÁINTE!*" the others roared back.

The ritual completed, the wild men sat down. Some took seats near the window to gaze out at the twilight. Others bellied up to the bar.

"Spruce beer!" the leader demanded. "And it's the black spruce we want!"

The Cailleach put bottle after bottle onto the counter, all steaming with heat. A sweet, putrid scent filled the room.

"Good woman, ye kept them in horse shite!" cried one of the men.

For the next few minutes the only sounds were those of corks popping, throats gurgling, loud sighs, and grunts.

"Any grub?" someone asked.

The murmuring amongst them was friendlier now.

"Salt herring, *ceann groppi*, blue potatoes, oatcakes, and bannock," the old woman announced.

There were cheers and shouts of "Good on ye, hen!"

From the cauldron on the fire, the Cailleach dished out a big mess of food for the men. It looked awful, especially the cod heads stuffed with liver; but the smell was hearty and, for the two upstairs, a welcome respite from the pong of bull hide and manure. As the men ate eagerly and noisily with drunken hunger, Jean and Dana conversed in low tones.

"They look like goblins," Dana said. *"Fir Dhearga* and *Fir Dhubha*. The Red Men and the Black Men. But they're very big. I didn't think their kind were found in this part of the world!"

*"Les lutins* we call them," said Jean. "This is not so good. They are *très dangereux*."

While the men were busy eating, the old woman clomped up the ladder and into the loft. She carried two large yellow bags, which she set down near the bed.

"Climb inside," she whispered urgently. "Be quick, be nimble. The night is falling. The moon is rising."

Neither of them moved.

"Why do you want us to do this?" Dana demanded in a low voice. "What's going on?"

"Do not seek to know too much about us," came the

stern reply. "This is the only way you will get what you want. You, especially, must take care," she said to Dana. "Raising the giant is man-magic. It's not safe for girls. Stay hidden till the giant rises, then remember this: you must call out to Fingal before the goblins do. Now, be of good courage and do what I say."

Dana and Jean hesitated, still fearing a trap and wondering if they might yet wind up in the pot. The Cailleach was growing impatient.

"Get in or get lost!" she hissed.

Fighting down feelings of panic and claustrophobia, Dana crawled into one of the bags. The material was soft like suede or pigskin, and there were air holes. Reluctantly, Jean got into the other. Once the old woman had tied the ends shut, they were in total darkness.

With astonishing strength, the Cailleach heaved the bags over her shoulders and carried them downstairs.

"Ho byes, the Hag has bags for us!" the goblin chief shouted.

"Haggis and baggis!" cried another.

"They're not for the likes of ye," she said shortly. She put the bags on the floor. "They're a meal for the giant. Little pigs for his breakfast."

Dana and Jean gasped at her words. One of the men came near. They could hear him snuffling.

"Fee fie foe fum, I smell the blood of a tasty hu-mawn."

A cacophony of howls and laughter followed.

Seized with the urge to get out of the bag, Dana started to kick wildly. She felt the Cailleach's hand on her head. The touch was strangely soothing, both firm and kind.

"It's no business of yours what's in the bag," the old woman told the goblins curtly. "Just mind you take it up the hill when you go."

"And who says we're going up the hill?" the chief demanded.

A tense silence fell over the room. They were seconds away from a hullabaloo. Suddenly the top half of the door burst open. The big ginger cat jumped up on the sill. In a high-pitched caterwaul it screeched into the room.

"Awake the Sleeper!"

Then the cat ran off.

The old woman looked triumphant.

"The *cat sith* has spoken."

The men exchanged glances. A low grumbling rose amongst them. One spoke up gruffly. "The wind's in the north."

Another nodded. "There be new moon tonight."

This elicited mutters of "aye" and "that's true."

The goblin chief slammed the counter. "We have no circle to dance in Her sight!"

The Cailleach distributed bottles of scotch and whiskey. Her tone grew warm and persuasive.

"So light a torch, bring the bottle, and build the fire bright."

The chief glared at her, then looked out the window at the darkening night. The first stars had appeared. He gave a hard nod to the others.

*"The giant will rise with the moon."*

It was the signal they were waiting for. They jumped up as one man. Coins were showered on the counter as they prepared to leave.

"Don't forget the bags," said the Cailleach mildly.

Dana and Jean were hauled over burly shoulders and carted out the door.

It was a rough passage down the road and up the hill. Inside the bag, Dana was jarred and jolted with every step. Whenever the men broke into a jog, it was all the more bruising, as she was bounced off bony backs and shoulders. There was a lot of loud talk and wild laughter and grunting and yelling. As well as the noise, there was also the smell: a heady mix of booze, belches, and body sweat. She began to feel as if she had been kidnapped by pirates.

After what seemed an eternity of discomfort, she was unceremoniously dumped on the ground. As the loud voices moved some distance away, she hazarded a low call to Jean. She could see nothing through the air hole.

"Are you there?"

*"Oui,"* came Jean's whisper. "You okay?"

"More or less."

They struggled to loosen the ties on their bags and

peeked out cautiously. The landscape rolled in dark shadows around them. They were in the hills overlooking Lake Bras d'Or. Below glinted the cold waters of the lake. Above shone the night sky, sprayed with stars and a sliver of new moon. But where was the circle of stones they had seen from the air? There was no sign of it.

They were on the highest hilltop. The ground was tamped earth with coarse patches of grass. Just beyond them, the goblins were busily building a bonfire. Some piled up sticks of driftwood and dried branches. Others lit torches soaked with petrol. One of them emptied a canister of gasoline over the kindling and threw in a match. The great WHOMPFF of flames made them all jump back. When they recovered from the shock, they screeched with laughter.

"Ye singed Black Murphy's ears, ye *omadhaun!*"

Red sparks exploded into the night air as the wood crackled and burned. The men stood around the fire, torches held aloft, gulping down whiskey by the neck of the bottle. A fiddle appeared amongst them, then a bodhran drum and a tin whistle.

Dana squinted through the dimness. The three musicians? Looking over the circle, she understood the Cailleach's warning. The goblins looked even bigger and wilder in the firelight. Their faces were flushed from heat and exertion, their eyes crazed with drink. These were hard men engaged in a hard man's ritual.

Up rose the shivery sounds of the fiddle, then the shrill of the whistle, and the thunder of the drum. Harsh voices sang out.

*Cold wind on the harbor*
*And rain on the road*
*Wet promise of winter*
*Brings recourse to coal*
*There's fire in the blood*
*And a fog on Bras d'Or—*

*The giant will rise with the moon.*

They began to dance as they sang, weaving around one another with surprising grace. They held their torches and their bottles high, footing it lightly over the rough ground, then stamping their feet down with great crashes. The ground trembled beneath them. Whether it was the firelight or the night shadows or the nature of man-magic, Dana found her sight wavering. In place of the goblins, a great circle of stones took shape to form a rampart around the bonfire. Then out of the stones stepped a new group of dancers—dark-robed men with gold torcs at their necks and blue spirals scoring their faces.

*'Twas the same ancient fever*
*In the Isles of the Blest*
*That our fathers brought with them*

*When they went west*
*It's the blood of the Druids*
*That never will rest—*

*The giant will rise with the moon.*

The music grew more frenzied, the singing more frantic, and the dancing increased in speed and complexity. The bonfire flared like solar explosions. The stars in the sky spun deliriously. A vortex of energy was mounting in the circle.

The stones and the Druids melted into the darkness. The goblins returned, drunk as lords. They stomped and bellowed and shook their fists at the moon.

*And crash the glass down!*
*Move with the tide!*
*Young friends and old whiskey*
*Are burning inside*
*Crash the glass down!*
*Fingal will rise—*
*With the moon!*

Now the dancing reached such a pitch of ferocity and aggression that Dana and Jean hung back, appalled. Where could this end but in murder? They were about to make a run for their lives when the circle turned again.

No longer stones or goblins or dark-robed Druids, they were ordinary men, familiar men. Yes, there they were, the three musicians she had met in Toronto! They played their instruments and they sang and they danced in the company of other men like themselves. Maritimers from the coasts and the islands, from Newfoundland, Nova Scotia, New Brunswick, Prince Edward Island, and Cape Breton. They sang with passion to a fever of music. They drank their bottles dry and crashed them to the ground till the glass splintered and sparkled like the stars above. In young and old voices, men's wild voices, they sang with ardent fervor to warm the cold heart of the moon. Throats hoarse with whiskey and cigarettes and age, they were men of the sea and men of the mines, hard men who lived hard lives, eking out a living, battling bad governments and poverty and hardship, their lineage not forgotten, the blood of the Druids in their veins, the memory of the ancient stones, the blood sacrifice, and the other world so close to their own. The fire was in their blood, in their voices, in their music, in their indomitable will to survive, to live on. Whooping it up around the bonfire, they waved their torches and their bottles of whiskey, roaring full-throated a song lusty with life.

*The wind's in the north*
*There'll be new moon tonight*

*And we have no circle to dance in her sight.*

*So light a torch, bring the bottle, and build the fire*
  *bright—*

## THE GIANT WILL RISE WITH THE MOON.

O see how he rises! Rising up from the waves! Rising
up from the deep! Up out of the deep of the great lake of
Bras d'Or! Wet and shining like the stars, dripping water
and kelp and sea-wrack, knobbled with barnacles, *wet
out of the sea and luminously wet*, gigantic and beautiful
against the night. FINGAL THE GIANT! He it was
who once strode between the northern shores of Ireland
and Scotland, who had crossed the broad Atlantic, wading
through the swell with massive legs like tree trunks, over
the heaving waves of the cold vast ocean to follow the
ships that bore his people, those who told his stories and
sang his songs. He couldn't let them go without him. Like
a faithful dog he followed, nearly drowning at times as he
sank beneath the water then rising again to plow the main
till at last he arrived in the new land, exhausted beyond
belief. He collapsed on Cape Breton Island where he heard
them singing in the Gaelic. It was early in the morning
and the sun was rising over Lake Bras d'Or. He saw the
gold light reach out like arms to greet him. He fell into
its warm embrace for the merciful sleep of the deep. And
there in his wet seabed he still lies at peace. But he will

rise, oh yes he will rise, on the night of the new moon if you sing his song with enough fire in your blood and your voice to wake him.

Now with slow, heavy tread, the giant waded out of the lake. As each gargantuan footstep landed on the ground, it sent tremors through the earth. He was huge beyond imagining. Bigger than the hills he crossed to reach the bonfire where they had called out his name.

Towering over the goblins on the hill, the giant lowered his head for a closer look. Expecting a terrifying visage, Dana and Jean were surprised to see a big, round, friendly face. He had a bald head, cauliflower ears, and a thick, bushy beard. The grin was broad and toothless.

"I do love that song, byes. We're havin' a party, eh?"

# Twenty-Two

D ana was so surprised by Fingal's affability, it took her a moment to act on the Cailleach's instructions. Then, heart beating wildly, she struggled out of the bag. As she ran toward the giant, she shouted as loudly as she could.

"Yoo hoo! Hello there! Help!"

The goblins went berserk. Screeching with rage, wielding their torches like cudgels, they charged at her.

Jean had just crawled out from his bag and saw the danger to Dana. He turned as he ran, face elongating to a snout, black hair sprouting from every pore in his body. Dropping on all fours, he faced down the goblins, baring his fangs and snarling and snapping. In the fiery shadows of the bonfire, he looked all the bigger and more savage.

Surprised, the wild men stopped in their tracks, but it didn't take them long to recover. Brandishing their torches, they circled the wolf warily.

By this time, Dana had run back to join Jean. They were hopelessly outnumbered. But before the goblins could move to attack, Fingal's big hands reached down.

"Now, lads, be pleasant!" he boomed as he scooped up Dana and Jean. "Ye know the rules. The lass got the first word in. Away ye go now and thanks for the song. See ye next new moon, if ye're up for it."

This was met with a blue streak of curses, but the men did as they were told, grumbling among themselves as they headed back down the hill.

Fingal lowered his massive face to peer at the two in his palm. His eyes were as big as moons. His nostrils were like caves stuffed with hair.

"Pay no heed to the byes," he said in a friendly tone. "They work too hard, them fellas. Take no holy-days. Makes wee Jock all cross and cranky."

He patted the wolf lightly with his baby finger. "Nice doggie, don't bite." But as Jean unraveled to his own form, the giant's eyebrows shot up. "That's a good trick. I never seen that before. A Frenchie, I betcha. *Loup-garou*, eh?"

Dana expected Jean to be offended by the remark, but he only laughed and nodded. Fingal turned to Dana.

"So, what is it ye want, lass? I'll do your biddin' this night."

Dana shouted to be heard. "The Cailleach said you could help me."

"An Cailleach Dubh? Aren't ye the lucky one to be gettin' advice from the likes of her. She be the sister of Aoife, her that was the wife of Manannan, the Irish Lord of the Sea. I shouldn't be tellin' ye this now, but I've always been partial to a bit of gossip. I've heard tell that Aoife stole secrets from her husband. The language of nature, it was, and all the wisdom it gives. Well he murthered her for that, didn't he? She was of the crane family so he made a bag of her skin and put the secret language inside it. Now her sister, An Cailleach Dubh, got ahold of the bag. She's not a crane, mind, she's—"

"A cormorant!" Dana burst in with sudden insight. Images of the old woman flashed through her mind: the feathery shawl, the hooked nose, the high-stepping gait. She wasn't human at all, but a bird-woman. "Of course! *An cailleach dubh*. The black witch. It's the Irish name for the cormorant, and they do look like witches with their raggedy black wings!"

"Anyhows," the giant continued, "once the Cailleach got the bag, she had to scarper from the wrath of Manannan. She flew all the way across the ocean till she dropped down here in Cape Breton, almost dead. And here she stayed. A bit like me own tale," he finished.

"She told us you can find things," Dana said. "I'm looking for the Book of Dreams."

Fingal scratched the top of his bald head. The rasping noise was like a saw cutting through a tree.

"Can't say as I've heard of it. But there's another one of your lot wandrin' about the place lookin' for a book. Brendan's his name. A saint from the Old Country, travelin' like a sailor in a wee boat. I could find *him* for ye. Maybe you're after the same thing?"

Without waiting for a response, the giant strode from the hills and headed straight for the ocean. He didn't slow down as he reached the seashore, but simply kept going, into the cold waves. Soon Cape Breton was but a shadow behind them.

Cupped in the shelter of Fingal's hands, Jean and Dana peered through the lattice of his fingers. They were striding over the water as if crossing a plain. On their left rose the jagged coastline of Newfoundland. In every other direction swelled the far-flung sea.

"I know some saint," Jean said to Dana. "Who is Brendan?"

"He's an Irish one, " she explained. "Very old. He sailed to Canada in a leather boat, long before the Vikings or the French and English."

She couldn't miss the snort of disbelief.

"It's not as daft as it sounds," she insisted. "An Irishman proved it was possible in the 1970s. Tim Severin. He wrote a book about it."

Jean didn't look convinced. Dana was about to argue the point when the giant made his announcement.

"We're goin' to drop by the girlfriend," he said. His face went red. They could actually see it glowing in the dark. "She'll point us in the right direction."

Now he popped the two of them inside his breast

pocket to protect them from the gale-force winds. The fabric of his shirt was coarse and warm. They could see where they were going by peeping over the edge. The coastline had disappeared. They were engulfed in the darkness of sky and ocean. The stars seemed to drown on the rim of the horizon. They were treading the cold lonely miles of the Atlantic.

When they finally spotted her, a distant figure on the waves, she was like a mirage in the dunes of a watery desert. Huge and stolid, like the Colossus of Rhodes, she stood alone on an outcrop of rock. A gigantic statue, she was coppery bronze, with a greenish sheen wherever the water had tainted her metal. Though she was dressed as a warrior in chain mail and helmet, she bore no weapons. Her features were strong and stern, with metallic eyes that stared blindly out to sea.

As they drew nearer, the great head swiveled on her shoulders.

"We'll be given a few riddles," Fingal warned his companions. "Ye know the drill. No such thing as a free lunch. Ye got to give before ye get."

A surprise test! Dana was alarmed. "What kind of riddles?"

Jean didn't look happy either. "In my *grand-mère's* tales, if you say the wrong thing, it's always bad."

"Don't let it bother a hair on your chinny chin chins," Fingal assured them, though he was gulping nervously.

"A few questions about life, the universe, and everything. Three will do the trick. The magic number. Don't suppose either of ye knows the *Saltair na Rann?*"

They shook their heads. He looked glum.

"Sure nobody reads the oul books nowadays."

He trudged up to the Bronze Lady till they stood face-to-face.

"Greetin's, hen, how's it goin' there?"

The metal jaws clanked as she opened her mouth to speak. Her voice had the timbre of organ pipes in a church.

*"What is the number of the hosts which the light of the clear sky reveals?"*

Fingal scratched his head as he mused upon the question. Dredging deep in his memory, he fished out the answer and produced it proudly.

*"The hosts of the air cannot be numbered."*

The Lady's impassive features warmed ever so slightly. Was there a hint of a smile on those great bronze lips?

*"That is correct."*

Fingal looked pleased as punch, but his face went blank at the next question.

*"What is the name of the multitudes which dwell there on the other side of the solid earth?"*

"Your turn," he hissed to the two in his pocket.

Dana and Jean conferred in a panic.

"Australian peoples?" Jean suggested.

Dana shook her head. Something she had read somewhere? A song or a tale she had heard in Faerie? At last the answer dropped onto her tongue.

"*The Antipodeans!*" she cried.

They were through to the next round and almost there. Jean waited nervously. In all fairness, he knew it was up to him to answer the last question.

"*And the bright sun, whither does it go?*"

Jean grinned with relief. He wasn't the weakest link.

"*À l'ouest*. It goes into the West."

The bronze head nodded for the third and final time.

Jean and Dana let out a cheer along with the giant. They had passed the test!

"Here's our question, m'dear," Fingal said to his girlfriend. "Has ye seen that little Irish monk fella, the one in the skin boat? He came this way once upon a time, if I'm not mistaken."

"Indeed I saw him," she said. "A holy man, a saint, and a mage of power. And he saw me."

A trace of surprise echoed in her voice.

"Can ye tell us where he went?"

"I can."

The Bronze Lady remained still for a while. Fingal waited placidly. He was evidently accustomed to long delays in their discourse.

At last she swiveled on her feet and pointed due north.

"He went thataway."

"Much obliged. Thank ye kindly."

Fingal leaned forward to plant a few slobbery kisses on the metal lady's lips. Hanging over the edge of his pocket, Dana and Jean were caught off guard and nearly fell out. Smothering their laughter, they clambered to safety even as they did their best to ignore the loud noises of the giant's affection.

At last the giant had finished with his farewells and they set off northward.

Dana looked back. In the clear starry night, the Bronze Lady stood stark and glittering above the cold waters. Arms akimbo she moved with heavy grace, pointing in different directions like a gargantuan weather vane.

"Who or what is she directing?" Dana called up to Fingal. "The wind? The waves?"

"Can ye no' see?" The giant was shocked. "That's a great shame now. Ye canny see the beauty of her work. What she does for the soul-birds who wander the world."

"Soul-birds?" Jean frowned. He translated the words in his mind, trying to make sense of them. "The souls of the dead people?"

"Ach no, they go elsewhere. The souls of the living. There always be parts of them flyin' to and fro."

"What?" Dana and Jean said together.

"It's a shame ye canny see them. Can ye not open your eyes a bit wider?"

The giant's words triggered a memory in Dana's mind. *You need but open your heart.* She made an effort to try harder, calling up her fairy sight. Gazing back again across the starlit waters, she finally saw what Fingal was talking about.

All around the bronze figure they flew, like spray from the sea, like flurries of snow. Hundreds and thousands of birds—white birds!—they flocked in circles and lines and spirals. From the four corners of the earth they arrived in droves, flying straight to the Lady. Over and around her and to her they flew, from the tiniest hummingbird the size of an insect to the great whooper swan. There were many that Dana could name—gulls and guillemots, razorbills and fulmars, gannets, puffins, skuas and terns—and there were many she couldn't. Exhausted from their journey, some rested on the Lady's head and shoulders. Others hovered on the wing, waiting for her instructions. What inspired her directions?

Dana was seized by a desire to understand, to know. Were these the birds she had seen in the Medicine Lodge? Were they singing her song? She couldn't hear them. She was too far away. The loss and longing was an ache in her heart. As the yearning to join them grew inside her, she suffered the strangest sensation. The yearning itself emerged from her body in the shape of a white bird. On a rush of wings and wind, it flew over the waves, to meet the others.

Dana found herself in two places at the same time and with two different perspectives. She was still with Jean in the giant's pocket even as she flew with the white bird toward the Lady. The first impression that struck her when she reached the other birds was the overpowering sense of loss. She could hear it in their cries. The call-notes were like sobs. All were grieving for something.

Now as she gazed on the Lady through the white bird's eyes, Dana saw a different figure. No longer a warrior made of metal, she saw a shining angel—*Cara Mia*, Mother Carey—all kindness and love and comfort itself. Her outstretched arms welcomed the weary travelers. She knew each bird and called it by name, knew whence it came and where it would go. Indeed she knew the very number of the feathers it had on each wing. And even as they came to her, she guided them in the right direction, sending them to the place where they would heal.

Like the other birds, Dana wanted to find her place. Could the Lady send her where *she* needed to go? Like a lost lamb to the shepherdess, she rushed toward the outstretched arms. Did the angel smile? There was no doubt that she knew who Dana was. The gentle arm pointed northward, directly at Fingal's back as he trod through the waves. Before Dana knew what had happened, she was fully back in her body.

A wave of disappointment washed over her. She had almost got it! A glimpse of the secret! Something that the

Lady knew. And the soul-birds too. And the Cailleach and her sister, Aoife. *Yes!* The knowledge that the crane sister stole from the Lord of the Sea and the cormorant kept in her black witch's bag. *What was it?* Dana had caught sight of it before, in the language of the land. The truth was all around her, encrypted in code, in the secrets of fairy tales. How could she decipher it?

"What are the soul-birds?" she demanded of Fingal.

"I canny explain, pet. It's too deep for me. Sure ye can ask Brendan when ye meet him. He'll be able to tell ye."

"But you must know something!" she insisted.

Jean frowned and murmured to her. "He don't know a lot. Maybe you ask too much."

Dana relented, aware that the giant was soaked to the waist with the dark waves breaking against him.

As if he had heard Jean's whisper, Fingal shrugged amiably. "Giants aren't the brightest pennies in the purse, doncha know?"

"Are there many giant in Canada?" Jean asked, curiously.

"Oh aye, there be giants everywhere! We were upon the earth from the very beginning. And there's lots of room here, eh? I've heard tell the Old Countries are all landfills and motorways. Here there still be wild places. That's what a giant likes. Plenty of room."

"You know the others?"

"Oh, aye, plenty of them. There be a whole French clan up in the big tunnels of Churchill Falls. Came from

Normandy they did, a long time ago. Used to live in the swamps of Labrador. Hard life, that. Ye get eaten alive by the black flies in the summer and freeze your butt in the winter. They were some happy byes, let me tell ye, when the hydroelectric plant was built and all them tunnels carved. Great place for a giant to live, all snug and out of the weather.

"Then there's Joe Mufferaw out in Renfrew County. Lives in them there hills in the Ottawa Valley. Half-giant, not as big as some, but a good lad. We have to lie low, ye know. Humans don't take too kindly to giants. Could be 'cause some are carnivores. Makes a fella unpopular. I'm vegan myself," he added quickly, when they both gasped audibly. "But there's some likes the taste of human flesh, if ye know what I mean."

"I'm hearing more than I want to," Dana whispered to Jean. She had given up hope of learning about the soul-birds.

But the giant's monologue came to an abrupt end as he let out a yell.

There ahead in the darkness a small boat bobbed on the waves. Absurdly small, it looked like a walnut shell afloat on the ocean. In the dim light, they could barely make out the design on the sail: a Celtic Cross emblazoned in crimson.

"Ahoy, Brendan!" Fingal called.

"Ahoy!" came a hoarse reply.

• • •

The man on watch was the first to see them. Another crawled out from the narrow shelter where he had been sleeping. Both gawped and rubbed their eyes. There was no mistaking what they saw before them: a gigantic grinning man with two small figures who had scrambled onto his shoulder, like tiny parrots.

"Visitors for Brendan," Fingal announced.

And before anyone could react, he deposited his two companions on the deck of the boat and, with a friendly wave, strode away.

# Twenty-Three

The strange boat was not unlike a floating bird's nest. Banana-shaped, with a flat bottom and square sails on double masts, it was an untidy muddle of ropes and equipment. Everything was wet or damp. It had obviously been at sea for some time. The smells were overwhelming: wet leather, musty wool, pungent sheepskin and grease. The astonished crewmen were as bedraggled as their boat. They were long-haired and bearded, and their eyes shone wildly from staring out at the Atlantic too long.

"*Cá bhfuill Naomh Bhreandán?*" Dana asked, assuming that Irish was their language.

The men looked back at her blankly. She and Jean were already suspecting the worst. They noticed the anachronisms around the boat. Yellow tarpaulins covered bow and stern. Sheets of plastic protected electronic equipment. There was a radio telephone and a life-raft dinghy. Hardly the gear of a saint who lived before the Vikings!

"I think," said Dana, slowly, "there's been a mistake."

"Brendan is here?" Jean asked the men.

Once again the sailors looked confounded. Two more

crewmen joined them. One was a tall young man with an easy air of command.

"I'm the skipper," he said in an Anglo-Irish accent. "Tim's my name. That's George with the flashlight, our sailing master. Trondur, there, with the head of curls, is an artist and hunter from the Faroe Islands. The gangly one with the big feet is Arthur. We call him 'Boots.' As for Brendan . . ." Tim made a sweeping gesture with his arm. "*Brendan* is the boat."

Their fears were confirmed. Fingal had left them in the wrong place! Jean looked dismayed. Dana didn't.

"This is the Brendan voyage!" she cried, delighted. "What's the date? What year is it?" she asked the captain.

"It's June 13," he said, puzzled, "1977."

"*Câlisse,*" Jean swore.

"The last trip!" Dana said, excited.

She knew the story well, it was one of her favorites, the life-saver that had helped her survive a dose of chicken pox at age nine. Gabriel had taken a week to read the book to her, as they pored over the maps and photographs in it. The author was the captain himself, Tim Severin. A true tale of heroic adventure, the book described how Tim built a boat of leather and wood, following instructions from a medieval manuscript. Then he set sail with a crew of three men to prove that Brendan the Navigator, an Irish saint, could have reached Canada in the sixth century A.D., long before the Vikings or any other explorers.

Regardless of the mistake Fingal had made, Dana was thrilled.

"You've an Irish accent," Tim said to Dana. He turned to the other Irishman in his crew. "Well, Boots, it's either my dream or yours."

Boots was well over six feet with a shock of yellow hair and a genial air of disorder. The youngest member of the crew, he was also the untidiest, managing to look even more disheveled than the rest.

"Can I not even get away from you lot when I'm havin' a kip?" he responded.

"You're both barmy," said George mildly. "It's not my form to fall asleep on watch. I must be dreaming wide awake."

The other men didn't argue the point. Tall and thin, George was a former English army man, and meticulous about his work and duties.

"Mass hallucination?" Boots suggested.

"Saltwater in the rations?" Tim worried.

Trondur continued to stare at the visitors without speaking. Big and burly, he had the hands of an artisan. He looked like a Norse god with his curls of chestnut hair and bushy beard. From an ancient Faroese family, he was a quiet man, shy to speak English.

"Strange things happen at sea," he said at last, "but I think they are not so much problem."

"Right then," Tim decided, nodding to the newcomers.

"We'll play this out and treat you as guests. Do please join us for supper. You can tell us your story and we'll tell you ours. The past week has been pretty dull. Dream or hallucination, we could do with the diversion."

The crew was pleased with the captain's decision. After braving gales, storms, and rogue waves in their perilous voyage from Iceland to Greenland, the men had found the journey to Labrador cruelly monotonous. Winds from the south along with calms and pea-soup fogs had slowed them to a crawl. With nothing to do and nothing to see, they were badly in need of some entertainment.

While the meal was being prepared, Jean and Dana conferred.

"Do you think the giant come back?" Jean said.

"He's got to," Dana pointed out. "Right boat or not, wouldn't he have to bring us home?"

"We don't ask him this. Only to help us find the book." Jean touched his head. "He's not too smart, eh?"

Despite their dilemma, neither could stay worried, for they were soon immersed in the *Brendan* voyage. The crew gave them sweaters, scarves, and mitts of oiled wool. These helped to ease the wet chill of the Atlantic. Sitting on damp sheepskins, they shared a night picnic, illumined by the ship's lantern high on the mast. All around them heaved the dark swell of the ocean. Overhead spread a vast panoply of stars. Though much of the larder had long been consumed, the offerings of food included smoked sausage and smoked beef with the green mold scraped off, hazelnuts, oat cereal, and the last of a truckle of cheese. There was also dried whale meat and blubber brought on board by Trondur. He hunted at sea, providing them with fish and fulmar.

Dana ate only the nuts and cheese, but Jean was ready to try everything, including a slice of strong-smelling blubber.

"Is good," Trondur assured him. "Very good."

Jean almost gagged. Rubber soaked in machine oil!

Hot drinks finished off the meal, a choice of beef extract, black tea or coffee, along with dessert. The "Skipper's Special" was a tasty sweet mush of stewed apricots, biscuits, and jam.

Jean and Dana leaned against the gunwales, sipping their drinks. They were getting used to the odd feel of the boat. Despite the creaks and the groaning of wood, the overall quiet was profound. The leather muffled the slap of wave against hull. Like a living creature, the boat flexed with the water, and its sides pumped in and out, as if it were breathing. Cupped inside, they felt curiously disembodied, like Jonah swallowed by a whale.

"*Moi*, I have a strange *canot* also," Jean said to the men, looking around with admiration. "How do you make her?"

"Heart of oak, bark of ash," Tim said proudly.

"And forty-nine oxhides to cover the frame," George added, "soaked in oak-bark liquor and coated with wool grease, then hand-stitched together. Our fingers ached for weeks."

"We're depending on two things to stay alive," Tim explained, "our sailing skills and the *Brendan*'s ability to survive at sea. In many ways it was easier for the original Brendan. For one thing, the weather was milder at that time. But more importantly, the saint and his monks were backed by generations of knowledge and experience in the building and sailing of skin boats."

Even as they talked, they heard the low roar of an airplane overhead. It was disorienting to be on an ancient boat out in the ocean with jet planes flying by.

"We are proving that Brendan and his sailor-monks could have done this," Tim insisted. "It's no longer a fairy tale recorded in an old book. Once we cast off in our *Brendan*, we became like Saint Brendan himself. At the mercy of wind and weather, we have delivered ourselves into the hands of Fate, like the *perigrinni* of old."

"*Perigrinni?*" said Jean. "What is this word?"

"Pilgrims. People who set out on a journey for sacred reasons. Usually they're looking for something special or holy, like the Grail or the Isles of the Blessed."

"*Ah oui, je comprends.* This is you, also, *non?*" he said to Dana. "You are *La Pèlerine.*"

Dana liked the title.

The crew wanted to hear their story. Dana and Jean took turns relating it. As the tale of the quest for the Book of Dreams unfolded, the men were enthralled to hear of fairy queens and portals, the *loup-garou* and *la chasse-galerie*, the Cree Old Man and the Medicine Lodge, the Cailleach and Fingal, the Giant.

"If this is a dream, someone here's got one hell of an imagination," said Boots. "Who's been boning up on Canadian folklore?"

Both George and Trondur shrugged. It wasn't them.

Tim regarded his visitors thoughtfully. He wasn't a superstitious man but he was a visionary, someone who was willing to go further than most in thought and action.

"If this is a dream," he said quietly, "it's what Carl Jung calls a Big Dream. We appear to have crossed paths in time and space, in a netherworld between realities. I can see why we've met. Both of us are questing between Ireland and Canada. I believe that each of us is born to do something special in our lives and it's our mission to find out what that thing might be. I was meant to go on this voyage. I've thought about it and planned it since the first time I read the *Navigatio Sancti Brendani Abbatis*. I guess in a way that old manuscript was the book of *my* dream."

Dana's mind was racing. What he said made sense to her. She was about to ask his advice about her own mission when George suddenly sat up, alert.

"We're moving faster!"

"Look lively," said the skipper.

The men were up in an instant and moving quickly. The

sailing master was right. They were no longer traveling a steady course through quiet waters. The boat was speeding along at a clip. The wind had risen and the sea was choppy.

*Crack-crack-crack.*

"Damn! What's that?" cried Boots.

George scurried up the mast with a flashlight to train it on the water.

"Hey, I do believe it's ice!" he shouted. "We're running into ice!"

The boat was hitting lumps of ice at speed. They rattled and crackled against the hull like ice cubes in a glass.

"Drop the sails!" Tim ordered. "We could be knocked to pieces! Our only chance is to stop!"

The crew worked frantically to lower the sails, but the boat was still speeding. George climbed higher up the mast and shone the flashlight over the water.

They were surrounded! Caught in a floe of icebergs! The grotesque sculptures were of every size and shape. They muttered and grumbled as they rubbed against each other on the waves. It was like a herd of sea monsters growling at the boat, out there in the cold night.

"This ice shouldn't be here," Tim swore. "I know the ice chart by heart." Then a slow horror dawned. "If a freak gale swept over the main sheet along Labrador, it could crack the whole thing open!"

Jean and Dana, who were doing their best to keep out of the crew's way, exchanged glances.

"Crowley?" Jean muttered.

"Could be," Dana said anxiously. "Didn't Grandfather say he could call up storm demons?"

"Big one dead ahead!" George cried.

Tim pulled the tiller as far as it would go to steer around the huge chunk, but no luck. *Crash.* It was like hitting concrete. Everyone staggered with the shock. Now a series in succession. *Thump! Thump! Thump!* A quick battering and the boat spun away. Worse loomed directly in front of them. A berg twice the size of the boat rolled in the water like a hippopotamus.

"Hang on tight!" Tim roared.

As they struck head-on, the boat tremored with the impact. George was flung off the mast. Hanging on to the halyard and dangling in midair, he was in danger of being crushed between the ice and the boat.

Trondur rushed to help him down.

*Crash!*

Another collision. The loud protest of wood.

Could the *Brendan* survive this punishment?

There was no escape. They were hemmed in by pack ice, mile after mile, floe after floe, driven toward them by gale and current. There was nothing they could do but fend off the attack as best they could, using wooden poles and their own hands and feet.

On the roof of the shelter, arm around the mainmast for support, George acted as lookout.

"Two on the port bow! Another to the starboard side! Mind the gap!"

Above all else, the *Brendan* had to avoid being caught when the ice bumped together. The boat would burst like a ripe plum.

For an interminable time, they wove in and out of the floes, clattering over tabletops of ice or scraping along the sides. As Tim said himself, it was "a cross between bumper cars and a country square dance."

Sick with worry, gazing out at the ice, Dana suddenly saw Crowley's features leering at her.

Then the squall struck.

Down came freezing rain and hailstones, cracking like bullets off the tarpaulins. The water rose ominously. Waves began to thrash and pound the boat. Deep troughs would threaten to swallow them only to toss them over the crests in a welter of foam. The full strength of the Atlantic was being hurled against them.

Veterans of sea storms, the crew reacted calmly and efficiently. They pulled on foul-weather gear and threw spare oilskins to Dana and Jean. With hoods drawn over their faces like cowls, all of them looked like monks.

"Trondur, handle the headsail sheets!" the skipper shouted. "Boots, take the mainsail and look after the leeboards. George, you're the best helmsman, take over steering. I'll handle the pilotage. This is going to be tricky."

The wind was rising rapidly. So, too, were the waves.

With a thunderous roar, a solid sheet of water crashed into the boat. *Water water everywhere.* The bilge was filled to the brim. The cabins were awash. They were too low in the sea. Water lapped over the gunwales, sloshing back and forth in the boat. As the bilge pump squirted it back into the ocean, Jean and Dana bailed with pots and saucepans. No one had to tell them that survival time in freezing water was five minutes or less. They could feel the threat of death lurking in the night.

Tim stood near Dana, eyes red with exhaustion and the sting of salt spray. His voice echoed a moment of despair.

"What on earth are we doing out here in this lonely half-frozen part of the Atlantic?"

"Following a dream," she said.

He managed a smile and nodded. "Times like this you really have but one choice. Whatever will happen will happen, so you either face it as a coward, or you face it as a hero. It's up to you."

The sinister dance with the ice went on for hours. Yet despite the battering and the drenching rain, the deadly cold and numbing fatigue, the little boat held. Three things kept them alive. Along with the *Brendan*'s ability to survive at sea and the skill of its sailors, there was a third factor. Courage.

Then their luck ran out.

And the worst that could happen did happen.

The *Brendan* was trapped between two icebergs as

if caught in a vise. The boat shuddered like a wounded animal. Everyone rushed to push the boat free. Too late. The damage was already done. Seawater swirled in the bottom of the boat.

"We've sprung a leak!" George cried.

Trondur agreed. His voice echoed doom. "I think stitching is broken by ice. Water in stern of *Brendan* is not so much problem. Water in bow is big problem."

Tim looked around frantically. "It could be anywhere! We won't find it in the dark."

Climbing under the protective plastic that sheltered the radio, he put in a call to the Canadian Coast Guard. In calm terse tones he warned them to stand by for a Mayday call. But they all knew the truth. If they went down, no one could reach them in time.

"We'll have to work the pump and wait for first light," he announced. "Then we find the tear and fix it."

No one groaned at the thought of more work. No one questioned how they could make repairs while the boat was still in the water. Whatever would happen, would happen.

Through the last hours of the night, while the storm raged around them, they worked the bilge pumps. Two thousand strokes per hour were needed to keep the boat afloat. Though they were all worn out from fighting the storm and the ice, they took turns.

Dana did her share. Holding her breath, she squirmed

through the dark wet tunnel of tarpaulin to reach the handle of the pump. They had told her to keep turning till her arm got sore, then switch hands. Already aching with tiredness before she began, she managed to follow instructions. The mechanical motion rocked her back and forth. Though wet and frozen with cold, she soon worked up a sweat. Her oilskins were discarded. The monotony of the action was almost as painful as the wear on her muscles. She counted her portion of strokes to help her keep going. No matter how bad it got, she wouldn't give up. She knew what the crew couldn't know: that she was to blame. The ice and the storm had been created because of her.

At last her turn was done. When she crawled out of the space, the men gave her a cheer. Eyes bleary, exhausted, she staggered to her feet.

"What's that?" Boots called from the bow. "Do you hear it?"

Something large was moving through the water toward them.

Dana's heart sank. What would Crowley send now? They couldn't take much more.

Then it emerged, through the hail and the waves, the big familiar shape of Fingal the Giant.

"Ahoy, *Brendan!*" he called.

"Ahoy!" Tim called back.

"Got the wrong boat!" Fingal shouted. His round face

hung over them like a friendly moon. "The girlfriend set me right. Got to go further back in time. So if ye don't mind, I'll just take my little friends, thank ye kindly."

Dana turned to Tim and the rest of the crew. They were long past questioning what was happening around them. Red-eyed and spent, they were barely managing to keep on their feet.

"It's almost dawn," she told them. "When the light comes and the weather lets up, you'll find the leak."

"We don't go!" Jean protested. "Like rats from a ship who sink!"

"We must," Dana argued. "Crowley sent the ice and the storm. He's after me, not them. They won't be safe till we leave."

Jean did not look happy. It was his turn on the pump. The *Brendan* needed the extra hands to work it.

"They'll be okay," Dana insisted. "I remember this part of the story. They find where it's torn and they mend it in the water. They survive and the boat survives. But maybe they won't if we stay!"

Though he still wasn't happy, Jean accepted her logic. Shaking hands with the men, he wished them all the best and safe home.

Dana attempted to reassure them as she said good-bye.

"The storm will stop as soon as we go. I'm sorry we brought you bad luck. Things'll get better. I can tell you this, honestly, I know all of you as heroes."

Their haggard faces lit up. Hope would keep them going.

Fingal scooped up Jean and Dana and popped them into his pocket. With a final wave, he strode away, leaving the *Brendan* behind in the mists.

Dana could see the guilt on Jean's face.

"They'll make it," she assured him. "At the end of the book, the Newfoundlanders threw them a *céilí*, a big party that went on all night."

The two snuggled inside Fingal's pocket. After the cold and wet of the boat, it was gloriously dry and warm. Outside, the gale howled.

"Will Crowley fight the giant?" Jean wondered.

It wasn't long before his question was answered.

"Hould on to yer britches," Fingal called to them suddenly, "here comes trouble!"

A violent lurch followed his words. The giant was under attack. The two scrambled to look out. As Dana had predicted, the storm had left the *Brendan* to pursue her instead. Now it raged against Fingal. The waves rose in a towering frenzy to match his size, then collapsed against him with vicious intent. Spume erupted like geysers. There was no doubt about who or what was driving the storm. Crowley's visage screeched in the squall.

"*No!*" screamed Dana.

Fingal floundered. His eyes were blinded by water

and he was thrown off balance. Arms flailing in the foam, he tried to tread water, but the waves pushed him under with malicious glee. It was a fight to the death. Though he struggled manfully, even the giant knew that the storm was killing him.

He sank beneath the surface. Water rushed into his pocket. Dana and Jean were thrown into the sea. They spluttered and kicked, attempting to swim. The water was too cold, too wild. There was nothing they could do to save themselves. Sucked into the icy foam, they were choking, somersaulting, drowning.

A big hand plunged into the deep and grasped the two of them. Now they were pulled from the brink and held high.

Fingal would not let them drown. Not while there was breath in his body.

A mountain of water crashed against him. It was the ninth wave. The one all sailors dread. The one that takes you down to Davy Jones's Locker. Despair darkened his eyes, as the giant began to sink for the last time.

But just when all seemed lost and the twist in the tale was a tragic ending, hope sailed over the horizon in a leather boat. From its mast flew a sail emblazoned with the sign of the Celtic Cross. In its bow stood a man garbed in the robes of a monk. His arms were outstretched to the heavens as he prayed out loud to banish the storm.

# Twenty-Four

Fingal's head was disappearing under the waves when the leather boat reached him. In the bow, the medieval monk stood fast, holding a wooden cross aloft. The monk's brown cloak swirled around him in the wind. His face was lost in the shadows of a deep cowl, but his prayers rang out with power and clarity.

The squall gathered in force like a tornado and charged toward him.

For a second, both were frozen in time: the monk holding his cross and the raging storm. Then came an explosion of light.

The sudden calm was profound. The seas lay still. A warm breeze played gently over the lapping water. Morning had arrived in a rosy glow.

The giant righted himself in the water and leaned over the little boat. Once again the monk lifted his cross.

"Death is above you!" cried the saint. "What is your ransom?"

"I hain't with the storm demon," Fingal hurried to explain. "I've a couple of pilgrims to join ye. Will they do? Ye're Saint Brendan the Navigator, am I right?"

The giant and the monk were both speaking Gaelic. Dana translated for Jean, and the two waited anxiously for Brendan's reply.

The saint's eyes flashed from the depths of his cowl.

"I have the Two Sights," Brendan declared. "I am able to see in the world of the body and the world of the soul. The Second Sight tells me that you are good. Your spirit shines brightly."

The giant blushed with pleasure. "Thank ye kindly. That's a great compliment comin' from a saint."

Gently, Fingal lowered Dana and Jean onto the boat.

"If he canny help ye, no one can," Fingal told them, switching to English. "He's a magus and a Druid. Ye saw his power over the winds and the water."

"I also have the Gift of Tongues," Brendan interjected in English. "That was not my power you saw, but the power of my God. He is *Dia duilech*, God of the Elements, even as he is *Coimdiu na nduile*, Lord of Creation."

"Well, ye've got power on your side, then. Would ye be on for givin' them a hand?"

"I will if I can," Brendan replied.

"I'm off, then," said Fingal.

"Thank you so much!" Dana called out to him. "Will we meet again?"

"When the Kingdom is restored," boomed the giant.

"*Merci beaucoup!*" called Jean.

"*À bientôt, mon ami.*" The giant's reply sailed over the water as Fingal disappeared into the distance.

How strange it was to find themselves on the original of the boat that would one day be called *Brendan!* Constructed of oxhide stretched over a wood frame, it was surprisingly like the one they had left behind in the future. But this boat was much greater in size, could almost be called a ship, and had a bigger crew. It was also more at home on the ocean. Dry and even cozy, the craft was not as open to the elements as the modern version. Two huts of woven wattle stood on deck, reminiscent of an ark. The large one amidships housed the crew, while the smaller one in the stern was the private quarters of the saint. The huts were round in shape, like the beehive cells hermits used in Ireland. Overhead, sheets of tanned leather hung between the masts to catch rainwater for drinking. Dried fish and plucked birds dangled from poles and lines. Bags of grain and other provisions were stowed under the gunwales.

Like Brendan, the crew were also monks. Eight were awake and manning the vessel, while an additional four slept off watch. Their clerical garb had been adapted for sailing. The wool tunics were like long sweaters over baggy trousers, all oiled and waterproof. Most of the crew were country men with raw red faces weathered by the elements. They moved about the boat with the ease of experienced sailors.

"You are welcome here," Brendan said to Jean and Dana. Only now did he uncover his head. As the cowl fell behind him, the two gasped. Dana almost laughed out loud. No wonder Tim was haunted by Brendan's voyage! For here he stood again, an older version of himself, still tall and slim, but with lines in his face and streaks of silver in his hair. The eyes were the same, shining with an unquenchable thirst for adventure. He was dressed like his crew with the addition of the broad mantle that marked his status as abbot. Like the other monks, he wore the Celtic tonsure, head shaven from forehead to mid-pate, with long hair falling onto his shoulders.

Taking in the plight of his visitors, who stood wet and shivering before him, Brendan gave orders to his men.

"Dry clothes for our guests, then bring them to my cabin. Bring also food and drink."

After their dousing in the frozen Atlantic, it was heaven to pull on the rough dry fabric of the monkish clothes. The weave was tight and thick, providing instant warmth.

"So Brendan is Tim!" Dana said to Jean. "I wonder if the others are here?"

"We look for them." Jean nodded.

After they had changed, Dana in the cabin and Jean out on deck, the two were taken to Brendan's hut. The wattle-and-daub structure was built to keep out wind and rain. It was warm and snug, with rush mats on the floor, woven hassocks for seats, and a brazier burning clumps of sod. A low table held the monk's writing materials:

feathered quills, sheaves of parchment, and pots of pigment and ink.

Brendan directed them to sit as their food arrived. There was hot mint tea sweetened with honey and a platter of fruit and unleavened bread. They were both exhausted, but the refreshment revived them, as did the mischievous grin of the cook. By far the tallest of the crew, he was well over six feet and had to stoop as he entered the cabin. He also had enormous feet encased in hide boots.

"Boots!" cried Dana.

"What name is this?" he said, laughing. "I am called Artán. 'Little Art' it means."

That made everyone laugh.

The food he brought was delicious. The grapes were as big as apples, and though the bread was unleavened, which called for a lot of chewing, it was seasoned with herbs. There was an odd purple-and-white fruit the size of a football that dripped with juice. It was like nothing they had seen or tasted before, with a mixture of flavors that hinted of strawberries, blueberries, plums, and oranges.

"A gift from the heavens," Brendan told them. "The fruit was brought to us by a flock of white birds singing celestial hymns."

"The white birds again!" Dana exclaimed.

The saint studied her closely. A silver rim formed around the irises of his eyes, like a corona around the moon. The Second Sight. In a melodic voice, he chanted.

*Are your horns the horns of cattle?*
*Are your ales the ale of Cualu?*
*Is your land the Curragh of the plain of Liffey?*
*Are you the descendant of a hundred kings and queens?*
*Is your church Kildare?*
*Do you keep house with Brigid and Patrick?*

Jean looked at her dismayed. More riddles? But Dana understood the nature of the questions.

"It's a greeting. He's just asking if I'm Irish and what province do I come from."

She answered the saint in the same formal manner.

"I am of Ireland and the holy land of Ireland. I am of the province of Leinster that is the plain of Liffey. But my companion is not. He is from—" She paused. What did the early Irish call the land to the west?—"*An tOileán Ur,*" she finished. The New Island.

The saint was satisfied with her response. "The giant declared you pilgrims, and the Second Sight tells me this is true. Are you practicing *ban martre?*"

It was Dana's turn to be dismayed. She could translate the words literally but had no idea what they meant. *White martyrdom?* They obviously referred to something medieval that she knew nothing about.

Brendan saw her confusion and explained, "There are three kinds of martyrdom that pilgrims practice. In *glas martre*, green martyrdom, you become a hermit or ascetic.

You give up the comforts and delights of life such as family, friends, food, drink. In *derc martre*, red martyrdom, you shed your blood in God's name. A noble death. *Ban martre*, white martyrdom, is exile. You leave your home, perhaps forever, and journey for a divine cause."

"You could say I'm in exile," Dana said, thinking about both Ireland and Faerie, "and what I'm looking for, the Book of Dreams, is something special."

"You are looking for a book?" Brendan's voice was both astonished and eager.

With great excitement, he produced a jeweled box from his desk. Inside was a manuscript of fine parchment. The vellum sheaves were inscribed with gold orpiment and illustrated with ornate borders and drawings in colored inks.

"The manuscript is composed of quinions," Brendan said proudly, "quires of five sheets laid on top of each other and folded. Hence a gathering of ten leaves makes twenty pages."

Dana's heart beat wildly. "Is it the Book of Dreams?"

She could hardly believe it. Her quest fulfilled! Just like that! But her joy was quickly dampened.

"No, my child," he said gently. "It is *The Book of Wonders*. The very reason why I am on this *imram*, this voyage upon the sea which is also a pilgrimage. I will tell you my tale."

As Brendan spoke, they followed his words through the manuscript, where pictures depicted what he described.

There he was, a younger man, the renowned abbot and founder of many monasteries. An accomplished sailor, he had already traveled to Wales, Scotland, and the Orkney Islands. One day he was doing his rounds in the great monastery at Clonfert, where three thousand monks lived under his rule. Psalms rose from the nave of the church. Pots and dishes clattered in the kitchens. Men delved with hoe and spade in the vegetable gardens.

When he came to the scriptorium, Brendan lingered a little longer. This was his favorite place. He liked to watch the monks at their work, dipping their goose-feathered quills into ink-horns and trimming nibs with their pen knives. The pages of vellum were carefully cut, then ruled with lines. Colored powders were mixed with water to make ink. Most of the young scribes copied psalters or gospels for use in the monastic schools. Only a chosen few, the most gifted artists, illuminated the manuscripts prized by Christendom. The monks wrote in Latin and Old Irish and a hybrid Hiberno-Latin. It was a labor of love, but once in a while they noted their complaints, jotting personal glosses along the margins.

*Is scith mo chrob on scribainn.*
My hand is weary with writing.
*Tria digita scribunt, totus corpora laborat.*
Three fingers write, but the whole body labors.

• • •

Brendan stopped at the desk of a young scribe new to the monastery. As he leaned down to peruse the monk's work, the shock on the abbot's face told a tale in itself. The scribe was recording the story of a fabulous journey across the sea to a magical land behind a rampart of fire.

Brendan was incensed. "I do not credit the details of this fantasy!" he cried. "Some things in it are devilish lies and some poetical figments. Some may be possible but others are certainly not. Some are for the enjoyment of idiots!"

As he finished his tirade, he seized the pages of the manuscript and flung them into the burning hearth. The young monk hung his head in shame. The others continued to scribble silently, without looking up. Brendan was the abbot. His word was law.

But that night, in his bed, the saint had a dream. He was standing at the front of the monastery chapel. From overhead came the sound of wings. A great bird settled on the altar. Shining with light, it had the shape of an albatross and the wingspan of a swan.

"A blessing upon you, priest," said the bird.

Brendan fell to his knees. "Are you the Paraclete?" he asked, bowing his head.

"I am the archangel Michael, sent to chastise you for destroying the book. Who are you to question the wonders of life? Between heaven and earth, more things exist than you can know of. Who are you to doubt the boundless power of the Creator?"

It was the saint's turn to hang his head in shame.

Now the angel charged Brendan with a mission. He was to set off on a sea voyage to seek out the marvels described in the very manuscript that he had burned. By recording all that he saw and experienced, he would restore *The Book of Wonders* for the glory of God. And not until he found the Land of Promise could he return home to Ireland, for only then would the book be completed.

Jean and Dana turned page after page of the manuscript. Each adventure on the voyage was more exciting than the last. There was an island where it was always dark, but the soil was lit up by glittering carbuncles. Then came the Liver Sea, a nightmare of still waters that held the boat fast. Only when prayers from Brendan called up a wind were they able to sail free. In a smoke-filled land where volcanoes spewed ashes, the inhabitants threw lumps of coal to chase the sailor monks away. Friendlier than humans were the herds of sea monsters who surrounded the boat.

"Whales!" said Jean, when he saw the illustration.

"This is the seventh year of my pilgrimage," Brendan said. "Many wonders have I seen and recorded, but *Tír Tairngire*, the Land of Promise, eludes me still. Thus my voyage continues without end, for a journey is not completed until one goes home."

He returned the manuscript to its jeweled box.

"And so you see," he concluded with wry humility,

"the penitent became a pilgrim and the pilgrim a writer. Today I shall transcribe the tale of the giant who brought me two young visitors. You will be part of *The Book of Wonders*."

Dana was taken aback. An idea struck her that made her head spin.

"Could I be like you?" she wondered. "Am I creating the Book of Dreams while I'm searching for it?"

"The dreamer is the dream?" murmured Jean.

Brendan folded his hands in front of him and gazed at Dana thoughtfully.

"To what end do you travel?" he asked her. "I know my destination. *Tír Tairngire*, the Land of Promise. It is a place where there is no grief or sorrow, no sickness or death."

His words sent a shiver through her. The description fitted Faerie exactly! Were she and the saint trying to reach the same place? The manuscript he had burned sounded like a book of fairy tales. Dana's head was spinning. He was in her tale even as she was in his! "If I'm writing my own book," she thought to herself, "I could be a third or even halfway through by now!"

"I think we're going the same way," she said, finally. "I think we're on the same quest."

The monk smiled at her serenely.

"Indeed, my daughter, we are all going the same way. We are all on the same quest. For life itself is a peregrination through a foreign land and we are all traveling Home."

"I understand what you say," Jean spoke up. "It make my heart want to fly like a bird."

The saint rested his hands on their heads. Though they couldn't describe what they felt, each suddenly wanted to be quiet and alone.

"Go now and rest, my children. Leave all your worries aside. I will pray and meditate upon this matter. The next step we take, we take together."

Out on deck, Dana and Jean were surprised at how mild was the weather and how tranquil the ocean. Warm breezes bathed their faces. The water lapped against the leather hull, rocking the boat gently like a cradle.

"It's just like Tim said," Dana pointed out. "The climate was nicer at this time."

A voice called out from the lookout near the top of the mainmast.

"*Na péistí! Ansin!*"

"Sea monsters!" said Dana.

The rest of the crew stopped what they were doing and hurried to see. Some looked frightened, but most seemed merely curious.

"There!" Jean cried.

The ocean was alive with leaping bodies. Their appearance was sudden and miraculous, a natural wonder of the far-flung seas. The first to arrive were dolphins, gamboling in the waves like calves in a field. Then came the white-bellied whales that surfaced in bursts of spray before diving again with a huge flick of their tails. To watch them was sheer delight!

One of the monks began to chant quietly. Words and phrases drifted through the air as he quoted from the Bible where it described the leviathan. *His eyes are like the eyelids of the morning. Sorrow is turned into joy before him. He maketh the deep to boil like a pot. He maketh a path to shine after him. Upon earth there is not his like.*

Jean's eyes shone like the sky. After the school had passed them, he breathed a deep sigh.

*"Magique, n'est-ce pas?"*

Dana knew what he meant. Wasn't this what the saint was sent to discover? The beauty of the world? The wonder of creation?

Nearby, two of the crew began to quarrel. One was a big burly man with curls of brown hair. He clutched a manuscript bound with wooden boards. The other was tall and thin with piercing eyes. He had taken a book out of a white satchel. Both were agitated as they pointed at the whales who swam in the distance.

"Never mind those two, they are always at it," Artán said, joining Jean and Dana.

He leaned on the gunwales with a genial grin.

"What are they arguing over?" Dana asked him.

"Brother Sigisbert has a book he copied in Wales. *The Liber Monstrorum,* a catalogue of curious and unusual animals. He's an unusual animal himself, being a Christian Saxon. All his people are pagans. Brother Fnör, from the land of Thule, has a book from his own country. The *Physiologus* is a bestiary of fabulous creatures. They like to argue, you see, over the names of the animals we meet in our travels."

Dana and Jean laughed as they recognized the two men. Sigisbert was a dead ringer for the sailing master, George, while Fnör was the spitting image of Trondur.

Some people are destined to be together, Dana reflected. She glanced sideways at Jean. Didn't she feel the same way about him?

"Do you get homesick?" she asked Artán, who was so like Boots.

"There are times when I long for the green hills of Ireland," he admitted. "It has been seven years since I last saw them. But I am a monk of Brendan. I would follow him to the ends of the earth. And I suppose," the eyes sparkled with mischief, "I am to blame for this voyage."

"How—?" Dana stopped when the truth struck her. "You're the young monk who was writing the fairy tales!"

"*Mea culpa,*" he said with a nod.

"Where do you get the story?" Jean asked him. "Do you make yourself?"

Artán's features softened as he gazed out to sea. It was obvious he was remembering something.

"I was not always a monk," he said with a little smile.

Jean grinned as he understood. *"Ah oui, je comprends."*

"What?" said Dana. "What?"

They kept laughing and teasing her, but at last Artán confessed.

"It was before I took orders," he explained. "I met a beautiful girl one day in the woods. She stole my heart and almost my soul. I had to choose if I would stay in this world or join her in another." He let out a sigh. "I made my decision, yet I never forgot the wondrous tales she told me, or the beautiful songs she sang. It was these I recorded in the scriptorium, when I should have been copying the Epistles of Saint Paul."

Dana smiled at his chagrin. "It's just as well you did," she pointed out. "Think of what you would have missed!"

"Did the abbot not order the two of you to rest?" Artán said suddenly. "On this boat, as in the monastery, we must obey him."

After all their adventures, a rest was welcome. They slept for hours in the crew's hut, on mattresses of down as soft as any duvet. At noon, Artán brought them steaming chowder, hot griddle-cakes, and cheese.

As it contained fish, Dana gave her soup to Jean.

"Do I dream this?" Jean said. "Hot food on the boat?"

"When the seas are calm we enjoy our comforts." Artán grinned. "I can light a fire in the big cauldron and cook over it with smaller pots. When you are finished here, you must go to Brendan."

Artán handed them their clothes, which had been hung out to dry earlier. Reluctantly, they traded the loaned woolens for their synthetic fabrics.

Refreshed from their rest, they returned to Brendan's cabin. The saint was looking livelier too. His eyes flashed with excitement.

"A new adventure awaits us! After deep prayer, I have been guided to the way we must go. In *The Book of Wonders* there was a tale about an Island of Glass. This island is the sacred abode of a mighty female spirit who is served by a Druidess. In that cold, white country, there comes a day when the sun does not rise and yet another day when it does not set."

Brendan closed his eyes for a moment as he chanted.

*There is an ancient tree in blossom there,*
*On which the birds call out the hours of life.*

"The birds again!" said Dana. "They've been following me from the beginning. Whatever they mean, they're important to the quest."

"What is this word 'Druidess'?" Jean asked.

"That is the Irish name for her," Brendan replied. "She is called *angakuk* by her own people. She has certain powers and can walk between the worlds."

"*Ah oui, jongleuse,*" said Jean, "like the Old Man."

"A shaman," Dana said thoughtfully. "Isn't that what you are too?" she asked Brendan. "Didn't the giant call you a mage?"

The abbot shook his head vigorously. "Before this journey, I did not even credit such things! I was a monk, a scholar, the founder of monasteries, but nothing out of the ordinary." His grimace was both rueful and amused. "Look at me now after one touch of an angel! I have the Second Sight and the Gift of Tongues, I am a sailor tossed upon the ocean in search of marvels, an explorer, and a writer of fabulous tales." He let out a chuckle. "But no, I am not a mage, though many think me so. I am simply a man who follows God's will."

Out on deck, Brendan barked his instructions like any skipper. Where the boat had been sailing in a leisurely fashion toward the south, they now tacked in the wind and pointed north. The change in course had an instant effect. No longer sluggish in the water, the craft took flight like a bird on the wing, clipping along at speed.

Brendan looked pleased. "As always when one goes in the right direction, things become easier."

They smelled the ice before they saw it, a cold breath

that frosted the air. It wasn't long before small chunks were rattling against the hull like cubes in a tumbler. In the distance, a jagged floe moved slowly like a herd of white beasts across the plain of the ocean.

"The Sea of Glass," Brendan said with quiet awe, "even as the book described it!"

The cold began to seep into their bones. Artán handed out blankets to be worn as cloaks.

Directly ahead of them a mountainous land came into view. As they drew nearer, they saw it was covered with snow. Between the land and the boat, the river of icebergs rose up like a barrier.

The crew needed all their skill to maneuver the boat through the floe. The deadly lure and majesty of the ice was breathtaking. Some pieces were sculptures of clear crystal; others were opaque white. The underwater ledges glowed a deep green, while the crags above the surface were a glacial blue.

"Look for a crystal pillar," Brendan ordered, "with a wide net. That will point the way to go."

Everyone kept watch till at last it was sighted: a shining column of ice surrounded by churning water. Flakes of frazil fanned out around it, looking indeed as if the ice were meshed. Landfall was in sight. In a straight line from the pillar, as if it were a transit buoy, they could see the sheltering fjord on the coast.

Not a word was spoken as the boat sailed into the

natural harbor. The stillness and beauty of the landscape was profound. They were approaching the edge of a glacier where bergs calved into the sea. The water was a silvery blue. A cliff of white ice towered above them. Behind it sheered a stark line of mountains draped in cold mist.

Sigisbert dug out a ledge in the wall of ice and rammed a plank into it, forming a gangway from the boat to the glacier. Fnör gave them fur jackets as well as crude snowshoes. The latter he hung from their backs until they had need of them.

"Gifts from the land of Thule," he said.

Despite the protests of his monks, Brendan insisted that only he and his guests would go.

The glacier was not as difficult to climb as Dana and Jean had feared. The ice was quite solid, and layered in places to grant their feet purchase. Where it was too smooth for climbing, the saint went first with a sharp knife to carve out footholds. Like Good King Wenceslas's page, the two younger ones followed in his steps. At last they reached the plain above.

An arctic panorama spread out before them. A vast land with a backbone of mountain. Frozen peaks and glacial valleys, ice fields and nunataks, all ranged silent and cloaked in snow. There was no sign of life, either human or animal, in that great white landscape.

"Where on earth are we?" Dana said. Her breath

streamed frostily in front of her. "Are we even on the earth?"

Jean glanced up as he strapped on his snowshoes. He knew where he was. The recognition had sounded in his heart and soul.

"It's Canada," he said. "*Le Nord.*"

# Twenty-Five

Jean finished lacing his snowshoes and stood up.

"This is Île Baffin, I think. Part of Nunavut. We sail north of Labrador, *n'est-ce pas?*"

"That makes sense," Dana said, thinking about it. "And it explains the Glass Sea and the pillars of ice in Brendan's legend."

She had finally managed to strap on her snowshoes and was ready to take her first steps. Moments later she was facedown in the snow.

Jean hurried over to help her up, trying not to laugh.

Her face was caked with powdery snow. She spluttered and spat as she laughed.

"It's all very well for you," she said. "You're used to this. We hardly ever get snow in Ireland. I feel like I'm wearing tennis rackets on my feet."

"It will get more easy," he assured her. "But if you walk too much you get *mal de raquette*. I tell you when to rest. *Mais vite*, we must hurry."

Brendan had gone ahead of them, gliding over the snow in his long monk's cloak like a ragged brown swan.

He wore a floppy-brimmed pilgrim's hat and carried a wooden staff. On his back was a satchel packed with provisions.

They set out after him, tramping across the snowy plain toward the craggy chine of mountains in the distance.

"Does anyone else live here?" Dana asked Jean. "I mean, besides the shaman? Are there Eskimos here?"

"This is the land of the Inuit. Their name mean 'the People.' They live here for many thousand of year. 'Eskimo' is a name the Montagnais give them that mean 'Fish-Eater.'"

Dana groaned. "There are so many races here. I'll never get them right."

Jean laughed. "This is good about Canada, *non*? All the peoples."

They chatted companionably as they hiked through the snow. It was their first chance in a while to really talk together, as the quest had taken up most of their time. Jean asked about her background. Dana told him about her childhood in a small town in Ireland, how she was raised alone by her father till she was twelve.

"That was a big year. Imagine discovering you're the daughter of a fairy queen!"

"Like I find I am *loup-garou*," he said. "At the same time wonderful and terrible."

"Exactly!" she agreed. "Then we came to Canada. I thought I would like it here. I left everything I knew behind, our house, our street, my school, my friends. Things just got worse and worse. I so wanted to go home. I hated it here."

Dana looked around at the glittering scene of snow and mountain, the clarity of blue sky and brilliant light. "I thought there was no magic here."

He stopped to gaze into her eyes that shone with the same blue brilliance as the sky above. "Who whisper this lie to you?"

She caught her breath. "My enemy?"

"Perhaps." He shrugged. "Or maybe it was you, eh? You tell yourself the lie because you want to believe it?"

She heard the pain behind his words, something to do with himself and not her. "What lie have you told yourself?"

He recoiled in that moment, caught off guard. Then he smiled sadly.

"That *grand-père* will one day be human again."

They continued chatting as they hiked, but eventually silence fell between them and the only sound was their breath rasping in the thin air. As the hours passed, their fingers and toes began to freeze, despite the thick wrappings. They could feel the chill of the air burning their lungs. The white glare of the snow threatened to blind them. They pulled their hoods down low over their faces. There was nothing to look at but their own feet stepping one in front of the other. The adventure was no longer exciting, but something to endure with every passing minute.

At last they reached the end of the ice field. Before them rose another wall of ice and snow, the end of a glacier that had streamed down the mountain. It was much higher than the one they had scaled in the fjord.

"We can't climb that," Dana said, dismayed.

Brendan agreed, and made no effort to ascend. Instead, he walked alongside the icy cirque.

They followed behind him.

"*It is enough to write the rough white cradles in the snow,*" he murmured to himself.

"That's lovely," said Dana. "What does it mean?"

The saint's features were ruddy in the cold. His eyes shone, silver-rimmed.

"It is something I dreamed. But I believe it means that she is somewhere here, cradled within."

More hours passed in that day of endless light and still they tramped beside the glacier. Dana had long since admitted to herself that she wished they hadn't come north. If only they had gone in a different direction! She could no longer feel her fingers or toes. Could she have frostbite? She was also beginning to doubt the saint's wisdom. Had he brought them on a wild-goose chase? Then at last they saw something.

It was like a miracle in that barren land: a branching tree rimed with frost.

"That is the sign," Brendan said happily, rubbing his hands together. *"There is an ancient tree in blossom there, on which the birds call out the hours of life."*

That there was neither blossom nor bird on the tree didn't matter, for they had spotted the opening in the ice just behind it. The jagged crack in the glacier was large enough for a person to enter.

Removing their snowshoes, they squeezed one by one through the crevice. Inside, they found a chamber with scalloped walls that emitted a cold blue light. Melodious sounds echoed frostily: the crinkling of ice and the chime of falling water. On every side, fissures laced the walls, branching out in snowflake patterns that made tunnels in the glacier.

Brendan chose a passageway and entered boldly.

"We must travel hopefully in the belief that all paths lead to the source."

Time seemed to stand still inside that translucent passage. From time to time they were startled to spy dark figures frozen in the ice: a woolly mammoth, an arctic fox, and once even a hunter, caught by death with his spear in his hand. Dana let out a cry when she saw him. Would they be trapped in the ice too? That was when Jean took her hand. She steadied herself. Somehow it was easier to accept hardship when he was beside her.

At long last the passageway brought them to what they sought. They knew they had arrived at the *angakuk*'s cave when they saw her handiwork, the first sign of humanity on the island. The archway into the cave was decorated with pieces of stone and bone in intricate designs that complemented the ice. Stooping to enter, they stepped inside.

It was like being at the heart of a frozen cloud. The cave glimmered with ice draperies and embroidered snow. Ledges in the walls held a profusion of objects—the whorled horn of a narwhal, the tusks of a walrus, stone implements and carved statues, harpoons and knives. The floor was covered with the furs of white seal and polar bear.

The strange beauty of the cave was captivating, but it was the woman who sat inside it that held their instant attention.

Brown and wizened like an autumn leaf, she appeared to be incalculably old. Her eyes were black stones set in Asiatic features. Her grin was toothless. The skins of the caribou hung loosely on her body. An ornate headdress of beads dangled over her face. Across her shoulders fell a mantle of gray-and-white feathers.

As she looked upon the *angakuk*, Dana felt a wave of terror. The power she could sense in the old woman was alien to her. Not of Faerie. Not of Ireland. Not even of Canada. Here was an ancient one of a different race, a different world. How dare they intrude on her? They had not been invited. They had no right to be here!

As if sensing her fear, the *angakuk* reached out to Dana. Tiny gnarled hands gripped her like claws. As the shaman spoke, the words echoed around the cave in clicks, whistles, and trills. Dana wanted to explain that she didn't understand, but her tongue seemed to be stuck to the roof of her mouth.

Brendan addressed the shaman in the same birdlike language.

Cackling to herself, the old woman nodded. The dark eyes flashed behind the strings of beads. She let go of Dana and rummaged through the feathery cloak. Now she drew out two smooth pebbles, handing one each to Jean and Dana. The stones were a bluish-gray color, round, and small.

She spoke to Brendan, a quick command.

"Put them under your tongue," he translated. "Then you'll understand her."

The pebbles had the slight salty taste of the sea. As soon as they put them in their mouths, Dana and Jean understood the shaman.

"Stones are the children of the earth," she told them. "They have been here since time began. They know all the languages of the world. Tell me why you have come."

"Wise and noble woman," Brendan addressed her formally, "before we declare our mission, may I offer you gifts from my people?"

The shaman's dark eyes lit up. She grinned with delight. "Are they things you found as you voyaged in your umiak?"

"They are." He smiled.

"Good. They will have power, for your journey is sacred. I have dreamed it."

Brendan took the gifts from his satchel and placed them before her, naming each and their origin.

"Four rods of yew with prophecies cut in ogham. They come from the branches of the lone tree that grows on Inis Subai, the Island of Joy. And in a land where the mountains glow like fire, these gold-and-silver leaves were forged by giant smiths. And the fruits of summer, *toirthe samruid*, were gathered on the island that is the Paradise of the Birds."

As the old woman accepted each gift, she held it to her forehead and bowed toward Brendan. Each time she did, he bowed in return.

When the greeting ritual was completed, the shaman addressed them frankly.

"Why have you come to me? I am the Angakuk of the People. When the Inummariit have a question they want answered—Where is the seal? Where is the polar bear? Where is the caribou?—they come to me. I journey to Adlivun to see the Goddess. She knows where all the animals are. They are her children and her gift to us. She tells me where they are and I, in turn, tell the hunter. What animal do you seek?"

An uncomfortable silence fell in the cave. Jean looked to Dana, his eyebrow raised. She looked toward Brendan, but he didn't speak. The question was obviously for her alone.

"Must it be an animal?" she asked, uncertainly.

Her voice was barely audible. She couldn't shake the feeling that something was wrong. That she didn't belong here. Though she was awed by the shaman, she was already doubting that the *angakuk* could help her. The old woman's magic belonged to the Inuit. Dana was a stranger and not of the People.

"The spirit of an animal is in everything you seek," the shaman said sternly. "If you cannot see this, you are blind. You will never find what you are looking for."

Dana blanched at the reprimand. She felt cornered. Apparently the *angakuk* wasn't going to let her off easily, stranger or no. Dana thought back over her quest. The angakuk was right, many animals were involved! The wolf that both she and Jean were kin to; the ravens who were Grandfather and Roy; the deer she had chased in the Medicine Lodge; the throng of caribou that showed her the secret language; the Cailleach who was a cormorant and her sister, the crane; the whales in the sea . . . Were there others? She was still reviewing her mission, when she found herself staring at the shaman's feathered cloak. *Of course!* It was like a burst of light in her head. There was one creature who had followed her throughout the quest, whose role eluded her, who seemed to convey some hidden significance she couldn't fathom.

"The white birds!" she cried. "The soul-birds! They keep showing up, but I don't know what they mean."

The *angakuk* cackled with glee and rubbed her hands. "You are not so blind after all. I will go to Adlivun. I will ask Taluliyuk about your birds. She knows a lot about birds."

Dana was overwhelmed by the offer. "But I'm not one of your people."

The old woman's response was immediate.

*"We are all family."*

No sooner had the shaman spoken than the stone lamp in front of her lit up of its own accord.

"It begins," she announced. "I go."

Closing her eyes, the *angakuk* began to shake her head till the long beads of her headdress swayed back and forth. A low humming came from under her breath. With mesmeric slowness, she rose to her feet and began to turn like a spinning top, twirling with ever-increasing speed. As she spun, she chanted. The high-pitched notes sounded like birdsong and the sigh of the sea.

Dana and Jean glanced at each other nervously. Brendan stood as still as a statue.

The air in the cave was dimming quickly till only the lamp shed light. The cave flickered with shadows, the greatest of which was the dancing shaman, cast upon the back wall. She seemed to tower over them. At first her song was unintelligible, arcane speech known only to her; but eventually words took shape to form a story and the story itself took shape in their minds.

*Once upon a time there was a beautiful woman named Taluliyuk, who spurned all the suitors who sought her love. Then one day a handsome young man came over the waters from a land far away. He wore gray and white clothing; his eyes were dark. His voice was as sweet as a bird's as he wooed her with promises.*

> *O lady, come with me*
> *To the land of my people*
> *There you will dwell*
> *In comfort and light.*

> *It is a land without sorrow*
> *Without sickness or death*
> *A land without hunger*
> *Without darkness or night.*

*Of course she went with him. He had promised so much. But when she arrived in his land in the North, she discovered his deception. He was not a king of the other world, but a king of the birds. For he was a fulmar who had taken human form in order to court her. He brought* her to his tent of fish skins. It was all torn and tattered and the wind blew through it constantly. She was always cold. There was no oil in her lamps. He fed her raw fish. After a year and a day of misery, Taluliyuk sent for her father to take her home.

Aja, her father, came in the season when the ice broke in the water. He grew angry when he saw the plight of his daughter, and he attacked his son-in-law. They fought long with each other till Aja killed the King of the Fulmars.

"You can come home with me now," he told his daughter.

Taluliyuk and her father were on the sea when the birds discovered the fate of their king. They cried and lamented till they raised a storm to kill Aja.

Afraid for his life, Aja relented. Crying out to the fulmars that they could have his daughter back, he threw her into the sea.

Taluliyuk clung to the side of the boat with all her might. Though Aja cut off the tips of her fingers with his knife, she still held on. The bits of her fingers turned into whales. Now he cut the middle joints of her fingers and they turned into seals. When the fulmars saw the animals in the water, they were appeased and they departed with the storm. The death of their king had been ransomed with new life.

Then the sea opened to swallow Taluliyuk and she sank down into the Underworld.

There she dwells to this very day, in Adlivun that lies under the waves.

• • •

The story ended, but the shaman's song did not. It seemed the tale was only the prologue, the antechamber to the throne room. Now they entered the dark heart of the matter. The *angakuk*'s voice rose higher still and she screeched out shrilly.

> *That woman down there beneath the sea,*
> *She wants to hide the animals from us,*
> *These hunters in the ice house,*
> *They cannot mend matters,*
> *Into the spirit world,*
> *I will go,*
> *Where no humans dwell,*
> *Set matters right will I.*

Dana found herself submerged in a heavy darkness at the bottom of the ocean. Around her moved two-dimensional creatures, flat eels and pseudopods and sleeping leviathans. Slowly she grew aware of something else in the depths, magnificent and misshapen, something so old and immense she could hardly comprehend it. At first she thought it was an idol from a giant city long lost underwater. Then came the beginning of terror when she saw it stir. The thing in the deep was alive.

*Taluliyuk.*

Dana was glad that Brendan and Jean were beside her.

It helped to ease her terror. The *angakuk* was there, too, singing and dancing in the water. With arms outstretched, she spun in the depths like a starfish. Slowly, reverently, the old woman approached the sleeping goddess. Taluliyuk's green hair swayed like seaweed. The shaman took out a whalebone comb and gently raked the tangles of long hair, all the time singing like a mother to her child.

> *Close your eyes, here I am,*
> *I'm right beside you,*
> *I'll close mine and together we'll dream.*

The lips of the goddess murmured with pleasure. Having lost her fingers, she couldn't comb her own hair. In turn, she would reward any shaman who requested her help in this way. And now, in the strangest moment of that strange journey, Dana found herself with the *angakuk* inside Taluliyuk's mind.

Inside her dreaming.

Dana felt she was here and there and everywhere at the same time. She was with every living thing that was upon the earth. She breathed, slept, hunted, and fed with countless numbers of animals. Every fish in the sea, every bird in the air, every creature great and small that walked, crawled, or flew. Wherever an animal was, there was Taluliyuk, living in them and with them and through them all their lives.

Subtly and courteously, the song of the *angakuk* changed inflection. A question was asked.

*Where are the soul-birds?*

In a dizzying ascension, like a plummet upward, Dana was hurled into the sky.

There! A great flock like a spread of clouds. A shining vista of white birds, brooding over the country with *ah! bright wings.*

Dana sensed the ripple of Taluliyuk's surprise. These were not her children, not of her body. She called out to the strangers.

In a rush of wings and wind, a mellifluous sibilance, the birds answered her call. Dropping out of the skies toward the shaman's cave, they alighted on the branches of the barren tree outside.

Even as the birds fell from the sky, so too did the shaman's three visitors. Back in the cave, they opened their eyes. The *angakuk* lay on the floor, deep in a trance. Her mouth opened briefly to whistle a word.

*"Go."*

It was only when they were in the tunnel and Dana looked back that she discovered the dream wasn't over.

"Look!" she cried to the others. "Our bodies!"

There they were, the three of them, eyes closed in sleep, still seated near the *angakuk*.

*"Tabernac!"* said Jean.

Brendan crossed himself hurriedly. "We are souls alone without their vessels. Another wonder to record! But we must take care. What happens to the soul, happens also to the body."

The *angakuk* called out once more. Her tone was urgent.

*"Go!"*

The three hurried through the tunnel and out onto the ice. There, another marvel awaited them. The branching tree had grown immense, almost touching the sky. Its boughs were laden with birds, hundreds it seemed, all white and shining, of every kind. And all fast asleep, heads tucked under wing.

As she gazed upward into the haze of feathered white, Dana felt a deep thrill inside her. The thrill of recognition. The Faerie blood that enlightened her veins knew the truth. These birds were kin.

"They belong to Faerie!" she said breathlessly. "What are they doing here?"

A single white feather floated down from the tree toward her. She caught it gently, holding it to her cheek. Her face was wet with tears. A longing for home surged through her.

As Brendan regarded the birds, the silver rim of the Second Sight seeped into his eyes.

"The souls of the just in the Mystical Tree," he murmured. He turned to Dana. "This flock of angel-birds hail from the Land of Promise. They came here for you. Hark to their message."

It was as if a wind had shaken the great branches of the tree. All the birds began to move, ruffling and rustling as they stretched and preened. As soon as they opened their mouths to sing, Dana remembered. The song she had heard in the Medicine Lodge. The message that tantalized in stray thoughts and dreams. Though she tried to grasp it, to understand, it was too grand, too lofty to be fully taken in. She could only catch phrases, like glimpses, of the Grand Design, the Great Song.

*Sleepers awake!*

*At the heart of the universe, we sing of a life lived in matter.*

*O nobly born, remember who you are!*

She knew they were singing her truth out into the world; the knowledge that was hers from the dawn of time, lost and forgotten at birth. Her heart's truth. Her soul's knowledge.

"Do you understand what they're saying?" Dana cried to the saint. "What are they trying to tell me?"

Brendan had closed his eyes as he listened to the choir of the birds. He was about to answer when Crowley struck.

In that moment, Dana realized her error. She had

relaxed her guard. She had forgotten that her enemy was able to track her. She should have warned Brendan and also the *angakuk*.

They heard him first, an eerie howling in the wind, then they saw the white tornado that sped toward them. Over the glacier it flew, hoovering up snow, firn, ice, and debris, gaining in bulk as it approached. Before Dana could even attempt to flee, the whirlwind struck her.

Everything went white. The song of the soul-birds ceased abruptly. Dana was sucked into a blizzard of snow and ice. The sensation of cold was so intense, it burned her skin. At the cold heart of the flurry, she sensed her enemy, sensed also his hatred. It was mindless and implacable. It wouldn't cease until she was dead. The malice itself began to erode her defenses, and she felt the touch of the deadly frost of despair. She, herself, was turning white and cold.

Then she heard it, high up in the air, the chant of the *angakuk*. The snow that was smothering her melted into water. The crystal flakes became bubbles as Dana sank down,

down,

down into the sea,

where she faced the gargantuan shape of Taluliyuk.

The shaman was still combing the green hair of the goddess. One of Taluliyuk's great eyelids opened. She stared at Dana.

Mirrored in the dark pupil, Dana saw herself trapped

in the whirlwind. She was being dragged across the ice field, alone. Already her body looked frozen. Still standing by the tree, Brendan lifted his arms in prayer. But where was Jean?

Now Dana's heart was gripped with greater terror as she spied Jean racing across the ice field. His eyes were golden. There was no question about it. He was about to turn. But the wintry sun shone pale and clear.

"*NO!*" she cried out to him. "No, Jean, you mustn't!"

She wanted to tell herself it was only a dream. But already she knew the truth. Dreams were never "only." Brendan's words echoed in her mind. *What happens to the soul, happens also to the body.* If Jean became a wolf now, he would be so forever.

"Please!" she begged Taluliyuk. "Please don't let him do this! I'd rather die!"

Now something huge stalked across the ice field with fantastic speed: a stone giant tromping over the glacier. It bore down on the whirlwind in which Dana was trapped. Head, limbs, and torso were massive rocks. The feet crashed to the ground. With each step it took, the earth shuddered, the ice cracked.

With stony ferocity, the *innunguaq* attacked the whirlwind. Crowley's screeches rang through Dana's ears. Tearing at the innards of swirling snow, the stone giant seized Dana. Now it reached down to snatch Jean, who had yet to turn. In one great movement, the stone giant hurled them both away from the glacier, away from Baffin Island, out of the North.

With a blur of light and a violent jolt, Dana and Jean landed body and soul on the shore of Ailsa Craig. Nearby, where they had left it, was the flying canoe.

After the white frost of the Arctic, the riot of smell and color was a shock. The landscape dazzled with blues, greens, and grays. The air was vivid with the scent of seaweed and pine.

"Taluliyuk, she save us," said Jean in a daze, looking around him.

His features were pale. He looked shaken.

Dana couldn't meet his eyes. Only a short while ago, he had made the same decision his grandfather had made. He had chosen to turn wolf in the daylight in order to save her. It was too much to take in. She clutched a white feather in trembling hands.

"We didn't get to thank her . . . or the *angakuk* . . . or Brendan . . ."

She was still stunned by Crowley's attack. He seemed to be able to follow her anywhere, like a relentless hunter tracking his prey. So far she had been lucky. There was always someone there to help her. Deep inside, she shuddered to think that a time might come when no one would intervene. When she'd have to face him alone. Her fingers closed around the feather.

Jean was studying his watch the way one does after crossing many time zones. It took a while to make sense.

"Monday morning!" he said at last. "Strange how time go, eh? If we leave now, I don't miss the turkey!"

She managed to laugh, though she was feeling dizzy and light-headed. Too much had happened. She could hardly think straight. There was something she needed to say to Jean, about his decision, but it was too big a thing to broach right now. She was too shy and awed by its significance. It was obvious that he himself wasn't ready to speak of it. He kept looking away, avoiding her eyes.

"Let's go home to Thanksgiving," she agreed.

# Twenty-Six

When Dana got home later that day, she let herself in with her own key. She was thinking of what she would say if there were any questions and how she might avoid lying. The quest had changed her that way.

Her father and stepmother were in the kitchen. She could hear their voices.

"Who'll tell her?" Gabe said.

Dana's heart skipped. Her father sounded anxious. Had her deception been discovered? She hesitated at the door and considered eavesdropping further, then changed her mind. That was something else she would no longer do. Instead, she barged into the kitchen before they could say more.

They were having Thanksgiving dinner. The table was adorned with a lace cloth and candles. There was no turkey, of course, but there was a feast nonetheless.

They were delighted to see her, and she was engulfed in hugs.

"You are returned in time! How wonderful!" said Aradhana. "Will you eat?"

"I'm starving!" she said, happy that things seemed fine.

Gabriel dished her out a bowl of hot chestnut soup. The main course had already been served, but she soon caught up. After a pineapple boat of curried lentil and tomato salad, she started on the almond croquettes with cranberry sauce and potatoes au gratin.

"I'm glad I didn't miss this!" she said, between mouthfuls.

When they questioned her about the weekend, she did her best not to lie. Apparently Ms. Woods had promised to bring her home without stating a specific time. Neither her father nor her stepmother had any suspicions about the "field trip."

"I learned a lot about Canada," she said. "Amazing things. But I'm really glad to be home. Really glad."

The warmth of her tone was obvious. Gabriel and Aradhana exchanged happy glances.

"Shall we have a game of Monopoly after dessert?" Radhi suggested. "We have not played for so long."

Gabe groaned. "You always wipe me out."

"Of course I do," said Radhi. "I am a businesswoman. You are an artist."

"What's for dessert?" Dana wanted to know.

"Spiced apples in chilled cider."

"Yum."

• • •

At school the next day, there was no sign of Jean. Alarmed, Dana tried to ring him between classes, with no success.

At lunch she tried again, but the line was busy. That was good news, she told herself, fighting down the waves of panic and worry. Sitting alone in the cafeteria, she wondered where he was. If something bad had happened to him, how could she find out? What could she do? She was haunted by the image of him about to turn wolf in the daylight to save her. Her heart beat rapidly at the thought. He had almost given up his human life for her! She felt awed and humbled by such a thing. And, though she fought against it, deep inside she was thrilled. What exactly did it mean?

Dana gazed dreamily into space. A shiver of joy ran through her.

Followed by a jolt of horror.

Her hands were shining with light!

Quickly she clamped down on the flow, then glanced around her in panic. No one was looking. What would she have done if someone had seen? She would have to be more careful!

Unnerved by what had happened, she hurried to finish her lunch. She wanted to try and call Jean again.

"Is it okay to sit here?"

Dana was about to point out there were empty tables nearby, but she didn't get the chance. Without waiting for permission, the other girl sat down opposite her. Dana frowned. She knew her vaguely. Georgia Cheung was a top student, as well as the class beauty with her long black hair and almond eyes. Though generally admired and popular with her peers, she didn't belong to any particular circle or group.

"Work away," Dana mumbled.

Georgia had her food on a tray, a noodle dish she had heated in the microwave. The smell of spices wafted toward Dana, making her mouth water. She was glad that Aradhana had made her lunch that day, or she would have been jealous.

Georgia took out chopsticks and began to eat, eyeing Dana's samosas.

"They look good," she said.

"My stepmother's specialty." Dana nodded. "When my dad makes lunch, it's peanut butter and jam. Sometimes I make lunch myself, but it's nicer when someone else does."

Georgia agreed heartily. "My great-granny always makes mine. She's better than a restaurant."

They munched together companionably for a while.

Then Georgia dropped her bombshell.

"I saw what happened with your hands."

Dana choked on her food. Georgia leaned over to clap her on the back.

"I don't know what you're talking about," Dana spluttered.

"Sure you do. You can't put me off. I know about magic."

Georgia continued to eat, giving Dana some time to recover.

"Don't worry," Georgia said at last, "your secret's safe with me." Then she giggled. "Don't you just love when you get to say clichés in the right place like that?"

Dana couldn't help laughing.

"You're Irish, right?" Georgia asked.

Dana nodded, glad that the subject had changed. "And you're Japanese?"

Georgia made a noise like a buzzer. "Wrong. Chinese ancestry."

Flustered, Dana began to apologize.

Georgia waved her hand breezily. "Don't sweat it. I can't tell the difference myself. I'm Canadian. My background's a real mix. Mom's Hungarian Irish. I told her about you. 'The quiet girl.' Dad's Chinese Jamaican. I know more about the Chinese side of things, because my great-granny lives with us. So, where's your boyfriend today?"

"My—?" Dana blushed furiously. "He's not . . . I mean . . ."

It was Georgia's turn to be apologetic. "Open mouth, insert foot! I'm always saying the wrong thing."

"Me too!" Dana exclaimed.

They laughed together.

"I don't know if he's my boyfriend," Dana confided. "I don't know that much about boys or going out with them."

"I could tell you a few things," Georgia offered. "He's really cute," she added. "Definitely boyfriend material."

"He is, isn't he," sighed Dana, and they laughed some more.

For the rest of lunch they talked about boys, school, the other kids, their classes, their teachers. Dana felt the happiness well up inside her. This was what she had missed for so long, a friend she could talk to and share things with. She appreciated that Georgia didn't mention the light again. And what could she have meant by that comment about magic? Dana was curious to know, but at the same time she was cautious. Their friendship was promising, but too new to test.

When the bell rang, Dana made a decision.

"Would you like to swap phone numbers?" she asked shyly. "You don't have to if—"

"Great idea. I was going to suggest it myself, but I thought you might think I'm pushy." Georgia grinned. "I am, in case you hadn't noticed."

They met on and off for the rest of the day as they shared several classes. Dana still hadn't reached Jean, but Georgia's steady stream of chatter kept her distracted.

"What about that Crowley guy, eh? Definite child-molester type. He picked on you, didn't he? I bet you're not sorry he's gone. Did you notice how we seem to lose teachers? Do you think they're buried in the basement?"

At the end of the day, Dana was disappointed to discover they lived in opposite directions.

"Call me!" Georgia shouted as she ran for her bus.

Dana was still waving good-bye when she noticed the young woman on the far side of the street. Her heart leaped in her throat. She *had* seen her that time, in the crowd near the musicians. Honor, the High Queen of Faerie!

Overcome with joy, Dana raced across the road.

"Your Majesty! How did you—?"

"Oh no, Dana," she said, "that name does not belong to me."

Dana was already realizing her mistake. The difference was subtle, but evident all the same. This young woman did not look as happy or as lighthearted as Honor. She was, of course, the High Queen's twin sister whom Dana had been told about before she left Ireland.

"I'm Laurel," the other confirmed. "Honor's sister. A mortal who lives in this world. Do you know where Gwen is? I've been trying to reach her. When I rang the school today, they were all strange about it and told me to contact the police. I know she was going east with you and—"

Laurel stopped when she saw the blank look on Dana's face.

"Ms. Woods didn't come with us," Dana said. "We were going to talk to her about the trip, but she wasn't at school."

Laurel looked as if she might faint. "Oh, God." Her voice shook. "When did you last see her?"

Dana thought back. She, too, was beginning to feel shaky. Something was very wrong.

"We left Friday. She wasn't there the day before . . . because that was the day the vice-principal took over. We thought she might be back today, but she didn't show up."

"She's been gone almost a week!" Laurel looked sick. She struggled for control.

"It's my fault," Dana said as the horror dawned. "She wanted to be friends, but I didn't trust her."

"Don't be ridiculous," Laurel said sharply. "How could it be your fault? You're only a child. You're not responsible for what's going on." She put her hands to her head, trying to think. "I'll have to contact the others and let them know what's happened. It's not your problem. We'll deal with it, don't worry. But right now, you and I need to talk. Are you on your way home?"

"Yes, I—"

"Fine, I'll go with you. I live near Brunswick Avenue."

"You know where I live?!"

"We've been watching you. Watching over you. Sorry, it was necessary. We've been trying to guard you, Gwen and I. That must have been . . ." Laurel bit her lip.

Dana began to shake. Had Gwen been hurt—or worse—trying to protect her? She told Laurel about the enemy who had come from Ireland to kill her, and how he had taken over her teacher's body to get near to her.

Laurel's voice was grim. "We suspected as much, but far too late to help you. I'm sorry. We did our best to guard you, but we didn't move fast enough. Thank goodness you were able to fight him yourself." Admiration echoed in her voice. "Now tell me everything," she said. "Gwen was convinced you know about the mission? The closing of the portals and the need to restore them by Halloween?"

Dana nodded dumbly, but she was slow to respond. Though she knew she could trust Laurel, she was reluctant to share her story. For one thing, she hadn't warmed to the High Queen's sister. Laurel's manner was adult and bossy, and she treated Dana like a child. Ms. Woods had been friendlier and more likeable. Dana regretted rejecting her. Worse still, that rejection may have doomed her teacher.

"I need to know what you know. What you've achieved so far," Laurel insisted. "I can't help you, or Gwen, unless I know the story."

It was the need to help Gwen that spurred Dana to speak. She told Laurel about Edane's visit and the quest to find the Book of Dreams. Then she related how Jean had brought her to Grandfather and his advice to travel the Four Directions. She described her adventures on Cape Breton Island with the giant and Brendan and the *angakuk*. Throughout her story she made it clear that Jean was her chief support, but she managed to exclude both the *loup-garou* and *la chasse-galerie*. Dana knew how fiercely Jean kept his secrets. With vague references to her own fairy abilities, she glossed over the question of how they had journeyed.

When she was finished, Laurel shook her head with amazement.

"You've done so well. Beyond anything we could have expected. I must apologize. I've underestimated you, I guess because you're young. To be frank, for the first time since all this began, I believe there's a real chance we might succeed."

Dana heard the approval as well as the apology and couldn't help but be pleased. The High Queen's sister was obviously not someone who was easily impressed.

It was Laurel's turn to tell Dana what she knew. She, too, chose to edit what she said. She didn't mention the fate of the Companions in Ireland. There was no point in burdening the girl with more bad news. Instead, she sought to encourage Dana with what support there was.

"There are others in the background working to help you. Even though we can't all come to you in person, you are not alone. Whenever your enemy strikes against you, it means we have failed to hold the line. But I want you to know that we will fight to the last for you and your quest."

"Thank you," Dana said, and she meant it.

They had traveled by subway, talking in low tones.

When they reached Dana's stop, Laurel continued to accompany her along Bloor Street and up Brunswick Avenue. As they passed the old convent, Dana stopped abruptly.

"What is it?" said Laurel.

Dana stared at the empty building. The dark hulking structure seemed vaguely sinister. Most of the windows were nailed and boarded. Part of the wall was charred, as if from a fire.

"I felt something," she said. She looked around warily. "Something cold."

Laurel shivered. She reached inside her pocket for the protective charms. Her heart jumped. Her pocket was empty! She had been so distracted and disturbed when she couldn't reach Gwen that she had forgotten to pack them.

Laurel caught Dana's arm. As they hurried up the street, she spoke quickly.

"I've made up my mind. We must travel west. There are two other Companions of Faerie in Canada: Findabhair, who's Gwen's cousin, and Finvarra, Findabhair's husband. He was once the High King of Faerie, but he's mortal now. They're musicians, on tour, in Vancouver at the moment. I don't know why they haven't joined us yet, Gwen was a bit vague about that, and right now I don't care. It's time they got on board. It can't be a coincidence that your instructions include traveling west too. You know yourself there's no such thing as coincidence in these matters. We'll go together."

The more Laurel spoke, the more dismayed Dana grew. She was glad to think of a line of support at her back, but she wasn't happy with the idea of others joining her quest. She preferred to think of the mission as something she and Jean did together. They were fine on their own. They didn't need anyone else.

"You should stay here and find Gwen," Dana said. "I can go out west with Jean."

Laurel's disagreement was instant.

"Listen to me, Dana. You mustn't involve Jean again. He's mortal and not a Companion of Faerie. This has nothing to do with him. I understand how you feel, he's your boyfriend and he has helped you through a lot, but if you care about him, you'll leave him out of this. It's too dangerous. He has no way of protecting himself. If he's harmed in any way, it will be our fault, yours and mine."

Dana felt a surge of resentment against Laurel. How dare she interfere like this! Then an image flashed through her mind: Jean lying unconscious in the hospital room, swathed in bandages. Another image quickly followed. Jean on Baffin Island, racing toward the whirlwind that was Crowley. His eyes glowed amber as he made his decision to turn wolf in the daylight. Dana's resentment changed to anguish. She knew Laurel was right. The quest put Jean in constant danger. She couldn't bear to think of him getting hurt or worse, losing his humanity because of her.

"All right," she said with a heavy heart. "I'll go west with you. Not him."

"Good," said Laurel. "Now we just need to convince your parents to let you go."

They had arrived at Dana's house and were standing on the sidewalk in front of it.

"I'll talk to my stepmother first," Dana said. "She understands these things better than my dad. It'll be easier for him when he hears you're going, but I'll have to decide how much to tell him."

"I'm sure you'll do fine," Laurel said. "If they want to meet me, I'm available. We have a slight connection, I believe, that might help matters. Your dad knows my grandfather, Professor Blackburn. You could mention his name. Here's my number. Call me tonight. I'm not far from you, at Massey College on Devonshire Place. If you need me, I can be here immediately. Oh, and tell your dad I'll be financing the trip. I'd like to book our flights tonight. The sooner we go, the better."

Laurel was about to leave when she stopped and looked up at the house.

"By the way, that's one powerful protection spell you wove."

Dana smiled. "Not me, my stepmother's guardian. She's from India. He's the Lord Ganesha."

"Ah, that's it," said Laurel softly. "You'll always be safe here."

Again she hesitated. It was obvious there was something else she wanted to say.

"What is it?" Dana asked.

"I know your story, I heard it in Faerie, but I get the impression you don't know mine or Gwen's?"

Dana shrugged sheepishly. "Actually, I didn't even know your names. I always went to my mother in Faerie. She's a *spéirbhean*, a Sky-Woman, not one of the Gentry. She didn't hang around the Court much, where the harpers tell the tales, and neither did I. To be honest, I was never interested in human tales, especially ones about Canadians and Faerie. I blamed the bond between the two countries for the reason I had to leave Ireland." She let out a sigh. "I didn't want to be here."

Laurel listened with sympathy. "I understand. I've had my problems with Faerie too. It's not always a picnic, eh? It's unfortunate, though. If you had known our stories, we might have met sooner."

Dana winced. And things would have been different. Gwen would still be there.

"I'm not accusing you of anything," Laurel said quickly. "Stuff happens. There's no point looking back. Believe me, I know."

Laurel's words surprised Dana. For the first time, she thought she could like this young woman.

"Perhaps you might tell me your story when we travel?" Dana said. "It's a long flight out west, isn't it?"

"Good idea." Laurel smiled at her thoughtfully. "I'm glad we're doing this together."

Dana hurried into the house, calling out for Aradhana, but a note on the table explained that her stepmother was working late. Gabriel was at home, practicing in his studio. The sound of the silver flute trilled through the house. She decided not to disturb him. She would wait for Radhi. When she rang Jean, his line was still busy. Where was he? What was he doing? She rang Georgia, but her mother said she was at a dance class. Though Dana was restless and anxious , she forced herself to do her homework. Then the telephone rang and she raced into the hall.

"I've got it!" she shouted to her father.

It was Jean.

"At last!" she cried, not bothering to hide her joy and relief. "Are you okay?"

"*Oui.* Yes. But I am in Québec. With the Old Man and Roy. *Grand-père est disparu.* No one can find him. I come as soon as they tell me."

"Oh no." Dana felt a cold grip on her heart. "Do you think it's Crowley?"

"I don't know. Each year *grand-père*, he is more and more wolf. It may be this. Tonight I go to the Shaking Tent. I find the truth."

"Can I help at all?" she asked.

Though she was overjoyed to know that he was safe, she was anxious about this second disappearance. Could it be connected to Gwen's? She was tempted to tell Jean about Ms. Woods and Laurel, but decided not to. She had already agreed to exclude him from the quest, to keep him out of danger. But was it too late? And what about *grand-père*?

"*C'est okay*," Jean assured her. "With Grandfather and Roy, I find him. And you? *Comment ça va?* What happen today?"

"I made a new friend at school," she said, avoiding an outright lie. "I'll introduce you when you get back. Don't worry about me. Find *grand-père*."

"*Bon*. I call you as soon as I know. But you, *fais attention*. Be careful, eh?"

"I will," she said. "And Jean? You'll take care, too, won't you?"

"I'm fine. This is the best place to be. But I worry for you. I don't want to be—*comment dit-ons 'chauvin'?*—chauviniste? You are strong, but still I worry. You will wait for me, yes? I ask you?"

"I promise," she lied. So much for good intentions.

There was nothing left to say, yet neither hung up. Dana could hear him breathing on the other end of the line. Her heart ached.

"Dana?"

"Yes?"

"I am missing you."

"Me too. I miss you too."

"*À bientôt, chérie.*"

"Yes. Soon."

When the line went dead, she stared at it awhile. Then she ran to get Laurel's number. She needed to tell her about *grand-père*'s disappearance. The phone rang for some time and then her call was redirected.

"Porter's lodge, Massey College. Can I help you?"

"Oh. Yes. Hello. I'm trying to reach Laurel Blackburn?"

"I'm sorry, she's not here. She's gone."

"What?"

"She left today. I don't know when she'll be back."

# Twenty-Seven

Dana couldn't believe what she was hearing. "What do you mean? I just met her a while ago. She told me to call her."

"It was some family thing," said the porter. "Sorry. That's all I know."

She could hardly think. Family thing? The other Companions? It didn't make sense. Why would Laurel go away without telling her? Unless, oh God, like Ms. Woods . . . As Dana hung up the phone, a fit of trembling came over her. The fear was overwhelming. She was drowning in it. Burying her face in her hands, she was lost for a moment in utter darkness. Then her palms grew warm. A golden light welled up to bathe her features like sunshine. *O nobly born, remember who you are.* She steadied herself. She was stronger than this. Tim Severin's words echoed in her mind. *Whatever will happen will happen. You either face it as a coward or you face it as a hero.* She wiped away her tears. Something terrible had happened and she had to face it.

Dana hurried to her father's studio.

"Sorry to bother you, Da, but I need your help."

Gabriel put down his flute.

"What's up, sweetheart?"

"Could you give me a lift? I have to meet a friend at Massey College. It won't take long. I could walk, but it's getting dark and I'd rather not."

Things had been steadily improving between them. He was obviously pleased that she had asked for his help, but he was also curious. Vaguely she explained that Laurel had come to her school to talk about Irish folklore.

"You know her grandfather. Professor Blackburn."

"Of course I do! He's the one who got me the job here. What a coincidence!"

"Hmm."

When they drew up outside Massey College, Dana asked her father to wait in the car.

"I won't be long. Maybe you could meet her some other time."

Heart in her mouth, she rang the bell outside the gates. *Please. Please.* She was still hoping desperately for a last-minute reprieve, a simple explanation, or even the return of Laurel herself.

The porter's lodge was directly inside the gates. The porter, a student working part-time, let her in. His office was a small cupboard of a room with notice boards and wooden mail slots.

"I'm Dana Faolan," she said, breathlessly, "a friend of Laurel Blackburn's. She didn't come back by any chance? Or maybe she rang? Or left a message?"

The porter looked contrite.

"You called earlier, didn't you? Sorry, I only remembered after you hung up. She left something for you." He took a thick envelope from Laurel's mail slot. "Said you might pick it up at any time."

A glimmer of hope. Perhaps Laurel had been called away by the other Companions? She could have tried to ring when Dana was talking to Jean.

"Someone came for her."

The porter shuddered visibly, though he tried not to.

"What did he look like?" she asked quickly.

Again he tried to hide his revulsion.

"He . . . badly scarred . . ."

The death of hope. Dana stood stock-still as she absorbed the news. Her worst fears confirmed. There was no mistaking the description. Again she fought off the terror and held on to her courage. She had to get help for Laurel. And Gwen too.

Oh, let it not be too late, she prayed.

"Everything okay?" Gabriel asked her as she got into the car.

"She's not there right now," Dana said quietly.

There was nothing else to say.

•••

Back home, Dana hurried into her bedroom and tore open the envelope. The contents gave her a shock. Wads of money! Thousands of dollars! There was also a note.

*Dear Dana,*

*I'm so sorry. If you are reading this it means I have failed you and this is the best I can do. You mustn't look for me or try to help me. There isn't time. If there's hope for any of us, it lies in the quest and the restoration of Faerie. Go west as soon as you can. Find Finvarra and Findabhair. Tell them to help you. Time is running out. The portals must be restored on Halloween when the two worlds cross. Use the money. It's yours. Again, I'm so sorry if you are reading this. Be of good courage. I can only trust that we'll meet again when the Kingdom is restored.*

*Yours,*

*Laurel Blackburn*

Dana wanted to cry. Somehow Laurel had known that Crowley was coming for her. Yet, despite the terror she must have been feeling, she still thought of the quest. A true Companion of Faerie. A true hero.

"I won't let you down," Dana murmured.

Attached to Laurel's note was a tour schedule with venues and dates. It took Dana a moment to understand what she was looking at: the itinerary of a musical group called the Fair Folk. Findabhair and Finvarra! She studied the dates. They had arrived in Vancouver a week ago and would be there over the weekend. Then they toured eastward with engagements in all the major cities. Dana frowned. They weren't due in Toronto till early November. If Halloween was the deadline, weren't they arriving too late? Had they other plans? She would soon find out.

Dana knew what she had to do. Yes, she would travel to Vancouver to meet Findabhair and Finvarra, but not to ask them to join the mission. Instead she would tell them to save Gwen and Laurel. She herself would continue the quest alone. She had done it in Ireland, she would do it in Canada. This was *her* mission. It was time she took full responsibility for it. According to Grandfather, something awaited her in the West. She would go to meet it.

With quiet resolve, Dana packed her bags. Then she went into the kitchen where Gabriel was making supper. It was spaghetti alla napoletana, a favorite of theirs from the days when they were a family of two. She joined him at the counter, cutting a crusty loaf in half, buttering the slices, and sprinkling them with garlic and basil. Gabriel had cooked the pasta and tomato sauce and was making a green salad. Loreena McKennitt sang melodiously on the CD player. *And now my charms are all o'erthrown. And what strength I have's mine own.* They smiled at each other as they worked together, humming along with the music. It was like the old days in Ireland, when they always made their meals together.

In that cusp of time, Dana allowed herself to feel safe and happy. This was the calm before the storm. The night before the battle. She knew that evil was at the gate, crouched and waiting, but she also knew it couldn't get in; for no dark thing could pass the Lord Ganesha's protection. She would enjoy this moment with her father. Gabe himself was full of cheer, looking younger and livelier than he had in ages.

When Aradhana came home from work, they all sat down to the meal. Though there was plenty of laughing and joking, Dana felt sad. Soon she would end this bright moment. Her bags were packed. She was leaving that night. No matter what they said or did, they couldn't stop her, as she was prepared to use her powers if necessary. She planned to tell Radhi first, then she would break the news to Gabriel. The three of them had faced a similar crisis in the past. She hoped that fact might ease the pain. On her last quest, Dana had left home without telling her father. At least she would give him fair warning this time.

It was when they were eating dessert that Dana noticed something odd. Radhi and Gabe kept exchanging furtive looks. Did they suspect something? But how could they?

After supper, Gabriel insisted on washing the dishes alone, ushering his wife and his daughter into the living room.

"For a talk," he said nervously. "That's what women do. Talk to each other. Talk."

Aradhana was trying to hide her laughter. Gabriel shot her a look.

Intrigued and a little anxious, Dana sat down. "What's up?"

Aradhana beamed at her stepdaughter and took hold of her hands.

"Dana, I will not beat about the bush. Your father is a typical man in such matters, that is to say, a coward. I am going to have a baby. You are going to have a sister or brother."

Dana fought to control her features. Her stepmother's face shone with joy. No wonder Gabe looked so happy! Her heart sank. If only she could feel the same way. But the timing was disastrous. She couldn't possibly tell them anything now. It would be far too upsetting. Her only choice was to leave without letting them know and then call from Vancouver.

The loneliness descended over her like a pall. Hiding her dismay, she hugged her stepmother.

"I'm really happy for you, Radhi. I really am."

Aradhana's embrace was scented with jasmine. Holding back the tears, Dana rested her head on her stepmother's shoulder. She could hear her father in the hallway, talking on the telephone.

"Thought you both should know. Yeah, aunties again!

Well, someone has to pass on the genes. Neither of you will ever be mature enough to have kids."

Dana's eyes widened. She wasn't alone!

Racing into the hallway, she grabbed the phone from her father and waved him back to the living room.

"Can I come over?" she demanded.

"Something wrong?" her aunt Yvonne asked immediately.

"We need to talk," Dana said, and her voice was urgent. "Invite me to stay the night. No, several nights. *Please.*"

Few adults respond correctly to the melodramatics of a teenager, but Dana knew she was talking to one who would.

"*Pas de* prob. Put Gabe back on."

Gabriel was sitting with Aradhana. He looked puzzled when Dana called him back to the phone.

"What—? But—" he stuttered into the receiver.

Dana could see the day was already won. She hurried back to her stepmother.

"Listen, Radhi. I'm going away for a few days. To visit my aunties. Please don't feel bad. It has nothing to do with your news. I'm really happy for both of you and for me too. But, believe me, I've got something I have to do."

Aradhana held Dana's face in her hands and gazed into her eyes.

"Dana? Does this—?"

"Don't make me explain. I can't say more. Trust me, please?"

Aradhana didn't look happy. She studied Dana's face intently. What she saw there evidently convinced her. At last she nodded.

Dana hugged her again.

"Your baby is going to be very lucky to have you. Just like I am."

Dana's aunts lived in the loft of a chic warehouse that accommodated an art gallery, a craft shop, and several artists' studios. Their loft was spacious, all skylights, wooden beams, and open planning. They had furnished it with futons, Afghan rugs, wall-to-wall artwork, shelves of books that reached the ceiling, and a music system any nightclub would envy. Having discovered they couldn't tolerate anyone else on a regular basis, the two sisters had been living together for more than a decade.

Yvonne greeted Dana with a hug. Casually shooing her brother out, she shut the door behind him.

"You've missed Mexican night, kiddo. You should have called earlier."

Her aunt was wearing a red-and-yellow poncho over embroidered mariachi pants. Behind her, the glass dining table was littered with leftover tacos and dregs of salsa. A half-empty bottle of tequila partnered a salt shaker and slices of lime. The lights were dimmed. Candles flickered around the room. The Gypsy Kings sang full-throated from the speakers.

"It doesn't matter," Dana said. "I don't eat meat."

"You could've had the refried beans," Dee called from the kitchen area.

She came out carrying a big bowl of nachos and a smaller bowl of guacamole. Dressed in black, she wore tight leggings with a tatty sweater torn at the elbows, and big clumpy boots. Her brush-cut had changed color from blue to pink.

"Refried beans," she repeated. "Could they have thought up a less attractive description?"

"Could be a direct translation," Yvonne suggested.

"You can eat this," Deirdre told her niece, setting the bowls on the table. "Suitable for vegetarians, and quite delicious. Also quite green."

She burst into song.

*How are things in guacamole?*
*Has the green gone brown and yucky yet?*

Dana looked puzzled. Between fits of laughter, the aunts attempted to tell her about an Irish-American stageplay whose theme song was "How Are Things in Glocca Mora?"

"*Finian's Rainbow*," Dee said with awe. "Classic kitsch. First it was a cornball Broadway musical, then it went bizarro-world when they made it into a movie."

"Oh, gawd, Fred Astaire's abominable brogue!" Yvonne screeched. "And Petula Clark was his daughter!"

They howled till tears came down.

"I bet Coppola gets nightmares remembering that one," Dee said.

"He was only twenty-nine," her sister pointed out.

"I'm twenty-nine and you wouldn't catch me making a clunker like that!"

Dana sank into a beanbag chair. Being with her aunts was always a leap into mayhem and madness.

"'Bout time you came to see us," Dee commented. "It's been forever since you were last here. Your first birthday in Canada, remember? We had to take a taxi to Gabe's and drag you out."

It was true. That was at the height of her rebellion. She had simply refused to go anywhere where she might enjoy herself. Most of the time she had stayed in her room, escaping to Faerie. How much things had changed!

"Don't mind her," Yvonne said, throwing her sister a look. "If you want to be moody, you go right ahead. It's a teenager's prerogative."

"I would like to visit more often," she assured them.

Dee grinned triumphantly at Yvonne.

"But I'm not really here for a visit," Dana announced. Time was running out. She had to state her case. "I'm here to ask for your help. I have to go out west, to Vancouver. I've got the money. I just need you to take me."

Producing the brown envelope, Dana emptied the pile of bills onto the table.

Her aunts' eyes went huge. The look that flashed between them spoke volumes. Both were evidently remembering the night she stole Gran Gowan's car.

"Who did you rob?" Dee asked outright.

"It's the baby, isn't it," Yvonne said gently. "It's totally freaked you out. You're being replaced and—"

"No," said Dana, exasperated. "I'm really happy about the baby. It's got nothing to do with it. And I didn't steal the money! This is something else, totally and utterly different."

Her aunts were exchanging looks again.

*Humor her*, their glances said. *The poor thing has cracked under the strain.*

Aware that she was fast losing her audience, Dana was ready to grasp at straws. She glanced at the bookshelves that lined the walls, cluttered with fantasy and mythology. There was an entire shelf of Charles de Lint alone. She saw her chance. An opening into the truth. She pointed to the books.

"Did you ever think, either of you, that this stuff— magic, I mean—could be real? Could exist in the world?"

They were caught off guard by the question. They had been concentrating on Dana and were suddenly thrown back on themselves. They started to giggle. Both looked younger and a little shy.

Deirdre rubbed the pink stubble on her head.

"Kiddo, you're looking at two people who spent a whole weekend in Ottawa searching for Tamson House."

Dana recognized the reference to *Moonheart*, which they had given her to read.

"Didn't find it," Yvonne said with a sigh.

"Yet," added Dee.

Dana took a quick breath. It was now or never. Putting her hands together, she offered her palms to the two of them. Light spilled out like liquid gold.

Deirdre's face drained of blood. There is always a moment of terror when the other world knocks. *Every angel is terrifying.* A healthy fear of the unknown is ingrained in every animal, including humans.

"Okay, breathe through it," Dee ordered herself quietly. She stood up to pace the room. "That's it. *Breathe.* Life just got a lot more interesting."

Yvonne sat so still she seemed to be in shock, but in fact her mind was racing.

"It's to do with your mother, right?" she said finally. "Gabe's first wife? I always knew there was something weird happening there. The whole thing was too odd and Gabe could never really explain it. Where she came from, who she was, why she had no family and then—poof!— she disappeared. Am I right or am I right?"

"I found her just before we left Ireland," Dana said. "She's . . . she's a fairy queen."

Both aunts let out a long-drawn *ahhhhh*.

Then Dee let out a whoop.

"That makes you half-fairy!" She grinned at her sister. "We're the aunts of a half-fairy! If we were her godparents, we'd be a fairy's godmothers. She'd be our fairy god-niece."

"You're babbling," Yvonne warned. "Get a grip. I don't want to slap you."

"'Cause you'd be sorry."

When they finally managed to calm down, Dana told her story. Except for the truth about Jean, she left nothing out. Her aunts were so thrilled and excited about the wonder of it all, she could see that the dangerous parts hadn't sunk in. But there was no question about them helping her. The three of them would go west and as soon as possible!

With that decision made, the aunts were galvanized into action, leaving their niece breathless.

The first call was to Gabriel. Dana would stay longer than a few days, maybe a week or more, nothing to worry about, they would get her to school, help with the homework. He and Radhi should enjoy the break. After all, they wouldn't have any time for each other once the baby was born.

Dana listened with awe as her aunts played their brother like a song. No doubt it had always been this way. They had always run circles around him.

The next call was to a friend who was a travel agent. Apologies for the late hour but this was an emergency, they needed round-trip tickets to Vancouver ASAP.

Dee had begun to count the money at this point. She yelled gleefully to Yvonne who was still on the phone.

*"First-class!"*

That made it easier. They could fly out in the morning.

"We'll call your school tomorrow," Yvonne concluded. "You've got a dose of something. You'll be back in a few days."

"You guys are amazing," said Dana.

"She said 'you guys'! Did you hear that?" Dee crowed. "We got to her at last! A fairy Canuck!"

Dee was pulling out suitcases from a wardrobe and tossing in clothes as she sang.

*My bags are packed, I'm ready to go*
*I'm standing here, on your big toe . . .*

# Twenty-Eight

Laurel's ordeal began shortly after she left Dana at her house. With the girl safely home, Laurel let herself feel the full shock of the news about Gwen. Bending over, she clutched her stomach as the dry retching began. An old wound opened. The guilt of the one left behind. She could hardly believe it was happening to her again. Why was she always losing the ones she loved? *It's my fault. I shouldn't have let her go off without me.* Their last argument came home to haunt her. The unkind words she had said. Her impatience. She hadn't apologized, even though she knew her friend deserved better.

Blinded by tears, Laurel stumbled down the street. Where was Gwen? What terrible thing had happened to her? It was when she passed the old convent that Laurel sensed suddenly that she was being followed. Turning quickly, she caught sight of a gaunt figure before he stepped behind a tree. Her heart jumped. She was being stalked! Instinctively she reached for the protective charms in her pocket, then remembered there were none. She quickened her pace. The day was still bright. She wasn't afraid. Yet. When she reached the busy thoroughfare of Bloor Street, she hurried to join the safety of the crowds. He wouldn't dare to attack her in public, would he?

At the corner of Bloor and Spadina, a young Native man had set up a stall to sell dream-catchers and beadwork. He was darkly handsome, with an easygoing smile. A sky-blue shirt matched his denim jeans, and his black hair was tied back in a ponytail, shining in the late sunlight. Snakeskin boots shod his feet.

Laurel stopped at the stall, feigning interest in the goods, to give herself the chance to look over her shoulder. She gasped audibly. There he was! A tall ragged man, with a disfigured face. As soon as she spied him, he stepped into a doorway, but not before she had caught the hatred that burned in his eyes.

She was about to rush away when the Native seller stopped her.

"Take this," he said quietly. Leaning toward her, he slipped a necklace over her head. The leather string held a smooth white pebble. "Moonstone. Protects the female."

Flustered, Laurel reached for her purse, but he waved his hand.

"The hunter teaches the prey to run. *Go*," he urged her.

She didn't need to be told twice. Laurel raced down the street.

• • •

Rushing away, Laurel didn't see her champion block Crowley's path.

"See something you like?" said the seller, indicating his merchandise.

Crowley's face twisted with fury. He spat out the words. "Be gone, Ojibwa."

The young man's eyes flashed. His voice was like a roll of thunder.

"If you're gonna use names, Shadow, try to get it right."

Crowley jerked backward as if struck by a blow.

Recognition passed between them like lightning before a storm.

"Nanabush!" hissed Crowley.

"Yeah, that would do. Or Nanabozho. Or, well, there's a lot more, but what do you care, eh?"

"I could crush you with—"

"I don't think so. You got no power over me or my people."

"I will call those who do."

"Go ahead. I'm in the mood for a fight. It's been a lousy day. No sales."

Crowley looked as if he might explode with rage, then he glanced down the street. Laurel was nowhere to be seen. With an exasperated cry, he dodged past Nanabozho and sped away.

Back in her room at Massey, Laurel moved quickly.

She didn't know how much time she had. This was the enemy who had got to Gwen, and now he was coming for *her*! Waves of terror and panic kept washing over her, but she fought them back. She had to think of Dana. The girl had to be protected. She tried to ring her, to warn her, but the line was busy. *What to do? What to do?* Frantically she rifled through the papers on her desk. *Where is it?* The tour itinerary of the Companions out west. Gwen had given her a copy as if to explain why the two had yet to join them. Well, regardless of their schedule, they were needed *now*. If she was taken . . . Laurel shuddered with horror . . . she steadied herself . . . the two out west were Dana's only hope.

Using all her willpower to concentrate on the task, she scribbled a note. *Oh, poor Dana! Just a kid. How will she manage this alone?* Stuffing letter and itinerary into the envelope of money, she ran to the porter's lodge.

"Could you keep this in my slot? If a young girl called Dana—Dana Faolan—comes asking for me, it's for her. I don't know when she'll come, today, tomorrow, but it's very important. Make sure she gets it. Okay?"

"Sure. No problem," the porter said, surprised by her vehemence. "I'll tell the night shift too."

As she left the lodge, Laurel glanced through the gates. Her heart stopped. A black sedan with darkened windows drew up across the road. It looked sinister. Could it be him? She wasn't about to take any chances. There was a back door out of Massey leading onto a side street. She would escape that way. Rushing back to her room, she grabbed her purse and some protective charms. She had no idea where she was going, she just knew she had to flee.

When the telephone rang, she froze. Should she answer or not? It could be Dana. Or Granny or Dara. Or even Gwen. Each ring increased the tension. But she was safe in her room, wasn't she? She locked her door. Picked up the receiver. A buzzing sound came through the telephone, so strong it shattered her eardrum. Her head spun. She staggered back dizzily.

"*Laurel.*"

The voice was oily. Hypnotic. Evil.

Mesmerized by Crowley's voice, Laurel left her room.

He was waiting in the porter's lodge from where he had made the call. The porter stood against the back wall, looking frightened and confused.

Silently, obediently, Laurel followed Crowley out of the college and into his car. He drove to the outskirts of the city to a deserted beach. She knew he was going to murder her, but she had no way of stopping him. A cloud had fallen over her mind, paralyzing her. The waspish sound rang continually in her ears. A sour metallic smell choked her nostrils. Though she wanted to fight for her life, she had no will to do it.

Now he leaned toward her. She cringed with horror. His face was skeletal, the skin shone with a greenish tinge, and his eyes were two black pits. Bony hands reached out to grip her throat.

A flash of white fire!

It came from the moonstone that hung around her neck.

With a screech of rage, Crowley jerked back. He couldn't touch her. But she felt no relief. For something awful was happening to his body. Tentacles erupted from his chest and tore at the air around her. Before she could even let out a scream, she found herself falling into darkness. The violence of the fall knocked her unconscious.

When Laurel woke, she had no idea where she was or how long she had been there. Scrambling to her feet, she staggered slightly. A nauseous feeling washed over her. She gulped for air and began to choke. As far as she could see, she was in a bleak and blasted wasteland. The air was gray and smoky. In front of her lay a bog that crawled with strangled trees. Beyond the bog rose a ridge of jagged ghylls and crags. There was no sign of humanity in any direction. A cold chill gripped her heart. She knew that she had been sent here to die.

In that moment of despair and loneliness, Laurel wanted to cry. But it was against her nature. Instead, she surveyed the land. If she climbed the ridge, she would get a better view. There might be a road on the other side that led to less hostile territory. Maybe a way out. At the least, she would escape the dreary bog. She noted the sluggish stream that crept past the trees. That meant swamp. There might be quicksand. She would have to be careful.

Once she had chosen a course of action, Laurel felt better. As the initial shock began to wear off, she considered her abduction. Could this be what had happened to Gwen? The thought gave her hope. She tried calling out for her friend, but soon stopped. The desolate echo of her voice was too discouraging.

How long she wandered in the Brule, Laurel had no idea. The view had been deceptive. Everything was farther away than it looked. Hours had passed and she had yet to clear the bog. Though she wasn't thinking of food, she was very thirsty. The ashen air parched her throat. She took a detour toward the stream, but any hopes of a drink died as soon as she saw it. The creek trickled over a bed of slime. The water was fetid.

She stood transfixed on the muddy bank, staring downward. What was in the shadows beneath the surface? She leaned forward to get a closer look. The image was distorted, sickly white and bloated. Terror crept into her mind as she recognized what she saw: her own body drowned in the snye.

Laurel tried to back away, but the stream seemed

to pull her toward it. Unable to stop herself, she waded into the oily water. Something flickered beneath the murky surface. Small wormlike shapes. As the first leech burrowed into her leg, Laurel went faint with horror and almost toppled over. As she pitched forward, the leather necklace fell out of her shirt.

The moonstone swung wildly, spraying white light around her. The leeches scattered. The snye released its grip. Almost weeping with relief, Laurel splashed her way out of the hideous stream.

Safely back on the bank, her hands closed around the moonstone. It felt cool to the touch. Her skin tingled. It was as if she were standing inside a waterfall. Silently she thanked the young man who had saved her life.

Still gripping the moonstone, Laurel headed back into the bog. Though her progress was slow, the stone seemed to give her the strength to go on. When she wasn't tripping over roots or beating back briars, she was pulling her feet from the thick, gluey mud. Someone less fit might not have been able, but Laurel was an athlete and in good shape. Still, the ordeal was taking its toll. Her limbs ached and she was covered in scratches as well as foul-smelling muck. At last she broke from the bog and faced the ridge.

Her moment of triumph was brief. Though the green orbs of light were not familiar to her, the buzzing sound was. A line of them had risen out of the earth to hover in the air, directly between her and the ridge she hoped to reach. The high-pitched noise they emitted was like that of killer bees. She had no doubt they were deadly.

Laurel retreated to the shelter of the trees. But she was not defeated. Breaking off branches, she finally found one hefty enough to make a bat. She grinned to herself. Softball was one of her favorite sports.

The green lights had moved closer to the edge of the copse, as if daring her to come out. Stealthily she approached them, gripping her stick. As soon as she stepped from the trees, one shot toward her. She batted it into the ridge, where it exploded against the rock. The next she doused in the river and the one after that as well. Two more hit the rock face.

"Come on!" she yelled. "I'm just warming up! Batting practice! Let's go!"

The remaining few hovered in the air without moving.

"Hah!" she called. "Not so brave now, eh?"

This was her chance. Bat held high, she made a dash for the ridge. But even as she ran, she realized the truth. They had only been playing with her. As the droning sound rose to a crescendo of screeches, more and more rose from the ground. Now they swarmed toward her.

Laurel screamed as the first struck her. Her shirt fabric burned away. Her skin was scorched. She batted away the second and the third, but the fourth hit her leg. She almost fell over. It was no use. There were too many.

Gulping back sobs, she turned around and fled back to the trees.

Again her hand closed around the moonstone. *Don't give up,* came the message, like a whisper in her mind, *you just need more weapons. Make a shield.* Clarity of thought gave her strength. Of course. A shield. Plaited branches would do. Soaked in water, they might even be fireproof. Dare she tackle that stream again? She would have to. As she hurried in that direction, her foot was caught by a hidden root. She was sent sprawling into a damp hollow. Black mud oozed around her. She could sense its malevolence. *Don't bother to get up. It's hopeless. You may as well surrender.* She clutched the moonstone. *Get up, gal, get up. You're not beaten yet.*

Gritting her teeth, she repeated the message.

"I'm not beaten yet."

Laurel clawed her way out of the ditch. That was when she spied it: a small mound of soil heaped at the foot of a withered tree. At first it looked like a fresh grave. Then she realized the mound had a discernible shape, as if sculpted in clay.

The hair on the back of Laurel's neck stood up. The shape was female. *Gwen?* Everything inside Laurel cried out not to look. But she had to. Breath held fearfully, she drew closer to the mound. As she recognized the body, a scream tore from her throat.

# Twenty-Nine

"We are so dead if Gabe ever finds out," Dee said mildly.

She looked out the airplane window. The sun shone palely above a sea of cirrus. The landscape below played hide-and-seek with the clouds. They had been flying for hours, over green and brown countryside, through various time zones, across plains and prairie.

"Yeah," said Yvonne with the same lack of concern.

"Do you feel as if you're wandering through a dream?"

Dee was still absorbing the fact that she was heading for Vancouver on someone else's money. The luxury of first class was as good as she had hoped. The flight attendant kept giving her things: delicious food, hot towels, free perfumes, expensive magazines.

Yvonne shook her head vigorously. "Not in the least. I feel exquisitely awake. As if I've been doused in the ocean. Every nerve is tingling. I'm totally alive."

Dee reflected on her words. "I have that too," she finally agreed. "That's a better description. It's the way I feel when I'm making a film, when it's all coming together but still at the stage where anything could happen."

"Absolutely," Yvonne concurred. "It's as good as art and nearly as good as—"

They grinned at each other and cackled like witches.

Dozing in the seat across the aisle, Dana couldn't help smiling to herself. Her aunts were worse than two kids. And in more ways than one. She couldn't believe it when Deirdre hogged the window seat. Gabriel always gave it to Dana on their travels. When her other aunt objected, Dana thought she was taking her side but no, Yvonne wanted the seat for herself. After a spirited exchange involving colorful words, the two came to a time-sharing arrangement that didn't include their niece.

"You need to rest," Yvonne had said, quite unfairly. "You're younger than us."

Only in years, Dana thought to herself, but she gave up arguing when she saw it was futile. Instead, she promised herself she'd be the first on the plane for the flight home. With her aunts, it was every woman for herself.

Now the two were discussing the adventure in low tones. They had finally reached the realization that there could be trouble and they were worried for their niece.

"Things could get hairy," Dee was saying. "Remember those strange little men screeching up and down the hall at night?"

"That was the dark rum," Yvonne pointed out. "You didn't see them again when you cut it out."

Again Dana smiled, but she also felt a pang of guilt. Was it right to endanger them this way? She had no doubt that it was only a matter of time before Crowley found her out west. He seemed to be able to track her no matter where she went. Did she have enough power to protect herself and her aunts?

Below lay the western province of Alberta. As they passed over the brown foothills of the Rocky Mountains, the flight got bumpy.

"I don't want to die," Deirdre moaned. "Not now. Not ever."

Yvonne didn't speak, but she looked anxious. Her knuckles were white as she gripped the armrests.

Dana wasn't afraid. It was far less turbulent than the flying canoe.

"Come on, let me near the window. You both have your eyes shut!"

Conceding defeat and welcoming the distraction, her aunts changed seats to let her in. Dana pressed her face to the window. The drifts of cloud had parted to reveal a vast mountain range powdered with snow. The stark peaks undulated like an ocean of living rock. Dana shivered with awe. There was power in these mountains. She had flown into the west to meet them. What would they teach her? What would she find here?

An ache gripped her heart. If only Jean could see these too! She had thought about him all the way across Canada, missing him, wishing he was there, and imagining him in her mind. At the same time, she was glad of her decision. She preferred that he was safe.

When the plane landed, the three took a taxi to their hotel. The driver was surprised when the aunts encouraged him to go the long way.

"Ah, Vancouver," Yvonne sighed, "Queen of Cities."

"Traitor," said Dee, though she was also looking around her joyfully.

"What?" said Dana, puzzled.

Yvonne explained. "If you come from Toronto you can't even hint that Vancouver might be better. Though it so obviously is and everybody knows it."

"Traitor," said Dee again.

"Don't you have that in Ireland?" Yvonne asked her.

Dana thought a moment. "There is a thing between Dublin and the west, but everyone pretty well agrees that the west is best. It begins when you cross the River Shannon."

"What is it about west coasts?" Yvonne mused. "Why do they have all the ambience? The *je ne sais quoi?*"

"Yeah, think of Seattle and California too," Dee added.

Beyond the cab window, the cityscape opened to embrace the Torontonians. On one side glimmered the pure blue of the Pacific Ocean, on the other sheered a grandeur of mountains. Cradled in between, like a sunburst of crystals, was Vancouver itself, with its elegant architecture and spacious streets, arched bridges and sandy beaches, museums and quaint pubs. Overhead, the Skytrain glided like a silver serpent. The weather was crisp and sunny, in contrast to the prairies where it was already snowing. Some of the trees still blazed with autumn color while others stood naked, leaves heaped at their feet like discarded garments.

Their hotel was old and old-fashioned. It had been a stylish apartment building in its day, but now the lobby and elevators looked worn and a little shabby. Their room had an antique charm. The furniture was 1950s, with oversized lampshades in beige and brown, stuffed arm-chairs, wooden furniture, and comfortable beds. The carpet was threadbare, the television huge, but the bath-room was spotless with an abundance of thick towels.

"We could have paid more for more," was Deirdre's comment.

"I just couldn't," said Yvonne. "I always stay here when I come to Vancouver. She's like an old lady friend. I would feel I was betraying her if we went to some tarty new place."

Dee rolled her eyes at Dana, but was obviously happy enough. Their room overlooked English Bay with a panoramic view of beach and promenade. Seagulls perched on the windowsills.

"Wait till you taste the food," Yvonne added. "Especially breakfast. Seriously yum. Bacon and eggs, fruit cup, pancakes with syrup, big pot of coffee."

"I want that right now," Dee decided, picking up the phone. "Why put off till tomorrow what you can eat today?"

"She knows nothing about deferment of gratification," Yvonne said to Dana, then she called to her sister, "The same for us!"

"No bacon for me!" said Dana.

When the food arrived, it was devoured with appreciative noises as they continued to discuss their plans. Dana had brought the Fair Folk's itinerary with her. The venue for the Vancouver dates was the Moon in the Bog, Whelan's Tavern, Gastown.

"I think it's safe to say the Moon in the Bog is a club on top of a bar," Dee said.

"New Irish bar," Yvonne said, nodding. "I've heard of it, but haven't got there yet. That means you can't go," she said to Dana. "They serve alcohol."

"Yahoo!" said Dee, but when she saw Dana's face, "I mean, boo-hoo!"

"We'll go there for you," Yvonne continued, after throwing Dee a stern look. "If we can't bring the Fair Folk back here, we'll arrange a meeting for tomorrow. We know the story, we can fill them in. Okay?"

Dana was not happy at all.

"Can't we just put loads of makeup on her?" Dee suggested. "She's taller than us. She looks at least sixteen."

"Which is still not the legal age," her sister said archly. "Look, we're in pretty deep here already. Can you imagine if we got arrested with a minor and they contacted Gabe?"

"Right," said Dee. Turning to Dana, she shrugged. "Watch TV till your eyes bug out and run up the room-service bill."

Dana opened her mouth to object, but Deirdre had already turned away to peruse the itinerary of the Fair Folk. A short blurb described their music: "Findabhair and Finvarra wow their audience with the eclectic electric sound of Celtic fusion."

"How do you pronounce this name?" she asked Dana. "Find-a-bear?"

Dana had to laugh. "It's an old Irish name, linked to Guinevere. You pronounce it 'Finn-ah-veer.'" But she wasn't distracted for long. "Can't we contact them before the show?" she insisted.

Yvonne looked sympathetic. "Keep trying if you want, kiddo. But you know how well that went before we left Toronto. Groups on the road are never easy to get ahold of."

While her aunts unpacked, Dana rang the tavern, the club, and the Fair Folk's hotel, all to no avail. She left messages at each number giving her name and "The

Companions of Faerie" for reference, but her lack of success left her crestfallen.

"They might call back," Yvonne said to comfort her. "And you'll be here to talk to them if they do. Bottom line, I promise you, we'll bring them to you as soon as we can."

It was too early for the club to open, so the three went for a walk along the promenade of English Bay. Crowds of people strolled along, enjoying the sunshine in the late afternoon.

"Very West Coast," said Yvonne approvingly.

There were musicians busking with guitars and fiddles, skateboarders, lovers walking hand in hand. Two old men played chess at a stone table beneath a big tree, while a young woman contorted herself into yoga positions. The pale sand on the beach was strewn with gray driftwood. Ducks bobbed on the waves. Gulls screeched overhead.

The three bought popcorn and ice cream, and sat on a bench to watch the world go by. Dana let herself relax. For now, there was really nothing else she could do.

Back in their room, Dana's good humor was dispelled as her aunts dressed to go out. Dee donned a black leather cat suit with a long zipper and metal jewelry, while Yvonne put on a slinky red dress with stiletto heels. Clouds of perfume wafted from the bathroom.

"You look divine, Mrs. Peel," Yvonne said to Deirdre.

"You too, Madonna."

"You're supposed to be on a mission," Dana accused them.

"You never know who you might meet on a mission," Dee pointed out.

"Heroes?" Yvonne said to her sister.

They grinned at each other.

"Now, don't wait up," Dee said to Dana. "We're bound to get tanked."

"Just try and remember why you're going," their niece pleaded as they left.

The club was not what Dee and Yvonne expected. The pub on the first floor was sleek and expensive. Upstairs, the Moon in the Bog was Celtic chic, a cavernous space with a big stage and dim lights. The walls were painted to look like stone adorned with ancient spiral designs. Afro-Celt music shivered through the speakers. A well-dressed crowd slowly filled the room.

"Not your average grotty, find-your-roots gig," Dee commented.

"Don't be cynical," said her sister.

"I am not 'doglike,'" she retorted.

Heading straight for the bar, they ordered pints of Guinness.

"Mmm good," said Dee after a long swallow of the cold black beer.

"You've got a mustache," Yvonne warned her.

"I should hope so," said Dee, licking the creamy froth from her upper lip. "It's bad Guinness if I don't."

When the show started, they turned to face the stage.

Dressed in black like the night, both Finvarra and Findabhair were tall, lithe, and beautiful. And there the resemblance ended. Where her hair was blond and spiked like icicles, his was a jet-black mane that fell in a blunt cut to his shoulders. Her skin was fair, with diamonds piercing her ears, nose, and eyebrows. His coloring was nut-brown, his eyes sloe-black. She wore a dark gown sprayed with stars and slit up the side to reveal a shapely leg. He wore black leather pants and a silken T-shirt that hugged his chest. Both had dark-blue spirals tattooed on their faces, and dusky kohl around their eyes. They were unashamedly flagrant and fey.

The aunts approved.

"These guys could give beauty lessons," was Yvonne's assessment.

"Seriously cutie-patootie," Dee agreed.

As soon as the music began, they were stunned into silence. It was haunting and exquisite. Finvarra played the fiddle like a gypsy king, with searing abandon and breathtaking virtuosity. Findabhair sang in high thrilling notes like a lark. When his voice entwined with hers, it was like a low dark stream running through the light that danced across the water.

*Traveler, do not tarry*
*For the moon shines so bright*

*Traveler, be not wary*
*For the Old Ones call tonight.*

Weirdly and subtly, other instruments joined the fiddle. The tingling tintinnabulation of the Celtic harp. The rapid-fire reverberation of a throng of bodhran drums. The full-bodied skirl of the uillean pipes, a hive of honeyed sound.

The audience looked around briefly for the other musicians, but returned their focus to the stage when they couldn't find them.

Dee and Yvonne raised their eyebrows at each other.

*"Where is the path my feet must tread?"* sang Findabhair.

*"Beyond the dark your heart doth dread,"* sang Finvarra.

In between the tunes and airs, the pair onstage took turns speaking. The lilt of Findabhair's Irish accent was evident, as was Finvarra's, but his speech was markedly different from hers. Though peppered with modern words, it was oddly formal and quaint.

As the first set progressed, something struck the two aunts. They nudged each other. Being artists themselves, they were sensitive to nuances of thought and feeling. Both caught the undertow of sorrow in the music; the dark grief that tore at its heart. At times the jagged edge of lament resounded with a bitterness that bordered on rage.

It was potent stuff.

"Grab your spear," Yvonne murmured.

"Look alive," said Dee, suddenly. "I think he's scanning for us!"

Deirdre was right. Finvarra's keen eyes were surveying the room. When his glance settled on the two of them, she gave him a little wave and Yvonne nodded. Finvarra's look changed to a piercing gaze. Both stepped backward, then his eyes looked away.

"Whoa!" Dee muttered. "What was that?"

"Magic," said Yvonne.

They could feel the electricity of that look still shivering through them.

As soon as the set was over, both members of the Fair Folk came to the bar.

"Is one of you Dana?" Findabhair asked.

"We are well met," said Finvarra.

Despite his words, neither Finvarra nor his wife was smiling. Their features were stiff. Their eyes, veiled.

Surprised by the vague hostility, the aunts were unsettled.

"No," they said together, "we're—"

They stopped, flustered.

"You talk," Dee urged Yvonne. "You're firstborn."

"We're Dana's aunts," Yvonne explained quickly. "She's back at the hotel. She's only thirteen. No amount of makeup was going to get her in here."

"*Thirteen?*" Findabhair looked at her husband, horrified. "She's only a kid!"

"She is no ordinary child," he said coolly. "She is the Light-Bearer's Daughter. She has power of her own."

The bartender brought their drinks. Findabhair was given a ginger ale, while a pint of Guinness with two shots of whiskey were placed in front of Finvarra. As he downed the whiskey in successive gulps, his wife frowned.

Yvonne and Dee exchanged glances.

"Do you know my cousin Gwen?" Findabhair asked them.

She saw the expressions on their faces before they could answer. She went pale. "Is she all right?!"

"I'm afraid she isn't," Yvonne said, tempering her voice. "She disappeared over a week ago. Dana suspects she was taken by some enemy who's been after her since this whole thing began. Gwen's friend Laurel is also missing."

Findabhair gripped the counter. She looked ill.

"Why didn't you tell me?" she demanded of Finvarra. "You must have felt something! You felt it when the others were hit."

His eyes darkened. "I felt the doom of Faerie, not the fall of our companions. I am as blind as you."

"Oh God, I should've joined her," Findabhair said. Her voice rang with guilt. "She needed us and we abandoned her!"

Embarrassed by the tension between the couple, Yvonne spoke up. "Dana wants you to find Gwen and Laurel. But we think you should join her quest as well."

"That's why we're here," Deirdre said bluntly. "To get your help."

"We must rescue Gwen!" Findabhair agreed.

Finvarra signaled to the barman to bring him more whiskey. He brooded over his drink.

"The blood of Faerie flows in Dana's veins," he said at last, without looking up. "She is more than any of you can imagine. It is her destiny to complete this task. The rescue of Fairyland is in her hands, as is the fate of our comrades who have fallen."

Even Findabhair looked astounded by his pronouncement.

"You can't expect Dana to do everything!" Yvonne objected.

"She's still a kid, no matter what you say," said Dee.

The aunts glared at Finvarra. But at the same time they were both overawed by him. Here was a former High King of Faerie. One who had lived in the world when the earth was young, before humanity was born. They recalled the power of his music and the keenness of his glance. Was this all that was left of his former glory?

"What's wrong with you?" Yvonne said. "What's your problem?"

"Aside from the fact that you drink too much?" Dee added.

Findabhair flinched at their words and was about to defend her husband when he cut her off.

"I do not expect you to understand," he said, looking up from his drink. In the fierce gaze of his eyes, they saw the same anguish they had heard in the music. "The nature of my grief runs deep. I could not have known what I would have to bear until my exile came upon me. To be banished forever from the Kingdom is to suffer a torment that eats away at my soul." He reached out to clasp his wife's hand. Her eyes filled with tears. "I do not regret the sacrifice I made for my Beloved. Were I to face it again, I would make the same choice. Still, it grieves my heart sore to live in the shadowlands that are not my home and to endure an existence that is not my own."

Yvonne's glare had softened to sympathy. Findabhair leaned against her husband in silent support.

Deirdre was not so easily hooked.

"Hey, you made your bed, you lie in it. It's not as if you've ended up in demonville. There are worse things than living in this world. It has a lot going for it. You've got a genius for music, not to mention a gorgeous wife who needs to read *Women Who Love Too Much.* Your music alone could sustain you if you let it; trust me, as one tormented artist to another. It's time you bit the bullet and stopped whining."

Yvonne gaped at her sister with admiration.

"Let's go," said Dee. "They're no use to Dana!"

Leaving the club together, Yvonne showered Dee with praise.

"You were amazing! I was completely sucked in by the Sad Sack routine."

"That's because you're an old softie. You'd never make a director."

Outside the tavern, they stood in the dark street and looked around for a taxi. It had begun to rain. The initial impulse to storm out on high horses began to wear off. Both were now attacked by second thoughts.

"Dana's going to be very disappointed," said Yvonne with a worried sigh.

"It's not as if they were offering to help," Dee said defensively.

"My dress is ruined," her sister groaned.

The quick shower had drenched the soft fabric. It clung to her skin. "I'm like a wet teabag!"

"I told you to wear a coat," Dee replied crossly. "Are there no bloody cabs in this place?"

"Don't start," her sister rejoined.

They were well into one of their usual spats when a tall figure approached them. At first they saw only the long coat and gray hat, but as he stepped in front of them, the streetlights of the bar lit up his face. Both drew back involuntarily. In the flickering neon, the scars looked even more gruesome. But it was the eyes that truly shocked them. Black pits of hatred.

*"Where is the child?"*

His voice was chilling, inhuman. It cut at their nerves like a jagged knife.

Their first reaction was to freeze in terror.

Their second was to run.

The two managed only a few steps before he caught them. With terrible force he threw them into the alley beside the tavern. The passage was dark and dank and smelled of garbage. They opened their mouths to scream, but long, bony fingers gripped each by the throat.

A horrible waspish sound rang through their brains. A sickening odor filled the air. Now their terror increased a hundredfold as his shape changed in front of them. Hands transformed to viscous tentacles. Features seemed to melt into a sickly, greenish mass. His grip tightened. Their veins began to swell.

From the club windows above pumped the sound of Celtic rock. Any hope that the Fair Folk might have followed after them, died.

There would be no rescue.

Slowly the monster lifted them into the air.

*"Where is the child?"* he repeated in a cold, remorseless tone.

They managed to catch each other's eyes, wide and terrified. Their strangled features were turning blue. Each saw the message in the other's look. They would say nothing of their niece and they would die. In that last glance of farewell, they sent each other praise and courage.

*Hang tough, sis. You're a hero.*

The acceptance of their deaths encouraged the final throe. With a surge of strength, they kicked out furiously to break his hold.

Caught off guard, Crowley dropped them.

The aunts jumped to their feet. Gasping for breath, they backed themselves against the wall. Yvonne pulled off her stiletto high heels and held them up like daggers. Dee was already wading in, kicking ferociously, glad of her boots. Yvonne joined her, jabbing with her heels. At the same time, they screamed for help with shouts that also served as war cries.

There was a moment when it looked as if they might succeed, when they drove the monster back. It was obvious that they had surprised him. That he was used to easier prey.

But it wasn't long before they sensed what he already knew: their struggle was hopeless. Though they were not as weak or as easily cowed as he had expected, still they were no match for him.

Hopelessly, courageously, they continued to resist, kicking, punching, screaming, scratching. They weren't going down without a fight.

Now the tentacles gripped their throats once more, lifting them off their feet. Now the darkness dimmed their sight as he cut off their breath.

Losing consciousness, the aunts weren't aware of the blast of wind that rushed through the alley, carrying with it an eddy of leaves. But they did feel the thump when they hit the ground again. Crowley had released them. Reeling and coughing, unable to get up, they saw a blur of shadows attack the monster.

The battle was quick and deadly. Was that the gleam of swords? Who was singing? Were they wearing bright cloaks?

Yvonne and Dee blinked dizzily.

Crowley howled with rage.

*"I'll find her no matter where you hide her!"*

Then he shrank into a trail of green slime and disappeared.

Yvonne rose shakily to her feet and leaned against the wall. She was willing herself not to faint from the pain. Her wounds were bleeding badly.

Dee was still sprawled on the ground, bruised and

battered. Every time she struggled to get up, she fell back down. Something was broken.

Hands reached out to help her to her feet. They felt firm and strong, but also kind.

"You fought well, Lady. We were tracking the beast and heard your cries. We came as swiftly as we could."

His voice alone revived her, echoing as it did of forest and mountain.

"I . . . not a lady . . . really," Dee stuttered, still in shock.

As the aunts steadied themselves and their vision cleared, they got a good look at their rescuers.

The two men were strikingly handsome, with earth-brown skin and flashing eyes. Their chestnut hair was tied back in ponytails. They looked like brothers, possibly twins. But where were their cloaks and swords? Both wore denim jeans with knives tucked into their belts. Despite the cold night they had no jackets, only T-shirts displaying muscled arms. The alley seemed less dirty and noisome in their presence. The scent of cedar lingered in the air.

Before the aunts could recover enough to thank them, the men took their leave.

"We gotta go now," said the one who hadn't yet spoken.

He lifted Yvonne's hand and kissed it gently.

The other did the same to Dee.

"Hope to see ya again, warrior gal," he said with a wink.

A gust of wind blew through the alley, kicking up debris.

The men were gone.

Yvonne recovered first.

*"Dana!"*

# Thirty

After her aunts left, Dana made a fitful attempt to do as Dee suggested. With the television on, a chocolate milkshake, and french fries with vinegar, she told herself to be patient and wait for news. Some part of her wanted to be the kid, to let the older ones look after matters, but it wasn't long before she knew that simply wasn't possible. Inside, the urgings grew stronger and stronger. This was her quest, and while she was disappointed that she couldn't meet the Fair Folk that night, they were not the chief reason she had come west. She began to pace the floor. There was something else she had to do here. What was it? Grandfather's words echoed in her mind.

*It is important to encounter and acknowledge the life of the land. From such encounters come power.*

Well, she had done the thing he encouraged her to do, traveling around Canada and meeting its spirits. And just as he had promised, she had learned much and gained in strength and power.

Dana's pacing increased. Things were growing clearer.

*The land won't yield its secrets to a stranger.*

And there in her hotel room in Vancouver, Dana suddenly caught sight of a huge truth. The spirits of the land knew all about the Book of Dreams. They knew what it was and where it could be found. But they would not reveal that secret to an outsider.

She had to convince them somehow. She had to make them understand she was not a stranger. That she belonged here.

Dana didn't stop to write a note. She had to go quickly. They were waiting for her. Throwing on her coat, she ran out of the room.

It was a balmy evening, much warmer than Toronto at that time of year. Dana strode determinedly along the boardwalk. Though it was less crowded than earlier, there were still a few strollers. Behind her rose the city towers. Ahead, the green shadows of Stanley Park. The sun had set over English Bay to drown in the waters of the Strait of Georgia. A flock of white gulls bobbed sleepily on the waves. Clouds moved in the sky to reveal a clear moon with a silver corona.

*Traveler, do not tarry*
*For the moon shines so bright*

The song was drifting on the breeze, whispered by the trees that bordered the path, leaves whispering and singing like dark tongues in the night. The farther she walked, the fewer people she passed. Alarm bells sounded in the back of her mind but she ignored them. There was no question of turning back. She had business there that night.

*Traveler, be not wary*
*For the Old Ones call tonight.*

The forest loomed ahead. Hurrying toward it, she plunged into the trees. The darkness inside was warm and inviting. A hush had fallen over the foliage. Slowly things began to move around her, to slip out of place, to shift and change. Colors competed with the darkness. Various shapes seemed to creep in her direction, then scurry away as if too shy to meet.

"Who's there?" she whispered.

The trees replied with a susurrus of sound: the crepitation of leaves, the crackle of twigs, the snap of branches. The night pressed against her ears like a seashell, whispering and sighing. She heard the scuttle of small creatures in the undergrowth and the rustle of wings in the boughs overhead. Her eyes darted here and there to catch sight of what moved. They were quick as a heartbeat! Everything was in motion yet somehow invisible.

She walked quietly, carefully, stalking her prey. Deep in the Canadian woods that night, she was hunting the answer.

Wandering through the park, Dana reached a clearing. Before her rose a stand of totem poles. Even in the darkness the carved features were striking; yellow beaks, white wings, black eyes, and red lips. She was able to make out the different animal beings—Raven, Eagle, and Bear. They looked proud and lonely. As she gazed upon them, she heard a loud crack on the wind.

There was no time to feel fear. The totem animals were waking up, moving, yawning, stretching. It was Raven who flew down from the top of the pole, no longer carved from wood, but flesh and bone. His wings closed around her in a flurry of black feathers. In the distance came the sound of a rattle and the beating of drums. Then a voice raised in song. There was something familiar in Raven's look, the wisdom and kindness that shone in his eyes.

"Grandfather!"

Like a small child she reached out to accept his embrace, to be lifted upward. He didn't hold her for long. She had no sooner been raised from the ground to the uppermost height of the totem than she was flung into the sky and far away. She flew through the night. The sensation was exquisite, far more wonderful than even *la chasse-galerie*. For there was nothing between her and the swift currents of air. She knew what it was like to be a bird. The stars hurtled above her. The land sped past below. Beyond the forest, over gorge and narrow passage, she crossed the North Shore Mountains and the craggy coast. Now the great islands slid away to the west as she journeyed deep into the interior of British Columbia.

Dazed but excited, Dana landed on her feet in another forest. The size of the trees was overwhelming, so too the sense of their age. Arboreal giants, centuries old. The air was rich with the scent of red cedar, Douglas fir, sitka spruce, and hemlock. It wasn't night here. Viridescent light filtered through the interlace of leaves. This forest was greener than any woods she had known in Ireland, more emerald than the Emerald Isle. Massive draperies of leafage cascaded from the boughs. The great trunks were shrouded with ivy and moss. Underfoot was a thick mat of old leaves, needles, and bracts laid down in layers over countless seasons.

Was this a forest in Canada or a primeval wood? The First Forest that begat all forests? It had an air of innocence, of paradise. A sense that no man had ever walked there. Black crows cawed from high in the treetops. Gray squirrels scrabbled in their dreys. A great spotted slug crawled over a leaf. As raccoons and skunks ambled past, some stopped to sniff her as if in greeting. They showed no fear. A black-tailed deer let Dana stroke its flank.

She could hardly describe how she felt in that forest. Somehow she felt very old and very young at the same time; new upon the earth and yet, as if she had always been there. For as long as life had existed so too had she; but now she was seeing it for the first time with new eyes.

Dana was attempting to orient herself when something rushed out of the trees to grab her. Though her mind cried "bear," she knew it wasn't. She had glimpsed features in the hairy face just before it threw her over its shoulders. The flat nose and lipless mouth were simian, like a gorilla or an orangutan. More than eight feet tall, with shaggy reddish-brown hair, it had broad shoulders, a barrel chest, and no visible neck. Against the first stab of terror, she had caught the apologetic look in its eyes.

The furry giant carried her along the trails, moving with the ease of one who dwelled in the forest. When they reached a wide clearing beside a river, Dana was set down.

Before her was a camp inhabited by similar creatures. Makeshift huts were arranged around a large campfire. The structures of leaves and branches had the temporary look of nomadic shelters. While the adults went about their work, gathering water from the river or tending the fire, children of all ages played nearby. They appeared to be a quiet and peaceful race. Dana could hear in their low murmurings a snuffling kind of language that involved grunts and snorts. As they glanced at her with big curious eyes, she found herself hoping they weren't carnivorous. Was she on the menu? There were no pots or cooking utensils to be seen.

Her captor had left her sitting on a rock. No one approached her. She wondered whether she should try to escape. A quick glance at the huge forest that crouched around her discouraged the thought. Where would she go? When more of the creatures entered the camp with baskets of roots, greens, nuts, and berries, she breathed a sigh of relief. Herbivores.

One of the children ran toward her to drop a bunch of wild strawberries into her lap. Caught off guard, Dana let out a yelp that sent her benefactress scampering away, yelping also.

"Oh, sorry, sorry," Dana called out, too late.

The longer she remained in the camp, the more relaxed Dana grew. She could see that the creatures were friendly, if shy. They showed no signs of aggression, either against her or amongst themselves. She noticed they kept looking into the trees. After a while she realized they were waiting for someone.

When he arrived at last, Dana thought she might faint with fear.

The ground trembled beneath him as he strode into the clearing. Even stooped with age he was much bigger than the others—at least twelve feet tall. There was no doubt he was ancient, the Elder of the tribe. Where the others had abundant red or brown fur, his hair was white and thin, even bald in patches. As he drew near, Dana caught the faint whiff of decay. His face was wrinkled like a dried riverbed. The dark eyes were wet and rheumy. Yet he was terrifying, far more so than the others. For while they were domesticated, he was obviously a wild man of the woods.

He did not sit down. His manner was brusque and impatient, like a king or a politician. He had come to perform a task and would leave again as soon as it was done.

He stood in front of Dana and pointed to the others around the fire.

"*Saskehavas.*"

Dana stared at him dumbly. Her mouth was dry. She fought against her fear to pay attention. He was trying to tell her something, but what?

He made a sweeping gesture that took in the forest all around them.

"*Klahanie.*"

Dana shook her head.

The others had gathered around and were watching curiously.

Now he made a drinking motion followed by feigned laughter and an exaggerated look of merriment.

"*Hootchinoo,*" he said, repeating the drinking gesture.

The furry audience burst into loud laughter, startling Dana. What madness was this?

"Hootch—?" Dana tried.

Another explosion of laughter. Dana was growing more confused by the minute.

Several more words were directed at her, each sounding

so different from the last that she finally guessed what was going on. He was trying out various languages on her.

"I speak English," she said, "and Irish. Also a bit of French."

The exasperated look on his face was almost comical. Had the situation not been so bizarre she would have laughed.

"Why did you not say so?" he said in a deep rumbling voice.

"I . . . I . . . didn't think—"

"Your kind never do," he said with a grunt.

He indicated the others, who were looking pleased and excited now that Dana and the Elder were talking.

"They called me here to speak with you. Do you know of the Sasquatch?"

Dana was embarrassed. "I haven't been very long in this country," she told him. "I've only begun to learn—"

"Bigfoot is another name your people use."

"Oh, wait! Yes! I know that one! You mean the North American version of the Abominable Snowman? The Yeti?"

"Tibetan cousins." The Elder nodded.

"Are you Sasquatch as well?" Dana asked, amazed.

"I am of the Firstborn. That is why I can speak with you. We have all the languages that are upon the earth. There are only a few of us, and we are solitaries. We live alone in the mountains. The Bigfoot, our descendants, are more sociable. They like to live in tribes, but they are also clannish. They shun human company and speak only their own language."

Dana smiled at the others, who smiled back shyly. Some still looked a little nervous of her. How could she have been afraid of them?

"Why did they bring me here?" she asked.

"They want to help you. Know this, even as the evil which has entered the land gathers allies to its cause, so those who oppose the darkness are called to your light."

"Like an army?" Dana said worriedly. "I don't want to drag people into a battle."

"There is no neutral ground in this war," the Elder said. "Battles must be fought, within and without, both big and small. You have been brought here for a reason. It is time for your initiation."

A rush of fear swept through Dana, but she fought it down. Wasn't this why she had set out that night?

"What must I do?" she asked the Elder.

"You will go into the forest. The Sasquatch will prepare you. You must seek out the Old Ones to ask their blessing."

Another wave of anxiety. What if she failed? Dana steeled herself. She was at the heart of her quest, the core of her mission. If she proved her worth to the spirits of the land, she would find the Book of Dreams. It was up to her how she faced this test: coward or a hero?

"Is there something I should bring?" she asked calmly. "A gift or offering of some sort?"

The dark eyes assessed her. She couldn't read the meaning of his gaze.

"You are the gift," came his reply, at last.

Before Dana could ask what he meant, the Elder's visit ended. With a grunt of farewell to the others, he stalked out of the camp.

As soon as he left, the preparations for Dana's initiation began. The female Sasquatch led her to the river where they indicated she was to undress and bathe. The water was icy cold and took her breath away, but she felt invigorated when she climbed out. Her skin tingled, her blood sang. Once dry, she was given new clothes; a shirt and leggings of soft, supple deerskin. Neatly stitched, they were embroidered with white quills and blue beads. A knee-length apron of cedar bark went around her waist. Her feet were shorn with moccasin boots. When she returned to the fire, a younger female braided Dana's hair into a single plait down her back. Then an older male painted her face with stripes of ochre. Two last things were given to her: a short cape of black feathers and a tall staff of carved pine.

When they were finished, the Bigfoot pressed around her with gentle noises of encouragement. For a moment Dana felt as if the forest were closing in on her. They were like tall shaggy trees with red-brown bark.

"I don't know how to say thank-you in your language," she said.

She gazed into their features, which no longer seemed alien. She saw their kindness and intelligence. With sudden inspiration, she placed the staff on the ground to free her hands. Bowing with respect and thanks, she placed her palms together till the light welled up. The flow was far stronger than at any time before. It poured out of her hands in a stream of gold.

They were neither surprised nor afraid, but they were obviously delighted. All beamed big smiles at her as they bowed in return.

It was the first time Dana really understood the phrase she had been hearing since her quest began.

"Yes," she said softly, smiling back through her tears. *"We are all family."*

Setting off into the woods alone, Dana wished some of the Sasquatch had come with her for company. But she knew it wasn't possible. This was her initiation and she had to do it alone. The forest was immense, a vast green country. While she had originally assumed her staff was a ceremonial object, she soon discovered it wasn't. Without it, she wouldn't have been able to make her way through the undergrowth. Again and again she had to beat back the sea of bracken, sallal, wild rose, and blackberry. Always the woods threatened to engulf her, the dank smells, the untrammeled growth, the clouds of insects, the density of trees. She could feel the weight of the massive greenery bearing down on all sides, creaking, sighing, muttering, groaning.

Hour after hour, she continued to hike through gigantic spreads of pine and cedar, rotting logs and forest debris, roots and stumps, toadstools and slugs, fallen branches and clumps of fern. Sometimes she stumbled into dips and hollows. Other times she waded through shallow streams. The forest soon left its mark on her. Her face and hands were scratched, her clothes caked with mud. Twigs and leaves clung to her hair. She was glad of the clothes the Sasquatch had given her, as they kept her dry and allowed her limbs free movement. Her own jeans and coat would have been destroyed long before this.

Though the monotony of the trek began to wear her down, Dana didn't halt or rest. She was driven to fulfill her vision quest.

Then the Old Ones came.

She had already begun to sense Their presence: something immense and profound in the forest itself. A great mystery that dwelled within it. An impenetrable strength. Slowly but surely the secret was revealed. They were here. All around her.

The first sound she heard was high in the air, so far above her it could have come from heaven. A great sigh on the wind. Then came the rivers of light exuding from the trees themselves, ribbons and striations of light that penetrated the green dimness like arrows and spears. They surged on the wind, a great movement through the forest, a force that sighed through every leaf and branch and blade of grass, surging through the undergrowth like the surge of the sea; a pacific force, urging the trees to explode into the sky, to swirl in spirals of green and yellow, terrible and rapturous, a great swell of light and movement and color and presence, a vast overflowing, a hugeness of energy, all of it coalescing into a trembling luminosity that only the word *God* could come close to naming.

How long Dana remained in Their ecstatic embrace, she couldn't know, but there came a time when she felt the struggle to emerge. Rising to the surface, like foam on the waves, an upsurge of consciousness, she felt the infinitesimal mote of awareness that split her from the whole as she remembered who she was. *O nobly born, remember who you are.* And in that rising which was epic and glorious she knew that she, like all the others, like all other things existing in the universe, she knew that she was important: a hero of life.

That was the moment when she plummeted downward
falling like a meteor
falling like a star
striking the ground with such force
she was embedded inside it.

She had landed in a bog and was buried beneath a tree. Sleeping there in the dark earth, inside the roots of the tree, she began to dream.

*Where is the path my feet must tread?*
*Into the dark your heart doth dread.*

# Thirty-One

She was in a cavernous house built of cedar, with one enormous open room. It was big enough to hold gigantic carvings of eagles with extended wings. The carvings dwarfed the inhabitants of the house: the chief and his family who lived there with their kin. Cradles hung from the rafters, rocking gently. Anyone passing by would give the cradles a push and the babies would laugh.

A storm was blowing outside the longhouse, but there were plenty of fires to keep the room warm. The air was smoky, sweet with the scent of burning wood.

Leaving the house, she wandered outside, unaffected by the wind and rain. Nearby was a rocky beach strewn with seaweed. Canoes lay upturned on the shore, elegant in design and painted with bright patterns. Their bows curved dramatically, like the crest of a wave.

When she glanced back, it appeared as if the village had grown organically from the dense tangle of forest. The houses were low and flat, with curled roofs, and connected to one another but with separate entrances. Each door was fronted with a tall carved pole. To enter the house you had to pass through the totem. Eagle was the most common, with hooked beak and feathered wings. Another was Beaver, with immense teeth and flat tail. The sacred animals towered over the village, reaching as high as the great trees at their back.

Now as the rain stopped and the sky blazed with sunlight, the village came to life. Hunters stalked into the forest. Women and children tended to the crops, cured skins over fires, and washed clothes on the shore.

She was drawn to steps leading up a high hill. More carved poles pointed to the sky, but these were crowned with wooden boxes. A whisper in her mind told her these were coffins, containing the bones of the tribal ancestors. And beyond the totem poles was a different kind of house. A burst of light on the roof made her look upward. Shielding her eyes, she saw a figure crouched at the edge. A halo of feathers spiked from his head like the rays of the sun.

.She was suddenly afraid. This house was not for the living. She didn't want to enter. Yet something compelled her inside. She was instantly aware that the interior was crowded. As her eyes grew accustomed to the dimness she was able to see, though she wished she couldn't. The bodies were piled on top of one another, up to the ceiling. They had all died horribly from diseases that had arrived with the white traders and missionaries. Whole families had been wiped out, almost entire nations. She felt the grief and the anger in that House of the Dead.

Returning to the village, she found it abandoned. An

*oppressive silence hung over the empty buildings. The totems leaned precariously. The wooden skeleton of a canoe lay alone on the shore. In the distance came the sounds of clear-felling, as great trees crashed to the ground.*

*She began to move swiftly, along the coast, past glowering hills and beaches of pale driftwood. The ruins of villages lay scattered like bones in the grasses. A gargantuan statue rose before her; the wooden carving of a woman bearing a child in her arms. No passage of time, no splintering or wear, could despoil the tenderness of those big loving hands, that mother's embrace.*

We do not believe in beating children.

*Now she found herself in a cold and unfriendly building. With drab furnishings and worn curtains, it had an institutional feel. Was it a school or an orphanage? It was filled with Native children with sad silent faces, filing through gray corridors or sitting at desks. The air was rank with the smell of misery, homesickness, and fear. They had all been taken from their families.*

*In the yard, a little girl was being comforted by her brother. As he whispered the words in their own language, a smile crossed her face:* Once upon a time Skokki the Spider traveled to the moon and learned from the Sky Dwellers how to weave. That is why the Salish people make baskets.

*She was back in the forest, at the heart of the darkness. Shadows blocked the light. Great curtains of foliage hung heavily around her. She was surrounded by totems. She felt as if she were falling upward into the sky, even as the sacred animals fell earthward toward her. She was lost in colors and shapes, faces and eyes, feathers and wings. Voices murmured in the air. And behind the voices came the steady beat of a drum and the hint of an eternal promise.*

Not all that is gone is gone forever.

*Traveling over the Rockies, she delighted in the breathless freedom of flight. So many mountains, towering skyward, some cloaked in snow, some covered in conifer, some brown, some blue, some barren rock, all shining like stone angels with limbs outstretched to embrace the clouds. Their presence, their very being was huge and overwhelming, vast amassings of matter, brooding souls. Such strength and longevity. Guardians of the earth.*

*She dropped to the ground for a run on the plains. After the gravity of the mountains, it was a lighthearted experience to race with smaller creatures. Gophers popped up and down from holes in the red earth. Chipmunks somersaulted in the air, leaping from tree to tree. Rattlesnakes basked in the sun.*

*She passed over plowed fields, furrowed troughs, calm dark sloughs, and tracks of wet gumbo turned to mud. In solitary treeless spaces rose the stark dark shapes of hoodoos, eerie spirits of rock. And as the starlit prairie fell behind her, she fled into the North, into a boundless shroud of black spruce and moose pasture and the broad sweep of muskeg sprayed with tamarack.*

*At last she sank exhausted into a bog, dreaming deeply and darkly of the world of wild things.*

Dana looked down at her own outline. Was she really buried in black soil at the foot of that tree? A disheveled figure knelt beside her, sobbing wildly.

"This is very weird," she said.

Laurel spun around. "*Dana!* What? How—!"

Grief and horror changed to shock as Laurel looked at the mound where Dana lay buried. Then back again at Dana who stood before her, alive and well, dressed in Native clothing.

"It's the quest," Dana said slowly. "I keep ending up in the strangest places." She looked around. "I think I'm here because I was worrying about you in the back of my mind. About you and Ms. Woods. Are you all right?"

But she could see that the other wasn't. Besides being covered in mud, Laurel's clothes were torn and there were livid burns on her arms and legs.

"I'll live. Gwen's not here. I looked for her, but I've been alone the whole time, except for these crazy fireball things. Are you really here? Are you . . . I mean . . . you look like a ghost."

"Don't worry, I'm not dead." Dana smiled faintly. She did feel a little vague and insubstantial. "I'm not sure where I am. Even while I'm talking to you, I seem to be moving through time." She shivered visibly and her voice echoed with wonder. "I'm on the prairies. There's buffalo everywhere. Thousands and thousands of them. I'm running with them."

Laurel was stunned. "Are you dreaming me? Am I dreaming this?"

"Yes. No. Maybe. Isn't life a dream?" Dana's confusion rang in her voice. She closed her eyes a moment, to listen. "Oh, I see." When she opened them again she looked clearer, more solid. "I'm wind-walking in the West. But I'm also dream-speaking with you. I've been sent to help you."

"Who were you talking to?" Laurel asked, amazed.

"I'm not sure. The wind, I think. It's too hard to explain. This is what the Native peoples do. I can't really describe it. Something like fairy magic. The Old Ones are teaching me."

"You don't have to explain," Laurel said, touching the moonstone. "I'm just happy we're being helped. Things have been going from bad to worse."

Dana closed her eyes again. "Things are bad, yes, but after the darkest hour comes the dawn." When she opened her eyes again, her voice was urgent. "We've got to go. If Crowley finds out I'm here, he'll come back. You need to get over the ridge."

"I tried that already. The fireballs—"

"The *feux follets*," Dana said, nodding. "I've fought them before. Can you run fast?"

"That is definitely something I can do." Despite her injuries and fatigue, Laurel was more than ready to try again.

Dana cupped her hands together till the light spilled from her palms. "Run behind me. Keep going no matter what happens. I don't know how long I'll be here."

It was a dash of hope and courage: Dana in front, streaming her light like a banner; Laurel behind, determined not to falter.

The *feux follets* were taken by surprise, but they recovered quickly. Buzzing through the air like giant wasps, they bombarded the runners. It was trickier this time, Dana saw. The crazy fires had learned their lesson. Avoiding her light, they wove in and around her, darting and diving.

One struck her arm. She winced in anticipation of the pain and was surprised to feel nothing.

"I'm not really here," she told herself. "I am with the Old Ones, dreaming."

Alas, it was not the same for Laurel. As fireballs hit her legs and back, she cried out in pain.

Dana had to do something. With all the effort she could muster she made more light, enough to cover the young woman with a golden shield.

As the *feux follets* came near, they were incinerated, like moths in a flame.

"Thank you!" Laurel panted.

They had cleared the bog and reached the ridge of jagged rock. Dana looked behind. Though she had destroyed the first barrage, more crazy fires were rising from the ground. They had increased in size. The buzzing sound was deafening. Yet they didn't move to attack. Dana's heart sank as she realized why. Their ranks were swelling by the minute. They were amassing a huge force. Their intention was to overwhelm her with sheer bulk.

"Go!" she urged Laurel. "I don't have enough light. I can't hold them all off."

Despite her injuries, Laurel attempted to scale the cliff. Her first efforts proved fruitless. As she scrambled upward, the rock crumbled beneath her feet and she slid back down again.

She leaned against the ridge. Her face was white with pain.

"I . . . I need to catch my breath," she said. "Look, if it gets bad, you've got to leave. Wake up or whatever."

"No," said Dana simply.

"Please," Laurel begged her. "The quest is more important than I am."

"No," Dana said again. "That's what you said when Ms. Woods disappeared and you were wrong. *Everyone* is important. Once I get you out, I'll look for her. If she's here—"

A voice suddenly shouted from above.

"Are you guys talking about me down there?"

High on the ridge overhead, Gwen peered down at them. She was about to laugh at their expressions when she spotted Laurel's injuries.

"Gwen! You're all right!" Laurel's voice shook, and to everyone's surprise, she burst into tears.

"Yes, I'm fine!" Gwen called out. "But you're not, by the looks of things. We're throwing down ropes. Can you climb?"

She called to someone behind her. The next minute two corded vines, heavy and strong, came tumbling down the cliff.

Now the *feux follets* charged toward them.

Laurel tried to tie the rope around Dana.

"No, you go!" said Dana. "I'll fight them off till you're safe."

"Stop being a hero!" Laurel cried. "You don't have enough light! Who knows what will happen if they engulf you. I'll follow after."

"You're injured!" Dana yelled. "I can fight. You can't."

"Would you two stop arguing down there!" Gwen roared. "They're coming. *Move!*"

A shrill screech pierced the air as the phalanx of *feux follets* bore down.

Dana had already thought up a new line of defense. *Fight fire with fire.* Even as she argued with Laurel, she compacted an orb of light in her hand. Now she hurled it at their attackers.

The globe of light hit the front line of crazy fire like a bowling ball striking a row of pins. There was an explosion of light. The front line broke and scattered.

Dana let out a whoop. Gwen cheered from above.

"*Go!*" Dana yelled at Laurel as she made another orb. "You're in my way!"

Laurel had no choice but to do as she was told. Grabbing on to the ropes, she clambered upward.

The second line of *feux follets* advanced. Again Dana knocked them back. A few managed to escape the explosion and charged at Laurel. One bounced off the cliffside. Another struck her back. Laurel cried out in agony but continued upward.

Gwen was now hanging over the cliff, apparently supported by someone behind her.

A third line of *feux follets* bore down.

Gwen reached out for Laurel.

Dana knocked out the third line, but the fourth was already near. There wasn't enough time to make another orb.

Gwen pulled Laurel up, onto the top of the ridge even as the fourth line smashed against the rock.

Weeping with relief, the two friends hugged each other.

"We came as soon as we could!" Gwen said.

"*We?* Who—?"

But Gwen had turned quickly to shout down at Dana.

"Wait a minute! I need to tell you something!"
Too late. Dana was gone.

*With Laurel safe, she expected to wake in the forest where she had begun her journey, but it seemed there was another wind to walk, another dream to speak. As she flew through the sun-spangled sky, she heard a whisper.*

This land is far more important than we are. To know it is to be young and ancient all at once.

*She journeyed with the wind that blew through the tawny grasses, the sweet-smelling forbs, fescues, and sedges. The land rose to meet her. She found herself walking a deserted highway across moonlit plains. She walked beside time as if it were a river where the seasons flowed past. Sometimes the fields were awash with the gold of summery sunsets. Then they changed color to charcoal-gray and the white frost of winter.*

*She spied a range of green hills ahead. As she crossed the stony field that lay before the hills, she discovered she wasn't alone. A woman walked there also, a rancher's wife dressed in jeans and jacket, with a scarf on her head. The woman was lost in her own musings, gazing up at the sky.*

*"This star-ridden, green, and scented universe," she murmured.*

*There was something about her that deserved attention. The way she walked, the way she touched the land as if it were precious, every blade of grass, every plant, every stone.*

*The woman turned at the sound of a soft footfall.*

*Dana stood in the feathered light of sunset, bathed in rose-gold.*

*"Am I dreaming you?"*

*"I think I'm dreaming you."*

*They both laughed.*

*"They told me you're a wise woman," Dana said.*

*The woman smiled shyly. "Who said that?"*

*"The wind."*

*"What's your accent? It has a musical sound."*

*"I'm Irish," Dana answered. Then she reconsidered. It didn't sound right. "Irish Canadian."*

*"Why are you here?"*

*"I'm looking for a book. It's somewhere in the land."*

*The woman smiled. "Well, that's a coincidence. I'm a writer. I write books about the land. I walk in this field and it whispers secrets to me."*

*"Because you belong here," Dana said, nodding, remembering Grandfather's words.*

The land will not yield its secrets to a stranger.

*"Actually, I'm pretty well a newcomer," the other responded, to Dana's surprise. "But there's something a Crow Elder once said. 'If people stay somewhere long enough—even white people—the spirits will begin to speak to them.'"*

*"I want to stay here," Dana said. "I want to belong to this land."*

*As soon as she spoke she was back with the wind, walking across the sky.*

*At first she thought she was looking at a vision, a mirage of infinity and timeless space. Then she realized she was looking at a country. She had grasped it in parts when she dreamed with the animals. Now she caught sight of something even grander. Miles and miles and miles of great plain sweeping to the horizon at the edge of the world. A summer land that shimmered in waves of baked heat. A winter land blurred behind the white veil of blizzards.*

*Place names echoed in the air like spirits.* Red Deer. Lonetree. Ravenscrag. Medicine Hat. Qu'Appelle. The White Horse Plains. Portage la Prairie. *The geography of the wild heart of the West.*

*From the four directions came the names of the Plains Nations winging on the wind.* Gros Ventre. Shoshone. Siksika Blackfoot. Plains Ojibwa. Assiniboine. Lakota. Crowfoot. Crow Absaroke. Plains Cree. *She saw them in the wind, riding wild horses. Scorned by history, beloved of the land, they moved like bright shadows in the prairie sky.*

*Wrapped in the vision of unbroken solitude, she mused to herself. What is the meaning of these images? This land? This journey?*

At the heart of everything is spirit.

It was time to return. Pulled away from the starlit prairies, she raced over the great mountain, and deep into the green interior of British Columbia. There was a brief moment when she passed the Sasquatch camp. Some of the Bigfoot looked up to see her. Then she was gone, flying over the painted totems in Stanley Park, and along the sandy shore of English Bay.

Gently as a leaf, she dropped onto the sidewalk in front of her hotel. Moments later, a taxi pulled up.

Dana's aunts jumped out of the cab, faces white and frantic. As soon as they saw her, they rushed over.

"We thought you were dead!" Yvonne cried.

The aunts smothered her in hugs, weeping with relief.

Dee stood back to regard her.

"Where did you get the cool gear?"

Only then did Dana see how bad the two looked.

# Thirty-Two

"You're hurt!" Dana cried.

"We're alive," Dee responded.

"Let's get inside," said Yvonne urgently.

Ignoring the stares of hotel staff and residents, the three hurried through the lobby and up to their room. Yvonne immediately ran a hot bath, while Dee ordered room service.

"What happened?" Dana demanded. "Tell me!"

She was the calmest of the three. Her aunts were moving around in fits and starts, taking off their clothes, donning bathrobes, checking their injuries. Both were badly cut and bruised. Their clothes were torn, spattered with blood and dirt. Some of their limbs looked twisted out of shape. There was a wild look in their eyes.

"We will," Yvonne assured her. "After we treat the shock."

"We've been here before," Dee said shakily. "A little rumble at our favorite club when it got raided by nasties. We had to hold our own till Toronto's finest arrived."

"This is a lot worse, though," Yvonne muttered. Her

voice trembled as she stared at a deep gash on her leg. "I think I might need a doctor."

"Me too," Dee admitted.

They slumped together on the edge of the bed. The reality of the attack was only sinking in. They began to shiver violently. The dark thing had left its mark; for though they called on all the liveliness of their personalities to rally against it, they were defeated. It was too hard. Too horrible.

Dana clasped each of them by the hand.

"I'm so proud of you," she said softly.

She gripped them firmly as she let the light flow. Like liquid gold, it seeped into their skin, slowly spreading like warmth throughout their bodies. As the light moved, it healed, not only the surface wounds but the ones deep inside; the nightmare of the evil they had faced.

When Dana let go, her aunts looked fully restored and refreshed, bursting with energy.

"Wow!" said Dee. "That was some rush!"

Yvonne had tears in her eyes. "Thanks, sweetie. It was lovely."

"I was taught things about my power," she said, a little shyly.

Before she could explain further, a knock on the door brought room service with the feast Dee had ordered. The three were more than ready to devour it. The tray was loaded with food: grilled cheese sandwiches, "western" omelets with fried peppers and ham, bacon-lettuce-and-tomato sandwiches, double-decker clubs, and a mountain of fries. There were also vanilla, chocolate, and strawberry milkshakes, and a pot of hot chocolate afloat with marshmallows.

They talked as they ate. Dana insisted on hearing their story first. She was dismayed at their descriptions of the Fair Folk.

"He's a lush," Dee concluded, "and she has co-dependency issues."

"Documentary on alcoholism," Yvonne explained to Dana.

"I know what I know," Dee asserted.

"So they can't help us," Dana said, shaking her head.

This wasn't good news. But worse was to come. The attack by Crowley. She could hardly bear to think of what might have been the outcome.

Her aunts shuddered as they recalled their ordeal.

"His tentacles were awful," Yvonne said.

"*What?*" Dee exclaimed.

"I said *tent*-acles."

"Oh."

"He couldn't find me," Dana said, thinking about it. "I was beyond his reach with the Old Ones. That's why he went after you two."

Her voice rang with guilt.

"We signed on for the whole kit and caboodle," Dee assured her.

"In for a penny, in for a pound," Yvonne agreed.

"Not anymore," Dana said. "It's too dangerous. I shouldn't have got you involved."

"We'd take a hit for you any day," Dee declared.

Her sister agreed. But it was the wrong thing to say. Dana's features hardened, as did her resolve.

"I can't let you. It's wrong. Laurel told me about this already. Other people can't get involved. If you don't agree to stay out, I'll use a spell on you and make you forget."

Her aunts looked shocked.

"That would be a violation of our basic human rights," Dee declared.

"And this has got nothing to do with humans!" Dana argued. "There are monsters, and you can't fight them off. Please don't make me use magic on you. I'd rather you agreed of your own free will."

"I can't believe you're doing this to us," Dee said with open admiration.

"She's right, but," Yvonne sighed, "we'd only get in her way. You know the plot. We'd be captured and held hostage, weakening her position et cetera et cetera."

They looked so dejected, Dana almost relented.

"I guess you didn't meet any heroes?" she asked, with a little grin.

"Oh but we did!" Dee cried.

She and Yvonne looked at each other, astonished.

"How could we have forgotten them?" Yvonne wondered. "Shock? Magic?"

They described their rescuers to Dana.

"Native guys, I think," said Yvonne. "With knives."

"*Gorgeous* guys," Dee said, nodding. "I wonder what they were doing there."

"The Old Ones must have sent them," Dana said.

It was her turn to tell her story. Her aunts listened awestruck as she described the Sasquatch and wind-walking and dream-speaking across the Great Plains. The two were also amazed by the rescue of Laurel in the Brule; but as soon as Dana mentioned the woman in the field, they were on familiar ground.

"I'll be damned," said Dee. "You met Sharon Butala!"

"Who?"

"She's a writer, well, a mystic really," Yvonne explained. "She writes about the land. We've read her books. The best is *The Perfection of the Morning.*"

"*Wild Stone Heart,*" argued Dee.

"The whole quest is about books," Dana said thoughtfully. "Like Grandfather said. We're all part of the Great Tale. And thanks to the Old Ones, the story is a bit clearer to me. I know where I'm going now."

"Where?" asked Yvonne, then she added quickly, "not that we'll follow."

Her assurance was unnecessary. Dana's answer was simple.

"Home."

# Thirty-Three

Dana and Jean sat together in the cafeteria, talking as usual in low voices. She was overjoyed to have him back. When he met her in the hall that morning, she had hugged him without thinking and he had held her tightly. Though she heard a few gasps around her, she didn't care. She was also happy and relieved to know that *grand-père* was safe and on Cree lands again.

"I find him first in the Shaking Tent," Jean told her. "Then I track him with Roy. He go near to Labrador City." The words were caught in his throat. "He try to go home."

"Oh, that's sad," Dana said softly.

"It is necessary I visit him more. He forget who he is and then he fight to remember."

Jean sat back in his chair and stared at Dana. There was a puzzled look on his face.

"You are *différente*. I feel it. What happen?"

Dana's heart skipped a beat. This wasn't going to be easy, but she couldn't avoid it. She had to tell him. Taking a deep breath, she plunged in.

"I went into the West. I met the Old Ones, the spirits of the land. They showed me things about my power, to help me on my mission."

She saw him register that she had broken her promise to do nothing till he returned. His eyes flashed. His lips pressed closer together. Things were about to get worse. She had thought long and hard about Jean in his absence. The attack on her aunts had confirmed her decision about others being involved. Laurel was the one who had first argued the point, but now Dana herself fully agreed.

"I'm sorry, Jean, but I've got to do the rest of this by myself. Believe me, I appreciate everything you've done, but I can't put you in danger anymore. If anything happened to you, it would be my fault. I just can't do that."

Though she had expected him to be angry, she wasn't prepared for the explosion that followed. He was already standing before she had finished, and he was furious.

"*Tabernac*, you decide for me? Who you are, eh? You think I don't know for myself that I go to danger or not? *Maudit, câlisse.* I don't like this! I don't like *you!*"

As he stormed away, Dana sat as still as stone. She was in shock. Her insides were twisted into a knot. Her world was collapsing around her.

"Boy trouble?" Georgia's voice was kind as she took the chair Jean had just vacated. "I caught the end of it. And you look as if you've been hit with a ton of bricks."

"I . . . I have," Dana said. Tears pricked the corners of her eyes. She wanted to run away and hide, to cry herself to sleep. "Oh Georgia, I've done something really bad. I've ruined everything!"

"Have you gone with another guy?" Georgia asked her directly.

"*No!* I don't even know anyone else!"

"Then you're okay. That's the only thing they won't forgive. Come on, we'll be late for class. Tell me what happened on the way."

Dana was already feeling a little better. Shamefaced, she realized she had barely said hello to Georgia since Jean's return.

"Where did you go at lunch?" Dana asked her guiltily.

"I sat with some other friends. Don't sweat it. You looked pretty intense. Two's company, three can be a crowd."

As they walked through the halls, Dana hurriedly explained that she had broken a promise—for very good reasons—and had then tried to exclude Jean from something she thought wouldn't be good for him.

"The situation sounds serious, but not hopeless," Georgia said thoughtfully. "I recommend some damage control. Groveling and apologies. With regards to the broken promise, you owe him one. You need to restore his trust. As for you deciding what's best for him, have to say

I'm on his side there. One look at that guy should tell you he's man enough to make his own decisions. Will I call you tonight?"

"Please," said Dana, with relief. "And thank you so much. You've saved my life!"

"What are friends for?" Georgia laughed.

When Dana left for home that afternoon, she was more than grateful to Georgia. Her friend had kept giving her pep talks in between classes, and she had needed them. Jean ignored her throughout the day and turned away whenever she tried to approach and apologize. When the final bell rang, he disappeared without a backward glance.

Outside the school, Georgia's good-bye was heartening. "I'll call you after supper!"

Half-glad, half-sad, Dana walked to the subway. While things couldn't be worse with Jean, things were great between Georgia and her. At the same time, Dana knew she couldn't get bogged down in her personal life. She had work to do. During her time with the Old Ones, she had learned a lot, including the fact that the Book of Dreams was to be found in the South, the final direction. *Like all things sought, it is near you,* they had said. That made sense, of course. The quest had brought her full circle. A journey was not completed until you returned home.

She would go hunting that night. She would journey out into the land around her.

Lost in thought, Dana didn't notice the bag lady right away. Seated on a bench in front of the subway station, the old woman was surrounded by plastic bags stuffed with clothes, bric-a-brac, dishes, and blankets. All her worldly possessions. Dana rummaged in her school bag for some money.

The bag lady appeared to be napping. Her head rested on her chest and her eyes were closed. She wore a tatty coat of glossy black fur that looked like old feathers. Wisps of gray hair escaped from a floppy wool hat. Her face was crinkled like a dried apple.

As Dana slipped the dollars into her hand, the old woman opened one eye to peep at her. A black beady eye.

"Stay out of the tunnels, dearie. There'll be trolls today."

"What! What did you say?"

The eye fluttered shut again. The bag lady tucked her chin into her shoulder, the way a bird tucks its head underwing.

Dana entered the TTC station and made her way through the turnstiles. Had she heard right? Did the old lady say "trolls" or "tolls"?

On the train, Dana looked around with more attention than usual. Everything seemed normal. It was a new train, sleek and silver, with plush red seats and a gray-and-white speckled floor. As if to prove its worth and youthfulness, it hurtled through the tunnels at high speed.

The metallic wheels squealed and scraped, the carriages tipped sideways as they careened around corners. The passengers looked normal, too, all ages and races, casually dressed as Canadians tended to be, some more muffled than others against the fall weather. The interior of the train was warm. Dana unbuttoned her jacket. Two kids ran up and down the aisle, swinging on the poles. Across from her, a young man petted the huge dog seated on the floor beside him. The animal had an intelligent face and was watching everyone closely. It gave Dana a particularly knowing look.

The train arrived in each station on a blast of wind and left the same way. After several stops with no surprises, Dana relaxed her guard. The rocking motion of the carriage lulled her into the train's routine: stopping and starting, doors swishing open and closed, automatic chimes heralding the recorded warnings. *The doors are now closing! Stand clear of the doors!* She fell into a half-doze. Shortly after St Patrick's station, she came to with a start.

The train had come to a halt inside the tunnel.

Darkness pressed against the windows like black water. In a calm flat voice, the conductor announced over the intercom that the delay was due to a mechanical fault. He asked for patience and would keep them informed. The other passengers seemed unconcerned, continuing to do what they were doing to pass time in transit. Some read newspapers or books. Others stared blindly at the floor or ceiling. A few read the ads for the umpteenth time, while one or two studied the other passengers surreptitiously. Most wore a look of patient boredom. A few were asleep.

Only Dana showed any anxiety. She knew something was wrong.

Peering out the window, she craned her neck in an attempt to see down the track.

A familiar voice sounded behind her.

"Troll attack, eh? They're always causing delays on the subway. They get bored and up to mischief. Idle hands are the devil's work, as my old mother used to say."

Dana spun round. The little brown man was grinning at her. He still had the Walkman and the dark glasses, but now he was dressed bizarrely in pink. A pink coat with padded shoulders and silver buttons matched pink baggy pants. He also sported a pink hat and kid gloves of pink leather. Even his running shoes were pink, with sparkly laces. Her jaw dropped as she gaped at his outfit.

"A secure man wears pink," he said, catching her look.

"I've been so hoping to meet you again! I'm always looking out for you. I wanted to thank you for the advice about my friend. What's your name?"

"Trew," he said. "That's my name. What's yours?"

"Dana," she answered. "But I thought you'd know that."

He peered over the rim of his sunglasses. The eyes were wide and innocent.

"How would I know your name? Aren't you a complete stranger to me?"

Dana was nonplussed. Were her suspicions wrong, or was he being coy?

"We gotta go," he said. "They're comin' for ya."

She jumped up immediately. The warning sounded sincere as well as ominous. She didn't think to doubt him.

"Don't get me wrong. It's not that trolls are bad," he explained. "They just get their kicks stallin' the trains. They like to watch people get all frustrated, lookin' at their watches, swearin' and whatnot." He did a good imitation of a harassed commuter. When Dana laughed he said, "See? Trolls find it even more hilarious."

All the time he was talking he led her through the train, opening the doors between carriages officially used by transit staff only. No one paid them any attention. Teenagers were always walking between the cars. When they reached the last carriage, Trew opened the door at the end of the car and jumped onto the tracks. He offered his hand to help Dana down.

"Don't go anywhere near that bar on the side or you'll be electrocuted. 'Fire-fried' as the trolls say."

The tracks were black as soot. With the fluorescent lighting, the tunnel glowed eerily, like a secret labyrinth. The walls crawled with wires and cables. A musty wind blew down the passageway. Trains rumbled like thunder in the distance. Far ahead, at the end of the darkness, the light of the next station flickered like a beacon.

Trew frowned as he looked up and down the track. A new sound echoed through the dimness. The low boom of drums. It was a threatening sound. The beat of ill intent.

Trew grabbed Dana's hand.

"As I was saying"—he puffed as they ran down the track, away from the drumming—"usually the trolls are not much more than a big fat nuisance. But they're easily influenced. And right now the troll patrol are under a very bad influence indeed."

"Crowley!"

"Who?"

"The monster who wants to kill me."

"That sounds about right."

Running hard to keep up with the little man, Dana was glad to note that he knew the tunnels well. He rushed her over tracks, around bends and twists, and along workmen's walkways. When the drums died out behind them, she sighed with relief.

But not for long.

More drums boomed. This time ahead of them.

Trew stopped abruptly and cocked his head to listen. Were they calling to the others? Sure enough, drums now beat on either side of them, growing steadily louder as they closed in.

"We're trapped!" Dana whispered.

Swearing under his breath, Trew searched the soot-covered wall beside them. Now he pushed against a large brick. A door swung open, revealing stone steps that ran downward into a pitch-black hole. A stale smell wafted upward.

Trew disappeared into the murk, but Dana hesitated. She could see nothing below.

"Come on! There's no time! They're coming!"

He was right. She could hear the drums on both sides. So near! And another sound accompanied them. The tramp of heavy feet. They would soon be on top of her.

The moment Dana stepped into the shaft, the door slammed shut behind her. She was plunged into darkness. Putting her hands together, she made enough light to see the stairway underfoot. The shaft went down at least twenty feet.

Trew's voice called up encouragement.

"It's brighter down here! Quick! The trolls know the doors too!"

Hurrying gingerly down the steps, she was amazed to find herself in an underground cavern as big as the subway station above. The walls and roof were of rock, covered with a phosphorescent lichen that glowed greenly in the dark. A maze of passages ran off in all directions.

"These tunnels are older than the human ones," Trew told her. "There was a lot of worry when the subway was being built. What if the workers dug deep enough to find us? Rumors of war were rife. 'The trolls will protect their own' and so forth." Trew let out a laugh. "The only thing that happened was entertainment. Trolls love causing trouble on the system."

They ran through cavern after cavern, each identical to the last.

"Trolls know tunnels like the back of their hand," Trew told her. "The way you know the streets you live on."

"Where do they live?" Dana wondered.

"Farther in and further down," came the answer as they hurried on.

After what seemed an endless chain of caverns, the ground began to rise. They were heading upward. Though she had managed to keep pace with him till then, Dana begged Trew to slow down. Her lungs were bursting. Her legs ached. She was certain they had covered a few miles.

"Nearly there," he panted.

"Where's . . . there?" she demanded.

"Scarberia. The east end."

To Dana's relief, they slowed to a quick walk.

"I think we shook them off," Trew said with a glance over his shoulder.

Then he let out a yelp.

Looking back, Dana cried out too.

Only a short distance behind was a band of trolls, quickly gaining on them. Dana's heart stopped. There were only four, but each was tall and broad, with hunched shoulders, belly-white skin, and black lidless eyes. All wore soot-covered Toronto Transit Commission uniforms, with jackets and caps. She might have laughed, if they hadn't looked so sinister. They bristled with crude weapons— hatchets, hammers, and even a broadsword. There was a mindless resolve to the way they charged. And now she saw why neither Trew nor she had heard them. Trouser legs rolled up, they were running in their bare feet. Somehow the sight of curled and dirty toenails made it all the worse.

"Up and out!" Trew cried. "They hate the light!"

Moments before, Dana was sure she couldn't have run another step. Now she sprinted off, with Trew beside her. Behind them came no drum or footstep, only the foul breaths of their pursuers.

"Where's the steps? Where's the door?" Dana hissed to Trew.

"No . . . amenities . . . the 'burbs . . ." he answered in fits.

At last she understood what he meant. There was no stairway to lead them out. The ground rose in a steep incline that finally reached a door with an iron bar across it.

Trew grabbed at the bar to lift it. Dana glanced behind. The trolls were there behind them! One reached out for her. Trew pushed the door open. With a scream, Dana hurled herself through the opening, on top of Trew. They tumbled out together on the other side, sprawling on the ground.

"Close it!" Trew roared, as a dead white hand clutched at the air.

Scrambling to her feet, Dana slammed the door shut.

They were back in the regular subway tunnels. Hurrying along the tracks, they came to the spacious and airy Warden station. But not until they were outside in the fresh air did Dana stop looking behind her.

Though it was late afternoon, the light seemed very bright after the dim tunnels.

"Stay out of the subway for the rest of the day," Trew said. "Once the troll patrols know they've lost you, they'll go bonkers altogether. Throw the whole system into mayhem, you betcha."

"I don't know how to thank you," Dana said. She rummaged through her pockets and pulled out a chocolate bar. "How about this?"

The little man admired the shiny gold wrapper and was even more pleased as he bit into the chocolate.

"I love this stuff," he said, "big-time."

"Can I ask you something?" She hesitated, not wanting to offend him. "Why did you help me?"

He peered at her over his shades. The earth-brown eyes regarded her thoughtfully.

"Do you think this is all about you, girl? You're not the

only one who cares about dreams, eh? There's no neutral ground in this kind of war. You sit on the fence, you get splinters in your bum. But it's a sign of just how desperate your enemy's gettin' if he's callin' on the trolls. Scrapin' the bottom of the barrel now. You've got him rattled, that's for sure."

"I think he's underestimated all the people against him," Dana said.

"He's underestimated *you*, that's for darn sure," said Trew. Again he peered at her over his glasses. "Now, there's one more bit I gotta do for you afore I go. You know the thing you're lookin' for? It's near all right, but it ain't here in Trawna. It's in a place called the Plain of the Great Heart."

"The what?" she said. "Where?"

"That's all I know." He shrugged. "A little birdie told me. I don't get out of the subway much."

He was shifting from foot to foot. Dana could see he was uncomfortable outdoors. Even with the dark glasses, he was squinting in the sunlight.

"That's Warden Woods," he said suddenly, pointing across the road.

Dana looked over at the plot of trees rising behind a tall wired fence.

"Your friend's in there. That's why I brought you. Between you and me, some last advice. I see a lot ridin' the Rocket. The good, the bad, and the ugly. He's good for you. Don't turn him away. Nobody said you gotta do this alone."

Dana shielded her eyes against the sun as she stared into the trees. She couldn't see anyone.

"Do you mean Jean?" she turned to ask, only to find herself talking to thin air.

A quick look around showed no sign of Trew. For a little man, he could really move fast. What exactly was he? Dana shrugged to herself. Whatever he was, she felt she could trust him.

Crossing the road, Dana found a gate in the fence that allowed her into the woods. The ground was damp and fragrant from the rain the day before. The October sun lit up the trees that still had their leaves. Red and gold flecks brightened the rusty brown of aspen and birch. Where the branches were bare, the autumn sky shone through. The sound of traffic beyond the woods grew muffled. In its place, she heard birds calling and the scurry of squirrels on the ground.

She found him leaning against a tree, staring up at the sky. He wore a navy-blue scarf around his neck and his hands were plunged inside the pockets of his jacket. Her heart beat quicker as she looked at him: the fall of dark hair over his eyes, the lean features. Every time she saw him, she felt the same skip of her heart, as if she hadn't seen him in ages.

He looked lost in thought. Deep, sad thoughts.

A twig snapped underfoot as she walked toward him. He responded to the sound, meeting her eyes, but he wasn't surprised. She knew the wolf in him had caught her scent on the air.

Neither spoke as they put their arms around each other. He rested his head on her shoulder even as she rested hers against his.

"I had to go west," she told him quietly. "Even though I made that promise to you. I couldn't tell you. You had your own problems. Everything's happening so quickly. I'm just trying to keep up. I'm sorry for telling you what to do. That was stupid. I'd really like if you would do this with me."

His features softened as he took her head in his hands and gazed at her. There was no anger in his look, only the same sadness she had noticed before.

"I am sorry also," he said. "You take a lot on your back. I don't want to add to the problem you have. I want to help." He touched her hair lightly and kissed her forehead. "I'm angry that time because I'm not there with you. I have fear for you. This is *chauvin*, no? You are strong, but still I want to save you."

His smile was wry and it made her grin. They both ended up laughing and then they stopped laughing so they could kiss.

"How do you know I am here?" he asked her as they walked through the woods, hand in hand. "This is a place I like to come when I am wolf."

She told him about Trew and about the trolls in the subway. When she described the tunnels beneath the tunnels, he shook his head, amazed.

"There is so much we don't see, eh?"

He put his arm around her. Her heart felt as if it might burst. It was so good not to be fighting, to be together again.

Since they couldn't take the subway home, they traveled the long way on buses and streetcars. Dana didn't mind. It gave her more time with him. And she was able to bring him up to date with the story.

"But Ms. Woods not come back to school, *n'est-ce pas?* Where is she now? And this other person, Laurel?"

"I don't know," said Dana. "With the Old Ones. Oh, and there's another thing. Trew says the Book of Dreams is nearby. In a place called the Plain of the Great Heart. Did you ever hear of it?"

Jean shook his head. "It sounds like a Native name. I ask Roy and the Old Man."

When it was time for them to go their separate ways, he caught hold of her again and held her close. She was the one who kissed him first.

"I call you tonight," he said, when they finally broke apart.

By the time Dana got home, dusk had fallen over the city and the streetlights were on. She hurried in the door, all apologies.

"Don't tell me, I know," said her father. "Radhi's only in ahead of you. It's all over the news. The subway's in chaos. Breakdowns everywhere. Were you hours in the tunnel?"

"It seemed like ages," Dana said truthfully.

"I've got a pot of ratatouille simmering. Grate me some cheese and set the table."

It was after supper, when Dana was doing her homework, that the telephone rang. Thinking it was Jean or Georgia, she raced to get it.

Gran Gowan's voice came on the line. "I'm getting in an early invite, what with you skipping out on my Thanksgiving dinner. Are you coming up to me for Halloween? I won't have you trick-or-treating in Toronto. There are all kinds of bad people there who put razor blades in apples and rat poison in the candies."

Dana laughed. "I don't go trick-or-treating, Gran. I'm too old for that."

She was thinking fast. She had to dodge her grandmother's invitation. There was no time for a visit, especially on the day she had to restore the portals!

"You'll love how we celebrate it here," Gran Gowan was saying. "The whole village turns out. There are bonfires and plenty of hot chocolate to keep the kids warm. There's a haunted house for the youngsters and the Headless Horseman gallops down Mill Street . . ."

Dana opened her mouth to speak, but in vain.

"The King of Creemore does that," her grandmother

continued. "Puts on a great show. We like to do the whole kit and caboodle here in the place of 'the big heart.'"

Dana nearly dropped the receiver.

Why was the truth always so obvious that you inevitably overlooked it? Why could one never see the forest for the trees? Despite all her questing and Grandfather's point about belonging to the land, she still hadn't grasped it. The answer was right in front of her, and in Irish to boot! There was a place in southern Ontario that she herself belonged to more than any other part of Canada. A place where her own family had stayed on the land for generations.

Creemore. *Croí mór.* Great heart.

Dana's mind raced. Halloween was two weeks away. She needed to get up there as soon as possible to search for the book. Surely Creemore would yield the secret to one of its own? As soon as the Book of Dreams told her how to restore the portals, she would use her power to do it on the feast of Oíche Shamhna.

"Gran, could I stay this weekend? And again at Halloween?"

"You know I'd love that!" Her grandmother was delighted. "We can make pumpkin pies. As long as your father agrees, of course."

"He won't mind," Dana assured her. "He and Radhi could do with some time together. With the baby coming, I'm sure—"

"The *baby?*"

The arch in Gran Gowan's voice crackled on the wire.

"Oops," said Dana.

"Put your father on this instant."

# Thirty-Four

D ana sat in the front seat of the bus to get the best view. In the midday light, the highway had a silver-gray sheen. On both sides of the road the land stretched outward like wings. The countryside seemed to be three-quarters sky over a thin line of brown earth. When she first came to Canada she had asked her father, "Is the sky bigger here?" "Definitely," was his answer. Signposts marked her passage through southern Ontario. *Wildfield.* Green and gray barns dotted the gentle slope of wide meadows. Farther north, dark forests came to meet the highway. *Caledon Highlands.* Here and there, tall flagpoles waved the red-and-white maple leaf flag of Canada. *Blue Church Road.* There was a little wooden church with a steeple painted blue. *Pink Lake.* There was a lake, but it wasn't pink.

Dana liked traveling by herself. Just before Gabe had put her on the bus, he had looked a little troubled.

"This is the second time you've left since we told you about the baby. Are you sure you're not upset?"

"Da, I already told you. It's not like that. I really like

the idea of a sister or brother. I just want to visit Gran. You know how much I love going to Creemore."

"She does spoil you rotten."

Dana grinned. "Thanks for letting me go on my own."

"A few months back, I wouldn't have," he admitted, "but you're really growing up, kiddo."

"I'm nearly fourteen," she pointed out.

"No, I mean . . . in a different way. You've changed . . . what I'm trying to say . . . you're a young woman now." He looked embarrassed.

Dana rolled her eyes. *Fathers.*

With Ontario farmlands flying past her window, she allowed herself the luxury of daydreaming about Jean. The week had passed quickly at school. When she introduced Georgia and Jean, they both liked each other instantly. The three of them had become a little gang, meeting between classes and sitting together at lunch. They couldn't help drawing attention to themselves as they talked and laughed so loudly. With Georgia there, Dana and Jean couldn't talk about the quest, but Dana didn't mind. She was glad to put it aside for a while. There came a moment in the cafeteria— the three of them were fooling around, Georgia had grabbed Jean's lunch and tossed it to Dana, while Jean swore in French—when Dana realized she was bursting with happiness. To have a boyfriend and a best friend was, for her, a dream come true.

As for the quest, she and Jean had made their plans by telephone. He would arrive in Creemore the following day and they would begin the search for the Book of Dreams together. She hoped he might be able to stay at her grandmother's house, but if all else failed he could go home at night by turning wolf.

Remembering the quest brought a flutter of panic. Time was running out. And even as she drew near to what she sought, the mystery deepened. Why was the Book of Dreams in Creemore? She had known from the beginning that she was connected to it, but she had always assumed that the bond with the book was through her fairy blood. After all, its secret would restore the portals of Faerie. But it seemed her human side was also involved. Why else would the book be near her family home? That couldn't be a coincidence.

There was another matter to consider. Crowley. He already knew about her connection to Creemore. It wouldn't be difficult for him to find her there. That thought sent her heart racing. Remembering the Old Ones, she managed to calm down. They had shown her she had power and that she wasn't alone. She had to trust that she could handle whatever happened. There was no going back. Her mission had to be fulfilled.

By the time the bus stopped in Creemore, Dana had stopped thinking in circles about the quest and had returned, instead, to daydreaming about Jean.

"Look at you, smiling away!" Gran Gowan said as Dana stepped from the bus. "We're going to have great fun together!"

At her grandmother's house, Dana discovered that her day was booked. A heap of pumpkins spilled over the kitchen table, surrounded by bags of flour, pie plates, rolling pins, and spices.

"I got the pumpkins from the Hamilton Brothers since the Farmers' Market is shut. Some of these will be jack-o'-lanterns," Gran Gowan said, sorting out the biggest pumpkins. "If they don't get smashed by hooligans, I'll make soup, scones, and muffins out of them after Halloween. It's a wicked waste to throw out a pumpkin without using it for something."

Dana was happy to bake. Her grandmother had often promised to show her how to make pumpkin pie. Though Gabe was a good cook, pastry-making was in a league beyond him.

"Of all the cooking skills, this is the one you have to be taught," Gran insisted. "The battle is won from the start with technique and confidence."

Dana knew she was learning from the best.

"Pastry dough can tell if you're afraid of it," Gran continued, "and if you are, it'll play up! You're a Gowan. Stand strong. Show it you're the boss, but not with an iron hand. That never works, not in pastry nor politics. The true sign of mastery is a light hand. Now, we start with good flour, none of that self-raising nonsense. There's something just plain wrong with flour that raises itself."

She sifted the flour from a height above the table and added a pinch of salt. Then the real work began.

"Everything must be cool, including yourself," said Gran. "Open the window if the room gets hot or steamy. Margarine and butter will have to do for the fat, as I'm guessing you and Radhi won't take lard. Pinch it in with your fingers. Softly. Softly. And speedily. The less you handle it, the better."

Lost in a mist of flour, Gran sprinkled and stirred and made up the dough. Move for move, Dana matched her actions till each was wrapping her own bundle in foil.

"Let it rest for half an hour in the fridge while we prepare the pumpkins."

This piece of work was messy but fun. They cut off the tops of the pumpkins and scooped out the orange gloop clotted with seeds. Being an easier job, it didn't demand concentration and freed Gran Gowan to vent her mind.

"Of course I'm over the moon about it," she said. "Radhi will make a wonderful mother and it's about time they started on a family, those two. I just don't appreciate being the last to know."

"He planned to tell you at Thanksgiving, Gran, but then we didn't come. He wanted to tell you in person."

"Hmph."

The pumpkins were chopped into chunks and the leathery rind hacked away. Rough and malleable like turnip, the pale flesh was cut into cubes and boiled till soft. Then they mashed it into a mix with Gran's ingredients.

"Sweetened condensed milk, that's the trick," said Gran, "along with brown sugar, eggs, cinnamon, ginger, nutmeg, and cloves. This is a melt-in-your-mouth recipe, a Gowan specialty."

It was time to roll out the pastry.

Gran Gowan held her rolling pin like a sword. Beside her, the knight's page, Dana wielded the dredger.

"Use it liberally," Gran ordered, "on anything that looks like it's sticking. Not on the dough, mind you. Never on the dough! Shake it on the pin or the pastry board. Here, you do one. Roll gently, gently—yes! you've got the knack!—now roll it right onto the pin. Good, now unroll it on top of the tin and press it in."

They worked for hours. Pie after pie went into the oven till the kitchen was filled with the sweet musky scent of baked pumpkin.

"There has to be enough to go around," Gran explained. "We'll freeze a batch for Halloween, then give the rest away. There's your family, the girls, Mrs. Mumford up the road who's too blind to bake anymore, Mr. Nalty who just loves my pumpkin pie . . ."

At last they were sitting down, exhausted but pleased, with cups of tea and scones in front of them.

"So, I hear there's a boyfriend?"

When Dana didn't respond right away, Gran fixed her with a stare.

Dana knew what the look meant. She would have to surrender some information about Jean. After all, she owed her grandmother. The Triumph Herald was once again in the driveway, shining like new since its restoration, paid for by Gabriel of course. Since the night it was damaged, not a word had been uttered about the incident. "Grandchildren are forgiven far more quickly than children," was Aunt Yvonne's assessment. But there was a price for everything, even forgiveness.

Dana mumbled. "He's a . . . a friend . . . from school . . . a boy . . . friend."

Gran raised her eyebrow, noting the faint flush. "Hmph. And your boy 'friend' is French, I believe?"

"*Oui.* I mean, yes."

"Roman Catholic, I suppose?"

"*Gran!*"

"Well, they all are, aren't they? I'm just saying what I'm saying. No need to get all het up about it. I married one myself, didn't I? It's in your blood, that's all. The Faolan streak."

It was an ideal opportunity to mention Jean's arrival the next day, but Dana couldn't do it. She was so used to keeping everything about him a secret, she could hardly bear to mention his name out loud. It didn't help that her grandmother was not the most sensitive of confidantes.

"Tell me about Granda Faolan," Dana said instead, creating a diversion.

"That Irish charmer." Gran sighed. She took a sip of her tea, smiled to herself. "I was in trouble the moment I clapped eyes on him."

Dana grinned. As well as changing the subject, it was a story she loved to hear.

"I was thirty-two years old at the time. Though I was a beauty in my day, if I do say so myself, it looked to be that I would stay a spinster. For one thing, there wasn't a man in the town that had caught my eye except young John Giffen, and he died in a car crash along with any hopes I had of marrying him. The family home was mine, even though it meant looking after Mother, who was in her seventies and cantankerous as a bag of cats. Father had died five years before, being a lot older than her. My two brothers were gone, one to ranch in Alberta, the other out east in Halifax with the Navy. I had a close circle of friends, did a lot of charity work, and was active in the Daughters of the Eastern Star. Didn't have to work, as Father had invested wisely. You could say my life was proceeding in a pleasant and orderly fashion.

"Then he showed up. Like a tumbleweed blowing down the main street. A real spanner in the works, that handsome Irishman with a tongue like honey. He was a poet and a painter, pretty successful with portraits, and he could do a fine sign. 'Looking for a quiet place in the country,' he said, didn't like 'the urban milieu.' Had a real way with words, that man. He rented rooms in the boardinghouse where the bookshop is now. He said the first day he walked up the street and looked around the town, he fell in love with it right away and told himself, 'I belong here. This is my home. I'm going to settle here.' Not long after that thought occurred to him—about five or ten minutes, he always maintained—he spotted me across the street, coming out my front door, and he said to himself, 'And there's the girl I'm going to marry.'"

Dana sighed. It was so romantic.

"He courted me shamelessly from that very day, starting right there on the sidewalk in front of this house, asking me questions, calling me 'darlin'.' What was my name? Did I have a beau? He just clean swept me off my feet with all his Irish blarney.

"I knew he was a Roman Catholic, you can always tell by the look of them, though he didn't practice his religion. He was a Freethinker, as we'd say. There's been Irish Catholics in Creemore right from the start, but not a whole lot. We've always been a Protestant town. True-blue Orange. Didn't the Hall go up before the church? Still, none of that mattered to me one whit. Lost the head altogether.

"The town was scandalized and I was coming close

to disgracing the family entirely. The only way to end the scandal was to marry him. So I did. Once he promised we'd marry in my church and I wouldn't be raising any Romans. Mind you, I was to regret that decision years later. Your aunts could've done with a good, strict convent school. They turn girls out like ladies, if the Dowlings and the Delaneys are anything to go by." She shook her head ruefully. "Might've put some manners on my two.

"Though the marriage was the talk of the town, the dust settled in time. He had married a daughter of one of the oldest and most respected families, they didn't have much choice but to accept him. And he won over the last of the die-hards himself. He was devoted to the village, did a lot of good work, even helped me organize the Trillium picnics. A hardworking man." Gran sighed sadly. "He had a big heart, like Creemore itself, but not a strong one. When he died too young, too soon, the whole town turned out for his funeral."

Dana heard the sorrow which time had made easier yet could never remove. She reached out to touch her grandmother's hand. Across the years and the generations, they smiled at each other.

"He used to write me love poems," she said softly.

"So, the artists are on the Faolan side," Dana observed. "That's where Gabe and the aunts got it from?"

"I wouldn't say that entirely. Didn't your Great-great-grandfather Gowan write the Book of Dreams?"

Dana was so utterly dumbfounded, she couldn't speak at first. Then at last she managed. "What . . . what did you say about . . . the . . . Book of Dreams?"

"Your great-great-granddaddy wrote it. Thomas Gowan. Fancied himself a bit of an author, he did. A bit of a ne'er-do-well, more like, in his early days that is. Must've broken his mother's heart. He didn't settle down till after she died. He traveled all over the country in his youth, collecting stories, having adventures. Then he did settle, of course, and became one of the pillars of the early Creemore community."

Dana could hardly breathe. "Was his book published?"

"Not at first. He was writing it most of his life, from the time he was young. He emigrated from Ireland with the rest of his family when he was eighteen years old. They were cleared at Grosse Île, where so many died, and journeyed on to Ontario. That's how we came to be one of the first families in Creemore. Anyways, the book was his diary; his journal I guess you should call it, seeing as he was a man.

"He decided to publish it when he was seventy-three. Age meant nothing to my granddaddy. Didn't he build this house in 1901, four years later? He paid to have the book printed up at the offices of the *Mad River Star*. Limited edition, but it sold pretty well. They even did a second printing as there was a lot of people liked it. But it didn't go far outside the community. Truth is, he wasn't much of a writer. Just had a lot of good stories to tell."

Taking a deep breath, Dana asked the crucial question: "Do you have a copy?"

The suspense was dreadful. Hope hovered in the air like a hummingbird.

"Don't know about any copies." Gran Gowan shook her head. "They all got ruined or lost here and there."

The hummingbird darted away. Of course not. That would be too easy.

"But we've got the original handwritten version right here in the house. His journal, that is. It was passed down along with the jewelry, china, and linen. Precious heirlooms and family history go together. I thought maybe we should give it to the museum in Toronto, it being part of our pioneer history, but your great-grandfather, my father, was very strict about that. He said his father told him in no uncertain terms that it wasn't to go outside the family. He wrote it for the ones to come. It's somewhere up there in the attic, wrapped in tissue paper and safely stored away in a trunk."

Dana had to use all her willpower not to race out of the kitchen and up the stairs to the little door on the top landing that led to the attic. How she managed to stay in her seat and finish her tea, she would never know. Her mind was reeling. Could it really be the book she was looking for? The title could hardly be a coincidence! But how could it be a human thing? How could a book written by her mortal ancestor contain a fairy secret? She had to find out. She had to know the truth.

Gran Gowan saw the look on Dana's face and cut her off before she could open her mouth.

"Don't even think about it. Not at this hour. You can hunt it out in the morning. Trying to find anything in that attic is like looking for a needle in a haystack, believe me. And it's already well past your bedtime."

Her grandmother was right. The hour was late. They had spent the entire day baking pies and then cleaning up after them. Though Dana could hardly bear the thought, she would have to be patient. And wait till Jean heard about this!

Dana kissed her grandmother good night and headed upstairs to her bedroom. There was a moment when she stood on the landing and considered sneaking up to the attic. She decided against it. She couldn't risk getting caught, not after the Triumph Herald fiasco. She would just have to wait until morning.

Despite her excitement about finding the book, Dana fell asleep easily in the big bed with the lilac quilt. Outside, the streets of Creemore were dim and quiet.

That night, she had a dream.

*She stood amongst a crowd on a large ship, waiting to disembark. Everyone was dressed in old-fashioned clothes. She wore a long skirt of homespun fabric and a bonnet on her* head. *The passengers were being lowered into small boats and rowed ashore. Dana recognized the island she had seen from the flying canoe. Grosse Île! Didn't Gran Gowan say her ancestor had survived that ordeal? Immediately she looked around for her great-great-grandfather, Thomas Gowan. Would she be able to recognize him? Of course she did! He looked just like Gabriel when her dad was eighteen, with dark wavy hair and laughing eyes. Her grandmother always said that Gabe was a true Gowan.*

*Thomas looked tidy, if not prosperous in his worn and faded clothes. He stood with his family, waiting to be cleared by the medical officers. She could see by his face that the voyage had taken its toll on him. Yet despite the signs of hardship and suffering, there was something irrepressible about him. The jaunty smile and the good-natured demeanor overcame the sickly pallor and the dark shadows under his eyes. He was obviously overjoyed to find himself alive and well in the New World.*

*She elbowed her way through the crowd to meet him. That's when she saw it under his arm: a book shining with light. The Book of Dreams? She was about to call out to him when something else caught her eye. She stopped and stared around her. All the immigrants on the ship were carrying books and all the books shone with the light of their dreams!*

Dana woke with a start. A sense of urgency overwhelmed her. Something she had lost! Something important she had forgotten! A silvery light drifted through the lacy curtains. The moon was luminous, almost full. She slipped out of bed and padded barefoot through the hallway, up the narrow stairs to the little door. Once inside of the attic, she cupped her hands to make her own light.

The task before her was almost impossible. The attic ran the width and length of the house. Every inch of it was covered with trunks and boxes. There was even baggage hanging from the rafters of the roof. But she was too excited to be daunted. Beginning with the nearest chest, she began her search.

An hour later, Dana was still making her way through antique dresses, hats, and moth-eaten furs, albums and costume jewelry, samplers and old paintings. It was time to come up with a plan. Ignore anything but paper. At last she found a brass-bound trunk full of books and papers. There were ladies' diaries with jeweled clasps and flowers pressed between the pages, perfume-scented letters, and all kinds of books, dog-eared and yellowed with age. In the midst of that pile, like a golden egg in a nest of tissue paper, lay her great-great-grandfather's journal.

The precious book was worn and well-traveled, with numerous stains and torn pages. At the same time it was bound in leather, meant to last. Slowly, reverently, she opened the book. On the first faded leaf, she was thrilled to see a big, friendly scrawl.

*The Book of Dreams by Thomas William Gowan.*

# Thirty-Five

*O*n this the 21st day of June in the Year of Our Lord 1841, I, Thomas William Gowan, find myself on board the good ship Horsely Hill asail on the ocean of the great Atlantic. It is a big ship, three-masted, with a crew of eighteen hands, over three hundred steerage passengers and several families with cabins of their own amongst whom mine is included. We have come with lock, stock and barrel, my parents, my two brothers and sister, our maid-servant and myself, the firstborn at eighteen years of age.

It has been two weeks since we departed from the port of New Ross bound for Montreal in the land of Quebec. I stood on deck as we left the harbor and bade farewell to my native country that I shall see no more. Others stood with me weeping copiously as they cast last lingering looks at the beloved green shores of the Emerald Isle. I did not weep. I was too filled with the glorious joy of adventure. Here was I off to the New World to a new life and new freedom, to try my fortune in a land of promise where dreams might prove true.

I have yet to tell Father or Mother that I do not intend to settle on a farm in the backwoods of Canada. I am no hewer of wood or tiller of soil. Such is not the destiny I envisage for myself. There is a vast land to be explored from coast to coast. How could I be content to bide in one small part of it when the whole cries out to enrich my knowledge and experience?

The voyage out has been long and arduous. This ocean crossing will not be speedily made. There is much sea sickness amongst our fellow cabin passengers as we plough the heavy swell of the great Atlantic. Many stay indoors, lying abed, moaning and sickly. The steerage passengers fare much worse. Some were already weak and ill from the trials and hardships of their life before they boarded. Fever and typhus rage amongst them. The majority are in bare feet and rags. Many are destitute and have only the most meager of provisions. If the journey takes longer than predicted, I fear they will suffer gravely from hunger and malnourishment. The very young and the very old are the most ill-affected. Only this morning we buried a small babe at sea still swaddled in her blanket. She was dropped most gently overboard while the Captain said prayers. The poor bereft mother had to be restrained from following her child into the Deep. It was a dreadful and piteous scene.

That was the moment when I decided to take pen and paper in hand and write this journal. Observing the crowd of unhappy humanity so sorely distressed without minister or priest to assuage their pain, I saw the truth. Against the vagaries of Fate and suffering in this life, we have only our hopes and dreams to bolster us. It is they which keep us from drowning in the black mire of despair. It is they which fortify us with the assurety that we are God's children blessed with the gift of immortal souls. Thus I shall record here, for my own good and that of posterity, all the hopes and dreams that I shall so encounter on this journey of my life.

—◌ ◌—

*June 23, 1841.* It is but two days since I last wrote in these pages. I have ventured below into steerage. The stench of unwashed bodies and sickness is most suffocating. I wonder why the Captain does not open more hatches to allow in fresh airs. Some of the more fastidious women have done their best to keep their quarters clean, constantly washing with buckets of sea water. However, they lack fresh straw to make new bedding. They tell me the crew mistreat them most cruelly often playing tricks on them and stealing their food. There are a few musicians amongst them who endeavor to keep up their spirits, a tin whistler, a fiddler and a lad with a skin drum. The three are of a most peculiar appearance, which in itself brings laughter along with the merry jigs and reels. They sing a sweet ballad concerning the land we are bound for.

Oh the green fields of Canada,
They daily are blooming,

It's there I'll put an end,
To my misery and strife.

*The creaking and groaning of wood is more cacophonous
in the bowels of the ship and the violence of movement more
severe. One fears at times that the ocean might break us
asunder. The rolling and rocking makes me quite sick. I can
rarely stay long below decks and soon find myself yearning
for the comfort of my cabin. How much worse off are these
wretches who have no other refuge!*

*Here let me record some of the dreams of my fellow
pilgrims on this voyage to a brave new world:*

*Josephina McAtamney, 16 years, from Newry, County
Antrim: I wish to find good employment in a nice house with
a kindly mistress. Then later to marry a good man and have
healthy children and my own wee home.*

*Seamus mac Mathuna, 25 years, from Bundoran,
County Donegal: I shall work as a laborer and save the
money to buy my own land. They say land comes cheap in the
wilds of Canada. I will build my own cabin and raise horses
and cattle.*

*Mrs Maggie Teed, Spanish Arch, 57 years, Galway
Town, County Galway: I just want to survive this voyage in
one piece, lad! That would be a dream come true!*

⸻ ◦ ◦ ⸻

*I no longer note the day or hour of our passage as we*

*are caught in a limbo of time and season. We were detained for weeks on the Banks of Newfoundland by heavy fog, stiff winds, and the foulest of weathers. We are short of fresh water and provisions. What we have left must be meted out with the greatest of restraint. The steerage passengers are deathly ill and starving. I have heard that the Captain, a decent God-fearing Scotsman, has released food from the stores to feed those below deck. Alas there is little to go around. It must be said there are stories of other Captains who have let their passengers die without raising a hand to aid them.*

*We have had our share of deaths, all in steerage. Many men, women and children have gone into the sea. There were times when I wondered sadly would it not have been best that they stayed in their homeland? Yet they were driven from the misery of their lives to seek new hope and better their condition. They died for their dreams.*

*✑ ✑*

*Landfall. Never shall I forget that first glimpse of this magnificent country. I waited long and impatiently for the sight. The shores were shrouded by a fog of inclement weather and there was nothing to be seen for many hours though the scent of pine traveled on the air. Then the gray haze lifted and there they were, like giants stalking towards us, the high rugged mountains of breathtaking beauty! Cloud-capped and rocky, they were cloaked with the foliage of a dark green* forest. I could only gaze with awe and reflection upon the scene of an ancient paradise untouched by man.

⁓ ⁓

At last we have traversed the great gulf of the Saint Lawrence to begin our journey up this mighty river. We are accompanied by ships of all nations flying their different flags. Many move under sail while others are steamers that shower the clear air with smoke and flame from their funnels. The waters are broken in many places with islands of all shapes and sizes. The shores to the south are low and rolling, while those to the north rise to lofty mountains. Along both shores are neat white-washed farmhouses, churches with tall spires and leafy orchards. This is country long settled by the French.

⁓ ⁓

Our ship has cast anchor off Grosse Isle and we have been boarded by health officers. They will determine who may continue the journey to Montreal and who must remain at the quarantine station on the island to await their death. There is no doubt that many will stay here, for the steerage passengers are rife with disease. We can only pray that there is no cholera-plague aboard. Clothes and bedding must be taken ashore to be scrubbed and washed. All of steerage have been ordered from the vessel to complete this task. The cabin passengers are not required to do so and we need only send our servants to clean what linen we have used. Apparently there are thousands of emigrants crowded onto the island. They say the sick are kept in sheds, like cattle. God have mercy on them all. Though the island looks picturesque from this distance with its wooded shores and towering bluffs overhung with evergreen, I am glad not to visit.

⁻ᴏ ᴏ⁻

It is a great discomfort to write in the failing light while suffering the jarring and jostling of the coach. However, I have asked my brother to hold the ink pot. For both of us this provides a diversion from the monotony and misery of our journey. We are closely packed into a narrow carriage. The wind whistles through the windows where design would have glass though it is lacking. The road is rough and plagued with a succession of mud-holes and corduroy bridges. This latter term is used to describe patches of ground on which logs are laid down over the boggy earth. Our teeth and our bones rattle as we traverse these dread patches.

The woods grow thick and dark on either side of the road. Giant pines rise to heights of over a hundred feet or more. Their trunks are surely six feet wide. This is bush country, gloomy with cedar and tamarack swamps, and infested with mosquitoes that would try the patience of Job. We seldom see signs of habitation now.

*When first we traveled northwards from Toronto we passed many stone and wood frame houses with little gardens of vegetables and flowers. They stood near inns, mills or smithy forges. Such comfortable homesteads are long left behind us even as the number of clearings has lessened. The few dwellings we spy through the dense growth of trees are no more than crude shanties befitting the occupation of cattle or pigs, not men. We have entered the backwoods of Ontario, the wilderness of Canada.*

—C⟩ ᴐ—

*September 28, 1841. There has been no time to write these past several weeks. Each night I have fallen into my bed with a tiredness beyond any of my experience. I have done my part as a dutiful son and stayed with my family to help them settle on the land. The work is hard and constant, clearing the trees to farm. The worst part of our labor is surely the stumps. What effort must be expended to remove each infernal one from its deep-rooted abode! I am more than proud to record that our cabin is built at last. It is a fine dwelling overlooking a lonely lake and a dark belt of pine. Summer has come to an end and while the days are still balmy, there is a chill of frost in the air at night. The rain is unlike that of Ireland where it falls soft and damp upon the green hills. Here it pours down in fierce torrents like the hammers of hell.*

*Do I regret this migration? Let me speak from the deep*

*of my heart. I have been bewitched by this land. What words can describe its stern solitudes and beauties? How can I write of the dark forest, the deep lake, the somber mountains? When I hear the call of the wild creatures, the loon and the owl, the deer and the wolf, I swear I am hearing the voices of mine own soul. As for the peoples native to this country who come to trade and converse with us, they are most courteous and kind. Indeed they are more decent than many a settler we have crossed in our travels. The affection shown to their children by both men and women is a lesson to us all as is the respect they grant to their aged. They are honest and truthful in their dealings and they never forget a kindness done to them. Alas, they are too often ill-used and cheated by the Christians who have come to settle in their land. How much they have lost by our arrival! Will they survive this meeting of the races, I wonder?*

⌒ ⌒

"I like this guy," Jean said.

"Me too," said Dana, proudly.

They took a break from reading the journal when their brunch arrived. The waitress set down plates of pancakes with maple syrup, along with a side order of peameal bacon for Jean. The two attacked their food hungrily.

Though Dana had dipped into the Book of Dreams the previous night, she had decided to wait for Jean before reading it properly. Tucking the prize safely under her pillow, she had fallen asleep satisfied. The next morning, she woke late to an empty house. A note to "sleepyhead" beside the box of cereal told her that her grandmother was visiting friends. There was no time for breakfast. With the book in hand, Dana grabbed her coat and raced out the door. The bus had already arrived. The door swung open just as she reached the stop.

Jean disembarked to find her breathless from her run, hair wild, face flushed.

"*Très jolie!*" he said, putting his arm around her.

He leaned forward to kiss her, but she pulled back, panicked.

"Small town!" she said quickly. "It's just like Ireland. Someone will see us and tell my gran!"

"Okay, okay," he said with amusement, putting his hands in the air. Then he plunged them deep into his pockets, as if to keep them restrained. "See? I am good."

Dana laughed at his antics. That was the wonderful thing about being apart; the excitement of meeting up again. She was thrilled to see him standing there, in his jeans and jacket, dark hair falling over his forehead, green eyes flashing. That he, in turn, looked so happy to see *her* made it all the more wonderful.

"Have you had lunch?" she asked him. "I'm starving. I got up late. I had a dream last night . . ."

• • •

By the time they were settled in the restaurant and their food was ordered, Dana had told him the story of her great-great-grandfather's book. Together they began to read the entries.

Everything Gran Gowan had mentioned was there, and more besides. Not long after Thomas arrived in Canada, he had grown restless, yearning to wander. He couldn't stay for long in the backwoods of Ontario. He was a dreamer, not a homesteader. Once he saw his family settled, he set off on his own to explore.

The journal was sporadic, skipping months and even years at times. Often the entries lacked a date. But it was a fascinating jumble of adventures, dreams, poems, and reflections interspersed with descriptions of the countryside and the people he met. Thomas described his various jobs with the Hudson's Bay Company that took him as far north as York Factory on Hudson Bay, and as far west as Fort Garry, near the Red River Valley, and then west again to Fort Edmonton.

*Though I hold these hunters and trappers in great esteem, for their bravery and resourcefulness knows no bounds, at the same time I cannot but be horrified at the ceaseless slaughter of wild animals. All summer long, brigades of boats and canoes arrive deep-laden with the skins and pelts of countless creatures. Surely this is greed beyond all necessity and comprehension.*

•••

"Oh I do like him so much," Dana murmured. "My dear great-great-granddaddy."

After their meal, the two walked to the outskirts of Creemore and stopped on a bridge that spanned the Mad River. The water was shallow, trickling slowly over a stony bottom. Trees lined the shore.

"The river got its name from one of the earliest settlers," she told him, remembering a story of her grandmother's. "Bridget Dowling was one of those tough Irish pioneers. She settled north of here with her husband and loads of kids. One day she was coming back from the mill with a sack of flour on her back and a baby in her arms and she had to ford the river. It was wild and rushing. She said later she almost drowned in 'that mad river,' and that's what everyone has called it ever since."

Jean smiled at the tale. "You are part of here, n'est-ce pas?" he commented. "You know all the story. This is what the Old Man say, I think."

She gazed into the waters below. "Funny thing. I always thought of myself as Irish, and I used to think of my family here as Irish too. But the Book of Dreams makes me see I really am part of Canada as well."

They were standing close together, leaning over the bridge. Well out of sight of anyone, Jean put his arm around her and gave her a long kiss.

"That's the hello I don't get at the bus."

She laughed. Everything around her seemed suddenly brighter.

"I missed you," she said, "even though it was only a day."

"Do you tell your *grand-mère* I come?"

"I didn't get the chance. I . . . ," she winced at the steady look he gave her and was driven to confess, "I chickened out."

"*C'est* okay," he laughed. "I go home as wolf."

They found a place to sit by the river and returned to Thomas's journal.

*July 2, 1850. Eight years have passed since I last saw my family and today I am restored to them. It is to my shame and sorrow that I have not returned until this sad occasion, the untimely death of my beloved mother. Father is broken-hearted and so too are my brothers and my dear sister. Despite Mother's goodly forbearance, I fear the hardship of life on a bush farm was too much for that brave woman. Father knew this too and I believe that is the reason he moved the family earlier in the year to the new settlement of Creemore. Alas, the move came too late for Mother's health. I shall bide here a while to help comfort the bereaved, though it is not my nature or inclination to linger long in one place.*

*I will write something of the settlement, for it is worthy of mention. Though it has not long been established, only five or a little more years, it is already a very promising village.*

*A flour and saw mill have been built on the south side of the river, making good use of its strength. A school and church have also been erected; there has been an Orange Hall since early days. The street names demarcating the allotments are that of Edward Webster's family, he being the distinguished founder. Though only a few houses have been constructed as of yet, there are many families on outlying farms who feel themselves to be members of the community. Most hail from either Ireland or Scotland, in this generation or the one preceding.*

—◦ ◦—

*Father and I had a mild but unhappy disagreement today. He was not pleased when I introduced the notion of my departure. While it grieves me to add to his pain, it is not in my temperament to settle. I am thinking of going east to Nova Scotia or Cape Breton. Or perhaps I shall visit the lands of French Canada. I know something of their language from my time in the Red River.*

"That's odd." Dana stopped reading for a moment. "Gran said he settled down after his mother's death. It doesn't sound like he planned to."

"Something happen to make him stay?" Jean suggested. "Do we come near to the secret?"

"I hope so," she said, flipping through the last pages. "There's not much left."

• • •

*July 12, 1850. This is the day so esteemed and respected by all Orangemen everywhere no matter their station. In truth I do not count myself amongst their number, for I am not of like mind with certain aspects of the society that would despise Roman Catholics. I have made many friends amongst Romish people in this country especially the Canadiens as the French settlers do call themselves. Still, I would not like to offend my father or my brothers by disdaining their celebrations, and I agreed to join them.*

*There being not much of a main street in Creemore to make a parade, the good members of the Purple Hill Lodge determined that we should walk to the home of one of their group, Mr. Edward Galloway. The Galloway farm is some distance outside of Creemore, thereby providing us with a worthy challenge. Both the Bowmore and Tory Hill Lodges joined the walk.*

*When we reached out destination, we were well rewarded for our efforts. What a feast awaited us! The fatted calf had duly been slain. Such well-laden tables as ever I saw stood amidst the trees. For our pleasure and consumption were dishes of venison, eel, legs of pork, roast chickens and ducks, fish of several kinds and plentiful potatoes or "pritters" as they call them here. Most delicious and varied were the pies of pumpkin, raspberry, cherry, huckleberry, gooseberry and blackberry currant. Fresh loaves of bread were served with new butter and green cheese, maple molasses, preserves and* pickled cucumbers. As is customary at these gatherings, a great deal of whiskey was provided along with the sober beverages of tea and coffee. The latter is a favourite drink in this part of the world and some say it will replace tea one day. I do not think so. It has a bitter taste and is only palatable when generously sweetened with sugar.

What trifles do I write here! It is done to calm the riotous state of my mind and emotions. Of all that happened on this day, I cannot bring myself to speak of the one event which lies at the heart of it.

"Come on, Thomas," Dana murmured, turning the page.

July 13, 1851. There is a belief in the Old Country that "a year and a day" is the spell of time necessary for the working of a "cure" or the lifting of a curse. A year and a day have passed since that fateful occurrence in the forest near Galloway's farm. Still I tarry in this place, unwilling to leave. What happened has marked me. I am a changed man. I cannot but look back on that day with awe and wonder. Was it a dream? A madness or delusion brought on by too much sunshine and whiskey? Though doubt assails me, in my heart I choose to believe that the events were real. For if they were, then all hopes and dreams are real and to know this is to be the most fortunate of men.

• • •

Dana and Jean stared at the next entry in disbelief. Holding their breaths, heads bent so close to the page they might have dived in, they found themselves reading a series of poems. The rhyming couplets were short and sentimental, conveying old-fashioned notions of romance.

"*Câlisse!* What this is?" said Jean, exasperated.

The poems were followed by an entry dated in the year 1876.

*"There is no fool like an old fool," my dear sister said to me today in a teasing but not unkind manner. I do not feel old, though perhaps I do feel a little foolish. A suitor cannot help but feel so, especially when he is courting a lady much younger than himself. Miss Harriet Steed has let me know that she is more than happy to encourage my attentions. I expect we shall be married before the year is out. I may be fifty-three years old, but truth to tell I feel as young as I did at thirty. I wonder sometimes if this youthfulness might not have been a gift that was bestowed upon me for the part I played that day.*

*Many years have passed since the Galloway picnic and I have lived a life of quiet and contentment. It seems to me, and I do not believe I am being too fanciful, that whatever once drove me in my ceaseless search for I-know-not-what was satisfied that day in the Canadian woods. Peace of mind and heart was granted to me. I have been blessed with good friends and neighbors as well as my family and I have helped to build this settlement into a thriving village. Whether big or small, we each have our part to play in the history of this nation as it unfolds in time. While I had thought to be a bachelor to my dying day, leaving the preservation of the Gowan name to my brothers, it seems not to be. I look forward to raising a family with my beloved Harriet.*

Another poem followed called "Our Wedding Day." Dana thought it was sweet and the best of the lot, but Jean snorted with impatience. They continued to read.

*The shivaree for my beloved Harriet and me went not as badly as I had feared. The usual ruffians were strangely absent. Those who sang so sweetly beyond our window had the voices of angels. While it may have been my own imagining, I thought I also heard the sound of silver bells, like those one hears on sleighs in the wintertime. Truly we both felt blessed that night.*

"What's a shivaree?" Dana wondered.

"*Charivari,*" Jean told her. "They make the word English. When the peoples marry, their friends come outside the house on that night and they make a lot noise. It can be not so good if they drink too much. They do it still now in Québec in the countryside. It's an old thing, a tradition."

"This is it," said Dana. "We're coming to the last page."

*Born March 17, 1878 William Patrick Gowan.*

"That's Gran Gowan's dad," said Dana. "My great-grandfather."

*Born April 1, 1880 Harriet Frances Gowan.*

*Born June 23, 1882 Caroline Maisy Gowan.*

*Born February 16, 1885 Thomas Robert Gowan.*

"What?" Dana cried. She turned the page over and stared at the blank sheet. "There's got to be more! Where's the secret? What happened in the woods?"

She wasn't sure if she wanted to scream or cry. How could they come so close and find nothing at all?

"Is this some joke?" said Jean, stunned. "This is the Book of Dreams we look for, *non*?"

"It must be," Dana said, trying to calm down. "Look, something happened to him that day in the forest. It made him stay in Creemore. Maybe even gave him youth and long life, as he said himself. The secret's here. Somewhere in this book. It's got to be!"

Frantically she rifled through the pages of the journal.

Then she noticed that the endpaper at the back was thicker than that at the front.

"Hey, wait a minute, what's this? Under the lining!"

"There is something there," said Jean, excited.

He took a penknife out of his pocket. At Dana's raised eyebrows, he shrugged. "In the bush it's good. In the city maybe too."

He slit the lining of the back cover and there they were, tucked away as if in an envelope, several sheets of folded paper.

The writing was still that of Thomas Gowan but it was scrawled and shaky; the hand of an old man.

*In the Year of Our Lord 1901, I enclose this addendum to my Book of Dreams for the sake of posterity, and the one in the future who will come to read this.*

"Oh." Dana shivered. "A goose just walked over my grave."

*Before I set to paper the record of events which did happen on that day, I must duly confess. There have been times these past many years when I have doubted the substance and reality of that extraordinary day. Indeed I have often wondered if such fancies were not the inevitable result of plenteous sunshine and the imbibition of homemade liquor. The sun did shine gloriously upon that day and it must be said I had taken more than my usual glass of strong whiskey. Perhaps it was these doubts which stayed my hand from putting pen to paper till now. What then do I credit for the peculiar reluctance I have suffered at each attempt to broach the matter with my dearest Harriet? For not one small part of my life save this have I kept privy from my beloved helpmeet. In truth I am more inclined to believe that the thing itself has commanded my silence through the years, even as now it insists that I write.*

*I remember that day as if it were but yesterday. It has a place in my memory as rich and as vivid as anything that has happened to me before or since. I have called my journal the Book of Dreams in honor of that which has brightened my life. Herein lies the tale of the brightest dream of all.*

*It was the 12th day of July in the Year of Our Lord 1850, that day when Orangemen everywhere celebrate the Battle of the Boyne. I was not a member of the Purple Hill Lodge nor had I any interest in it, but I was happy to walk through the forest with my father and brothers to the Galloway farm. There we feasted and drank well into the day.*

*What was it that called me away from my companions and into the woods? There was something in the quality of the light that I remember. It was not yet twilight but I had noticed a change, a faint glimmering in the trees that impressed my eye. Then I heard the drumming, low and quick like a heartbeat. I turned to my brother seated beside me and asked him, "Do you hear the drums?" He laughed and did accuse me of consuming too much whiskey. I had taken a few* glasses but not as many as the others. It was soon apparent to me that no one could hear the drums but I.

Here I will explain why it was with no great surprise or difficulty that I answered the call from the woods. In my childhood back home in Ireland, there were times when I heard a sweet music rise from the old spinney behind our house. I would follow the high piping sounds into the tangle of trees and there I would see swift darting shapes dance amongst the leaves. I knew better than to remark upon these strange occurrences. I accepted them as part of my own converse with Nature. Such moments came to me also in my new land. One time I stood on the shore of a dark lake far in the northern woods of Ontario, and I heard a loon cry my name. No matter where I have traveled, wherever I have gone, be it deep in the forests or high on the mountain tops or alone on the windy plains, I have heard the Voice which speaks in a tongue above that of mortal men.

So it was on this day that I recognized the call and I left the picnic and walked into the woods. The talk and laughter of my companions faded behind me and then disappeared. I was soon lost in the forest of ancient white pine. The trees were like pillars in a great cathedral. The surge of wind in the branches was like the blast of an organ. I saw a deer leap ahead of me through the trees. Ravens cawed in the boughs overhead. When I heard the cry of wolves I grew anxious but still I continued on my way, following the drums.

It was not a wolf that awaited me on the forest path but

an old Indian. He was a Chief, I knew, for he wore a fine blanket over his shoulders. At that time the Ojibway tribe still made their summer camp on the ridge south of Cashtown Corners. His blanket was a crimson red with various designs in black, depicting wolf and raven. His countenance was noble, but I knew by his pallor and the dullness of his eyes that a sickness was upon him. I sensed that he had not long to live.

Unlike many of my race, I am not repelled or frightened by the natives of this land. They are a proud and decent people, laid low by their encounter with us. It is the tragedy of human history that whenever two races meet, it must inevitably mean the downfall of one. The curse of Cain and Abel. Will we never meet as brothers and share the Earth?

I bowed my head to honor him, for he was a leader amongst his people and deserving of my respect.

"I do not speak your language," I told him, with regret. "I know words of some of the northern and western tongues, but I have not dwelled long in these parts."

The Chief raised his hand to end my apologia and replied in perfect and mellifluous English.

"I know your language. I have traveled a long way to meet you. You must do something for one of your family who is to come."

On mature reflection, I remark with what readiness I accepted his words. No doubt or contest entered my mind, for deep in my heart I knew he spoke the truth. A profound silence had fallen over the woods, as if the moment were of such gravity it weighed upon the very trees. In that holy quiet there came to me a sudden and steadfast belief that it was not by chance or without purpose that I was born into the world. Whatever else I may have done or yet might do in the course of my life, this day would be the cornerstone. I had no doubt that it was ordained in that other Existence which I had experienced from time to time, that I was meant to meet this man and do his bidding.

I nodded my head to show my assent, for I seemed to have lost the power of speech. The Chief opened his arms wide, enfolding me in his blanket. To my utter astonishment and by some miracle or magic, his cloak had sprouted feathers to become the dark wings of a raven! How it came to be I cannot know, but we were then of a sudden transported from that place. Indeed we flew through the air as witches are said to do, and it took all my concentration not to swoon with terror.

Happily we did not traverse any great distance and soon alighted in a field. Despite my wonderment and the weak state of my mind, I recognized the place to which I was brought. I knew it at first glance to be one of Edward Webster's allotments. On a low rise of land, it overlooked the hills that surrounded Creemore. Yet at the same time it was not Edward's land. Upon it lay the shadow of something greater, a wide plain that shone with the lustrous light of the gloaming. At the heart of this plain stood the greatest marvel of all: a stone monument of stern grandeur. I had never seen its like in this country before, though they are numerous in my homeland. Yet not even the Old Country could boast one of this colossal stature. With its awesome pillars and capstone overhead, it looked for all the world like a giant's doorway.

"I had a dream," the old Chief said to me. "Listen, for this is sacred. With your blood you will seal the door today, so that only one of your kin may ever open it again."

I do confess I was quite fearful when he produced a knife. I steeled myself for some dreadful sacrifice, but his eyes were mild and he looked kindly upon me. In the most gentlest of tones, he bade me make a cut in my finger and mark the stone.

This I did with little pain to myself.

There was a moment before I touched the stone doorway that I peered into its depths. What words could I use to describe what I saw? Only those from the Holy Book could do the scene justice. A fountain of gardens. A well of living waters. In that brightest of moments I stood at the threshold of a world so beauteous that it awoke in me the highest emotions of reverence and delight. Here was a Kingdom that revived the spirits and nourished the soul.

Alas, it was but a glimpse that I caught of that Land, for I had no sooner placed my injured finger upon the monument than the whole disappeared from sight.

Once more the old Chief wrapped his blanket around me and I was again engulfed in the softness of wings. When at

*last he set me back down in the Galloway woods, these were*
*his parting words.*

*"There is one who will come many years from now, blood*
*of your blood and blood of the Summer Country. She will*
*follow your trail across the land. She will look in many places*
*to find this secret and she will gain knowledge and power.*
*If she proves true, the spirits will speak to her and they*
*will give her many teachings. She will be a wind-walker, a*
*dream-speaker, and the key to the door. All this you will tell*
*her and a final message: 'On the Plain of the Great Heart,*
*where the living meet the dead, you will find the portal that*
*will take you home.'"*

*Dazed and confounded, I made my way back to the*
*picnic, but I soon left the festivities. At first I repeated in*
*my mind all that I had seen and heard lest I forget. For no*
*matter how often I attempted to record the events on paper,*
*I proved unable to do so. As time passed my mind rested easy*
*as I came to understand there was no fear of my forgetting.*
*That day was burned upon my memory for all eternity.*

*And now here at last, as I sense permission and even*
*persuasion, I do make my record for the one to come.*

*As a final note, I will add that before I took my leave of*
*the Chief, I could not restrain myself from asking a question.*
*He had come to meet me despite his grave illness. Why would*
*he help those who were not of his tribe or people? Again I was*
*struck by the kindness in his eyes, and I found his response*
*most touching.*

*"We are all family."*

*Thomas William Gowan*
*July 12, 1901*

By the time they had finished reading, both Dana and Jean were dumbstruck.

Jean let out a low whistle.

"The Old Man! *C'est certain!*"

Dana nodded mutely. She couldn't find her voice. Yet it wasn't Grandfather's presence in the past that left her speechless, but the meaning of his visit to her ancestor and the message he had left for her.

There was a portal that couldn't be destroyed. A portal only she could open. And it was right here in Creemore!

# Thirty-Six

"A portal in Creemore!"

Dana was in a daze. The news was almost too great to absorb. To think that her ancestor had recorded the secret for her all those years ago! A secret hidden in the past to protect the future, as if time meant nothing at all. The thought made her dizzy.

"Why don't the Old Man tell us?" Jean wondered.

"Maybe he doesn't know in this life," Dana reflected. "Or maybe he felt I wasn't ready to hear it. Because I didn't belong to the land."

Jean nodded thoughtfully. "These things are a *mystère, n'est-ce pas?* I hear him say, 'It's best I don't tell and you learn for yourself.'"

They both laughed. Both were flushed and excited. They knew they were close to the heart of the quest.

"It *is* a mystery," Dana agreed, "but we're very close to solving it. Where do you think 'the living would meet the dead' in Creemore?"

They shouted the answer together.

*"The graveyard!"*

• • •

The Creemore cemetery was at the south end of the village, in a hilly wooded area beyond Collingwood Street. The site was sheltered on all sides by tall stands of pine. A bone-white pathway meandered through the rolling grounds. Tombstones of pink and white granite were scattered over the clipped grass. The view from the height took in the hills that cupped the valley in which Creemore nestled.

Hand in hand, Dana and Jean wandered through the cemetery, looking for any sign that might indicate a portal or something magical.

Dana noticed immediately how many Gowans were there. *Separation is our sorrow. To meet again our hope.* Granda Faolan was buried among them. *Gabriel Patrick Faolan 1931–1981.* Fifty years old when he died. A terrible tragedy for his wife and children. *Till the day break and the shadows flee away.* Dana thought of her own father. Gabe was just her age when he lost his dad, while her aunts were only eleven and nine. It must have been so hard for them. *Yea, though I walk through the valley of the shadow of death, I shall fear no evil. For thou art with me.*

Standing amid her ancestors, Dana felt something nag at the back of her mind. Something she was overlooking. In his journal, her great-great-grandfather said he recognized the place where the portal stood, yet he didn't call it a graveyard. He said it was land belonging to Edward

Webster, the village founder. Perhaps it wasn't yet a cemetery at the time? But when it did become one . . . wouldn't Thomas have chosen where he would be buried?

"Look for his grave!" she said suddenly to Jean. "Where Thomas is buried! That's where the portal will be!"

She broke away and ran through the tombstones, checking the dates. According to Gran Gowan, Thomas had lived to a ripe old age. After building his new house at the age of seventy-seven, he had enjoyed it for more than a decade, dying at eighty-nine years old in 1913. The oldest graves held the oldest names, the pioneer families whose descendants still lived in the village. Along with the many Gowans were Giffens, Galloways, Kellys, Hoggs, Caseys, McDonalds, and Langtrys. When Dana finally found her great-great-grandfather's grave, she knew she was right.

His memorial was striking and unusual, quite unlike any other. Instead of the customary square shape with a cross, it was an obelisk of white marble crowned with the sculpture of a bird in flight. Words from Psalm 91 were carved on the stone in curlicue lettering. *He shall cover thee with his feathers and under his wings shalt thou trust.* The names on the gravestone included Thomas Gowan and his beloved Harriet, as well as some of their children and grandchildren.

Dana stood at Thomas's graveside, remembering her great-great-grandfather's life. Here lay the young man who had sailed to Canada, recording the dreams of his fellow emigrants; the intrepid adventurer who had traveled the length and breadth of the country in search of his own destiny; and finally the one who had settled in the backwoods of Ontario once his dream was fulfilled; for here lay the man who had been given a glimpse of that other Existence he had sought all his life.

As she stood there thinking of Thomas, Dana knew without a doubt that he had kept faith with that other world even unto death. Her skin tingled. The air around the grave felt charged with electricity. With no effort on her part, her hands were shedding light.

The portal was here.

She stared at the bird on top of the tombstone. Had Thomas been thinking of the raven who carried him here? It was fashioned from snow-white marble. A soul-bird of Faerie? A great longing came over Dana. Faerie was near, just beyond the veil.

Holding her hands outward, she poured light over her ancestor's grave. But though she felt the portal's presence, it didn't appear. Something was wrong.

"It's here!" she called to Jean, turning around, "but I can't seem to—"

Intent on her find, Dana hadn't noticed how far away Jean was. Nor had she noticed the shadow creeping out of the trees.

• • •

From the time they entered the cemetery, Jean had been keeping a wary eye on the woods. The wolf in him was alert and on guard. When Dana ran off to find Thomas's grave, he decided to patrol the perimeter. The site was ideal for an ambush. Surrounded by a rampart of trees and shrubs, it was isolated and well-hidden. There were too many nooks and crannies, too many places to hide. As he scanned the woods, they seemed to darken before his eyes. Neither he nor Dana had given much thought to the possibility of an attack in broad daylight. He suddenly realized how foolish that was.

He called out to Dana to suggest they leave.

Deep in the gloom of the woods, something dark had been watching them. Called by an evil akin to itself, it had come down from the midnight lands of the North. Its ravening hunger craved human flesh and it knew the name of its prey.

Dana heard the cold whisper on the wind and shivered. The air had darkened suddenly, as if night were coming or a storm approached. She stared into the trees. A bleak feeling fell over her. What spell was being cast from the black heart of the woods? A disturbing odor crept through the air, something rotten and decayed. Following the smell came a low mournful sound, both seductive and chilling. She stirred uneasily.

*Daaa-naaa.*

There was a cry in the voice, tortured and desolate, yet it also echoed with abominable power.

*The wind through the trees, the sigh of a restless soul, the waves of the waters are the unquiet spirits. The white man asks, "What is that sound?" We who know the answer cry, "The We-ti-ko."*

Dana knew nothing about the spirits of the Canadian North, those who roamed the wilds of the taiga and the tundra. Though Grandfather had spoken the name of the We-ti-ko, she didn't know the giant cannibal whose heart was ice. Its hands were gnarled with crooked fingers that had nails like claws. Its feet had long pointed heels and a single toe. The face was the most dreadful thing to behold, black with frostbite and lips gnawed raw. The yellow eyes rolled in sockets of blood. Through jagged teeth it hissed and whistled before letting out screeches and blood-curdling yowls. Worse was the voice when it chose to speak. Nothing could be more awful than to hear it call your name.

*Daaa-naaa.*

Only in those last minutes did both Dana and Jean realize the extent of their foolhardiness. Was their love to blame? Were they too happy together to imagine catastrophe? Were they too clouded in their thoughts to make a proper plan? The truth was, they had come to the heart of the quest with no preparation or defense. Now it was too late, even for regrets. They were under attack.

As soon as the demon broke from the trees, Dana raised her hands to make light. She would use it as both shield and weapon. With Thomas's tombstone at her back, she stood her ground on her ancestor's grave. Though she quailed at the horror that charged toward her—the hideous eyes, the clawed hands, the frostbitten lips howling her name—she did not run.

Jean knew of the monster that raced toward Dana; knew that no human could fight it off. He made his decision. It was the second time he had faced this moment and, once again, like his grandfather, he suffered no doubt. It was his nature to act this way, his love for Dana simply made it easier. Still, the sacrifice was a bitter one, for he knew what it meant and what he would lose forever. As the midday sun beat down on him, he willed the change to come upon him.

Dana hurled her first fireball at the creature. A direct strike at its chest. The We-ti-ko screamed with pain, but didn't slow down. She was about to throw another when Jean cut in between her and the demon. His eyes were golden. He was pitching forward, about to land on all fours. By the time she opened her mouth to scream —*NO!*—he had turned.

In a flying leap that arced through the air, the great black wolf struck the We-ti-ko.

The demon was an abomination of winter, an evil spirit that stalked the frozen lands of the North. It liked to grip its prey by the head or feet and lift it from the ground, high into the air. Horrified witnesses would describe in dismay how the victim's cries grew muted by distance; a melancholy wail that faded away in the night. Then hidden in the farthest wilds, in a foul lair fashioned of human bones, the demon would devour its prey alive.

The We-ti-ko recovered quickly from Jean's assault. With an ear-splitting screech, it exploded to its feet, hurling the beast away from it. The wolf yowled with pain as he hit the ground with force. Before he could recover, the monster leaped upon him, claws extended like knives. The talons slashed and raked. Black fur flew with red spurts of blood.

Helplessly Dana watched, sick with horror. The two were locked in a death grip. She couldn't strike at one without hitting the other. Rolling frenziedly over the ground, they clawed and bit, howled and screeched.

But if the We-ti-ko had otherworldly power and strength, so too did the *loup-garou*. And the wolf was wild with rage, insane with the knowledge that he had lost his humanity, that he would never again take the form of his own kind. The form that matched his beloved's. Till the day he died he would be separate and different. The rage coursed through his veins. As it burned away all sense of his humanity, Jean gave himself over to the pure power of the wolf. *A strength that would die fighting, kicking, screaming, that wouldn't stop till the last breath had been wrung from its body.* With tooth and claw he tore at the monster, ripping flesh and muscle, biting bone and tendon. In the end, his sacrifice was not in vain, for the We-ti-ko lay dead.

There was no time to celebrate, no time to mourn. Other creatures were issuing from the forest, spectral and malevolent.

Dana cried out to the wolf. Together, they fled from the cemetery and into the woods that bordered the Mad River.

Like a pack of hounds, the dark things bayed in pursuit. Wicked and grotesque, they moved with the swiftness of shadows, hiding behind the trees and calling out to each other. Sinister shrieks rang through the woods as more joined the hunt. Some slithered through the undergrowth. Others leaped from branch to branch.

Dana's heart beat wildly. Her breaths came in short gasps. Their enemies were increasing in speed and number. And even as she ran, she suffered torment and shock, anguished by the enormity of a loss that hung over her. A grief that threatened to defeat her before death itself caught up.

In the wild flight and the fear and the anguish of her heart, she was the Hunted One. And so, too, was he, the great black wolf that ran beside her.


Neither Dana nor Jean saw the arrows that rained behind them. Arrows that flew with uncanny speed and unerring marksmanship. Arrows that struck with silent and deadly purpose. Arrows tipped with burning light.

Nor did they see their enemies fall.

Deeper and deeper into the woods the two ran, till they reached the heart of the forest where the oldest trees stood. Ancient white pine rose tall and majestic, perfuming the air with resinous scent. Green boughs reached downward as if to embrace them. Shafts of light warmed their faces. Both began to sense they were no longer pursued. As the trees thinned out, they stepped into a clearing.

Dana looked around her. She knew this place! It was the same glade to which the deer had led her the night she journeyed in the Shaking Tent. Even the ring of stones and the ashes of the campfire were there. The air was hushed with a special stillness and peace. *Sanctuary.*

Dana sank to the ground beside the black wolf and put her arms around him. Then she threw back her head and howled.

Somewhere in the midst of her sorrow she grew aware of his injuries. Still weeping without restraint, she let the light flow that would heal him. As the blood stopped and the deep wounds closed, her own pain increased, for she was forced to acknowledge what her power couldn't do.

"You shouldn't have done it," she whispered. "I could've fought it. And I'd rather have died."

She saw the tragic look in his eyes, but he shook his great head to show his dissent.

There in the glade, they leaned against each other, both silently grieving: a girl who was almost a woman and a wolf who would never become a man. As they knelt on a mat of red and gold leaves, the soft light of the day illumined their sorrow.

Out of respect for their pain, the others came quietly, with gentle footfalls barely touching the ground. They had arrived too late at the Plain of the Great Heart. Hastening there to aid the Light, they could have turned the tide. They had the power. But before they could loose their burning arrows, the *loup-garou* had transformed, changing in the daylight to save his love.

It was a tragic sacrifice, and for this they mourned; but it was also a noble one, for which praise was due.

All drew near to the wolf. They wanted to honor him. Trueheart. Braveheart. They wished to sing of his act of heroism. With magnificent voices they began to tell his tale; for they would set his name among the constellations, his story to be told as long as they lived.

And they would live forever.

It was a while before the song reached Dana's ears and she grew aware of the circle that had formed around her and Jean. She stiffened in alarm, ready to flee, but the wolf didn't growl. These were not enemies.

The voices were melodious, like the whisper of rain falling on leaves, or the plash of water over pebbles on the seashore. The song was a glossolalic air, a medley of languages. Dana heard the tongues she knew best, Irish and English, while Jean heard French and Cree. In all the languages, the words were the same. It was a love song and a paean, a song of praise. A song of heroism, romance, and sacrifice.

Dana looked around at the singers. Her vision was blurred by her tears. She saw flickering flashes; columns of light that kept shifting and changing like cascading water. She wiped at her tears. She wanted to see. There was something here. She was overcome with a sense of familiarity. Again she remembered the glade in her journey in the Medicine Lodge and the vague forms around the campfire, like trails of mist in the morning. She had almost understood the message, then, the secret of their existence, but the moment had been fleeting. As soon as she had reached out to grasp the knowledge, it had eluded her. Even now, she was struggling to accept what she saw, for she knew them and yet she didn't know them.

There were several tall males with reddish-brown skin and a brush of green hair like feathered needles. When she blinked, Dana found herself looking at a stand of red pine. Beside the men were equally tall women of a silver coloring with bristles of hair. Elegant cones dangled from their ear lobes. When the wind blew, they shivered like white pine. What were the ones with the wrinkled skin? They were grayish brown with a tint of purple and their hair was shiny green. Eastern hemlock! There were others she slowly began to recognize: a fair-skinned lissome birch, three shy and trembling aspens, many sweet-smiling maples with scarlet locks. Their clothes were woven of wild daisies, black-eyed Susans, and white trilliums. At times they rustled and whispered like a small wood in the wind. Then they would return to a state of deep repose, like sleeping trees.

Some had large birds perched on their shoulders or wrists, a glossy black raven, a golden eagle, a blue jay.

Smaller sparrows and woodpeckers nestled in their hair. Along with the birds, there was a host of wild animals who sat or lay beside them: a beaver, a badger, a great black bear, several families of squirrels, a raccoon, and a white-tailed deer.

Though the animals were unperturbed by Dana's scrutiny, the tree people appeared to be caught fast in her gaze. *Human-struck.*

Dana continued to struggle with the huge fact of their existence. She found herself comparing them to the ones she knew in Ireland. Like their Irish counterparts, they reflected the landscape in which they dwelled. These had a stern beauty that spoke of dark forests, deep lakes, and vast mountains. They were incredibly old and wild and free.

When Dana finally accepted the truth, it was shattering. A shock that reverberated through her heart, mind, and soul.

"You're fairies!" she cried out. "*Canadian* fairies!"

# Τhirty-Seven

The beautiful creatures looked both wary and shy as they suffered her gaze. The eyes that stared back at her were a luminous green, like stars from Ireland.

"You're *gorgeous!*" she breathed at last.

A ripple ran through the group. They looked happy, pleased, proud. As if eased by her tone, they diminished to human height, some shrinking even smaller still.

One of the pine women stepped forward to speak. A daisy chain crowned her long green hair. Her skin was a silvery hue.

"I'm Daisy Greenleaf of the Clan Creemore. Pleased to meet you, Light-Bearer's Daughter."

More came forward to greet her, some bowing, some shaking her hand. Others timidly stated their names and then scurried off. Those too shy for even that, slipped away into the woods like bright shadows. But soon a little band of the brave were seated in the grass around her. Tall and lithe, Stanley Moon had eyes that flashed with mischief. He looked like Pan with his pointed ears and evergreen skin. His arm was draped lazily around Daisy's shoulders.

Fern Moon, Stanley's sister, was the same green color with a head of bushy dark hair. She was quiet where her brother was brazen. Brown as an oak, Big James Tweed was robust and kindly. Flora Bird was blue, tiny and quick-witted, flitting here and there. Honeywood was a beauty with long yellow hair and dreamy eyes. Her voice was mellifluous, her movements languid like boughs in a warm breeze. Lavender was pale mauve, the size of a flower petal. She was the only one who had chosen to wear wings, and she fluttered around Dana like a lilac butterfly.

The more at ease they became, the more the fairies shape-shifted at will, from creatures of light to earthly guise to various animal forms. The divisions of nature were nothing to them.

The *loup-garou* remained at Dana's side as the fairies settled around her. Flora Bird brushed his coat with a golden comb. A family of ravens, ever friend to the wolf, nestled against him as they preened their feathers.

"I've been here for over a year," Dana said, astonishment ringing in her voice. "Were you hiding? Why didn't I see you?"

They looked at each other, then at her.

"You know the rules," Daisy said. "You can't see what you don't believe."

"I believe in fairies!" she said indignantly.

"Canadian fairies?" they chimed.

Dana's huff deflated. A thousand questions buzzed

in her mind like bees, but before she could ask them, Lavender called out in a chirp.

"Eat as we talk! Where's the feast?"

"Yeah! Bring it on!" the others clamored while the animals hooted, barked, and cawed.

Daisy, evidently the leader, clapped her hands. In the blink of an eye, they were surrounded by a cornucopia of treats. Baskets of birch bark spilled over with every kind of fruit: rosy apples, blueberries, fat gooseberries, cranberries, wild cherries, and currants. There were hot dishes of roasted corn on the cob and yams. These were followed by cold desserts of sugar cakes dripping with dark molasses and every kind of maple confection.

Dana and the wolf joined in the feast while keeping a watchful eye on the forest. Big James Tweed noticed their wariness.

"You needn't worry. These woods are safe. This is Dun Croí Mor, our fairy fort. No minions of evil can come here. It is well protected."

As the picnic got under way, they told her about themselves.

"We emigrated with the Irish," Daisy said. "We couldn't bear to see our good neighbors leave without us."

"We're scattered across North America," Stanley Moon declared. "Wherever the Irish went, we went too."

"At first we were homesick," said Honeywood in her sweet golden voice. "Like the settlers themselves, we pined for the hills and woods of Ireland. And then, just like them, we grew to love it here. That's when we took on the colors and shapes of the new land."

"The clans in British Columbia are huge!" Lavender piped up. "Rain-forest fairies!"

"They went west with the Guinness family," Fern added.

"In time, many of us forgot about the Old Country," Daisy said. "By that I mean Faerie. Some ran off into the bush or into the Far North, never to be seen again. None of us has gone back in over a century. We've all gone native. This is our home now."

"I guess that's why I never heard of you," Dana murmured. She let out a sigh. "But then, there's so much about Faerie that I don't know. I was really surprised to hear about the queen who brought summer to Canada. Did she come through the portal in Creemore?"

"Oh no," said Daisy. "She came through the oldest one here. It stood in Newfoundland at the heart of the Rock. There were gateways in every corner of the world before they got destroyed. But they're all gone now."

"Except for ours," Stanley stated with pride.

"Ours stood strong," Daisy agreed. "For the portal of *Magh Croí Mor*, the Plain of the Great Heart, was sealed long ago."

"Thanks to the Old Ones," Flora Bird chirped up.

A solemn air fell over them all, including Dana.

"You know the Old Ones," she said at last.

"How could we not?" said Daisy. "All of Turtle Island—what you call North America—belongs to them. They are the spirits known to the First Peoples of this land."

Dana saw the looks that passed between the fairies. Their features were difficult to read.

"They've been helping me," Dana told them.

Daisy nodded. "Since long before you were born. They were the ones who sealed our portal, though we didn't know why at the time. It was all a big secret. But we were happy to do their bidding. At their request, we called your ancestor to meet with the Chief Druid—"

"You mean Grandfather?"

"He has many names," Daisy said. "He is not an Old One, but they speak through him. He has great power."

"He could see us," said Stanley Moon, "from the time we got here. That's how we knew he was a Druid. He said he was going to die soon but that his soul would migrate to another body. We brought your great-great-grandfather to meet him, here in our rath."

"We drummed till Thomas followed us!" Lavender said. "He was a man with a big heart."

"We liked him for that," said Big James Tweed.

"We sang at his shivaree," chirped Flora Bird, "and we blessed his children and their children and their children . . ."

Dana had to smile to herself. No wonder her father ended up marrying a fairy queen.

"We are the guardians of Magh Croí Mor," Daisy explained. "We have always kept watch on the Plain of the Great Heart."

"We're the ones who got Edward Webster to donate the site for a graveyard," Stanley Moon explained with a little grin. "He had a dream that the land should be secluded and peaceful."

"A good neighbor he was," Fern said with a sigh. "I cried buckets when he went away to California. It was so sad that he lost all his money and had to sell everything."

"We tried to help as best we could," Flora added, "but in the end mortals got to live their own lives."

Though they were talking about something that happened long ago, it was obvious the matter still upset the fairies. Dana was trying to get them back to the subject of the portal when a small group broke from the trees.

"Ms. Woods!" she cried. "Laurel!"

The two young women rushed over to hug her. They looked like forest-dwellers, twin Maid Marians in mottled clothing of green and brown, with leaves caught in their hair. They were escorted by more of the Creemore troop. Alf Branch was like Daisy, a natural leader, short and stocky with an air of command. Weatherup was fat and jolly, while Gaelyn Tree-Top was tall and dignified. Christy Pines looked half-girl, half-hedgehog with a mane of spiny bristles. Like the other fairies, they wore clothes of fern, bark, and wildflowers.

Joining the circle, they helped themselves to the feast.

"Isn't it wonderful?" Gwen said to Dana. "Fairies over here and we didn't even know!"

"How could we?" Laurel pointed out. "They've been in hiding for years!"

"Some of them are so shy they still won't come near us," Gwen added.

"It's our nature to be elusive," said Alf Branch. "And modern people don't believe in fairies."

"That's not true!" Gwen argued. "I keep telling you. More and more of us believe. If you showed yourselves from time to time that would help the cause."

"How did you find them?" Dana asked Gwen.

"Actually they found me."

Alf Branch told the story of how the Creemore fairies saved Gwen.

"The day the portals went down, we all got a shock. Though we hadn't gone home in a hundred years we felt the cutting of the cord, and it hurt, I can tell you. In that terrible moment we understood why our gateway was sealed so long ago. It was the only one left standing. We were slow to act, I'll admit that now. In our defense, we knew nothing about what happened between Thomas and the Chief. All we knew was that they shut the door between them.

"I guess we were waiting for someone or something

to come to us. Then rumors and strange tidings started to drift in. Dark things creeping through the countryside. Bad things happening in the city. By the time we got wind of your quest, you were already on the move. Once we heard you were a Gowan of Creemore, we put two and two together. It was time to end our isolation, not to mention our procrastination. We knew we had to go into the city to find you."

Alf Branch stopped and shuddered visibly.

"We'd rather go into battle than into Toronto!" Big James Tweed stated with conviction.

The others echoed his sentiment.

"We're woodland fairies," Alf Branch explained. "The Big City is just too big. The crowded streets and the traffic and the noise . . ."

He shuddered again.

"You should've seen us cringing round the corners of those skyscrapers." Honeywood breathed with soft horror.

"And unfortunately we don't know any urban fairies," Al Branch went on. "They hide even better than we do. But thanks to the city pigeons and squirrels we finally got our bearings. They told us there was an evil thing squatting in an empty building on once-holy ground. And when we discovered it was near to a house protected by a Sacred One, we knew we were on the right trail. And not a moment too soon! We were in the area when we heard the cry. Gwen's spell of succor brought us to her in an instant."

It was Gwen's turn to shudder, and it was obvious she preferred not to speak of it.

"Poor girl, she was near dead," Daisy said gently, squeezing Gwen's hand.

"He was about to deal the fatal blow." Alf's look was grim. "Good thing there were so many of us. We got right in there and lathered him good-oh, till he fled the scene. Then we took her back here as fast as we could."

"We thought she was you," Daisy explained to Dana. "Her wounds were terrible and she was close to death. It took all our healing skills and many long days before she was conscious. Only then did we discover the full story."

"We hurried back to the city," Alf Branch said, "but we couldn't find hide nor hair of either you or Laurel."

"I thought you were both dead for sure," Gwen said, eyes dark as she recalled the nightmare of that time.

"I would have been," Laurel put in, "if one of the Old Ones hadn't acted to save me. I didn't know who he was then, but I realized it later. The amulet he gave me protected me from death, but then Crowley flung me into the burnt place."

"The Brule," Dana said, nodding, "where I met you when I was with the Old Ones."

"We were over the moon to find you both there," said

Gwen. "Messengers had been looking everywhere for you. Laurel's body was found on a deserted beach where Crowley had abandoned it. That was a bad moment. I thought she was dead, but the fairies could see that her spirit had been stolen. We had to find it."

"That was some search," Daisy Greenleaf said softly. "With the doorways closed, he couldn't hide her in some dark part of Faerie; but he had made a lair in the shadows between time and space."

"And that's where you found me," Laurel said.

Now Daisy turned to Dana with a look of deep regret. "We saw you were with the Old Ones and that you had fairy powers. Alas, we assumed you were safe and didn't need us. We were caught off guard when we heard you were in Creemore and under attack."

"What!" said Gwen and Laurel together.

It was Dana's turn to tell her story. When she came to the part where Jean had lost his humanity, Gwen wept openly while Laurel looked stricken. Up till now, neither of them had known anything about the wolf in the circle.

Dana didn't cry. She had no tears left. As she spoke in a calm and quiet voice, her hand rested on the wolf's head. The golden eyes gazed back at her without blinking.

"Faerie is the Land of Dreams and Promise," she stated with sudden fierceness. "Once I open the door, I will bring Jean there where I believe he can be cured.

I've found the portal. It's at my great-great-grandfather's grave. But for some reason it was beyond my reach."

"It's out of alignment," Gwen explained. "As I mentioned in my note to you, the worlds have been drifting apart without the gateways to bridge them. When they cross again on Halloween, the portal will appear. That's your chance to open it."

Gwen hesitated, though it seemed she had more to say.

Laurel finished for her. "It's your one and only chance. If the door isn't opened on Halloween and the worlds drift again, they will stay apart forever."

Dana felt the weight of the truth on her shoulders, but she preferred to know it. She nodded gratefully to Laurel.

"The Book of Dreams described how my ancestor sealed the gateway with a drop of his blood. Only the blood of his family can open it again. I'll do what he did. That's easy enough, I think."

They all looked at her. There was a gravity to their silence that made her catch her breath. She knew that she was missing something.

"It won't be easy at all," Daisy said to her. "As you discovered today, your enemy has called many dark things to the Plain of the Great Heart."

"By the time the portal appears," Alf Branch finished, "a great army will stand between you and the door."

The wolf growled low in his throat.

Dana looked back at them, stunned. She had expected a battle of some kind, chiefly between herself and Crowley, but she hadn't imagined something this huge.

"The secret of the portal was well kept through the years," Alf pointed out, "but even as you uncovered the truth, so too did your enemy. Having failed to kill you, he will stand between you and what you seek. His forces are closing in on Creemore. Many are already here, as you know yourself."

Dana looked stricken.

"You have allies also," Daisy assured her quickly. "We've been gathering our own army far and wide. That's why we were away and didn't know of your peril. You'll be happy to know that you've made many friends on your travels across the country. You've passed many tests, received many blessings. Word of your quest and your cause has spread. Stories are being told about you. Even as the dark forces draw together, so do the bright hosts who will stand against them. You are not alone."

Dana was steadied by Daisy's words. Her arm tightened around the wolf's neck. They would do what they had to do to open the door.

"Now, your report," Daisy said to the latecomers. "What news?"

"We steered clear of Creemore," Laurel told her. "As Alf Branch said, the dark is rising there. We went to Collingwood. We were told about a great hosting at

Algonquin Park. They're coming from as far as Fort Severn and Lake of the Woods. All the northern Ontario troops will march down together on Halloween."

"Excellent," said Daisy.

There were smiles all round.

"There's good news from Ireland too," Gwen told her. "We rang from town. The hold on our Irish Companions has been broken at last. All are restored to health and ready to help. They'll gather in a sacred place on the eve of Samhain and send us power."

"Good news indeed." Daisy nodded. "And I can report that at the Grand Council held today on White Island, there were heralds from every province and territory. All will send troops to join the battle."

A lively cheer rose up from the circle.

"The giants are in," Gaelyn Tree-Top announced. He was a quiet man who rarely spoke, but when he did everyone listened. "Fingal has called them."

"The trolls too," Weatherup declared.

"Really?" Dana said, surprised. "They'll fight for us?"

"Natch," said Weatherup. "They're not bad, you know, just thick. Their king says he's a friend of yours? Little fella, half-troll, half-leprechaun?"

"Trew!" said Dana, even more surprised. "He's the King of the Trolls?"

"Will the dragons come?" Lavender interrupted. "I'd love to see them!"

"Lots of power there," was Big James Tweed's comment.

"Would they want to join us?" Fern wondered. "After what happened?"

A silence fell over the group. Stanley Moon let out a sigh.

"What is it?" asked Dana.

"The Irish and the Chinese built the railways together," Stanley Moon explained. "Right across Canada. They got along most of the time, except when the Irish took to the drink on their days off. Then they thought it was funny to cut off the pigtails of the Chinese workers."

"Dreadful behavior," said Fern, shaking her head.

"We used to pinch the blackguards black and blue," said Christy Pines, "but it made no difference. They just thought they fell over when they were drunk."

Dana frowned. History was a terrible thing. *The sins of the father.* It had an awful habit of coming back at you. "None of you sounds Irish," she pointed out. "You've all got North American accents."

"Will we approach them as Canadians, then?" Alf Branch suggested.

"Yes and no," Dana decided. "We must be honest. Say I belong to both Ireland and Canada. That's the truth. See if they will accept that."

With or without the dragons, they had reached the full tally. Dana sensed an uneasiness in the circle. Was there enough?

"What about the Old Ones?" Laurel suggested. "They've helped us already."

The fairies frowned. Their reluctance was obvious.

"They seldom intervene in such affairs," Daisy said quietly. "When they do, it's on their own terms and not at anyone's request. They see a bigger picture, a Grand Design beyond our comprehension."

Even before Daisy had spoken, Dana had already decided against the notion.

"We won't ask them," she said. "It wouldn't be right. Why should they fight our battles? They've already been more than generous."

Flora Bird looked as if she might speak, so too did Gaelyn Tree-Top, but Alf and Daisy both shook their heads as if to say *keep quiet.*

"We will leave that decision for now," Daisy declared with finality. Then she turned to Dana. "When you traveled in the West, did you receive a blessing of any kind?"

"I . . . I don't know," Dana said. "I visited many places and was taught many things. Most of all, I was given a vision of my own power. What do you mean exactly?"

"Was there any mention of a gift or ransom?" asked Alf.

"Oh yes!" said Dana. "The Sasquatch Elder told me. He said *I* was the gift."

Some of the fairies went pale at this. All looked deeply sad. They couldn't meet her eyes. Again, their leaders shook their heads. *Say nothing.*

"So be it," said Daisy tersely, and her voice sounded pained. "But it may not come to that and we shall do our best to ensure it doesn't. Whether big or small, we all have a part to play."

The wolf stood alone at the edge of the forest, unable to deny himself one last look. His amber eyes were dark with grief as he gazed back at his beloved. Her black hair shone in the afternoon light. Her eyes were like blue stars. Despite the burden that weighed upon her, she had never looked so radiant or so strong. Her hands rested in her lap, glowing faintly. She had found her people. It was time he returned to his.

On hearing the battle plans, he had decided what was best for him to do. He would head north to Roy and *grand-père*, and most of all to the Old Man. He would ask them to help Dana.

He was about to set out when she was suddenly there, blocking his path.

"How could you go without saying good-bye?"

Her face was streaked with tears, but her voice was steady.

"You can't stop the pain, Jean."

She knelt down to put her arms around him his neck. He rested his great head against hers.

"Don't give up," she whispered to him. "There's still hope. If I open the portal, we have a chance."

She could hear his thoughts as if he had spoken to her.

"Stay alive for me," he said. *"Je t'aime."*

"I love you too," she whispered back.

When Dana returned to the camp, the fairies were singing around the bonfire.

*She's like the swallow that flies so high,*
*She's like the river that never runs dry,*
*She's like the sunshine on the lee shore,*
*She loves her love forever more.*

"I've got to go," she told them. "It's getting late. My gran will be worried."

"Not a good idea," Gwen argued. "Creemore is crawling with creepies."

"I'm going home," Dana insisted quietly. "I've got seven days till the battle, and I'm going to spend it with my family. I'm not afraid of Crowley. I can protect myself."

Both Laurel and Gwen were about to say more, but Daisy held up her hand.

"The Light-Bearer's Daughter has power of her own."

Alf Branch agreed. "He won't risk attacking her now that she has gained strength from the Old Ones. He'll wait till he's gathered his full army. The servants of evil are always cowards."

Dana took her leave of the fairy troop of Clan Creemore.

"Till we meet again on the battlefield," Daisy Greenleaf said, kissing her on the forehead.

"See you next week," was Dana's response.

As she left the camp, guided through the forest by Alf and Christy, she heard them singing behind her.

*She's like the swallow that flies so high.*

# THIRTY-EIGHT

"Is our *garçon* a bad-boy truant, or what?"

Georgia plunked herself down at Dana's lunch table and took out her chopsticks. The first thing she noticed was her friend's untouched sandwich. Then she saw the look in her eyes.

"Omigod, what's wrong!"

Though she had managed to avoid her friend all morning, Dana was beyond dodging the question. Coming to school had only worsened the nightmare. Jean wasn't waiting for her in the hall. His desk sat empty, an agonizing reminder of what she had lost before the battle even began. She knew it was crazy, but she wanted him there to talk about the situation, to help her figure out how to save him. Her grief kept rising up in waves, threatening to engulf her. She struggled to stay calm. To be strong. His only hope rested in her opening the portal. Surely the Land of Dreams could return him to humanity?

"Something awful has happened," she mumbled.

"Not again," said Georgia, dismayed. "Another mugging?"

"Worse."

Her friend frowned. With a quick look around them, she leaned forward to whisper. "What about your magic? Will it help?"

"I . . . I can't . . . I'm sorry . . ."

Dana stood up to leave.

Georgia pulled her back down again. Her voice was low and insistent. "Look, I've kept your secret and I haven't bugged you about it, but something's come up. We need to talk, and I mean talk." Again Georgia took a quick look around and leaned even closer. "It's my great-granny. She's special. The way I figure you are too? She talks to dragons. She says they're all over the place, but no one can see them because we're too modern and scientific. She's been telling me stories about them since I was a little girl. I believe her, and I don't care what anyone else thinks. She's the smartest person I've ever known."

Dana heard the tremor in Georgia's voice. It was obvious that her friend had never spoken about this to anyone else. Distracted from her own woes, Dana felt honored. She knew what a risk it was to admit such things.

"Your great-grandmother's right," she said softly. "There are dragons here. I've seen them."

Tears welled in Georgia's eyes. Her voice rang with gladness. "I knew there was a reason I wanted to be your friend! It felt so right! Here's the thing. The dragons told my great-granny about a girl from Ireland who's facing a big battle. They've been asked to fly to Creemore to help her. As soon as Granny told me the story, I knew it was you. It is, isn't it?"

There was no use lying or hiding the truth. They were well past that point. Dana was surprised and deeply happy. She no longer felt so alone.

Georgia was waiting for her answer.

Overcome with emotion, Dana simply nodded. She expected an immediate barrage of questions. There was only one.

"Will you be all right?"

"I don't know," she answered truthfully. "Did the dragons say they would come?"

"They're still debating the matter. They asked my great-granny for advice. Seems something happened a while ago? Between the Chinese and the Irish . . ." There was an awkward pause. Dana sensed that Georgia was being diplomatic. "Dragons have long lives and long memories. Do you know much about them?"

"Not a lot," Dana admitted. "I never met one. The dragons in Faerie live in the sun with their cousins, the salamanders. They don't come out that often. From what I can tell from fairy tales, it's just as well. They can be wild and destructive, breathing fire and burning towns and villages."

"Eastern dragons aren't like that at all," Georgia told

her. "For one thing, they're water spirits. Only a few of them breathe fire. In our stories, they're always noble and friendly, peaceful and wise. And they bring good luck. In China and Japan, they've got their own temples."

"They sound wonderful! I hope they'll join us."

That was apparently all Georgia wanted to hear. "You've got to come and meet my great-granny. If she likes you, I'm sure she'll put in a good word with the dragons. They respect her opinion."

Dana felt a stab of anxiety. "What if she doesn't like me?"

"Hey, no sweat. You'll pass. You're good people."

Dana was feeling better already. As she started on her lunch, she gave Georgia a quick summary of the quest.

"What a fabulous story!" Her friend was enthralled. "It's like the Hsi Yu Chi! That's a legend my great-granny's been telling me since I was small. It's all about Hsuan Chuang and his pilgrimage to the Western Paradise to find the Buddhist scriptures for the Emperor of China. It's a long chronicle about demons, ghosts, and fairies."

A shiver ran through Dana, a thrill of recognition. She caught a glimpse of a truth so profound it left her breathless. She was only one of the People of the Great Journey. There were so many of them, in so many stories.

"What about our missing buddy?" Georgia prodded her. "I notice you left him out of the story, but I have a feeling he's in it? I could tell he was special too, you know.

You've both got the same thing around you that my great-granny has. Some kind of aura, I guess, without getting too weird about it. What happened to him?"

Dana hesitated. She really wanted to tell her. After all, Jean was Georgia's friend as well. They could comfort each other about him.

"I . . . I can't say," she said, at last. "That's his stuff. His secret. I'm sure he'll tell you himself if—*when*—we get through this. But I can't do it for him. I'm sorry, I really am."

"Don't worry about it," Georgia said, shrugging. "I'm not pushing you. I'm just glad you could tell me your side. I'd like to help if I can in my own little way."

"You've helped me already," Dana said, fervently.

"Well, maybe I can do a bit more. I'll call you tonight about my great-granny."

That night, Georgia rang Dana with the news.

"It's all set. We're to meet her on Wednesday first thing after school. We're going to *yum cha* in her favorite restaurant."

"To what?"

"*Yum cha*. Drink tea. You'll love it. If we hurry, we'll be in time for *dim sum*. Have you had that before?"

"No."

"You'll love it!"

• • •

On Wednesday, Dana and Georgia left school together and headed for the old Chinatown on Spadina Avenue. They hurried through the bustling streets past outdoor stands of exotic fruits and vegetables; small shops cluttered with porcelain statues, paper parasols, and ironware woks; clothing stores with their wares displayed on sidewalk rails; and butchers with barbecued pork and duck hanging from hooks in the windows. The air was pungent with the scents of incense, raw fish, cooked meats, and spices.

"This is it," said Georgia, stopping in front of a large restaurant.

The Dragon Palace was a grand old establishment near an Asian mall. Two stone lions guarded the doorway. A silken banner above the lintel displayed a golden dragon with Chinese lettering.

"*Lung tik chuan ren.*" Georgia read out loud. "Children of the dragon. That's what Chinese people call themselves."

A wide stairway covered with a red carpet led upward into a cavernous dining room decorated with tasseled lanterns and delicately painted screens. The music of a two-stringed lute, *baa-u*, flute, and hand bell chimed behind the tumult of voices. The restaurant was packed to the brim. Round tables seated entire families. In among the diners, waitresses wearing embroidered cheongsam dresses pushed handcarts of food. From bamboo steamers and kettles of boiling water, they served the small delicacies that made up *dim sum*. Moving between the tables, the waitresses called out the dishes in Chinese and English. *Ha gao!* Shrimp dumpling! *Nor mai gai!* Sticky rice in lotus leaf! *Sui mai!* Pork dumpling! *Wu gok!* Taro cake!

Georgia and Dana hovered in the entranceway till a beautiful hostess glided toward them. When Georgia spoke to her in Chinese, Dana noticed the change in the young woman's expression. The gracious smile faltered. Was there a trace of fear in her eyes?

She led them down a corridor lined with paintings of dragons.

"I should warn you," Georgia whispered to Dana, "if you see anything strange, it isn't your imagination. There's two of her."

"What!"

"You'll see. Maybe. Just remember I told you and don't freak out. Oh, and she doesn't speak English, so I'll be your interpreter."

At the end of the hall was a doorway draped with a heavy red curtain. The hostess drew the curtain aside and ushered them in, then hurried away with visible relief.

In contrast to the noisy restaurant, the private compartment was dim and hushed. The rich furnishings were of mahogany inlaid with ivory. A thick red-and-gold carpet covered the floor. Dragon images were everywhere, in carved red wood, bright ceramics, green jade, and pale porcelain. Against the back wall was an altar with joss sticks in brass holders. A musky incense smoked the air. In the center of the room was a lone dining table with high-backed chairs. Seated at the table was a tiny, wizened woman.

Dana was surprised. After the edginess of the hostess and Georgia's warnings, she was expecting someone fierce. The little old lady with wrinkled eyes and beaming smile was the picture of a beloved great-granny. She wore a high-collared trouser suit of a flowered pattern, with buttons and toggles. Her wispy gray hair was pulled back into a bun. Except for the tiny golden dragons that dangled from her ears, she wore no jewelry. When Georgia ran to hug her, she cackled with delight.

Georgia waved Dana over to be introduced. Relaxed and smiling, Dana put out her hand. In that moment, she became aware of the other.

As the shock ran through her, Dana was glad of Georgia's warning. It stopped her from crying out. For there behind the little great-granny, like a ghostly shadow, stood an imperious figure. Her features were haughty, her gaze cold and stern. She was formally dressed in the sumptuous robes of a Chinese noblewoman, padded silk and brocade finely worked with gold-wrapped thread. Her shining black hair was bound up with jeweled combs. Her throat and ears dripped with pearls.

Instinctively, Dana bowed toward her.

Georgia's great-granny responded quickly in Chinese.

"Good move there, girl," Georgia said to Dana. "She says you have good manners. But you needn't address the Dragon Lady again. Don't worry, you're not being disrespectful. She's the secret part of great-granny. No one else can see her, but I figured you might. I can only see her when Great-granny sleeps. No one else can, but they sense her sometimes. That's what scares them, eh?"

The two girls sat down as various waitresses arrived, wheeling carts. Dana could see how nervous they were and how they avoided coming too close. Yet none looked directly at the Dragon Lady.

The little great-granny herself bantered away in Chinese as she chose different foods, while Georgia did her best to guide Dana.

Before she had even looked at the dishes of food on the carts, Dana was stumped by the plethora of small bowls, cups, chopsticks, and china spoons laid out in front of her.

"There's actually a method to *dim sum*," Georgia explained. "It means 'light heart' or 'touch the heart.' You start with the steamed stuff, then you move on to the more exotic, like the chicken feet—no?—then the deep-fried, and finally the dessert."

Dana's heart sank as she studied the portions of chicken, pork, shrimp, and beef.

"I'm vegetarian."

"No sweat," Georgia assured her, "there's lots of things you can eat."

Soon Dana was tasting turnip croquettes, red bean cake, water chestnut and taro root dumplings, sesame seed balls, and crispy egg tartlets. All went down happily with tiny cups of tea.

"This is delicious!"

As they ate, Georgia kept up a stream of conversation and translation between her great-granny and her friend. Like the little dishes of food, the talk was light and varied, and seemed to center for the most part on Dana's family and background. Mindful of the Dragon Lady's ever-watchful eye, Dana did her best to be truthful. Neither Georgia nor her great-granny showed any surprise when she spoke of her fairy mother.

"Great-granny's like you," Georgia said. "She's the daughter of a human woman and a Dragon King. That's how come she's the way she is and why she's able to talk to dragons. She said everyone in the olden days could, but things are different now."

By the time they had finished their dessert of almond pudding, Georgia's great-granny was looking sleepy. Her eyes kept closing, then fluttering open again, till finally they stayed shut. Her breath came in low whistles.

Georgia sat up straighter. There was an expectant look on her face, mingled with awe. Now she bowed her head toward the Dragon Lady.

Dana knew immediately it was time for the other to speak.

The Dragon Lady didn't move from behind the chair, yet it seemed as if she had stepped out of the shadows. Her silken robes rustled. Small white hands appeared from inside her wide sleeves. Dana stared at the long red fingernails. When the Dragon Lady spoke, her voice was cool and aloof. Her language sounded different from the little great-granny's, more formal.

"She's speaking Mandarin," Georgia told Dana. "We were using Cantonese before. She has only one question for you. It's not a trick or anything, so just answer as honestly as you can."

"Work away," said Dana, as her stomach tightened.

"She wants to know," Georgia said, enunciating each word carefully, "do you respect your ancestors?"

Though Dana found the question odd, it wasn't difficult to answer. She thought immediately of Thomas Gowan, the story of his life, and the Book of Dreams. She liked what she had read, what he had written, how he had thought, and she was proud to be descended from him. She thought also of his "beloved Harriet" and their children from whom Gran Gowan had come. On the other side of her family was her mother, Edane, the Light-Bearer, a *spéirbhean* and a queen in Faerie. Behind her was the fairy ancestress of whom Edane had spoken, the White Lady of the Waters.

"I'm very proud of my people," Dana said. "I hope to do them honor when I face my destiny."

Georgia looked delighted and quickly translated the answer.

The Dragon Lady nodded curtly but gave no other response. From deep in her sleeve, she produced three bronze coins. They had square holes in the center and were inscribed on one side.

She handed them to Dana.

"Keep throwing them on the table till she tells you to stop," Georgia said.

As Dana obeyed, the Dragon Lady watched the falling coins with keen eyes. After the sixth throw, she raised her hand to stop Dana. Retrieving the coins, the Lady went to the altar and stayed there awhile, writing on sheets of gold paper.

"Have you heard of the *I Ching?*" Georgia asked Dana, who shook her head. "*The Book of Changes.* It's so old, some people say it was the First Book. They also say it has a soul of its own and when you throw the coins, you're asking questions of that soul."

"A book with a soul!" Dana breathed. "But how can you talk to it?"

"It's kind of complicated. Do you believe in coincidence?"

"There's no such thing as coincidence," Dana said automatically. Then she added, "That's what they say in Faerie."

Georgia nodded. "That's what the *I Ching* says too.

When you throw the coins, there are patterns in the way they fall. The heads and tails are lines of yin and yang. You throw six times to make a hexagram. The book describes the sixty-four hexagrams that three coins can make. The patterns you throw mean something specific to you. Not a fluke or coincidence, but something true and important."

"I should have asked a question!" Dana said, disappointed.

"The Dragon Lady already did." Georgia said in a low voice.

"What did she ask?" whispered Dana.

Before Georgia could answer, the Dragon Lady returned to them. She handed Georgia a piece of paper and went on at some length.

Now Georgia interpreted for Dana.

"The reading's good! You get two with the moving lines. They're the changes. I'll explain that later if you want the details. The first pattern is Hexagram Ten, called *Lu*, meaning 'Treading.' The small and cheerful *Tui* here—that's the Lake—treads upon the large and strong *Ch'ien*—that's Heaven. It shows a very difficult situation ahead, but the message says *For the weak to take a stand against the strong is not dangerous here because it happens in good humor.*"

Dana looked skeptical. "I can't imagine there'll be anything to laugh at in this battle."

Georgia caught her mood and wavered uncertainly.

"You said there's another one?" Dana prompted, not wanting to discourage her friend.

"Yes, the first one changed to this, Hexagram Sixty-four. *Wei Chi.* 'Before Completion.' Now, this is amazing," Georgia insisted, as if hoping to convince her friend. "It's the last pattern, the one that ends *The Book of Changes.* That's auspicious in itself. But see how the two parts mirror each other? Fire and water. *K'an* over *Li.* The message says there is order inside chaos regardless of how bad things look. That's the step 'Before Completion'—get it?"

"The darkest hour is before the dawn?"

"Yeah, kind of. *The Book of Changes* ends with the promise of new beginnings and that's the message it's giving to you."

"I like it." Dana nodded. "Sounds more probable than the first one. So, do you think the readings will affect what she says to the dragons?"

Georgia glanced askance at the Dragon Lady, who had resumed her position behind the great-granny's chair.

"You want to ask her?"

"Nope," said Dana. "You?"

"No way."

"Chicken."

"Steamed chicken feet."

Dana took a deep breath and was about to ask the question when the little great-granny yawned. She was waking from her afternoon nap.

The Dragon Lady withdrew into the shadows.

"Time to go," said Georgia.

Before the girls left, the little great-granny gave each a fortune cookie. On their way down the stairs, they broke open the cookies to extract the slips of paper.

"You first," said Georgia, popping the crisp biscuit into her mouth.

"*O nobly born, remember who you are.*" Dana felt a little shiver. "I keep hearing that all the time! What is it?"

"It's a saying from the Buddha," Georgia said, as if the answer were obvious.

Dana's mouth dropped open. "You've got brains to burn. So, what's your fortune?"

Georgia's eyes widened as she read the piece of paper, then she burst out laughing and nearly choked on her cookie.

"I don't believe it! From the sublime to the ridiculous. Just my luck!"

"Come on. Tell."

"*May your life be as long and useful as a roll of toilet paper.*"

They laughed all the way to the subway.

# Thirty-Nine

*The hounds raced ahead to drive the wolf back. Back
toward the hunter who shouldered his rifle.*

*"NO!" Dana cried.*

*The shot rang through the mountains. The wolf somer-
saulted in the air.*

*Then fell to the ground, dead.*

Dana woke, calling Jean's name. Though her eyes
were open, the last trails of her nightmare lingered in
her mind. Weighed down with grief, she lay in the bed
without moving. A tear trickled down her cheek. The
only one she allowed herself. For today was the day of
her destiny. The day she would succeed in restoring the
portals or die in the attempt. She would do this for Faerie,
for Ireland, and for Canada. But most of all, she would
do this for Jean. It was an enormous task for one person,
let alone a young woman, but she was ready to face it.
Half-fairy, half-human, wind-walker, dream-speaker,
she had the power to do it.

By the time Dana got out of bed, she had wrestled

the last of her fears to the ground. Dressing quickly, she headed downstairs and into Gran Gowan's kitchen.

Her aunt Yvonne greeted her. "Hey, sleepyhead!"

Dee was also there, popping up waffles from the toaster and whipping them onto the table like Frisbees.

"We're better than you," she sang, exultant. "Those who rise first are morally superior. It's a universal law."

"What are you doing here?" Dana demanded.

"We got in late last night," said Yvonne. "As soon as we heard you were in Creemore for Halloween we knew something was up."

Dee sat down to pour a river of maple syrup over her waffles before attacking them. In between bites, she burst into song.

*But the night is Halloween, lady*
*The morn is Hallowday*
*Then win me, win me, an ye will*
*For weel I wat ye may.*

"You promised to stay out of this," Dana said accusingly.

"Like we keep our promises," Deirdre mumbled, her mouth full.

"We considered behaving," Yvonne admitted, "but it's against our nature. You can't leave us out," she added quietly. "It wouldn't be fair. Not after Vancouver."

"And especially since we're skipping a hot party to be here," Dee put in.

Dana sat down at the table and helped herself to some breakfast. Her feelings were mixed. She loved being around her aunts, they would cheer up a corpse, but there was no question of leading them into danger.

"And you're not to worry about our safety," Yvonne said. "We're old enough and ugly enough to look after ourselves."

"Just accept the fact," said Dee, reaching for more waffles. "We're in this with you, whether you like it or not. We intend to shadow you all day. You're not going anywhere without us."

"That's what you think," Dana muttered, but she couldn't help laughing all the same.

The dark cloud that hung over her brightened a little. She told them about some of the latest developments. Typically, they heard the good news and skipped the bad.

"Fairies in Canada!" Dee cried. "Hooray!"

"Our own great-granddaddy at the heart of it!" Yvonne said, amazed. "No wonder we're crackers. And there's Mom trying to blame it all on the Catholic side. Hah!"

"I've got to see that book," Dee said. "I feel a doc about families coming on."

Dana didn't tell them about Jean. Even now, in the final hours, she protected his secret. No matter what happened, she would never betray him.

• • •

By lunchtime, Gabriel and Radhi had arrived from Toronto. After salads and quiche, the pumpkin pies were presented with fanfare and fresh cream.

"Dana was as much the baker as I," Gran announced to the table.

"Her talents know no bounds," said Dee knowingly.

Yvonne threw her a warning look.

"I'm glad we're all together today," said Gran, as she sat down at the head of the table. "Besides Halloween, we should also consider this a celebration of the new member of the family soon to join us."

"The gang's all here, the gang's all here," sang Dee.

"I'm so glad you're into having kids," Yvonne confided to Radhi. "Dee and I have decided to girl it out to the end. We do love being aunties, however," she added, winking at Dana.

Dana sat between her father and stepmother, drinking in the warmth and security of her family circle. It was just like in the old stories, she reflected; when the warriors were fêted and pampered before going into battle. As it was then, so it was now. She felt strengthened by the feast.

"You are very quiet," Radhi said.

"I'm just happy to be here," she said softly.

The day itself had been dreary since morning, with a steely gray sky and fits of cold rain. Dana suspected that Crowley was working his ill will with the elements; but as the afternoon waned, other forces came into play. A warm southerly wind blew in to sweep the clouds away.

Outside on the streets, in the last hour before dark, the smallest children set out for their Halloween trick-or-treats. Dana thought of how the night was celebrated in Ireland. Oíche Shamhna. The beginning of the Celtic new year. First there would be potatoes and colcannon for supper, followed by apples and nuts and a barmbrack cake with a gold ring inside. Once the night grew dark, there would be bonfires on the streets and fireworks. In the Faerie world, it was a bigger festival still, one of the special feast days when the two worlds collided and mingled in full. There would be feasting and frolic, and sorties into the Earthworld to cause mischief and mayhem. It was a time of great power when anything could happen, for good or ill.

As twilight drew near, Dana went to her room to change. She had brought the clothes the Sasquatch gave her: the deerskin shirt and leggings embroidered with white quills and blue beads, the cedar bark apron that fell to her knees, and the high moccasin boots. The short cape of black feathers felt reassuring around her shoulders. *Under his wings shalt thou trust.* The staff of peeled pine felt like a weapon. She braided her hair in a single plait down her back, as the Bigfoot females had done. Finally, she took the white feather from the soul-bird in the North and attached it to her braid.

A quick knock on the door. Her aunts barged into her room without waiting for permission.

"Whoa, I love it!" said Dee. "Seriously shamanic."

Yvonne eyed the clothes thoughtfully.

"How about costumes for us?" she asked her niece.

"Yeah, come on, do some magic," said Dee, more directly. "We want to be fairies. Not little pixie things. The gorgeous naughty kind."

To the same tune she sang at breakfast, she added more lines.

*Just at the mirk and midnight hour*
*The fairy folk will ride.*

Dana frowned. She was about to tell them she wasn't playing a game, when she stopped. Behind their irrepressible humor, she sensed something else. Her aunts were using jokes to ease the tension. They were determined to stay by her as long as they could. If they had magical garb, it might give them an edge, bring them closer to her. She was touched by their loyalty.

As for working a spell on them, it wouldn't be difficult. The quest had given her confidence in her gifts and abilities. Fairy glamour was a simple matter.

"Any particular colors?"

"You have to ask?" said Dee, dressed in black, as usual.

"Fire and brimstone for me!" was Yvonne's request.

In the blink of an eye—and a spray of starry dust—the two were transformed. Dee wore a body suit of midnight satin, filigreed with silver. Yvonne got a flouncy dress that changed colors as she moved, shimmering from rose to orange to crimson and back again.

"I'm wearing a Tequila Sunrise!" she cried.

"This is fairy glamour," Dana warned them. "A simple spell, really. And it isn't real. You could be wearing tatty old rags. Or nothing at all."

The two aunts raised their eyebrows.

"Who cares? We're gorgeous!" cried Dee, twirling in front of the mirror. "But what's at the back?"

She twisted her neck to see. Yvonne did the same. Both gasped as they caught sight of the leaf-thin, pale-veined wings that fluttered from their shoulders.

"Are they truly ours?" Yvonne asked breathlessly. "Can we—?"

"Not in public," Dana warned, "and only till the stroke of twelve."

"When we turn into pumpkins," Dee said, nodding.

With squeals of delight, they attempted liftoff. Their wings were like another pair of limbs, but they had difficulty coordinating movement along with direction. Bumping in midair, they were soon tangled up. As they landed on the floor with a thump, their screeches of laughter bordered on hysteria.

Gran Gowan shouted up the stairs. "What's all the racket up there?"

Snorting and hooting, the aunts disentangled themselves and smoothed out their new clothes.

Dana was holding her stomach from laughing so hard.

"Come on, we're dressed to kill," Dee announced. "Let's blow this pop stand."

The sun was setting below the horizon. A dusky light suffused the air. Along the main road, fires burned in steel barrels to provide heat and light. The streets of Creemore were crowded with witches, goblins, vampires, fairies, princesses, and warriors, all trooping from house to house to collect their due. Jack-o'-lanterns flickered with orange light on every porch. Paper skeletons dangled in the windows. Shrieks and howls rang through the night. There were plenty of adults in costume too. The first full moon on Halloween in fifty years was due to rise. Everyone felt the magic.

But they also felt something else. There was an edge to the night that shivered in the air like a chill. People glanced over their shoulders. Some frowned anxiously. Those with children held on to them tightly.

Only Dana knew what the others sensed: not all the creatures who moved through the crowd were in fancy dress. She could see them slithering in the shadows, peering around corners, hurrying through the streets.

Some were knurled and grotesque, toothed and clawed; others had tails and leathery wings, distorted bodies and baneful eyes. They had been called to this place to increase the darkness, to join the battle. And all were moving in the same direction. Toward the cemetery.

Dana knew it was time to go. It was already twilight. But she needed to escape her aunts. Where was her grandmother? A simple distraction and she could slip away. At last Gran Gowan arrived with Gabe and Aradhana, bearing cups of hot chocolate. They admired the costumes of Dana and her aunts.

"You've really outdone yourselves, guys," Gabriel said to his sisters. "How did you construct those wings? They're fantastic."

"It's a whole pulley-system thing," Dee said. "You know, special effects. Film stuff."

Aradhana looked from the aunts to Dana, but said nothing.

"We'll stop here," Gran commanded. "This is a good spot. Now, there's something special on the way, Dana. A real surprise. Wait till you see him."

In the midst of her family, Dana felt the pain of regret. She would have to leave them soon, not knowing if she would return. Though she had considered writing them a letter, she couldn't think of a way to explain the situation or to make things easier. Sipping her hot chocolate and listening to their banter, she wished for a moment that she could forget the whole thing. Oh, to be an ordinary girl enjoying Halloween with the rest of them! Then an image of Jean flashed through her mind and the little fantasy died. Because of her, he was out there in the night, lost to humanity. She had to do what she could to bring him back.

A church bell tolled, as if for a funeral.

"Is it him?" said Dee, craning to see down the road.

"*Ssh!*" said Gran. "Don't ruin it for Dana!"

The main street was lined with people waiting expectantly. A hush of suspense fell over the crowd. Now a sound broke the night.

Hooves striking the road at a gallop!

He came from the north, charging down to the south, a tall dark rider on a great black horse. Children screamed. Adults cheered. Everyone applauded. For the horseman carried his head in the crook of his arm!

"He's the local carpenter," Gran was saying to Aradhana. "He's also the King of Creemore at Oktoberfest."

Remembering the real Headless Horseman she had seen in the East, Dana joined the applause. But she was already inching away from the others. Here at last was the diversion she was waiting for. Like everyone else, her aunts were enthralled by the spectacle. But now as the rider approached them, Dana felt suddenly ill. A chill knifed through her. She almost fainted. As the horseman paused on the road nearby, her legs buckled under her.

The dark horse reared up, eyes white and maddened. The cheers of the crowd swelled.

Weak and dizzy, Dana could hardly move. It was as if she had been seized in an iron grip. That's when she knew. The rider was no Creemore man. This was the real thing, an ally of her enemy: the Dullahan!

Everyone's eyes were on the horseman. They had all been mesmerized. It was only when Dana staggered against her aunt's wing that Yvonne turned around. Her reaction was instant. Catching Dana in mid-fall, she quickly poked her sister. Between the two of them, they supported their niece and moved her back from the crowd.

The Dullahan's horse reared again, letting out a high-pitched screech.

"We must get away," Dana gasped.

"I can see that," Yvonne said, grimly.

"Home!" said Dee.

"No!" Dana said, struggling to stand up. Away from to the horseman, she was beginning to recover, but she still felt weak. She leaned on her aunts. "The cemetery. I must get there. Others will help."

They hurried down the street, behind the crowds, with Dana still supported by her aunts. But the horseman shadowed their movements on the road.

"Shortcut to the graveyard," Dee suggested to Yvonne. "Remember?"

"You read my mind," her sister answered.

Dana was steadier now and they broke into a run. With the echo of hooves behind them, they raced down Mill Street and onto Edward. It was only when they reached Collingwood, not far from the cemetery, that they dared turn around.

Their throats gorged with terror.

Head back on his shoulders, the parade abandoned, the Dullahan was gaining on them fast.

Linking arms with Dana, the aunts took to the air. But they hadn't enough practice. Before they could go beyond his reach, the horseman bore down on them.

With quick sharp blows, he knocked the aunts to the ground. Then he grabbed hold of Dana, pulling her onto his horse. She kicked wildly to fend him off, but his grip was like iron. The horse sped down the street, away from Dee and Yvonne.

Though they had cried out in pain as they struck the pavement, the aunts scrambled to their feet. With sheer will and resolve, they steadied their wings and took to the air again. Now they flew after the horseman like harpies.

Distracted by Dana's struggling, the Dullahan was caught off guard by the rear attack. Dee landed a swift kick in midair that sent his head rolling. Yvonne reached out for Dana and plucked her from the horse.

"Shortcut nearby!" Yvonne hissed to Dana as they fled.

Half-running, half-flying, the three ducked down the narrow lane that led directly to the graveyard. But when they came out at the other end, their hearts sank.

There in front of the cemetery gates stood horse and rider. The Dullahan's eyes blazed as he watched the road.

"There's no other way in," Dee said with a little moan as she fought to catch her breath.

The three huddled in the shadows.

"We'll have to fight our way past him," Dana told them. She was already rubbing her hands to make a fireball.

Shouts rang out from the street. Two lithe figures raced into sight. With shining swords drawn, they charged at the Dullahan.

"Hey, it's the Fair Folk," Dee said, with approval, "arriving like the cavalry."

"Class act," Yvonne agreed. "They're off my hit list."

The horseman charged away without stopping to fight.

Dana and her aunts raced across the road.

"Didn't expect to see you two again," said Dee with a grin.

"Not that we're not glad," Yvonne added.

Findabhair grinned back. "Let's just say the royal bollocking was effective. Tough talk can work sometimes. You're both looking gorgeous, I might add."

"Fairy glamour," Yvonne said airily.

"Admiration's mutual," was Dee's comment.

Both Findabhair and Finvarra were dressed in black with silver chain mail, helmets, and swords. Both glittered like stars in the night.

Neither Finvarra nor Dana had spoken. They stared at each other. Blood called to blood, as they acknowledged their kinship. In the formal manner of Faerie *courteisie*, Finvarra bowed to her.

"Greetings, Light-Bearer's Daughter. We are well met. Late is the hour that I come to thee, yet I would place my sword at thy command if thou wilt receive it."

Dana bowed her head in turn. She had spent enough time in Faerie to know the protocol.

"I am more than honored to be served by a High King. Let it always be the time of your own choosing, Sire."

"No more a High King," Finvarra said with a wry shake of his head, "but a mortal who is prepared to die in your cause."

"Once a king in Faerie," Dana said quietly, "always a king."

"We must go," said Findabhair, looking around.

"To Magh Croí Mor," Finvarra said, nodding. "The Plain of the Great Heart."

As they stepped through the iron gates of the graveyard, Dee sang under her breath.

*Gloomy gloomy was the night*
*And eerie was the way . . .*

"Would you stop with the Tam Lin already," Yvonne hissed.

"I love that song. Besides, it's very appropriate. Music heightens the atmosphere in an action scene."

"This is not a movie!"

Seconds later, the two stopped dead in their tracks.

The cemetery was gone.

In the twilight of the Eve of All Hallows, in the crossing of time and the collision of worlds, Magh Croí Mor, the Plain of the Great Heart, had descended upon the site. An immense level plain of moonlit grass, it was surrounded on all sides by primeval forest. A bluish mist whispered over the ground. Yet it wasn't the plain itself that shocked them, but the sight of the great megalith that brooded there.

Stone upon stone it stood, a massive dolmen, two colossal standing stones with a giant capstone overhead. Stark and silent, it arched against the sky, dwarfing the muted shapes and shadows around it. Though fashioned of granite, it gleamed with a dark metallic sheen that reinforced the impression that it was a gigantic gateway.

"It looks so near," Dana said softly. "A quick run across the field."

"Before this night is done," Finvarra said gravely, "this space will be a battlefield. Come. We must join our friends before we are joined by our enemies."

They hurried into the ancient woods that bordered

the plain. When they arrived at the rath of the Creemore fairies, Dana found it utterly changed. No longer a secluded clearing, it was the stronghold of an army.

Stretching away into the distance, crowding the great forest, were tents and leafy shelters on the ground and in the trees. Stores of arms were piled in gleaming heaps of swords, spears, shields, and axes. A great assembly had gathered there, with more troops arriving every minute. Heralds rushed from tent to tent. Parleys were called and meetings held, as the various leaders debated the battle plan.

Findabhair let out a cry when she spotted Gwen outside a pavilion. The cousins ran to greet each other with tearful hugs.

"I was so afraid you were dead!" Findabhair said. "I only heard the good news a short while ago."

"I'm over the moon you've come," Gwen cried. "What do you think of the fairies? Here all the time and we never knew!"

"Finvarra did," said her cousin. "Of course they all disappeared over a century ago and he had completely forgotten about them. Why is it that fairies are always going missing and no one seems to notice?"

"They're not like us," Gwen sighed.

"Tell me about it," said Findabhair, her eyebrows raised. Then she added warmly, "And I was glad to hear

Dara and the others are well too. I only wish they could be here."

Gwen agreed heartily. "We could do with the Company of Seven right now."

Even as the cousins chatted, another reunion was taking place. The fairies of Clan Creemore were clustered around Finvarra, kissing his hand and murmuring their affection. As more of the troops caught sight of him, they swelled the throng. The last time all of them had been in Faerie, he was their High King.

Daisy Greenleaf threw her arms around him.

"Sire, your people are overjoyed to see you again!"

As the warmth of their welcome touched Finvarra's heart, the bitter years of his exile fell away like withered leaves.

"I am no longer your king, dear hearts," he told them gently. "No longer immortal."

"Whatever you be, our regard for you will never lessen," said Daisy. "We got the story from Gwen," she added with a grin. "It's a good one. Losing all for love—of that we approve!"

Finvarra let out a laugh. "Ever the romantic, dear Daisy. Are you still with that mad Midsummer Moon?"

"He's called 'Stanley Moon' now. Some of the others have changed their names too. In keeping with the new land. And, yes, we're still a couple. He still makes me laugh."

Finvarra grinned. "That's two millennia now? And your own troop as well, I see. Well done. You've kept the fairy faith."

Daisy shook her head. "I share the captaincy with Alf Branch, the one you knew as *Craoibhín Ruadh*. We got voted in. It's called democracy."

Hovering on the sidelines, Yvonne and Dee were drinking in the scene with wide-eyed enchantment. It was as if every fantasy they had ever read had come to life around them! At the same time, they felt a little awkward and out of place.

Till the clans of British Columbia arrived.

The B.C. fairies were huge, the same height as the great trees in which they dwelled – the giant red cedar, Douglas fir, and western hemlock. Beside them strode their furry neighbors, the Sasquatch Nation. All shyness cast aside, the Bigfoot were armed to the teeth and fearsome.

"Hey, it's our heroes!" Dee said suddenly.

There in the troop from the West were the two young men who had come to their aid in Vancouver. No longer clad in T-shirts and denim, they wore hide leggings and forest-green cloaks. Swords fell at their sides, quivers of arrows hung at their backs, and they carried tall bows slung over their shoulders. At first they appeared gigantic, but as they entered the camp, they diminished to human size.

Dee and Yvonne wasted no time in running to greet them.

"We are met again, fair maiden," said the one who liked Dee. His dark eyes flashed as he bowed to kiss her hand.

Yvonne snorted. *"Maiden?"*

But now his companion bowed to her and kissed her hand also.

"I am Andariel. He is Tomariel, my brother. There is surely joy in battle when it brings such beauties to our side."

"Za za zoom," said Dee.

"Are you kin to us?" asked Tomariel, glancing at their wings with surprise.

"Nope. Just queens for a day," Yvonne said ruefully.

"Pumpkins the rest of the time," Dee said with a little sigh.

The two fairy-men looked baffled.

"Fully human and fully alive," Yvonne confessed.

They expected their heroes to be disappointed, but the brothers exchanged grins of delight.

"It has been long since we made merry with mortal women," said Andariel.

"We used to have great sport and play," his brother agreed.

"We're into sport," said Dee, brightening.

"And play," Yvonne added.

• • •

As her aunts dallied with their admirers, Dana was also being reunited with someone she knew. She had recognized the beat of the big skin drums long before Trew marched into sight, leading a battalion of trolls. How different they looked now that she knew they were allies! Where they had appeared alien and horrifying in the dark tunnels, here they seemed simply big and pasty-white; friendly soldiers tramping to join her cause.

Trew was dismissing his troops when she joined him.

"Build yourselves hootchies, boys," he commanded. "Use good strong branches and braid them with plenty of leaves, in case it rains. I'll go get the chocolate."

The pale faces of the trolls lit up and they let out a cheer. All were kitted out in TTC uniforms with great axes and spears gripped in each hand. Trew himself was uncharacteristically somber in the gray jacket of an inspector, but he wore his peaked cap at a jaunty angle and still sported his shades.

"You're the King of the Trolls!" Dana said. "And you didn't even tell me!"

"Means nothin' in the subways," he said with a laugh. "Half the time they don't remember. But as long as they get plenty of chocolate, they'll do what I say. Who's the quarter-master round here? The one who provides the grub?"

"Daisy Greenleaf is the one you want," she said, pointing out the Creemore captain.

"See you in a tick," Trew said, tipping his cap, "after I get these boys settled."

The ground trembled underfoot as a corps of giants arrived, led by Fingal.

"There you be, little one!" he roared happily. Reaching down, he scooped Dana into his palm. "Where's the boyfriend?"

The big smile died on his face when she told him.

"Oh, that's bad," he boomed, scratching his bald head with concern. "But we'll get him back for ye, hen. Just see if we don't!"

As more and more troops and clans arrived, the ache in Dana's heart increased to anguish. Despite the hilarity and excitement, she couldn't ignore the truth. Many of these would die before the night was through.

For as surely as forces gathered to defend the Land of Dreams, so too another army was massing. On the far side of the plain, a gloom hung over the ragged treetops. A sickly vapor seeped from the ground. Through the air came strange cries and moans, shrieks and growls. The wind carried a foul stench in its wake. There on the opposite side of Magh Croí Mor were the allies of her enemy, those who stood with him against life and light.

In the center of the plain was the prize to be won: the great portal. It stood alone and shining at the heart of the battlefield.

• • •

Dana was called to the pavilion where the leaders were holding their Council of War. Dee and Yvonne followed her in. There was a long table spread with a feast, but the food was untouched and the goblets of wine remained full. Everyone was standing, their faces stern and grave. Gwen and Laurel were there beside Finvarra and Findabhair.

Daisy Greenleaf told Dana the battle plan.

"There is no need for complicated stratagems or tactics. The plan is simple. The army is here for one purpose only: to hold back the tide while you go forward to reach the portal. Step by step, inch by inch, you must make your way toward it, even if that means climbing over us, injured or dead. You are the key. Only you can open the door. You must not be distracted by what happens around you. We have come this day to defend our dreams. We gladly offer our lives for the sake of the cause. And even as we play our part, so must you."

Weighed down by the thought of what lay ahead, Dana couldn't speak. She simply bowed her head to show her agreement.

"Wait a minute," said Yvonne. "You mean you guys can be harmed? What about your magic? Your immortality?"

Alf Branch waved in the direction of the enemy forces.

"They're immortal, too, and they've got their own magics. Truth is, we can maim and kill each other . . . and we will."

Both aunts paled. They were just beginning to realize the true nature of the situation. This was no adventure fantasy or exciting daydream. This was real and dangerous. If the fairies could be hurt or killed, then horrible things could happen to them also. Each faced the stark fact that they might die that night.

They looked at their niece with sudden regret.

"We should have stopped you from coming," said Yvonne.

"We were being selfish," Dee agreed. "Chasing the fun as usual and hang the consequences."

"You couldn't've stopped me, even if you tried," Dana said quietly. "This is my destiny. But you shouldn't be here. You've got to leave now. Both of you. Before the battle starts."

There were murmurs of agreement around the table.

Yvonne reacted first, speaking directly to her niece. "You think we're going to desert you like two big cowards? Not a chance."

"We're the fairy's godmothers," Dee declared to the assembly. "We stick by her. And don't try whisking us away. We've got wings till midnight. We'll come back." She surveyed her silken body suit with a grimace. "I just wish I had my boots."

In the blink of an eye they were there on her feet: her heavy black boots with the steel plates on the toes. The ones that made her feel safe when she walked home late at night, and had done her proud against Crowley in Vancouver. Scuffed and battered, they were an interesting contrast to the shimmering fabric of her fairy clothes.

"I like it," she said, turning her heels to admire the look.

"Be careful what you wish for," Gwen said quickly. "Everything is awry around the fairies. Reality is fluid. Anything can happen."

The aunts stiffened as they clamped down on all the wishes that suddenly clamored into their heads.

"Johnny Depp begone," Yvonne muttered.

"You are not warriors," Alf Branch spoke up. "Nor have you any powers or abilities."

"Hey, we fought the Headless Horseman," Dee argued.

"And Crowley before that," Yvonne pointed out. Then she added in a firm tone, "Look, we don't have powers or abilities, but we've got courage. Not the fearless kind— we're both afraid, very afraid—but the kind that feels the fear and does it anyway. No matter what you say, we won't abandon our niece."

Findabhair smiled with approval at the two aunts. So too did Gwen and Laurel.

"The Companions of Faerie are mortal," Laurel spoke up suddenly. "And we have no special abilities. If they choose to stay, I say let them."

"I'd be proud to fight by their side," Gwen agreed. She turned to the fairy leaders. "Humans have always rescued Fairyland. It's our mission. Our duty. And it's our battle too. All our hopes and dreams are linked to Faerie. This very day, across the ocean, four Companions will add their strength to ours. I only wish that they were here. Together, a Company of Seven can wield great power. Still, if we—"

"Excuse me," Yvonne interrupted, putting up her hand. "Sorry to butt in but, while I realize we don't know a lot about this stuff, I can sure count. It seems to me there are seven of us already. Seven mortals, I mean. Am I right or am I right?"

A shiver ran through the company as the head count was made.

Dana. Gwen. Laurel. Findabhair. Finvarra. Yvonne. Deirdre.

Seven.

Finvarra's voice rose with excitement. "She will not cross the plain alone. Six of us will make a queen's guard and the seventh herself to march at the center: the Light who is the key to the portal."

Gwen's voice rang out with new authority. The leader of the first Company of Seven, she spoke the words to bless their fellowship.

"*Seven were the days of Genesis. Seven are the pillars of life. Seven will be the fires of the Apocalypse. No better number can ride the storm. As a Company of Seven we will forge our destiny."*

It was at that moment that Gaelyn Tree-Top entered the tent with a face like thunder.

"It has begun."

# FORTY

*B*ehold a tempest raged upon the earth and throughout the heavens. All elements, visible and invisible, and every creature seen and unseen, were provoked into a murderous frenzy. Earth, air, fire, and water clashed together, broke open, erupted. Lightning flashed across the sky. Thunderous explosions wreaked death and destruction. Mountains collapsed, forests burned, seas boiled. The air was choked with noisome gases.

In the murk of twilight, the Battle for Magh Croí Mor unfolded. Grotesque hordes, monstrous and terrifying, poured from the dark forest and onto the plain. They carried flaming torches or spat fire themselves. Some moved with slow and mindless purpose. Others darted here and there with swift malevolence. There were many Dana recognized, denizens from the dark side of Faerie, known to the Scottish, Welsh, and Irish. These creatures, too, had migrated across the sea to infest the New World. The Redcaps were a cruel clan of brutal goblins who normally lived in the ruins of old castles. Their name referred to the habit of bathing their caps in the blood of their victims. Small and swarthy, they came with all their kith and kin: Redcombs, Bloody Caps, Dunters, and Powries. Above them flew the wraiths of the Unseelie Court, night shades of evil that inhabited the air. A pestilence, an ill wind that blew no good, they added their screeches to those of the green ghastly Banshees. Shoulder to shoulder by a fang-toothed Black Annis tramped the West Coast behemoth called D'Sonoqua. Both cannibal, both ravenous, they had come to feed on the living and the dead. Swarms of hags and specters, gargoyles and demons marched alongside them. And there were even more nightmarish beings whom Dana had never seen nor heard of. With a sinking heart, she realized what they were. *Les esprits du mal* of whom Grandfather spoke: the dark spirits that plagued the First Peoples of the land. Her enemy had allies in every part of the world.

*There were voices and thunderings and lightnings and an earthquake. There followed hail and fire mingled with blood. The third part of the trees was burnt up and the green grass was ashen. A great mountain burning with fire was cast into the sea and the third part of the sea turned to vapor. An angel flying across the firmament cried out with terrible voice—Woe! Woe! Woe to all!*

Now the dark ones were met on the battlefield by an

army of light; all those who had come to fight the cause of hopes and dreams. In the first onslaught of the conflict, in the first charge and engagement, it seemed the two sides were evenly matched. Neither side made headway either forward or back. The initial clash was a draw.

The battle raged on.

Dana surveyed the scene with quiet dread. Where was Crowley? The leader of the enemy was strangely absent from the field. What deception was this? What terrible weapon or secret would be revealed?

The Company of Seven gathered together. Dana stood in the center of the phalanx of her guard. On her right and slightly ahead of her stood Gwen. No longer the plump and pleasant Ms. Woods, she was armed and armored like a warrior-queen. Years had passed since she fought the Great Worm as Captain of the first Company of Seven, but the old courage shone in her face. As it was then, so was it now, she was ready to fight for the Land of Dreams.

For a moment, Dana blinked. Was that the faint outline of a hawk on her teacher's wrist?

Finvarra took up position on Dana's left, again just ahead of her. Once High King in Faerie, he was a master of the art of *Bruion Amhra*, the Wonderful Strife, the game of war that the fairies liked to play. Now he would use his skill in a war that was no game.

In the middle ranks, on either side of Dana, were

Yvonne and Deirdre. Breathing deeply to swallow their terror, they exchanged looks with each other. *I'm dying here. Me too. Can we do this? We're about to find out.* Like the others, they wore chain mail and were armed with shields and weapons. Both still sported their fairy wings, now stiff and rigid, as if standing to attention.

The rear guard was composed of Findabhair and Laurel, who would defend Dana's back. *"Death is not the enemy,"* Laurel whispered to herself, remembering the great battle she had fought on the island of Hy Brasil. Across from her stood Findabhair, who gripped two swords, one in each hand. She thought of the battle against Crom Cruac in which she had almost died. If she had to face that again, so be it, she was ready.

In a voice that rang with spirit, Gwen called out the Company's blessing once more.

*"Seven were the days of Genesis. Seven are the pillars of life. Seven will be the fires of the Apocalypse. No better number can ride the storm. As a Company of Seven we will forge our destiny."*

At the center of the Seven, at the eye of the storm, Dana grew calm. Rising within her was the strength she had gained in her travels and the courage she had garnered from her quest. She felt the power swell. As the light surged from her hands, she cast it over her guard like a golden cloak.

They moved out as a unit toward the battle; but before

they could go far, Trew came running. His face showed his panic.

"Something's not right at Ground Zero. I've lost half my gang. Whenever we get near the portal, it's always the same. Screams of pain, bad burns. We can't see who or what's doing it, but something's there!"

"An invisible enemy!" Gwen said with dismay.

"Crowley!" said Dana. "It must be."

Before they could act on the news, a cry went up at the edge of the forest behind them. It came from the ford where the Mad River flowed, wider and deeper on Magh Croí Mor.

"Now what?" said Laurel, impatient to join the battle.

White sails shone in the dimness as a leather boat glided up the river. Lanterns hung from the masts, illuminating the great emblem of the Celtic Cross.

"It's Brendan!" cried Dana.

Breaking out of formation, she ran to the riverbank.

A plank was lowered from the boat to allow the abbot ashore. His smile was quick as he greeted Dana. He rested his hand gently on her head.

"We have been at sea for many months since I last saw you," he told her. "We sailed down a river as wide as an ocean, then a number of freshwater seas. For the past seven days we have been lost in a fog. Only now as we made our way up this passage did the mist begin to clear."

Brendan gazed upon the Plain of the Great Heart. His features darkened as he took in the apocalyptic scene. The silver rim of the Second Sight seeped into his eyes.

"This is the end of my pilgrimage," he declared solemnly to Dana. "Even as it is the end of yours. Tír Tairngire is near. I see what was written in *The Book of Wonders*. The Land of Promise is behind a rampart of fire; an eldritch fire that cannot be quenched."

Inspired by the saint's words, Dana lifted her hands to the night sky and sent her light forward, like a shooting star. It swept in a great arc across the plain, shedding golden rays onto the battlefield. A howl of anguish rose up from the ranks of the dark creatures, even as Dana's forces were heartened. And as the shafts of light rained down, it exposed the invisible wall that surrounded the portal.

An inferno of hellfire.

"My brother monks and I shall join the battle," Brendan declared. "The dream I seek is on the other side of that fire."

"But . . . you're clergy!" Dana said, surprised.

The saint's smile was rueful. "Do you not know of the warrior-monks of Ireland? Often we have to defend our monasteries. We can acquit ourselves in battle. If there are fiends to be fought, then we shall fight them."

Leaving Brendan to assemble his crew, Dana rejoined her guard.

Just as the battle took a turn for the worst.

Swarms of Bag o' Bones flew from the treetops to descend on the plain. Screeching and chattering, they dived like hawks. As they snatched up their victims in bony claws, they carried them to the fire and flung them in. The stench of burnt flesh choked the air. The cries of torment were wrenching. Against the malevolent magic of the flames, the children of Faerie had no defense. It murdered them slowly without pity or remorse.

The fairy response was swift. All over the plain, bright-winged creatures took to the air to fight off the skeletons. Now the battle raged on high as well as below. The fairy defense was brave and furious, but the Bag o' Bones were not beaten back. Their initial success had made them daring and, despite their losses, they continued to prey. Many had already gone into the fire. Many more would be added.

Sick with horror, Dana looked around wildly. Trew was missing, so too were many of the Clan Creemore. And where were the Sasquatch? Not a single member of that nation could be seen on the field.

"We've got to do something!" she cried. "We've got to rescue them!"

Bloated with triumph, the enemy forces surged forward.

The forces of light were facing defeat.

"We must move now," Gwen said quietly to Finvarra, "before the battle is lost."

"Heads up!" Fingal shouted.

A ragged cheer followed the cry.

There in the sky, passing the moon like winged shadows, flew a vast squadron of dragons.

Beneficent beings, life-giving and valiant, chief of the three hundred and sixty scaled reptiles, fathers of the emperors of ancient times, their numbers were astounding. Every dragon clan had sent a troop. There were *Tien-Lung*, celestial dragons who protected the heavens and the mansions of the gods; *Shen-Lung*, spiritual dragons who caused the wind to blow and the rain to fall; *Ti-Lung*, earth dragons who directed the course of rivers and streams; and *Fut's-Lung*, underworld dragons who guarded the hidden treasures of precious metals and gems. They came in every shape and size, from hundreds of feet long to as small as a silkworm. Their sinuous bodies had the head of a horse, the tail of a snake, and the claws of an eagle. Some had horns and antlers, others long whiskers trailing from their snouts. Many flew by the grace of great wings. Many more were airborne by their own power. Their glittering skin was scaled in all colors, golden, purple, aquamarine, ruby red, and emerald green. Their eyes shone with wisdom and humor.

As they swooped to attack the Bag o' Bones, the fairy hosts cheered.

"Thank you, Georgia," Dana whispered. "Thank you, Georgia's great-granny."

The rout was swift and sharp. Dragon talons ripped the skeletons apart, scattering their bones on the wind. In a matter of minutes, the skies were won.

Now the Dragon Commander hovered over the firewall to assess the situation. Chien-Tang, from the city of Winnipeg, had blood-red scales and a fiery mane. With sorrowful eyes, he regarded the suffering of those trapped in the flames. Then he made his decision.

Dropping out of the sky, he flew into the fire.

A gasp rose up from the fairy army, though his own troops did not react. Their Commander's bravery was famed and unsurpassed.

A cloud of steam burst around Chien-Tang, obscuring him from sight. It seemed an eternity before he appeared again. But though his flanks were scorched as he flew from the flames, he held his head high. And in his claws he clasped a small bundle: the unconscious body of Trew.

"Go!" he commanded his troops. "Free the prisoners!"

Following their chief's orders and his lead, the other dragons went willingly into the fire. Many were badly burned and injured, but their watery natures protected them from death.

Before long, all in the hellfire were carried to safety.

Now Chien-Tang ordered his squadrons to surround the firewall. In a spectacular display of elemental power, they unleashed torrents of rain, black clouds of storm, and thunder and lightning.

To no avail. There was nothing they could do to quench the flames.

Acknowledging that the firewall was impervious to their magics, the dragons returned to the field, attacking from the air.

Back and forth, the battle seethed, with each side winning and losing by turns. There was no break or lull or cease-fire in this war. The enemy forces were unrelenting; their onslaught merciless. They didn't stop to tend their wounded or their dead, but left them on the battlefield, if they didn't devour them.

The Company of Seven held a hasty council.

"We need another plan," Laurel pointed out. "There's no use getting to the wall and being trapped there."

"It would be suicide," Findabhair agreed. "There's no hope of success as long as the fire burns."

Dana's guards were wavering. Gwen looked distraught and Finvarra uncertain. The aunts were biting their lips, not knowing what to say. Dana left them once more. She had to know if Trew survived.

When she found him in one of the healing tents, she almost cried out. He was so badly burned, she hardly recognized him. His small body was livid with blisters that bubbled on his skin. Despite fairy ministrations, he was delirious with pain. The malignant magic that had caused his wounds was not easily dispelled.

"Oh, Trew, *mo chara, mo stór*," wept Dana, lapsing into Irish in her grief.

He was too raw to touch, so she held her hands above him. Gently she showered him with light. Though the burns seemed unchanged, he brightened visibly and was able to speak.

"Was that the Old Tongue?" he whispered. "Can't say I know it. I'm a new kid on the block. Born in Trawna."

Dana smiled through her tears. "I called you 'my dear one' and 'my treasure.'"

"You goin' sweet on me?" He tried to smile back. "I must be bad, eh? No more riding the Rocket?"

Their eyes met. Each acknowledged he was dying.

Dazed with sorrow, Dana looked around at the slain and injured. She knew there were countless tents like this.

"Too many," she said, soul-sickened.

Daisy Greenleaf entered along with Alf Branch. They had obviously come looking for her. Both bore severe wounds that had been tended. But it was their faces that told her the truth.

The battle was lost.

"What should we do?" Dana demanded.

Before Daisy or Alf could answer, Trew signaled to her.

Dana bent over as he struggled to say the words.

"You gotta call them in. The Old Ones."

"I agree," Daisy said, behind her. "Only the Firstborn can fight that fire."

Dana frowned. "I thought we agreed. This is not their battle. We are not their people. We don't have the right to ask them. We can't expect—"

"They will come," Alf said.

Daisy took Dana's hand. "We *are* their people. Everyone and everything that lives in this land belongs to them. It's up to us to acknowledge that. To open our hearts to the truth."

Her words echoed in Dana's mind, reminding her of what others had said.

*Your gods are all around you, child of Faerie, you need but open your heart to them.*

*The land, the plants, the animals, and the people all have spirit. It is important to encounter and acknowledge the life of the land. From such encounters come power. The power of the spirits rises up from the land.*

*If people stay somewhere long enough—even white people—the spirits will speak to them.*

"They'll come for you," Alf Branch said quietly. "You have their blessing."

And Dana suddenly knew. It was like a sunburst in her head. *You are the gift. You are the ransom.* Again and again she had heard the others say that they were willing to offer their lives for the cause. She had never really thought about dying. She was too young to dwell on such things.

But now she understood. A ransom had to be paid for Faerie. A gift had to be offered to keep the dream alive.

The other members of the Company arrived.

"We must do what we set out to do," Dana told them. "We must reach the portal. A gift will be offered. A sacrifice will be made. Once the hellfire is destroyed, I can open the door."

There were several in the Company who knew immediately what she meant. Findabhair had once offered herself as the sacrifice, though her cousin Gwen fought against that decision. Finvarra was the one who finally paid the ransom with his immortality and the High Kingship of Faerie. Though these three looked stricken, they didn't argue the point. They knew all too well the universal law. *For every dream to exist, there must be a sacrifice.* And no matter how much they wanted to, they couldn't take Dana's place. She was the key. The only one who could open the door.

Along with Laurel, the aunts weren't certain what Dana meant, but they were already suspecting the worst.

"Wait a minute," Yvonne began.

"What's going on?" Dee demanded.

"Don't," said Dana.

There was no time for explanations or disagreements. Too many were dying. She had to go.

"You should have told me sooner," was all she said to Alf and Daisy.

They shook their heads, eyes wet with tears.

"We couldn't, dear heart," Daisy said. "We were all agreed on that. We have lived long upon the earth. We would rather have sacrificed ourselves instead."

Gently Dana said her farewell to Trew and kissed the others good-bye. Then she turned to hug her aunts. They were both in shock, hoping against hope that what was happening in front of them was not actually happening.

"No," said Dee, in a whisper.

"Yes," said Dana firmly.

As she left the tent, the others followed.

For the third and last time, the Company of Seven fell into formation. Dana was about to cast her shield of light when Gwen raised her hand.

"Wait! Can you feel it?"

Images flickered across their minds.

*A high green hill in the north of Ireland. A gray stone wall rims the peak like a crown. The Grianan of Ailech. The ancient fort overlooks the Donegal mountains and the wide bay of Lough Swiligh that empties into the sea. Four figures stand upon the ramparts. Matt, the businessman, has parked his Mercedes at the base of the hill. Katie, the farmer, rode her motorbike all the way from County Clare. Dara, the young King of Inch, supports Granny Harte, the fairy doctress who will lead the ritual. Stooped with age and weariness, she is still recovering from the Enemy's attack.*

But where the gray hair sweeps over her face in the wind, her eyes are keen with an indomitable will.

"Four is the sacred number of Turtle Island," she says. "We will forge a chain of power to cross the ocean."

Each takes up a position in one of the four sacred directions, north, south, east, and west. They raise their arms to the midday sun, knowing it is evening on the other side of the Atlantic.

As Granny begins the incantations, power rises from the earth and swirls around them.

Even as the circle was formed in Ireland, another four met in northern Canada.

A full moon shines on a forest of tall spruce and pine. A newly built Medicine Lodge stands in a clearing. Inside the tent, tobacco smoke curls with sweetgrass and sage. Roy beats the drum as the Old Man rattles to the four directions. Two great wolves complete the circle, the silver-gray and the black.

As Grandfather begins to sing and chant, power rises from the earth and swirls around them.

"They're sending us power!" Gwen cried. "Stand ready to receive it!"

Like a blast of wind, the power surged through the Company of Seven, clearing away all doubts and fears.

They were buoyant with a sense of strength and purpose, with the confirmation of their role in life, the knowledge of their place in the cosmos. Suddenly they were taller, stronger, and shining with light.

Imbued with new courage and battle skills, Yvonne and Deirdre felt like Amazons. They threw each other a look of triumph. *We can do this.*

At the center of the phalanx, Dana felt the surge of power that bolstered her guard. She was pleased for their sake. It would help them bear what lay ahead. No more power had come to her, for she had enough. She was ready to do what she had come to do. She was ready to forge her destiny.

A cheer rose up from the fairy hosts as the Company of Seven moved onto the field.

The last battle for the Plain of the Great Heart had begun.

# FORTY-ONE

L ike a great golden scarab, the Company of Seven inched
across the plain, shielded by the carapace of Dana's
light. But though they were protected from black magic
and spells, they still came under attack. The fairy forces
thronged to their side to increase the guard, but the outer
circle was soon overwhelmed by a ferocious onslaught. The
news had spread through enemy lines. *The key has entered
the field.* As a groundswell of animosity seethed against the
phalanx, the Company was pressed on all sides.

Dana's guard fought tooth and nail to hold their
places around her. There was no time to think or feel. All
acted on instinct; the will to survive. The din of battle
was deafening. The fog of war was red. Their swords and
spears flashed in the dimness.

With all her strength, Dana upheld the shield of light.
She could feel the other force that strove to break it: a
relentless malice that emanated from the firewall.

Slowly but steadily, the shining Company cut a swath
across the plain. Grim-faced and silent, they beat back the
waves of murder and mayhem that broke against them.

After what seemed an interminable span of time, they reached the rampart.

Immediately their spirits flagged. The flames gave off a deadly cold as well as intense heat. The cruel extremes worked to disturb and disarm. The golden shield wavered.

And then collapsed.

The moment their defenses fell, the guard were struck full force by an overpowering enmity. They couldn't hold ranks. Falling apart, they staggered under the weight. Every effort was spent just keeping on their feet.

"Go!" Dana ordered them. "We'll meet again when the Kingdom is restored."

Her hands were shaking, but she made enough light to surround herself.

The others backed away from the wall. It was impossible to stay close. Neither dark nor light forces could bear to be near it.

"The light will keep you safe, right?" her aunt Yvonne cried.

Dana didn't answer.

Gwen and Findabhair were crying openly. Laurel and Finvarra looked ashen.

"Isn't she safe?" demanded Dee.

There was no point in lying when one battled for the truth.

"The light may protect her," Laurel said. "That's our hope. But we can't know for sure."

"We should go with her!" cried Yvonne. "We're her guard!"

Finvarra moved quickly to block her path, even as the others stopped Dee.

"She's only a kid!" screamed Deirdre, struggling against them. "She can't go alone!"

"We can't help her! We don't have the power!" Gwen shouted. Her voice rang hollow with despair.

"Don't you think we would if we could?" Laurel said in the same tone.

The aunts had no choice but to accept what was happening. The die had been cast, the decision made. Only one could go into the fire. There was no time to protest. No time to grieve. Weeping out loud, they were in the thick of battle, fighting for their lives.

There was a brief moment when Dana glanced back at her guards. And wished she hadn't. A series of terrible sights assailed her. Her aunts, standing back to back, were surrounded on all sides by hideous creatures. Laurel, seized by the Black Annis, was being dragged deep into enemy lines. Gwen raced after her, sword slashing and hewing. Finvarra fell to the ground as an arrow pierced his chest. Findabhair cried out his name as she ran to defend him.

Dana turned away. She had no choice. The sense of urgency was overwhelming. There was only one way she could hope to save the others. From the moment she had stepped onto the battlefield, she had sensed who lurked inside the flames. The time had come. To do what she had dreaded for so long. She had to confront her enemy. Alone.

She licked her lips. They felt dry and cracked. But she forced herself to speak.

"Are you hiding?"

Her legs were shaky, threatening to buckle, but the words rang out, encouraging her to say more.

"Playing it safe in the back while your soldiers die? I see you couldn't touch the portal."

For there, just beyond the firewall, on an island of green grass, stood the gateway. Pristine and intact.

Without stopping to think, Dana stepped into the flames.

As soon as Dana entered the firewall, Crowley's face appeared. It leered at her from the flames with grotesque glee. As the first stabs of pain pierced her armor of light, she sensed his triumph; his belief that he had won even as he was killing her.

His voice hissed around her.

*"Idiot! What good is a door without a key? Once I have destroyed you, the portal can stand here forever, sealed and useless. The Earthworld on one side, Faerie on the other. Never the two shall meet and both will perish alone."*

His words rang out like a funeral knell. The flames

seared her skin. As her immortal self struggled to contain the pain, Dana acknowledged the truth. Her light might keep her fairy self safe, but her human body could not withstand the fire.

It was the final irony of the quest. Before she had begun her journey, Dana would not have mourned this loss as deeply, for it was her humanity that always called her out of Faerie. Now there was so much to grieve as she left behind the new life she had only begun to live. In her mind she bade farewell to them all, her family, her new friends, and most of all, her beloved Jean. Heartsore, she lamented what she and he would lose, all the time they should have had together.

And even as her mortality slowly burned away, Dana's fairy self moved inexorably toward the portal. The flames seemed to stretch for an eternity. A fiery plain to traverse. An endless gauntlet to run. It was important that Crowley believe this was her sole intent. He mustn't know the part he himself would play. Not yet.

Drawing near to the heart of the matter, near to the malevolent heart of her adversary, she was confronted by a mindless will to destroy. This was nothing like the imaginary evil so often depicted in stories. Neither epic nor exciting, it was barren and monotonous and utterly dismal. *The banality of evil.* There was nothing lively or imaginative about it, for it sought only to kill liveliness and the imagination.

Knowing instinctively what she had to do, Dana reached out to grasp hold of Crowley. He wavered and changed in her grip, one minute reflecting the human body he had stolen, the next, a monstrous tentacled thing. Underneath the two was another presence, an oily form, darker than night. This was the one she concentrated on. The waspish buzzing exploded around her, now recognizable as the cries of the countless creatures he had killed. Despite her distress, Dana kept her grip. The immediate backlash was horrible. Like a malignant worm, her enemy burrowed into her mind. Worse than the physical revulsion was the mental anguish that came with the onslaught. She had to contain his malice without falling prey to the darkness itself.

*Truth shall be thy shield and buckler.*

The whisper fluttered through Dana's thoughts like wings. It was time. Time to know the evil that had come to her.

A series of images appeared in the firewall. Some echoed secrets and rumors she had heard in Faerie. Others were entirely new and unknown, resonating with the mystery and significance of a dream.

*From a lake of black water rears a monstrous serpent with thousands of eyes; he who curls around the Tree of Life that bears both Faerie and the human world like golden apples.*

• • •

*The same creature lies motionless on the shore of the lake, eye sockets gaping, blood trickling from its wounds. With sudden shudders and great spasms, it swallows its own tail. Then, rolling into the water, it sinks beneath the waves.*

*Finvarra, High King of Faerie, follows the Great Worm into the waters of death.*

*There on the sand is a dark stain. A skin of the Great Worm shed and forgotten. It begins to bubble like oil, seething with rage: a demon born of the shadow of the Destroyer of Worlds.*

*Shock waves strike Faerie at the loss of the First King. Power is needed to restore equilibrium. The Midsummer Fire must burn in the West.*

*The shadow of the Destroyer enters Faerie. Snaking through the cracks that rend the land, it lays down spells on every gateway. But one portal is sealed and beyond its reach.*

*Even as the shadow swells with rage, it smells the blood. The key to the last portal. The one it must kill.*

*As the Midsummer Fire is lit, waves of energy heal Faerie's wounds. The demon is caught in the fiery light, yet it does not die.*

...

*Honor, the High Queen of Faerie, must find the one the demon seeks. Where is the light to bridge the darkness?*

*The demon enters a human body to pursue its prey, but by the time it catches its victim, she has discovered her power. The shadow of the Destroyer is cast into the sea.*

*Once again the demon survives. Even as it dissolves in the brine, it clings to life, feeding on the toxic water. Sinking into the depths, it captures an ancient creature that broods on the sea floor. Now a green and tentacled thing, the demon slowly, inexorably crawls across the ocean: toward the one it is destined to kill.*

"Your task is done," Dana whispered. "I'm dying."

Reveling in his victory, Crowley was merciless. He bombarded her with more visions to feed her despair. She saw how evil ruled the Earthworld, how it triumphed continually in every corner, both big and small: the greed of the powerful who squandered their riches while so many starved; land and air polluted by industry; forests felled and waters poisoned; animals tortured for human gain; women and children enslaved; racism and murder; war and war and war. Everywhere she saw the face of the Destroyer, the murderous shadow that dogged mankind. *Where there is no respect for life, there you will find evil.*

In a lightning flash, she saw the true nature of the war being waged in humanity's history. The battle fought on the Plain of the Great Heart was the battle fought in the hearts of all men and women. The monstrous forces pitted against the Land of Dreams were shadows and projections, misshapen creations of the human mind; fairy-tale versions of the real evil in the world that came from humanity, not gods or spirits.

"We are the enemy," Dana whispered, "and we are the battlefield."

Weighed down by hopelessness, Dana searched in her heart for something bright to offset the dark. Deep in her mind a faint image flickered. As she strained to see it, the vision grew stronger. A beautiful woman, tall and pale and as luminous as the stars. She rode a white horse that trod upon shining waters, and she carried a spear. Dana knew who she was, though she had never met her. *You belong to that tribe who herd the stars across the heavens, who have light in their veins, who are descended from the White Lady of the Waters.* The Lady was her forebear, her fairy ancestress. But though Dana was inspired by the vision, it wasn't enough. Drowning in the darkness that was human despair, she needed more than a distant ideal to cling to. She needed something real.

The image of the Lady wavered and changed. Another woman emerged.

There before her stood Gran Gowan, steady as a rock,

a staunch Protestant who had married a Catholic for love. With the raw courage of the pioneers that ran in her veins, a true descendant of the intrepid Thomas, she had walked a broader path than many. Dana could see the lines in her grandmother's face, and the hardship she had suffered, left to rear her children when her husband died young. Despite adversity she had lived undefeated, a woman proud of her life. As she smiled at Dana with infinite love, she wielded her rolling pin like a weapon. *Pastry dough can tell if you're afraid of it. You're a Gowan. Stand strong!*

The image was so bizarre, so contrary to what was happening that Dana burst out laughing.

And the laugh echoed like music, like freedom, like light.

As the cool clear laughter washed over the flames, Crowley shrank back in shock. Only now did he glimpse the depth of his failure. The ruin of his mission. With the first stab of doubt came tremors of fear, even as Dana spoke the words that marked his doom.

"I am the gift. I am the sacrifice. I am the key to the door."

Though he raged and screamed against it, the shadow of the Destroyer was slowly dispelled. By accepting Dana's death, he had appeased the betrayal from which he was birthed. He had restored the balance. For here was a deeper truth that could not be denied. *Evil is but a small and passing thing.* He was part of a whole much bigger than himself. A strand of story in a Great Tale.

As the struggle with Crowley ended and the shadow faded away, Dana collapsed. The flames still burned around her as she clung to her light, but everything was different. Like perfume in the air, she caught the scent of *promise.*

Vague figures moved in the firewall. She sensed they were real, not visions. Some looked human, others appeared to be animals, and there were those who seemed a mixture of both. Human heads on animal bodies. Animal heads on human bodies. More and more arrived. They were a shining assembly, multitudinous, living, glorious. They were speaking among themselves. The murmurous sound was like that of an ocean. They were discussing her quest. For a moment Dana shared the same experience as her enemy, as she caught sight of her own small part in the immensity of a Grand Design.

With a rush of joy, she felt the goodwill directed toward her and the promise that was made. They would come. They would help. She had defeated the demon, but the hellfire was beyond her power; for she was in her death throes.

Everything was fading around her. The sounds of battle

on the plain receded like the tide. Now a howl echoed on the wind. One last time, Dana glanced back into the red night of war. High in the air, the spirit boat flew past the full moon. Grandfather and Roy paddled the canoe. Two wolves sat between them. They had come in the last hour for one reason only. They had come for Dana.

She heard Jean's cry inside the wolf call. Heard also the fear and despair that echoed through that howl.

*Stay alive. I love you.*

The ground trembled underfoot. The beat of drums sounded over the plain. Deep and loud, reverberating through the air, the pounding drowned the din of war.

*O for a voice like thunder, and a tongue*
*To drown the throat of War!*

The drumming quickened like a thousand heartbeats, call-notes throbbing, pulsing louder and louder. Then came the Voices. Singing a song that was carried by the wind.

*O Siem*
*We are all family.*

# Forty-Two

Over the rim of the horizon they came, rising up from the earth. Bounteous, multitudinous, living, glorious. The Old Ones of Turtle Island. The gods and spirits of the land.

The beat of innumerable drums reverberated through the air. The cadence of countless rattles rained down from the sky.

Some came in human form, tall and noble. Others wore the magnificent shapes of animals. As they descended upon the Plain of the Great Heart, they danced and they sang.

*O Siem*
*We are all family*

There was Old Man Coyote, Trickster of the Great Plains. He howled at the moon to announce his arrival. Beside him ran Grandmother Spider along with Fox, Hare, and Possum. Through the night air flew Raven of the Pacific Tsimshian, who made the western waves flow free by tricking the Old Woman who held onto the tide line. And with Raven came Crow of the Tagish-Tlingit who cast sand on the earth when it was flooded with water.

"Become the land!" Crow had cried.

*O Siem*
*We're all the same*

Tall and beautiful, White Buffalo Calf Woman walked so lightly that her feet barely touched the ground. It was she who gave the gift of the Sacred Pipe to the people so they would know the unity of all things. The bowl of the Pipe was fashioned of red stone, the color of the flesh and blood of mammals. The wooden stem harkened to trees and plants and all things green and growing. The smoke from the Pipe was the sacred wind, the breath that carries prayers to Wakan Tanka, the Creator. It was White Buffalo Calf Woman who taught the people to offer the Pipe to Earth and Sky and the Four Directions.

*O Siem*
*The fires of freedom*

In the sky above, the night was shadowed by an immense winged shape. It was Pe-ya-siw—Thunderbird—Lord of the Heavens. His plumage gleamed with the colors of the rainbow. His eyes flashed lightning. His voice rumbled thunder.

Below on the plain stepped the humpbacked Flute-Player. He was the one who brought the seasons and gifted the people with the seeds of plants. Beside him walked Fisher the Hunter, who dwelled in the sky amidst the stars of the Big Dipper. Once upon a time, he broke into Skyland with his friends Otter, Lynx, and Wolverine. They released all the birds who now flew in the world.

Strong winds came sweeping over the plain. White Bear, the north wind, brought the cold breath of ice and snow. Moose, the east wind, shook rain from his antlers. Gentle Fawn, the south wind, blew warm sweet air while Panther, the west wind, struck with sudden force.

*Dance in the burning flame.*

Glooskap, he who was also called Koluscap and Gluscabi, was dressed for war. Fierce and robust, he had painted his face half-black, half-white. He rode upon a stallion that was also black and white. In his hands were a shield and spear of the same colors. A great eagle perched on his shoulder. Glooskap lived in a tent with Woodchuck, his grandmother. Another of his names was Odzihozo, "the One who made Himself." For after Tabaldak made human beings of dust, there was one last bit that got sprinkled on the earth. Glooskap took form from that bit and sat up and looked around.

"Well, here I am," he said.

It is the Mi'kmaq in the east who tell the story of the time Glooskap went to the Summer Land to get help to stop Old Man Winter. Glooskap told his friend Loon about his plan.

"There's a land where the sun shines all year and it's always summer. I'm going there to meet their queen. Maybe she can help us deal with Old Man Winter."

"Good idea," said Loon. "Try singing her a song. Women like that."

*Siem o siyeya*
*All people of the world*

There also came one whom Laurel knew, the one who had helped her in her hour of need: Nanabush, Trickster-Hero of the Anishinabe Ojibwa. It was he who brought the gift of fire to the people. After he stole it from the Fire-Keeper, he ran fast and far in a great relay with Cougar, Fox, Squirrel, Antelope, and Frog. Nanabush was the son of the West Wind and he had many powers. When he was a child, he lived with his grandmother, Nokomis. One day he was so hungry he turned himself into a rabbit so that he could eat the grass. Nokomis cradled him in her arms and called him Nanabozho, her "little rabbit."

• • •

*Siem o siyeya*
*It's time to make the turn*

These were but some of the Old Ones who arrived on the plain, laughing, invincible, fearless, joyous. As they crossed the battlefield, singing all the while, the dark army fled before them. The warriors among the Old Ones smote the baneful creatures down. Those who were animals swallowed them up. Everywhere the enemy was in turmoil and despair, for here was beauty and light that could not be defied.

The Old Ones continued to sing as they vanquished the dark till not a trace of the foul army was left on the plain. Now the Singers advanced on the fiery rampart. Without pausing their song, they walked into the fire. And they danced and they sang at the heart of the flames.

*Siem o siyeya*
*A chance to share your heart*

The song they sang within the flames was one of triumph over pain and loss. They sang of the wounded side of humanity, of the many peoples who walked the trail of tears upon the earth. For the most powerful songs and the most enduring are those that rise to overcome adversity, to survive and prevail. They sang the song of the Risen People.

• • •

*Siem o siyeya*
*To make a brand-new start*

And as they sang they quenched the fire till there was
nothing but ashes that blew away in the wind.

*And watch the walls come tumbling down.*

Their song finished, their work done, the Old Ones
left the plain.

*And so the battle ended that night. The claps of*
*thunder and the winds and the storms had ceased their*
*disturbance. The uproar of the elements and the sky and*
*the land had been stilled. A great peace and harmony*
*settled over everything. For all had been cleansed and*
*healed and whatever was foul had been banished. There*
*arose the greatest tranquillity to play its part in the Divine*
*Plan.*

Dana lay on the grass in front of the portal. She had
no strength left to move. Vaguely she sensed those who
reached out to help her: members of her guard, the black
wolf that was Jean, fairies of Clan Creemore. But they
couldn't touch her. She was already beyond them. She
heard their calls, heard the wolf's howl, but there was no

turning back. They were in the Land of the Living. She had gone into the Dreaming.

Only Grandfather was calm. He stood on Magh Croí Mor, but he was also in the cemetery beside Thomas Gowan's grave. A brief smile crossed his lips as he touched the white bird carved on Thomas's tombstone. With a rush of pale wings, the bird flew into the air. Flying high like a lark, it let out a call-note of sorrow and joy.

From the great forest around the plain, the cry was echoed a hundredfold. Up from the trees, in a blur of white flight in the moonlight, rose the soul-birds of Faerie. The night resounded with the sibilance of wings. Feathery voices rang through the air.

Swooping down on the plain, the birds flew toward Dana and lifted her into their midst. Without substance or weight, she was lighter than a feather. As they carried her to the portal they sang a Homecoming song. With melodious voices, unearthly and sweet, they sang of her quest, her mission, and her sacrifice.

Lost in the daze of her dying, Dana saw faces on the heads of the birds that carried her. They were the faces of those she knew, both human and fairy: her family, her friends, and all who had helped her. Jean was there beside her. And it was Grandfather who led their flight. Everyone she had ever loved was in that shining flock. In that moment she knew they were a vision to accompany her death. Dana accepted the honor with gladness, for it showed the wealth of her life however brief.

Once upon a time she was the light to bridge the darkness. Now she was the key to open the door.

As the soul-birds of Faerie bore her through the portal of the Great Heart, Dana sensed an infinity of doors opening everywhere, in minds and hearts, in distant lands, on distant worlds, all bursting open like flowers as she went Home.

# FORTY-THREE

Dana was walking in a green and radiant garden. The scent of flowers sweetened the air. Butterflies flitted around her. Her mother, Edane, was with her and so also was Honor, the High Queen of Faerie. They linked her arms as they walked beside her, speaking gently as if to coax her awake. She felt light and airy, like a puff of thistledown on the breeze. Her mother's voice rang with gladness, but Honor's was tinged with regret. Words and phrases floated in Dana's mind. They were explaining her new reality, the nature of her being. Her human self had died. She was purely fairy.

Of course she could visit the Earthworld now that she had restored the portals. She could even dwell there if she chose. But she would do so as a fairy, like those of Clan Creemore, and not as a mortal. She could no longer live among humans as one of their race.

Dana felt the protests rising inside her, but she was unable to speak. She was trembling all over. Where was she? What was going on? She pulled away from the fairy-women. Though she was weak and dizzy, she struggled in her mind to call up the portal. She needed to get away, to go back.

The portal took shape immediately, responding to her command. The good news penetrated the fog in her mind. She *had* succeeded. The doorways were open! Now she lurched toward the portal. In the shadow of the great arch, she could see the Plain of the Great Heart. It was still night on the other side. Bonfires lit up the darkness. But the battle was over. The wounded were being carried from the field to the healing tents. The dead were being taken away to be mourned. She could see the luminous face of the full moon and the spray of white stars in a Canadian sky.

Behind her shone the bright meadows of Faerie, the Many-Colored Land of dreams and enchantment. In the distance, a golden palace crowned a high hill. Banners flew from the pinnacle. A great crowd was gathered on the parapets and around the walls, cheering. She could hear her name rising on the swell. A celebration awaited her. She had rescued Fairyland.

Dana was devastated. This was not how she had imagined the end of her quest. This was not what she had hoped for, not what she had dreamed.

She pleaded with her mother and Honor. "I thought if I got back to Faerie everything would end happily! Isn't that how fairy tales are supposed to go? I thought I'd get Jean's humanity back and we'd be together. This is supposed to be the Land of Dreams. Where everything is possible. I don't want things to end this way. This isn't my dream! It's a nightmare!"

Edane was bewildered by her daughter's reaction. "You were unhappy in the Earthworld, daughter! You fled to us constantly and did not want to return. It was your humanity that ever pulled you back. Now that it is gone, you can stay with us forever!"

The High Queen was more understanding, for she too had died as a human, leaving the world of her parents and her twin behind. *For any dream to exist, there must be a sacrifice.* Her voice rang with sympathy.

"We cannot restore your mortal life, Dana. That is beyond our power."

"I don't want this! This is not my dream!"

No sooner had Dana spoken than she found herself in a different place: a small island floating like a lily on the waves of a warm sea. The clarity of light was intense. The rim of the horizon was very close, dominated by the giant face of the Faerie sun. Dana was standing on a green hillock at the foot of a great tree. The tree was bare of leaf or flower, but its branches were covered with countless birds. White birds like blossoms. Fast asleep, their heads were tucked under their wings.

"The soul-birds of Faerie!" she said, breathless.

Though Edane had vanished, Honor stood beside her. The High Queen gazed upward. "I didn't really know what I was doing when I woke them. All I knew for certain was that they would change things. Everything seemed so hopeless. It was the only way I could think of helping you. Desperate times—"

"Call for desperate measures," Dana said, remembering the High Queen's motto. "But I don't understand. What kind of birds are they? What do they mean?"

Honor frowned. "I don't quite understand myself. They are something very ancient. A part of Old Magic."

"There were soul-birds in the Earthworld, too, different from these ones. I met them on the ocean."

"There are soul-birds in every world. They are coming into being all the time, but they also existed before the worlds were born. They are part of what made the worlds come into being." Honor shook her head. "I'm saying this all wrong." She frowned, tried again. "There are things that have no limits—they are boundless—and as soon as you put words on them, the description is wrong because it contains them, like putting something that should fly into a cage." Now she held herself upright as she donned the mantle of sovereignty that brought her wisdom. "The soul-birds are fleeting, like thoughts, yet their power is immeasurable. They are the dreams of the Creator, they are the hopes of the Old Ones, they are the hopes and dreams of everything that exists. They are the utterances that make things come into existence and that hold things together, but they are also the bringers of change. They are the unravelers, the undoings, the unmakings . . ." Her shoulders slumped. She gave Dana a rueful grimace. "It's all that 'life, the universe, and everything' stuff that gives me a royal headache sometimes."

Dana grinned back, but in fact she understood. These were echoes of the teachings she was given when she was wind-walking and dream-speaking.

"The soul-birds in the Earthworld are often lost and suffering," she said softly. "Because life is difficult there. Hopes and dreams go astray all the time. While the soul-birds of Faerie rest easy in the Land of Dreams."

"Not if you wake them," Honor pointed out, "which is why no one does, as my husband has reminded me. I knew I was taking a huge risk. By sending them to you, I started a chain of events with no guarantee that things would get better. Change is change. Hope can be a burden. And people die for their dreams." She looked at Dana sadly. "It is my fault you died."

Dana was about to respond when something caught her eye. She stared up at the sleeping birds. There was something wrong. Something missing. She touched her hair where she had tied the white feather when she dressed for battle. It still hung from her braid.

"It's not here," she said, suddenly. "The bird who gave me this feather. It's still in the Earthworld."

"Ah," said the High Queen, catching her breath, "hope is still on the wing."

...

Word had reached the Court that Dana would attend the celebrations later that night. The news was met with joy. The revels commenced in earnest. Music filled the air. Bright lords and ladies twirled over the marble floors. The hall blazed with the light of a thousand candles. Green garlands draped the walls and pillars. The long tables clothed in snowy lace groaned beneath the weight of a fabulous feast. Gold and silver dishes offered every kind of sweetmeat and savory, delicacy and dainty. Fountains bubbled with champagne and spiced wine.

Many who had fought on the Plain of the Great Heart came to enjoy the victory ball. The Canadian fairies were greeted with a tumultuous welcome. Time had passed in both worlds since they were last seen. Friends and family embraced them with open arms. When a troop of Chinese dragons arrived, they were hailed as heroes. Stories and songs were already being composed to praise their part in the battle.

Dana's aunts were brought to the palace by Daisy Greenleaf. To their own huge surprise, they had acquitted themselves well on the battlefield, suffering only minor wounds. Coloring the air with curses as they fought back-to-back, they had proved both skilful and lucky at war.

"We can't go to the ball like this!" Yvonne said with dismay.

"Cinderellasville," Dee agreed.

Both their wings and finery had disappeared at midnight. Their own clothes were in tatters.

Daisy waved her hand over them. Now Yvonne wore a dress of sparkling red, while Deirdre sported a black satin gown sprayed with silvery stars.

After being told that they would see their niece later, they were ready to party. Both looked around the hall, overcome with the dazzling beauty of it all.

"There's Andy and Tom!" said Dee suddenly.

The handsome brothers were also scanning the crowd. As soon as they spotted the two sisters, they hurried toward them.

"Sport?" said Dee, raising her eyebrow.

"Play," Yvonne concurred with a nod.

There was one of Dana's guard who couldn't come to the feast. When the battle ended, Gwen was discovered deep in enemy lines, badly wounded and unconscious. Brought to a healing tent, she finally woke to find Dara leaning over her.

"Are you really here or have I died, beloved?" she asked.

His eyes darkened as he relived the terror of that moment when he came through the portal and couldn't find her.

"No, you haven't died, *mo stór*," he said gently. "You're made of stronger stuff than that."

His Irish accent fell gently on her ears. She smiled to hear it. He took her hand in his.

"I've been watching over you," he said quietly, "and I've been thinking. It's time you and I were married. No more nonsense about it. We can sort the rest out as we go along. What do you say to that?"

Her smile widened. "Yes, of course. Yes! What else could I say?"

Despite the pain that wracked her body, she managed a small laugh.

"You have a brilliant laugh," he murmured.

When Laurel entered the fairy hall, she did so with a divided heart. Surveying the great assembly, she wasn't sure whom she hoped to see first, Honor or Ian. As it turned out, the High Queen had gone missing along with Dana, which saved Laurel from choosing.

He came to her as the Summer King, resplendent in a crimson mantle. A golden circlet bound his raven-black hair. The blue eyes of Faerie regarded her with careful concern.

"Art thou well, Lady?"

She was dressed in a long green gown seeded with pearls. Her fair hair fell to her shoulders. Though one of her arms was bandaged, most of her wounds had been healed.

"I'm feeling better, thanks. My friend, Gwen, got the

worst of it when she rescued me. There were so many . . ."
Laurel choked. "We're lucky we survived. Many didn't."

She managed to appear calm as she spoke, but inside she was in turmoil. Overjoyed to see him safe and sound, she wanted to throw her arms around him. But she knew he had every reason to be wary. She was the one who had ended their relationship.

"All the time the worlds were divided, I thought of you," he said quietly. "I knew there would be a great battle and that you, being you, would be caught up in it somehow."

Remembering her original refusal to join the mission, Laurel's smile was wry. "It wasn't my quest, but I played my part."

She saw that he was about to leave. Was he hesitating? Would he forgive her? Or reject her? It was now or never. She would have to put aside her pride and take the risk. Either she reached for her dream or lost all hope of getting it. The words tumbled out.

"When I thought you might be dead . . . or even injured . . . I . . . My heart was broken. The thought of never seeing you again. It was the reason I took the mission. When I went into battle, it was for *you* I was fighting."

He looked as if he couldn't believe what he was hearing. With a pang, she realized that in all their time together, she had never spoken so honestly to him. He searched her features. Could he see that she was different? That she had changed?

"Come, Lady," he said, catching her hand. "Dance with me."

When Dana arrived, a hush fell over the great hall. Everyone knew that something was amiss. It had been announced before she arrived that she would not join the feast. She had come only to seek an audience with Midir, the High King. This had caused a lot of whispering and speculation. Refusing to eat or drink in Faerie was the customary sign that one didn't intend to stay.

Dana made her way across the marble floor toward the dais where the High Majesties were enthroned. She was not garbed in shining raiment, nor was she bedecked in jewels. Instead, she wore the clothes the Sasquatch had given her; her battle-dress. The black feathered cape folded like wings over the deerskin shirt and leggings. The cedar-bark apron fell to her knees. On her feet were moccasin boots. In her hand, she carried the staff of carved pine. Her hair was braided and draped with the feather of the soul-bird still on the wing. On either side of her loped two great wolves, the silver-gray that was *grand-père* and the black that was Jean.

A ripple of shock ran through the gathering. The North American clans grinned their approval. She didn't look like an Irish fairy. She looked like a *man-i-tou*, a spirit of Turtle Island.

When she called out her challenge, her voice was steady.

"I have rescued Fairyland. I request a boon for my companions."

The High King frowned. His red-gold hair fell in a mane to his shoulders. His eyes were solemn. Though he wore no crown, the star of sovereignty glittered on his forehead. At his left hand stood Edane, watching her daughter anxiously. On his right was Honor, his wife. The High Queen sat stiffly, her features a mask of control, but her eyes sparkled with mischief.

Midir's frown was not directed at Dana, but rather at the wolves.

"This enchantment is not of Ireland or Faerie."

"It's a French-Canadian thing," said Dana.

"We have no power over magics that are not our own," he told her.

"The High Queen is or was Canadian," Dana pointed out succinctly.

Clan Creemore let out a cheer. Honor barely managed to stifle a giggle.

"Also, as I've recently discovered," Dana continued, "there has long been commerce between Turtle Island and Faerie. The two are bonded in many stories."

Dana thought she saw amusement and admiration in Midir's look. He nodded his head, an encouraging sign. After what seemed an eternity, he answered.

"I will take counsel with the Old Ones of Ireland: the Salmon of Assaroe, the Old Woman of Beare, Blackfoot the Elk of Ben Gulban, the White Lady of the Waters, and Laheen, the Golden Eagle, King of the Birds. The Five Ancients came before Faerie and the New Magic of our realm. They will know if the spell can be broken."

Dana was overjoyed. This was definitely a "maybe" as opposed to a "no." They had a chance.

"I'm not finished," she said quickly. "I haven't stated my full request. There's three parts to it. I'm asking not only that Jean and *grand-père*'s humanity be restored, but mine too."

Before Midir could accuse her of asking too much, the High Queen spoke up.

"Three is the sacred number of the Summer Land. It befits the boon requested, my Lord."

Midir glanced at his wife with sudden suspicion. She made an admirable effort at returning his look with some semblance of innocence. His features showed his struggle not to laugh out loud. Like his subjects, the High King took great delight in the way his wife flaunted the rules. Yet, these were serious matters.

"You agreed to be the gift," he said gravely to Dana. "You offered yourself as the sacrifice."

"And I died willingly," she agreed. "But there is another law in the universe. *Love is as strong as death*."

Midir, indeed, was impressed.

"So be it," he declared. "The three-fold boon will be put to the Ancients. You shall have your answer before the night is done."

Dana didn't feel like joining the ball. The suspense was too great. Instead, she sat by a fountain in the palace gardens with the two wolves at her side. Gazing into the falling water, she could only wonder: what did Fate hold in store for them?

One by one, the others came to express their support.

"We'll raise blue murder if you don't get what you want," Dee told her. "Nothing short of a happy ending is acceptable."

"Being a fairy is all very well, but we'd rather have you in our world," Yvonne agreed. "They say even the gods want to be human."

"*They* say a lot of stuff, don't they," Dee remarked.

When Laurel arrived with a handsome young man by her side, Dana noticed that the two were holding hands. Laurel looked more like her sister now, lighthearted and happy.

The Summer King bowed to Dana.

"May you be restored to your beloved, Light-Bearer, as I have been to mine."

Wild shouts heralded the arrival of Clan Creemore. In a blast of wind they appeared around her.

"It's our wish that you return home with us!" said Daisy Greenleaf.

"Home to Creemore," Alf Branch added, "where Gowans belong."

Brendan came to wish her well before he set sail for home. As he sat down beside her, he clasped her hands.

"I have prayed that your intentions be granted," he said, "and that your book ends as joyfully as mine."

"So *The Book of Wonders* is finished, then?"

Dana was pleased for the saint. Brendan nodded happily.

"As soon as I stepped through the portal into this wondrous land, a rider approached me on a white horse. She wore a purple mantle and gold-embroidered gloves and her feet were shod with sandals of white bronze. In her hand she carried a silver branch that dangled three golden apples. I bowed before her.

"'You are the Queen of Tír Tairngire, the Land of Promise,' spake I, 'as described in the book that I am restoring.'

"'Indeed that name belongs to me,' she said in her melodious voice. 'I have come to tell you that your work is done. Your pilgrimage is fulfilled and you may return home.'"

Dana smiled to herself as she imagined Honor enjoying that task.

Gwen had requested to be brought to Dana, though

the healers had yet to release her. Still pale and weak, she was carried on a silken palanquin supported by her friends from Ireland. Her eyes shone with happiness as she introduced Dara and the other members of the first Company of Seven. Dana thanked them for their help with her mission.

"We all had our part to play, whether big or small," said Granny, the fairy doctress. Her visit to Faerie had fully restored her health. She looked younger and livelier.

"I was glad to do more than throw money at the problem," Matt stated.

"Thank God we woke up in time to do something!" were Katie's heartfelt words. "We nearly slept the whole thing out!"

Gwen leaned over to Dana and spoke quietly just to her.

"It was an honor to be your guard in battle, but you know what? I'd rather be standing in front of you in class, with Jean there as well. Would that be too dull for you?"

"It's a dream of mine," said Dana fervently.

It was almost dawn in Faerie when their Royal Majesties returned. The festivities had waned, but everyone was still there. All had remained in solidarity with the Light-Bearer's Daughter, for whom they wished only happiness.

Dana saw immediately that the news was not good.

The faces of the High King and High Queen were sorrowful. Beside them, Edane looked distraught as she leaned on her husband, King Lugh.

Silence gripped the hall. The air crackled with tension. Dana went down on one knee to put her arms around the wolves.

"The humanities of the three may be restored." As soon as he made his announcement, Midir raised his hand to stay the applause.

"Here comes the 'but,'" Dee muttered.

"However, it is not a simple matter. The boon requires both High Magic and Old Magic. As it has been since time began, High Magic calls for a noble sacrifice and Old Magic calls for a death."

Dana's hold on the wolves tightened. Jean and *grand-père* bared their teeth.

"What must be done?" she asked steadily.

"The three of you will go beyond the Black Gates of Faerie to meet Crom Cruac. The Great Worm is the guardian of the balance between the worlds. It was his shadow you appeased, for he is the one who presides over death and sacrifice. The death is twofold. The wolves must die to allow the men to live. They will be fully human and *loup-garou* no more."

The High King's eyes grew darker. It was obvious that what he had to say next caused him great pain.

"The noble sacrifice is the act of an immortal. To

regain your humanity, you must offer up your fairy self."

Edane let out a little cry. Dana was stunned. Having steeled herself for a straight yes or no, she wasn't prepared for complications. She was staggered by the proposal, the price to be paid. How could she give up her birthright? Her glorious inheritance? And yet she yearned to be human, to live out her life, to be reunited with Jean and her family and friends.

*For every dream to exist there must be a sacrifice.*

As difficult as it was for her, so too would it be for Jean and *grand-père*. They would lose a part of their souls to become human again; all the wildness and freedom of the *loup-garou*.

Kneeling beside the two wolves, Dana bowed her head against theirs. All three were shaken to the core of their being.

The High King of Faerie gazed upon them with compassion.

"Each of you is free to choose your own destiny. One decision is not bound by the others. But choose you must, between your magical selves and your humanity."

# FORTY-FOUR

It was still Halloween in the Earthworld, for both the Plain of the Great Heart and the Land of Faerie were beyond time. Gabriel stood beside his wife on the streets of Creemore, laughing with the crowd as the Headless Horseman disappeared down the road. Suddenly he found himself elsewhere. It was a place he recognized instantly: a forest in Ireland, in the Wicklow Mountains, on a high ridge overlooking a narrow road. The trees were a tangle of old oak and holly. He was sitting on a fallen tree trunk, his silver flute in his hand.

Bewildered, he looked around him. Was this a dream?

Then she stepped out of the trees and walked toward him. Her gown was pale and shining, her feet and arms bare, and her head was wreathed with a crown of white blossoms. For a moment he thought she was Edane, his first wife, but her hair was raven-black. Then he realized with a shock that the glimmering girl was his daughter.

"Gabe . . . Da . . ." Her voice echoed with a touch of sadness and regret.

He felt a sharp ache in his heart. Despite his confusion,

he knew what this meant, the thing he had always secretly dreaded. She was going to leave him, his fairy daughter, even as her mother had.

As Dana reached out to him, her hands spilled golden light.

"This is what I am, Gabe. I can't hide it anymore and I can't protect you from the truth. I'm going away for a while. Something has happened and I'm no longer able to live in both worlds. I've got to choose one or the other. I need to think about it, but I promise to return and let you know my decision. I don't want to hurt you, but you know it's my life and I've got to be the one who makes the choice."

Gabriel dropped the flute from his hands. His heart was breaking. Yet even as he looked at her with love and awe, he knew her words were true. She was more than a child.

"I love you, Da. Take care of yourself and Radhi and the baby."

With tears in his eyes he held her tightly, hoping it wasn't for the last time.

"You'll always be my baby," he murmured, "my firstborn."

By the time Dana caught up with Findabhair and Finvarra, they were in their hotel room in Toronto. Finvarra had removed his shirt so that his wife could change the dressings on his wounds. The sweet scent of fairy herbs wafted on the air.

"You should've stayed in the healing tent." Findabhair chided her husband, but her voice was gentle, as was her touch.

"You have power of your own," he said with a smile. "And it is best we go back onstage as soon as possible. Our honor must be restored. We broke our pledge with the tour."

"The show must go on," she agreed. "A makeup concert should fix things. We're not the first musicians to go astray. *All's well that ends well.*"

Neither looked surprised when Dana appeared beside them. Both were saddened to hear her news.

"You must know the full consequences if you choose humanity," Finvarra told her. "You will be banished from the Land of Faerie. Once you lose your immortality, you cannot return."

This was the reason she had come to see them. She needed to talk with someone who understood her dilemma.

"But I'll still be able to see fairies, won't I? If they show themselves to me? Like Clan Creemore? And my mother will visit me and show up in my dreams?"

"That's the theory," said Findabhair.

She and her husband exchanged glances.

"I need to know the truth," said Dana, sensing that they were holding something back. "To help me make the right choice."

Findabhair sighed. "The bottom line? Fairies are flighty. You know that yourself. Life is a game for them, feasting and frolic, music and dancing. They never grow old and I'd say they never grow up. And that's another thing. Time. Because of their immortality, they don't notice it passing in their world or ours. They don't mean to forget to visit, but years can pass before they remember. You need to understand, Dana, that if you choose to be human, you're not in for a penny, you're in for a pound. Faerie will play a very small part in your life. It may even disappear from it altogether."

Dana's eyes filled with tears. This was her worst fear.

"But the others, like Gwen and—"

"It is a different thing for the Companions of Faerie," Finvarra explained. "They have right of passage to the Realm and are ever a part of it. For you and me and any other immortal who falls out of the Great Time, the door is closed. We are exiles in this world."

*Life is a peregrination through a foreign land.*

"Is it forever?" Dana asked. She held her breath.

Something flickered in their eyes. A glimmer of light.

"Actually, that's something we don't know," Findabhair said. "Immortals who have fallen—like humans who hold no belief—face death as a mystery."

"Hope is still on the wing," Dana murmured, releasing her breath.

Georgia was asleep when Dana arrived at her house. Instead of waking her, Dana slipped into her friend's dreams. She found herself outside a ruined building in a darkened city near a river. Georgia crouched nearby with a gun in her hand. As shots rang out, Georgia stood up to fire back, then hunkered down again. She didn't look surprised to see Dana. After all, it was a dream.

"What's going on?" Dana hissed at her.

Explosions sounded across the river.

"Don't you dream you're on secret missions fighting some mysterious enemy?" said Georgia. "No wait, that's your real life."

She stood up to let off another round, but she had run out of ammunition. Crouching again, she reloaded.

"According to dream books, I'm fighting the dark side of myself," she commented. "So far, we're even."

Dana snickered. Even in her dreams, Georgia was hilarious.

"Could we go somewhere quiet?" Dana asked her. "We need to talk."

Now Dana found herself perched beside Georgia on a high wall overlooking a hilly countryside. The sun shone on their faces. Their legs dangled over the warm stone. The wall stretched away on both sides as far as the eye could see, rising and falling with the roll of the land. There was no sign of habitation or people or animals, only brown soil and green bushes and the wall going on forever.

"Wow," said Dana. "Is this the Great Wall of China?"

"Yep," said Georgia, banging her heels off the stone. "Isn't it neat? I love this place, but I can't always get here. Lucid dreaming is tricky."

"You're not actually dreaming *me*," Dana said. "I'm really here."

Georgia sat up straight, her look serious.

"Is it all over, then, the battle and everything?"

Dana nodded.

"Great-granny said the dragons went," Georgia told her. "But they didn't come back yet to tell us what happened."

"They were brilliant. They saved a lot of our army."

"That's great! So, how come you're not keeping this news to brighten an otherwise boring day at school?"

Dana saw the concern in her friend's eyes. Georgia might be hilarious, but she was also very smart. Dana hesitated. In that pause, Georgia's worry turned to fear.

"Did you die? Is that why you're here?"

When Dana paused again, Georgia's eyes filled with tears.

"I'm still alive as a fairy," Dana hurried to say.

"It's not the same!" Georgia cried. "I thought we were

going to do the best-friend thing: you know, graduate together, go to university, be each other's brides-maid. All that corny stuff."

She started to cry. Dana did her best to comfort her, explaining the situation and the choice she faced.

"Well, that's easy." Georgia sniffled, recovering quickly. "Do the right thing. You were born here. The human option is the only option."

"Then I won't be special anymore," Dana pointed out. "Isn't that why you picked me for a friend in the first place? Because I was like your great-granny?"

"Yes and no," Georgia argued. "I just wanted someone I could talk to about that stuff. Someone my own age. It's lonely having a secret you can't share. I can still do that with you as a human."

"This is so hard," Dana murmured.

She stared down at the ground far below her and found herself thinking of Humpty Dumpty. There were other elements to the choice she hadn't mentioned to Georgia. The question of Jean. If he remained a wolf, it would be easier for both of them if she stayed a fairy. She could shapeshift into a wolf herself, whenever she wanted. But what if Jean chose to be human? She knew from her father and mother that mortal and immortal didn't work. But though Jean's decision added to her dilemma, Dana was aware of the deeper truth. No matter what Jean did, she had to choose her own destiny.

"I'll lose so much if I stop being a fairy," she pointed out to Georgia. "And what do I get in return? Old age, sickness, no power over anything . . ."

"Hey!" her friend interrupted. "Don't forget the other things, Ms. Glass-Is-Half-Empty. Friendship, love . . ." Georgia waved her hand over the vast expanse of wall. "All the wonders you can find in *our* world. These belong to *us*. The lowly mortals. Not them."

Dana smiled. "I knew you'd be a help."

"Speaking of love, how's our *garçon?*"

Dana was about to answer when she stiffened. The sound of an alarm clock rang through the air, like loud bells.

"I've got to go. It's time for you to wake."

"Whatever you decide, don't forget me!" Georgia cried.

The two girls hugged good-bye on the Great Wall of China.

Laurel made her way to the High Queen's solar. It was an airy chamber high in the palace, overlooking a vast rose garden and ornate fountains. Honor was reclining on an embroidered couch. Beside her was a lacquered table with a china tea set, a plate of seedcakes dripping with honey, and a bowl of red berries. The High Queen nibbled restlessly on the tidbits as she gazed out the window. When Laurel entered the bower, Honor jumped up with delight.

"Here you are at last!"

The twins embraced joyfully.

"I was looking for you, but I couldn't find you," Laurel told her.

"I was out and about with royal duties. It's not all party-party, no matter how it looks."

Honor smiled at her sister proudly as she poured the tea. "I knew you wouldn't abandon us."

Laurel sighed. "It seems you can take the girl out of Faerie, but you can't take Faerie out of the girl."

Honor laughed. "And did I see you walking in the garden with the Summer King?"

Laurel wasn't ready to discuss that subject yet. "What do you think Dana will do?" she said, changing the subject.

Her sister's face clouded. "I was dwelling on that matter just before you arrived. She has so much to gain and so much to lose. My heart goes out to her."

"Can't you help her decide? You, more than anyone else, can understand her position."

Honor disagreed. "It was different for me. I didn't have a choice. In truth, I'm glad I didn't. How can one choose between two worlds? Two homes?"

On Iynu lands in northern Quebec, where the snow lay white and glistening in the dark of night, they waited for Dana in Grandfather's kitchen. Roy leaned against the wall, too restless to sit. The great black wolf that was Jean lay in front of the stove. On either side of him sat two old men, smoking their pipes. *Grand-père* was a stately gentleman with short gray hair and the same wintergreen eyes as his grandson. He wore a big woolen sweater over his trousers. From time to time he looked at Grandfather and they would nod their heads through the curl of tobacco smoke. The Old Man was cloaked in his black-and-red blanket. All of them remained silent, in the stoic manner of men who didn't talk when there was nothing to say.

Outside in the cold night, high in the clear starry sky, Dana was playing with her mother in the Northern Lights. *Aqsarniit*, soccer trails, was what the Baffin Islanders called the shimmering strands. One moment the lights were swirls of silver, the next sheets of green and lilac rippled like veils. The sky was the playing field for a game of soccer in which thousands of spirits took part, singing and laughing as they raced across the firmament.

Breathless and barefoot, with stars in her hair, Dana ran among them, kicking the ball and shouting to Edane. All the time she played, the questions rang through her mind.

*Are you or are you not? Have you the taste of your existence or do you not? Are you within the country or on the border? Are you mortal or immortal?*

When the game was over, she parted from her mother with the same words she had said to Gabe.

"I promise to return and let you know my decision."

Falling to earth, Dana landed in the snow near Grandfather's house. Though she walked in her bare feet, she was impervious to the cold. It was early in the morning, the darkest hour before dawn. Were anyone to look in her direction they would see only a pale wisp of light.

With every step she took, Dana felt the weight of her decision. How could she embrace humanity? To grow up in the mortal world, she would have to accept so much pain and sorrow, failed dreams and lost hopes, inevitable change and inevitable tragedy. There would be so many things she couldn't control, both in herself and in her life.

On the other hand, there was so much to gain, all the joys and wonders of being alive on the Earth, learning and growing, finding friendship and love. And what a great mystery was human life itself, when you can never really know what might happen next!

She stopped before she reached the door. Her hand paused in midair and didn't knock. *Not yet.* Turning suddenly, she ran from the settlement. With the ease of a shape-shifter, she dropped to the ground and took the form of a wolf, as white as the snow. Now she let out a howl. It woke all the dogs for miles around and set them barking furiously.

The door of Grandfather's house opened. Light spilled onto the snow. Out bounded the black wolf in a rush to join her. When he reached her side, they touched noses in greeting. They played a frantic game together, chasing each other in frenzied circles in the snow, dashing back and forth around the trees, snapping and barking in the sheer fun of being wild.

Then, without a backward glance, they ran into the North.

The next evening, the two old men sat drinking tea by the stove. It was dark outside the window, but the moon glittered on the snow. The Northern Lights were swirling across the sky. Heads close together in easy companionship, they spoke in a mixture of French and Cree. A jeep pulled up in front of the house. Footsteps sounded. Roy came in the door, stomping the snow from his boots. He looked sad and dejected.

"I tracked them to Lac à l'Eau Claire."

Grandfather and *grand-père* regarded him with sympathy.

"They came up to me. There was plenty of jumping and barking and they let me hug them, but they didn't change back. They ran off. Is that their choice, do you think?"

He looked stricken.

The old men exchanged glances.

"Some things don't get decided right away," Grandfather said.

"It's not possible to know for now," agreed *grand-père*.

"But they are your friend forever, Roy. *C'est vrai, n'est-ce pas?* This you know. Whatever happen, they are your friend."

Far in the North, on a promontory overlooking the lonely tundra, two wolves howled at the moon. Across the clear sky, the Aurora Borealis illumined the night with multicolored lights. *Les chèvres dansantes,* the French Canadians called them. *The dancing goats.*

The two wolves exulted in the wild beauty of the night, the wild freedom of their nature, the wild magic of the land.

Farther north again, beyond the Northern Lights, in a place some Native legends call Skyland, the High King and High Queen of Faerie arrived. They bowed before the Old Ones, the Firstborn of Turtle Island.

"Because of you, the Battle of the Great Heart was won," said Midir.

"We are here to express our gratitude," said Honor.

"There is no need," came the reply.

*We are all family.*

# Postscript

A year and a day later, Roy went to bed at midnight, having failed to talk his grandfather into doing the same. The Old Man sat at the stove, smoking his pipe and drinking tea. The wise dark eyes gazed out the window at the night beyond.

"No point us waitin' forever," Roy had said quietly, more to himself than to Grandfather. "They made their choice. We gotta let them go in peace."

That very night, Roy had a dream. He was playing soccer in the sky with wolf-people and goat-people who sparkled like the constellations. The blue shining ball they were kicking around was the planet Earth. Running beside Roy was Jean, who kept changing from wolf to young man and back again. On the same team, racing across the vast plain of the firmament, was Dana: one minute fairy, the next wolf, the next again, a young woman.

The three went into a huddle together to review the Game Plan. It was so profound and exhilarating that Roy kept losing track of their strategy, yet somehow he knew it and understood it in the deepest part of him.

*At the heart of the universe, we talk of a life lived in matter.*

Then he found himself plummeting from the sky, shooting out of the darkness, like a falling star.

Did the others fall with him?

Roy surfaced from his dream to stare groggily at the ceiling. A final image lingered in his mind: his two friends, in jeans and parkas, walking out of the forest, hand-in-hand. As he lay there, heart aching, familiar sounds reached his ears. Voices talking and laughing. Feet crunching on the snow outside. His name being called out. Loud knocks on the door.

Roy was already out of bed. Pulling on his jeans. Running into the hall, yelling.

# Glossary
## Key to Words in Languages
## Other Than English

*À bientôt.* (French)—See you soon.

*À gauche! À gauche!* (French)—To the left! The left!

*Abú* (Irish)—Forever! Hurrah!

*Allons! Allez!* (French)—Let's go! Go ahead!

*Allons-nous!* (French)—Let's go!

*Alors* (French)—then, in that case

*Alors, regarde, chérie* (French)—Then look, my darlin'

*Âme soeur* (Canadian French)—Like the Irish term *anamchara*, this means soul-friend. It tends to be translated as "soul-mate" but it transcends romantic connotations though it may include these. As a Québécois friend explains, it refers to *"une grande amitié, une forte relation amicale et très respecteuse."*

*Anamchara* (Irish)—soul-friend

*Angakuk* (Inuktitut)—shaman, medicine man/woman

*Aqsarniit* (Inuktitut)—soccer trails, the name used by Baffin Islanders for the Northern Lights. Another Inuktitut name for the Lights is *Aqsalijaat,* meaning "the trail of those playing soccer."

*Attention!* (French)—Watch out!

*Aventure* (French)—adventure

*Aya* (Hindi)—anglicized to "ayah." A nursemaid or governess.

*Ban martre* (Old Irish)—white martyrdom

*Beaucoup de magie* (French)—lots of magic

*Bí ar d'fhaichill ar an strainséir!* (Irish)—Beware the stranger!

*Biens le temps* (French)—plenty of time

*Bienvenue, Loup.* (French)—Welcome, Wolf.

*Bon* (French)—good

*Bravo!* (French)—Good work! Well done!

*Buíochas le Dia.* (Irish)—Thank God.

*C'est bon.* (French)—This is good.

*C'est ça.* (French)—That's it.

*C'est certain!* (French)—For certain! It's definite!

*C'est incroyable!* (French)—It's incredible!

*C'est vrai?* (French)—It's true?

*C'était merveilleux!* (French)—It was wonderful!

*C'était très beau* (French)—It was very beautiful.

*Cá bhfuill Naomh Bhreandán?* (Irish)—Where is Saint Brendan?

*Ça va?* (French)—How's it going? (How are you?)

*Cailleach Beinne Bric* (Scots Gaelic)—The Hag of the Speckled Company

***Canot d'écorce qui va voler!*** (Canadian French)—The bark canoe/boat that is going to fly!

***Canot d'écorce qui vole, qui vole!*** (Canadian French)—The bark canoe/boat that flies, that flies!

***Cara Mia*** (Latin)—My dear/beloved lady

***Caribou*** (Canadian French of Algonkian origin)—large deer in Arctic regions of North America. Both male and female have antlers. The same deer in Asia and Europe is called reindeer.

***Cat sith*** (Scots Gaelic)—fairy cat

***Catholique*** (French)—Catholic, as in Roman Catholic

***Ce n'est rien*** (French)—It's nothing. Used as "you're welcome" in reply to "thank you."

***Ceann groppi*** (Scots Gaelic)—stuffed cod head. A Cape Breton delicacy. The cod head is stuffed with cod livers mashed with cornmeal, flour, and rolled oats, then boiled or steamed. Yum.

***Chauvin*** (French)—chauvinistic

**Chercher une aiguille dans un botte de foin** (French)—
to look for a needle in a haystack

**Chez toi** (French)—(at) your house

**Coimdiu na nduile** (Old Irish)—Lord of Creation

**Comment dit-on?** (French)—How do you say?

**Complainte** (French)—lament, sad song

**Comprends-tu?** (French)—Do you understand?

**Conte merveilleux** (French)—wonder tale, fairy tale

**Craic agus ceol** (Irish)—crack and music—Crack means
great fun, as in "having the crack."

**Craoibhín Ruadh** (Irish)—Little Red-haired Branch

**D'accord** (French)—agreed, okay

**Dangereux** (French)—dangerous

**Dans l'bois!** (Canadian French of *dans les bois*)—Head
for the trees!

**Dehcho** (Dene)—The Big River (the original name for the MacKenzie River in the Northwest Territories)

**Derc martre** (Old Irish)—red martyrdom

**Dia Duilech** (Old Irish)—God of the Elements

**Diablotin** (Canadian French)—demon

**Dis-moi** (Canadian French)—tell me (informal of *dites-moi*)

**Esprit du mal** (Canadian French)—evil spirit

**Et toi?** (French)—And you?

**Excus'-moi** (French)—excuse me, sorry (informal of *excusez-moi*)

**Fado, fado** (Irish)—long ago. Usually found at the beginning of a fairy tale, as in "once upon a time."

**Fais attention** (French)—be careful

**Fais-nous voyager par-dessus les montagnes!** (Canadian French)—Let's journey over the mountains!

**Famille** (French)—family

*Fatigué* (French)—tired, weary

*Garçon* (French)—boy

*Gentille* (French)—nice

*Glas martre* (Old Irish)—green martyrdom

*Go raibh míle maith agaibh.* (Irish)—Thanks ever so much (literally "a good thousand to you").

*Grand-père est disparu.* (French)—Grandfather has disappeared.

*Guru* (Hindi)—A Hindu or Sikh spiritual leader or teacher. While the term has taken on derogatory connotations in Western society, it is one of great respect in India. From the Sanskrit *guruh*, meaning "weighty."

*Hootchinoo* (Tlingit)—distilled liquor, shortened to "hooch" and now North American slang for liquor, particularly illegally distilled

*Innunguaq* (Inuktitut)—This is the proper term for the human-shaped stone figures (*innunguait*, plural) most of us call *inuksuk* (*inuksuit*, plural). *Innunguaq* means "in the likeness of a human." The *inuksuk* comes in many shapes. It means "acting in the capacity of a human," e.g., as a navigational aid, marker to hunting grounds, indicator of food caches, doorway to the spiritual world.

**Inummariit** (Inuktitut)—"the real people," those who live on the land in the manner of their ancestors

**Irlandais** (French)—Irish

**Irlandaise! Magnifique! C'est un très beau pays, l'Irlande.** (French)—You're Irish! Great! Ireland is a beautiful country.

**Is scith mo chrob on scribainn.** (Old Irish)—My hand is weary with writing. (Found in the margin of an old manuscript, medieval monkish graffiti.)

**J'ai peur.** (French)—I'm afraid.

**Je comprends.** (French)—I understand.

**Je m'excuse.** (French)—I'm sorry.

**Je n'sais pas.** (French)—I don't know (short for *je ne sais pas*).

**Je pense** (French)—I think

***Je suis ancien, pas invalide.*** (French)—I'm an old man, not an invalid.

***Je t'aime.*** (French)—I love you.

***Jongleur*** (Canadian French)—Native medicine man/ shaman *(sorcier indien)*. Also used in the book is *jongleuse*— Native medicine woman/shaman *(sorcière indienne)*.

***Klahanie*** (Chinook jargon, a Native-based trade language used west of the Rockies and as far north as the Yukon)—the great outdoors

***L'histoire*** (French)—history, story

***La chasse-galerie*** (Canadian French)—Often directly translated into English as "witch canoe" or "spirit boat," but this is incorrect. *La chasse-galerie* is the process of flying a canoe. One "runs *la chasse-galerie*" *(courir la chasse-galerie)*, but there is no direct translation for the term itself. The boat is *canot* or *canot d'écorce*.

***La Pèlerine*** (French)—the female pilgrim

***Le Brûlé*** (Canadian French)—"The burnt place." Anglicized to the Brule. A patch of wasteland or swamp created by a forest fire.

*Le canot* (French)—boat

*Le Diable* (French)—the Devil

*Le Diable, beau danseur* (French)—the Devil, a great
dancer and handsome too

*Le Nord* (French)—the North

*Les fantômes* (French)—ghosts

*Les lutins* (Canadian French)—goblins

*Liber Monstrorum* (Latin)—*Book of Marvellous
Creatures.* Probably written in England (they don't know
for sure) early seventh century, but maybe earlier.

*Loup! Enfin! Ça va?* (French)—Wolf! At last!
How are you?

*Ma grand-mère* (French)—my grandmother

*Magh Crí Mór* (Irish)—the Plain of the Great Heart

*Maintenant* (French)—now

*Mais non* (French)—of course not

**Mais oui** (French)—(but) of course

**Mais peut-être** (French)—but perhaps

**Mal de raquette** (Canadian French)—leg strain caused by heavy snowshoeing

**Man-i-tou** (Algonkian)—spirit of the land, sacred force

**Mea culpa.** (Latin)—(It's) my fault.

**Merci beaucoup** (French)—thank you very much

**Mo chara** (Irish)—my dear one, my friend

**Mo stór** (Irish)—my treasure

**Moi aussi.** (French)—Me too.

**Mon ami** (French)—my friend

**Mon amour** (French)—my love, beloved

**Mon frère** (French)—my brother

**Mon grand-père** (French)—my grandfather

**Monsieur** (French)—mister

**Mystère** (French)—mystery

**N'est-ce pas?** (French)—Isn't it? Another way of saying "eh?"

**Na péistí. Ansin!** (Irish)—Sea monsters! Over there!

**Naturellement.** (French)—Of course/naturally.

**Navigatio Sancti Brendani Abbatis** (Latin)—*The Voyage of Saint Brendan the Abbot.* Written in Latin around A.D. 800, it tells the story of the sixth-century Irish monk who set sail for the Island of Paradise on the other side of the ocean. It was a "best seller" in medieval Europe.

**Nous risquons de vendre nos âmes au diable!** (Canadian French)—We risk selling our souls to the devil!

**Nous sommes ici!** (French)—Here we are!

**Nunatak**—Anglicized version of *nunataq* (Inuktitut)— an isolated peak of rock projecting above a surface of inland ice or snow.

*Nunavut* (Inuktitut)—"our land." Canada's new territory, which officially came into being April 1, 1999.

*Ogham* (Middle Irish)—ancient lettering of the Celtic peoples based on straight lines drawn perpendicular or at an angle to another (long) straight line. Usually found on stones or carved on wood. Related to the God Ogma, inventor of the alphabet.

*Oíche Shamhna* (Irish)—Halloween

*Omadhaun* (Irish)—anglicized version of *amadán*, meaning "fool."

*Oui* (French)—yes

*Oui, c'est ça! Exactement!* (French)—Yes, that's it exactly!

*Oui, je connais.* (French)—Yes, I know/recognize it.

*Oui. Bien. Très bien.* (French)—Yes. Fine. Very well.

*Ouvre la porte! Vite!* (French)—Open the door! Quick!

*Pas de problème* (French)—no problem

**Perigrinni** (Medieval Latin)—pilgrims

**Physiologus** (Latin)—*Natural Science*. Originally a
Greek work of late antiquity about the natural world.
Popular in the Middle Ages in Latin. Icelandic version
written later.

**Poudrerie** (Canadian French)—drifting or powdery snow

**Prends garde.** (French)—Take care/be on your guard.

**Qu'est-ce que c'est?** (French)—What is it?

**Qu'est-ce que c'est que ça?** (French)—What's that?

**Qu'est-ce que tu fais?** (French)—What are you doing?

**Qu'est-ce qui se passe?** (French)—What's happening?

**Regarde, chérie, regarde mon pays.** (French)—Look,
sweetheart, see my country.

**Roth Mór an tSaoil** (Irish)—*The Great Wheel of Life*
(Note: this is the Irish title of Micheal MacGowan's book
about his adventures in the Yukon's gold rush called in
English *The Hard Road to Klondike*.)

**'S FOSGAIL AN DORUS 'S LEIG A 'STIGH
SINN!** (Scots Gaelic)—Open the door and let us in!

**S'il te plaît** (French)—please (informal of *s'il vous plaît*)

**Sadhu** (Sanskrit)—literally meaning "good." The name given to a Hindu holy man or woman who wanders throughout India. They have renounced material life and live in a state of perpetual pilgrimage.

**Saltair na Rann** (Medieval Irish)—*Psalter of Verse,* a tenth-century manuscript containing songs and poems about "life, the universe and everything."

**Salut** (Canadian French)—Hi

**Saskehavas** (Coast Salish)—Sasquatch in Canada, Bigfoot in the U.S., and in Tibet, the Yeti, or Abominable Snowman

**Sensible** (French)—sensitive

**Son nom?** (French)—His name?

**Tabernac** (Canadian French)—swear word referring to "tabernacle." Many French-Canadian curses refer to the Roman Catholic Church. Also used in the book are *câlisse* for *calice* (chalice) and *maudit* (damned).

**Tabula rasa** (Latin)—blank/clean slate

**Toujours** (French)—always

**Tria digita scribunt, totus corpora laborat.** (Medieval Latin)—Three fingers write, but the whole body labors. (More graffiti written by another monk long ago.)

**Umiak** (Inuktitut)—skin boat

**Un peu** (French)—a little

**Une chanson irlandaise** (French)—an Irish song

**Vite! Rapidement!** (French)—Quick! Hurry!

**Vitement** (French)—quickly

**Voyageur canadien** (Canadian French)—woodsman, guide, trapper, boatman, explorer. Literally "Canadian traveler."

# Permissions

Lyrics from *"Le Canot"* and *"Les Canayens sont Toujours Là"* are used with the kind permission of the Centre franco-ontarien de folklore, Université de Sudbury, Ontario.

Lyrics from "GIANT," Stan Rogers (SOCAN) © 1977, used with the kind permission of Fogarty's Cove Music and Ariel Rogers.

The following material found in Chapter 21 is used with the kind permission of Ronald Caplan, editor of *Down North: The Book of Cape Breton's Magazine*, published by Doubleday in 1980 and reprinted by Breton Books: the Scots Gaelic poem *"An Calluinn"* transmitted by Mr. Roderick MacLeod, the Acadian song from Miss Marguerite Gallant (English translation by O.R. Melling), *ceann groppi* recipe from Mrs. Sadie MacDonald, spruce beer from Mrs. Lillian Williams, and larrigans from Mr. Donald Garrett MacDonald.

References to and dialogue quotes from Tim Severin's *The Brendan Voyage* (various publishers) used with kind permission of the author.

References to Sharon Butala and her work used with kind permission of the author and her publisher, HarperCollins Canada.

Lyrics from "Kathy I" (Chapter 25) and *"O Siem"*

(Chapters 41 and 42) used with kind permission of the artist and songwriters: Susan Aglukark, Aglukark Entertainment Inc (SOCAN), Chad Irschick (SOCAN), and Kelita Haverland Music (SOCAN).

Throughout the book there are quotes from other sources such as the Bible, Shakespeare, Farid ud-din Attar's *Parliament of the Birds*, Hildegard of Bingen (as translated by Matthew Fox), Hannah Arendt, Scott Peck, Henry David Thoreau, and various poets such as Rainer Maria Rilke, Gerard Manley Hopkins, Samuel Coleridge, William Blake, and Wallace Stevens. These are found in italics.

Most of Grandfather's statements are teachings of Elders given to me or found on record. His words concerning the land are from the written brief *In the Spirit of the Land: Statement of the Gitskan and Wet'suwet'en Hereditary Chiefs in the Supreme Court of British Columbia, 1987–1990.*

Quotes from the *I Ching* or *Book of Changes* are taken from the Richard Wilhelm translation rendered into English by Cary F. Baynes (Penguin Arkana).

Lyrics from *"Vive la Canadienne!"* and "She's Like the Swallow" are found in *The Penguin Book of Canadian Folk Songs* compiled by Edith Fowke (Penguin Books, 1973).

Any songs or poems not acknowledged above were written by the author.

# About the Author

O.R. Melling was born in Ireland and grew up in Toronto with her seven sisters and two brothers. At eighteen, she hitchhiked across Canada to California, seeking adventure. A year later, she was off to Malaysia and Borneo on a youth exchange program. That set her motto for life, "to travel hopefully." She has a B.A. in Philosophy and Celtic Studies and an M.A. in Medieval Irish History. To date, her books have been translated into Japanese, German, Chinese, Russian, Czech, and Slovenian. She lives in her hometown of Bray in Ireland with her teenage daughter, Findabhair. Visit her Web site at www.ormelling.com.

# Keep reading! If you liked this book, check out the rest of the series.

**The Chronicles of Faerie:
The Hunter's Moon**
978-0-8109- 9214-6 • $8.95 paperback

**The Chronicles of Faerie:
The Summer King**
978-0-8109-9321-1 • $8.95 paperback

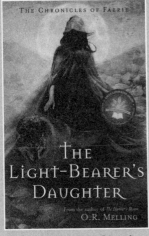

**The Chronicles of Faerie:
The Light-Bearer's Daughter**
978-0-8109-7123-3 • $7.95 paperback